"How did I get here? don't remember." Her work, I walked home thr wrinkled in the most adorable way as she rambled disjointedly through the succession of events. "I heard chanting. I followed the sound. And then I saw—" She broke off, shaking her head as her words came faster and faster. "I ran, and this dark shadow. And then—" Eyes wide, she peered at him. "And then. Then that huge *m-monster*—"

He didn't want to give her time to dig herself further into the fear. Didn't ask to which monster she referred, Ronové or himself.

"You aren't crazy," Niklas soothed. "This night and all you witnessed was real."

Now she looked at him as if *he* were the crazy one. She glanced to the door again. He could all but see the wheels turning in her head. Could she make it before he caught her? Would he try to stop her?

"You've seen something you shouldn't have this night. Something not meant for human eyes."

"Uh-huh." She nodded in a placating sort of way. A weak smile pushed at her lips, thin and unconvincing.

A storm cloud of gray bled through her aura, darker, denser than before.

Heaving a sigh, he resisted the urge to roll his eyes. She might not be a screamer, but she had *runner* written all over her. That was just terrific. He had better things to do than chase her all over creation tonight.

Unobtrusively—at least, he imagined she *thought* she was doing it on the sly—her right foot slid back, angled, planted for traction.

And three, two, one...

Praise for Brenda Huber and...

THE SEER: "Thrilling, dangerous and seductive... Brenda Huber has done it again with her continuation of a fantastic plot, amazing characters and sizzling passion."

~Fresh Fiction Reviews

~*~

THE SLAYER: "With danger, passion, sexy demons, and a lot of action, [this book] is a new favourite of mine."

~Fresh Fiction Reviews

~*~

SHADOWS: "Brenda Huber is an author to watch. The way she paints a scene is fantastic."

~Catherine Bybee, New York Times and USA Today Bestselling Author

~*~

SHADOWS: "Huber's serial killer is truly twisted and readers will be guessing the person's identity until the last pages of the story."

~Romantic Times

~*~

MINE: "The turbulent, fast-paced plot leaves readers holding their breath while turning the page."

~Coffee Time Romance

The Seer

by

Brenda Huber

Chronicles of the Fallen, Book 2

The Seer

Cover Art by *Rae Monet, Inc. Design*

The Wild Rose Press, Inc.
PO Box 708
Adams Basin, NY 14410-0708
Visit us at www.thewildrosepress.com

Publishing History
Previously Published by Samhain Publishing, 2015
First Black Rose Edition, 2019
Print ISBN 978-1-5092-2666-5
Digital ISBN 978-1-5092-2667-2

Chronicles of the Fallen, Book 2
Published in the United States of America

Dedication

I would like to dedicate this book
to my circle of friends:
Angie Kinzle, Kris Ostwald,
Kim Meyer, and Sandra Teachout...
you are my rocks, my shelter in any storm,
my sympathetic ears, my sanity, my comic relief,
and my partners in crime.
You are my chosen family,
and every day I am grateful for you.
Thank you for always being there...
and always being as crazy as I am.

"You believe that there is one God. Good! Even the demons believe that—and shudder."

~James 2:19

~*~

"Nietzsche once said, 'If you gaze for long into an abyss, the abyss gazes also into you.'...I am the abyss."

~Niklas

Chapter One

The scent of smoke and sulfur tickled her nose. Flinching, Carly turned her head in a vain attempt to evade the acrid smell. Her head throbbed. Her mouth was dry. No, something dry was *in* her mouth.

A gag? Why am I gagged?

Splaying her fingers, she gripped the rough bark pressing against her back. Rope, thin but unforgiving, bit into her flesh just below her breasts and across her stomach, binding her wrists tight enough to threaten her circulation. Woozy, she struggled to focus. Wiggling her wrists and squirming gained her no freedom.

What happened to me?

Oh, her head hurt.

This was bad. *Really* bad.

Why was it so difficult to focus?

Slowly, she forced her eyes open. Flames, blurry at first, then brighter, leaped before her. The heat of the fire warmed her bare legs, licked invitingly at her chest, neck and face, despite the chill of foreboding settling into her bones. Bodies swayed and gyrated. Dark shadows danced across a brilliant orange and yellow canvas. A twisted, impossible form came into view. Goat legs, horns, a slithering forked tongue, furry yet humanlike upper body.

A monster stepped out of the shadows. A hush swept over the clearing as the dancers bowed low and backed away. Whispers of "Master" floated to her on the smoke scented breeze. It all came back in a jolt of sudden awareness.

She'd been walking home, taking the same route past the park that she'd taken a hundred times before. They'd come at her from every direction, melting from the shadows like the boogeymen of nightmares. She'd run. She'd thought she'd escaped.

But she hadn't. They'd only been toying with her, surrounding her, letting her exhaust herself before they moved in for the bag and tag. There was a large gap in her memory that was more than a little unsettling. But her current circumstances took precedence over what may or may not have happened after they'd knocked her out.

She'd been gagged and trussed to a tree, a sacrificial lamb waiting to be slaughtered. And the creatures dancing around her defied explanation. When they'd burst from the trees, she'd assumed, as any sane person would, that they were wearing costumes. Elaborate, grotesque costumes.

Now she could see they weren't costumes at all.

"Help me," she tried to scream. The putrid gag prevented anything but muted garble from escaping. "Let me go," she mumbled, struggling against her bonds with renewed purpose. But the more she fought, the more the ropes bit into her flesh.

The Master uttered something in a guttural, foreign language, and the other creatures resumed their dancing and chanting with frenetic vigor. A flutter of diaphanous white in the periphery of her vision caught her attention. A woman lay sprawled in the grass a few yards away, unmoving, eyes closed. The Master gave a jerk of his head and snarled something in that language she couldn't understand. The dancers swarmed over the unconscious woman. They fell upon her like a pack of feral animals lost to a ravenous frenzy and tore her to shreds with bared teeth, slurping and suckling at the crimson flow of her blood.

Gagging, Carly scrunched her eyes closed and whipped her head to the side. But she could not strike the image from her mind so easily. That sight would haunt her for the rest of her days. Not that she expected to live much longer, all things considered.

And then she felt it. The Master's presence in front of her. Too terrified *not* to look, she opened her eyes and faced him. He wasn't human. Of that she had little doubt. He dwarfed her by a solid two and a half feet, if not more, and had to outweigh her by at least two hundred pounds. He was enormous.

The Master began chanting; his voice was unimaginably deep, layered as if multiple voices spoke in unison. The words he called out were a jumble of syllables and grunts, but his intonation held a discernible, mesmerizing rhythm now. And his face held more than a hint of smug pleasure.

At his sharp command, the frenzied creatures ceased their feeding with swift obedience. The group scuttled back, but Carly couldn't bring herself to look at the woman, or rather what was left of her. She didn't dare glance away from the cold, black eyes staring down at her.

The Master stretched out an enormous hand and slowly lifted a lock of Carly's hair. He examined the shoulder-length tresses for a moment before flicking her hair away with idle indifference.

The tip of one cold, black claw skated down the side of her neck, and paused at the base of her throat where her pulse pounded erratically. He gave a deft twist of his wrist and searing pain scored her flesh. Just a scratch, but the wound burned like it had been splashed with rubbing alcohol. As if he had all the time in the world, the Master raised the talon in front of her face. His tongue slithered out, and he licked her blood from the claw, his expression grotesquely blissful.

Tears of terror welled, blurring her vision. But she was made of stronger stuff than that. Forcing steel into her spine, Carly blinked the tears away and thrust her chin up. This beast would feed off her fear as the others had fed off that poor woman's flesh and blood. She'd be damned if she'd give him the satisfaction.

He lowered his razor-sharp claw and paused at the first button on her blouse. He watched her with an evil, lecherous gaze, pushing her for a response, waiting to feed on her terror. With another flick of his claw, the Master sent the small button flying. Her blouse sagged open. Another flick, another button. Slow. Torturous. But she refused to respond. Refused to react. Those cold, black eyes narrowed as he surveyed all that he'd uncovered. His breathing changed subtly, coming faster now. His interest had finally been stirred. By her rebellion or by her body, she couldn't say. It didn't really matter. Either way she wanted nothing to do with what she'd unintentionally sparked in him. Carly pressed her head back against the tree. A lone tear slipped past her control, sliding down her cheek.

Her flesh crawled as a thick finger slipped under the edge of her blouse, sliding the thin material out of the way, first one side, and then the other. Soon the pale pink lace of her bra was the only thing concealing her breasts from the Master's lewd stare. Trembling, Carly shook her head and a whimper escaped her, a mute plea the Master ignored. His intentions were clear, and she gagged again.

Death might be better than what this monster's lust-filled obsidian eyes promised.

That long, black talon skimmed over the curve of her breast, down her stomach, and stopped just inside the edge of the waistband of her shorts. She no longer trembled. Instead, she shook like a tree in the aftershocks of an earthquake. Her heart pounded so hard, she wondered how it hadn't already exploded.

A bloodcurdling roar tore through the unnatural silence. A roar worthy of a feral, rabid beast. Carly jolted against her restraints and jerked her head around, looking for the source of that God-awful sound. The Master froze. His black eyes widened. His body tensed. And then he vanished, only to reappear on the other side of the bonfire, a dozen feet away, feet braced apart, arms spread as if preparing for attack. Carly gaped, not believing her own eyes.

How had he…?

Another dark roar split the night. The Master crouched in a battle stance, jerking his head around as he too searched the shadows. His otherworldly eyes narrowed, and he surveyed his minions, as if counting how many obstacles stood between him and whatever it was that had made that horrendous sound. What could make this monstrous beast react like a cornered rabbit?

The air blurred, distorted. Another monster appeared not three feet from her, wavering into reality, like a desert mirage taking form. This monster was more frightening than the first, if that were possible.

Short, thick, slightly curved, black horns sprouted from either side of his head. Wicked, black claws tipped each finger, and vicious fangs—longer and thicker than the Master's—gleamed in the firelight. His skin was jet black, from the top of his bare head to the waist of his ragged, tight jeans. His shoulders were massive, his arms and thighs bulged with raw strength.

Defined ridges of muscle roped across his stomach, disappearing into the narrow waistband of his jeans. Red runes glowed upon his flesh, strange symbols she'd not seen before, as if lit from within, pulsing with a life of their own.

Tied as she was with her arms behind her, Carly plastered herself to the tree, eyes wide. Fear choked her silent as she struggled to make herself smaller, praying this new threat wouldn't notice her.

The newcomer glanced down at the ravaged body near the bonfire. His nostrils flared, his brow crushed together in a harsh scowl. Then his gaze slid to Carly.

She swore, in that sliver of time, her heart stopped dead. Simply ceased to beat.

His eyes arrested her. They were brittle chips of ice blue, pure as a cloudless summer sky. His unwanted attention raked over her, pausing for a moment on her exposed, heaving chest. A low, appreciative growl rumbled in his throat, like the deep snarl of a lion. Sparks of interest flared in the icy depths as he devoured her with his stare.

But then the Master moved, shifted to the side as if he intended to flee. The newcomer's eyes changed, burning fiercely as he turned to the Master and then to the minions cowering around the fire. Throwing his head back, taking her by surprise, the newcomer let out a savage roar. Balls of pulsing yellow liquid-like energy suddenly danced above his palms as he faced off against the Master. Challenging. Lethal.

The Master's followers scattered in a crazed flurry. Some scurried to their overlord, seeking protection. Others fled into the night. A brave few rushed forth to face the newcomer. The Master turned upon those who fled or sought his protection, cutting them down with great sweeps of his massive arm and lethal slashes of his deadly claws.

The Master's loyal minions shrieked as they hurled themselves at the dark newcomer. He took two of them out with glowing orbs of pulsing yellow plasma. Screaming, they fell to the ground, engulfed in flames. He stepped over one writhing figure with casual disregard, batting others aside like nuisance insects. He was on a mission, and his mission was the Master.

The sight of him as he crashed through the bonfire, unscathed, left Carly in an odd state of shock. He looked like a nightmare called forth from the bowels of Hell, something born of brimstone and hellfire. A whirlwind of sparks shot into the dark sky as he left a trail of branches and thick, burning logs in his wake. Carly watched, helpless, as the two monsters faced off, head to head. Roars and bellows rent the night. Massive fists pulverized flesh. Blood sprayed. Though they rolled through the fire, the blistering heat didn't appear to affect either of them. Claws slashed, fangs snapped, blood ran.

Carly gaped in horror, tugging frantically at her restraints. Her wrists burned where the ropes cut her skin, and still she struggled, beyond desperate to slip away while the two were locked in battle.

The dark fiend landed a particularly vicious blow, sending the Master flying through the air. He crashed into a huge tree, snapping it in half. Chunks of bark and massive splinters exploded into the air around them as the tree toppled.

And then the Master was gone, vanishing before her eyes.

The dark fiend slammed his fist into an enormous boulder, cracking it right down the middle. A frustrated snarl tore from deep in his chest. Carly scanned the small clearing. Not a single one of the Master's followers had survived.

She remained to face the beast alone, tied to a tree. Unable to run. Helpless.

And then he turned to her. He was every bit as terrifying as the Master. His focus dipped to her chest, lingered, heated as he closed the distance between them. And he snarled that lion's purr again. Lifting a huge hand, he cradled the side of her head with unexpected tenderness, his gaze probing.

"Do not be afraid, *tá'hiri*," he growled around those huge fangs. His voice was deep and layered as well, the words tripping from his tongue as if the language were foreign and unwieldy. The timbre of his voice stole through her, soothed her, lulling her into compliance despite all common sense.

"It is best that you sleep now," he commanded. "Do not fear. I will keep you safe."

Carly blinked against the hypnotic pull of those odd, pale blue eyes. And then out of nowhere, a huge fist clipped her chin. Fear abandoned her. Terror had no hold upon her. Not anymore. Darkness swam over her vision. Her eyes slid closed, and she sagged against her bonds.

Chapter Two

Niklas sat on the edge of the scarred coffee table and stared at the unconscious woman on his sofa. Lost in thought, he lifted a towel to his head and rubbed the moisture from his hair. He'd worried she might wake up before he was through with his shower, but it looked as if he'd hurried for nothing. She hadn't moved a muscle since he'd laid her on the couch.

He grimaced when he spied the bruise forming on the ridge of her jaw. She was far more delicate than he'd thought. Unable to resist the temptation, he trailed his fingers from her temple to her jaw and down the length of her throat. Warm. Soft. Creamy perfection. He gritted his teeth as rivers of lust surged through his blood and jerked his hand back as if he'd been burned. Best not to touch her anymore. He didn't dare stretch his already tenuous control. She'd stirred something in him. Something dark and...primitive.

The air around her pulsated a soft, peaceful white. She wasn't ready to wake yet. Probably just as well. He needed a few moments to marshal his wayward thoughts. He'd had several unexpected surprises tonight. Not the least of them, her.

Or rather, his reaction to her.

Sighing, he pinched his thumb and forefinger on the bridge of his nose. A dull throb persisted just behind his eyes and at the base of his skull, as it always did whenever he went demonic. He would deal with the headache. He'd rather fight in demonic form. Though it constantly, painfully regenerated, his human body sustained damage too easily.

He just couldn't maintain demonic form for very long. The allure of *staying* demonic, the appeal of giving in to sinful depravation, was too powerful. He'd tossed back a few painkillers on the way out of the bathroom. He'd count himself lucky if the pills took the jagged edges off the migraine he had tonight. Usually, a good day's sleep would cure him, but he didn't have time for that luxury now.

He had traps to set, demons to kill.

And now a woman to protect.

The woman in question drew a deep breath, shifting. He opened his eyes to gauge her aura. Still white. She shifted again, restless, and the gape in her shirt sagged open. Groaning, he forced himself to look away, but he found himself drawn back to her creamy flesh time and time again.

Pressing a fist to his aching forehead, he held himself in rigid check. He would not do this. He wouldn't listen to that dark, layered voice of sin echoing in the back of his mind. He would *not* give in. He'd fought too hard, come too far to fall back to his old ways now.

His body continued to respond to her, despite his best efforts to curb his desire. That fact alone left him shaken to the core. He needed to get his mind off her. Now. He glanced around the tiny apartment, taking in the full-size bed in the corner. The sheet and blankets were a jumbled mess, one corner trailing onto the floor. The single, balled-up pillow made the bed look all the more desolate. He'd grown used to the isolation. Used to sleeping alone. He'd been sleeping alone for almost two hundred Earthbound years now. Denying himself the pleasures of the flesh had been one of the more difficult aspects of his penance. But he'd managed.

Of course, he'd never chanced upon a woman this beautiful before. He couldn't quite put his finger on it, but something about her drew him like a moth to a flame. Was it only skin deep? Or had it been the way she'd resisted the fear and raised her stubborn little chin in defiance of Ronové? Whatever it was, he couldn't shake it.

Seeking a safer train of thought, he surveyed the kitchenette. A small, dented, dorm-size fridge hummed softly in the opposite corner, near the single-basin sink. It was, he knew, nearly empty. He only kept it stocked with essentials for times like this, when his head was already throbbing too much, and his concentration was too jumbled for him to conjure anything else. He'd just have to wait 'til she woke up, and then—somehow—he'd manage to call forth whatever she requested. Provided his head hadn't rolled from his body by then.

He turned to survey the rest of the apartment. Anywhere but the woman. The walls were a dull brown, the carpet worn and stained from decades of traffic. The room was Spartan at best, located in a rundown dive in the only seedy neighborhood in town. He could have altered the dimensions of the room, conjured anything he wanted, made the inside of this pitiful apartment as large and as opulent as the Taj Mahal. He could have taken her to his flat in Paris, but why bother? It wasn't as if he were contemplating keeping her. Even if she was the most entrancing creature he'd ever come across. He didn't care what she thought of him. He had a single, all-encompassing purpose.

Absolution of his sins.

Redemption.

And no room for a woman.

Finally glancing down at the fragile female he'd saved, steeling himself against the unwanted desire she kindled without effort, he realized bringing her there, trapping himself inside the tiny apartment with her, was a disaster of epic proportions. Even now, the scent of her crept inside him, stealing into the deepest, darkest corners of his tarnished soul. Disconcerted, he pushed to his feet and strode across the room. He draped the towel over the back of the chair and made his way to the dingy window.

After prying the pane open, he pushed it up and braced his palms on the peeling windowsill. Niklas leaned out into the night, dragging in a gulp of stale air in a vain attempt to clear his head. And still, the fog of lust lingered. He caught himself peering at her over his shoulder.

It was no use.

He couldn't *not* watch her.

It had been so long since he'd been with a woman, so long since he'd touched one or lost himself in soft, feminine flesh. So long since he'd simply sat and just watched one, with her fluid grace and delicate mannerisms. His fingers itched to caress her. Was the rest of her skin as soft as he'd imagined, or had his mind played cruel tricks on him after all these years of abstinence?

Fearing his unexpected weakness, Niklas stood

there, digging his fingers into splintering wood, praying his feet might grow roots so he wouldn't go to her, seduce her.

Get rid of her, that was what he should be doing. Ditch her somewhere and put her from his mind, never think of her again. But he couldn't do that now, thanks to that bastard Ronové. Now he had to question her, pump her for whatever information he could get from her. There was too much at stake to let a valuable opportunity like this slip through their fingers. Dragging in a great breath of humid night air, he weighed his options. Much as he disliked admitting it, she presented him with too much temptation. He was going to need help on this one. But who to call?

Mikhail? Hmm.

No, that might not be wise. Witnessing Ronové and himself had, no doubt, been traumatic enough for the female. More than likely, Mikhail would send her right over the edge, screaming the entire way. No matter *which* form he chose, demonic or human.

Sebastian?

With his immeasurable patience, Sebastian would probably be the best candidate. But last Niklas had heard, Sebastian was off the grid somewhere in South America tracking a horde of demons that was devastating small villages, leaving behind nothing more than rubble and desecrated bodies in its wake.

Gideon then?

No!

Much as he considered Gideon his brother-in-arms, unwarranted jealousy fisted deep in his gut and twisted. Granted, Gideon could no longer physically touch or *be* touched by human hands. But these odd stirrings inside

Niklas didn't bode well. What if Gideon held too much appeal for the woman to resist? Besides, lately Gideon had been...*unpredictable* at best. No, he wouldn't call Gideon.

The last thing he needed was to have to worry about some unexpected, treacherous thing like jealousy rearing its ugly head. Not that he had any right to be jealous where she was concerned. He'd willingly accepted abstinence as part of his penance. Penance wasn't meant to be comfortable, or something you could shrug on and off when it was convenient.

Niklas reached down and readjusted the bulge behind the straining zipper on his jeans.

Heaven knew *this* wasn't comfortable. Not one damned bit.

Since Niklas had clapped eyes on the woman, since the moment he'd caught her scent, he'd been experiencing the strangest urges to protect her. To possess her. To lay her down and thrust himself inside her, fast and hard, slow and deep, and every measure in between. To fill her body and her mind with nothing but *him*. Brand himself upon her very soul.

Until he got those baffling urges out of his system—or, at the very least, got a leash on them—it would be best not to test his limits.

Relations between his small legion of fallen demons had withstood much. But none of them had great quantities of patience, except for Sebastian, of course, and Niklas didn't want to strain the bond they shared any more than necessary. They provided a support system of sorts, a network of aid in times of temptation, and were useful allies in their ongoing war against their former compatriots, demons of hellfire and damnation, Lucifer's soldiers. That didn't, however, mean they always played well together.

With the right provocation, things could get nasty. Real quick.

Xander it is.

At one time the right hand of Lucifer, feared by all in Hell and beyond, Xander had hunted down and slain any demon that rebelled against Lucifer's rule. No matter how powerful, no matter how cunning or resourceful, there wasn't a demon alive that could evade the Slayer for long.

Right now, it looked as if Xander was his only hope.

And, that being the case, he was well and truly screwed.

Biting back a curse, Niklas reached into his hip pocket and drew out his phone. Having to admit to weakness was galling. Revealing that weakness to another demon went against the grain. After thumbing in a quick sequence of numbers, he waited impatiently for the call to connect.

"Speak," Xander rasped.

"I need your help. I'm in Ridgefield, Iowa. I've already interrupted a summoning. There's some weird stuff going on down here, and I've got an added..." Niklas peered over his shoulder at the sleeping woman "...complication."

"Friday. Noon." Short, sweet and to the point. Well, maybe not so sweet, but definitely short and to the point. That was Xander. Not one to waste words.

Not anymore. Not since the Great Fall when Gabriel and the others had not only torn his wings from him but desecrated his voice as well.

Niklas ran a splayed hand through his hair. Three days. Heaven help him. He shot a nervous glance at the woman on his sofa. What was he going to do with her until then?

"Can't you make it any sooner than that?" Hell's bells, he sounded desperate.

He turned to the woman again, his focus dipping to her exposed, lacy bra.

Damn it, he *was* desperate.

"Miss me?" Xander's dry sarcasm crackled over the phone line.

Not even the fact that he'd recently found his own shining piece of Heaven right here on Earth in the form of a leggy blonde beauty had softened Xander one bit. *Asshole.*

Normally, Niklas would have fired back with some snide remark, but his hunger for the woman on his couch was growing by the moment. Every second he spent alone with her was one second closer to another fall. And, damn it, he'd kept his nose clean for too long to slip up now.

She moaned, shifted, drawing his attention. Her creamy breasts, plump against that thin scrap of lace, literally made his mouth water.

Sweet Christ, he could all but taste her.

"Ronové gathered an Earthbound legion, just as we feared." Desperate to turn his focus to something—*anything*—else, he tore his attention from her alluring flesh. Niklas scrunched his eyes closed, scrubbed a hand over his face and prayed Xander would change his mind and agree to come directly to the apartment in the next five seconds.

Dead silence met this pronouncement. Niklas

pulled the phone from his ear and glanced at the display, just long enough to ascertain the call hadn't dropped. Gripping the back of his neck with one hand, he pressed the phone to his ear once more.

"They're performing ritual sacrifices in the middle of the frickin' city park. *Ritus Niger Noctis.*" *Sweet Mary!* That reminder succeeded in dampening some of the heat coursing through his veins. He got chills just thinking about it. "A woman was killed tonight. And another woman saw the whole thing, Slayer."

"Who are they summoning?" That single question was as dark and as vehement as any curse Niklas had ever heard.

"Ronové is a warlord, and a powerful one at that. With the number of minions he was using...and the blood sacrifice...he has to be summoning one powerful SOB." He didn't even want to speak the consequences aloud.

Xander was silent for a moment, and then, in a voice gone deadly cold, said, "Stolas?"

Niklas weighed his response. The mastermind behind the plot to overthrow Lucifer was the only demon he could come up with. "Gut instinct tells me yes. If Ronové is working for or with Stolas, then we have an even bigger rebellion on our hands than we first thought. I took out most of Ronové's minions without breaking a sweat. A couple fled, but I doubt he'd rely on them anymore. My guess is he'll hunt them down himself and fry them for abandoning their master in the middle of a fight. Either way, it'll slow him down considerably. But that doesn't mean we're off the hook."

An aggravated growl rolled through the phone line,

Xander's elegant way of voicing his opinion. If Ronové was trying to summon Stolas…if he eventually succeeded, well, it wasn't gonna be pretty.

"The witness?"

"Currently, she's passed out on my sofa."

"And?" Impatience dripped from the solitary word.

Over the course of the last few centuries, Xander had achieved a great respect for free will. He probably figured if this woman wanted to leave Niklas's protection, she should be allowed to waltz right out the door the moment she woke up. No matter the risk.

Niklas glanced at the woman again. Those cursed primitive instincts stirred deep in his gut once more.

She's not going anywhere, that dark voice deep in the pit of his black soul snarled.

He wouldn't let himself consider the logic behind his determination to keep her. Wouldn't let himself examine the fierce need to possess her. He'd chalk it up to keeping an innocent safe and leave it at that.

That was logical.

That he could deal with.

Huchtaé ma'k, locti'vars, Niklas had once told Xander. *Choose your battles wisely, my brother.*

This was one battle he had a feeling he should avoid at all costs.

Niklas dragged his hand down the side of his face and around to the back of his neck once more, kneading the stiff muscles there. "Ronové has tasted her blood. She's in danger. You know how he is. To make things worse, *I* was the one that took her away from him. He won't just let it go. He won't stop until he gets her back, if for no other reason than to get back at me."

"And?" How could Xander infuse one word with

such a wealth of accusation?

Leave it to Xander to slap the cold, hard facts directly in your face with the smooth finesse of a fist to the nose. Niklas had assumed Xander would be the most understanding of all of them, all things considered. He himself had a woman now that he'd die to protect. Not that this was the same kind of situation. Because this was *so* not the same. Xander's mate was special. Hell, they'd all developed a soft spot for Kyanna. This woman was just another innocent. Totally not the same thing *at all*.

Was he protesting too much?

Yes. Yes, he was.

And he'd never been good at lying to himself.

"She's probably in more danger from me than she is from Ronové," he grudgingly admitted. "Or I'm in more danger from her. Either way, this whole situation is screwed beyond all hope."

A lengthy silence followed. "Had some new developments on this end as well. Had another visit from an old friend."

"Who?"

"Samuel."

That gave Niklas pause. Xander had one mission now, to protect the Arc Stone and its guardian. A simple enough task in theory, given the guardian was now his wife. But Xander's mission was going to Hell in a handbasket if he was being visited by angels. Niklas didn't envy Xander.

But the memory of big, brown eyes, staring trustingly up at him, flashed in his mind. He wasn't all that fond of his own situation just now either. "Just don't drag your feet, all right?"

Silence. Niklas very nearly checked his display again.

"Thursday," Xander conceded with a deep, aggrieved sigh.

"Thursday," Niklas echoed unhappily. Xander, after all, had his own demons to fight. And now, apparently, angels as well. "Don't shimmer directly into the apartment. I don't know how she'll handle all this yet."

A disparaging snort taunted him through the phone. He could well understand Xander's cynicism. Since when had Niklas been overly concerned with human sensibilities?

The line went dead.

Niklas thrust the slim device back into the pocket of his ragged jeans. He closed the window and stared at his reflection for a moment, silent and pensive. Icy blue eyes, eyes once a brilliant, sapphire blue, stared back at him, a cold and pale ghost of their former glory. Flat and emotionless. Wary and piercing. He did not look upon beauty for the sake of beauty alone. Hadn't for a long time, not the way he used to do.

Oh, he could still see.

He just saw things *differently* now.

The woman stirred again, moaning softly. He peered over his shoulder. The air around her slowly began to change from peaceful white to purple, an oppressive shade of fear. Streaks of gray, anguish and despair, started to snake their way through her aura.

She wasn't going to wake up with a smile on her face.

The throbbing gray around her grew stronger, a churning, angry, storm cloud nearly muting the purple.

At this rate, he'd be lucky if she didn't wake up screaming. Niklas heaved a great, put-upon sigh.

He hated the screaming.

Niklas went to the fridge and pulled out a bottle of water, wishing he had something stronger to offer her. But she was stuck with whatever he had on hand. No way was he tapping his energy, conjuring anything else randomly, not with the migraine pounding through his head. He returned to the coffee table. How long would it take her to wake up? The sooner he got all the hysterics and the explanations out of the way, the sooner he could get on with tracking Ronové.

The sooner he could get rid of her.

As he sat there waiting, he studied her colors. Gray and purple weren't the only colors swirling around her. The closer he looked, the more puzzled he became. He'd never seen someone wearing that much emotion before. She was like a rainbow to him. Complex. Compelling. But there was more. *She* was more. She was this *canvas*, a solid base of color that tinted all the other swirls of color.

A bright and sunny yellow-gold.

The purest glimpse of raw hope he'd ever seen.

Since his fall, his *vision* had become both blessing and curse. He saw humans, saw their physical being as others did, only he possessed an added perspective most did not. He saw vivid layers of color pulsing around every living individual. Their anger and their joy. Their despair and their hope. Their fears and their love. All a kaleidoscope of emotional hues.

Her colors swirled faster.

And three, two, one...

Between one heartbeat and the next, the woman

gasped aloud, lurching into an upright sitting position. Arms swung up, tiny fists clenched like a boxer squaring off, she scooted down the length of the sofa, eyes wide and darting.

But she didn't scream.

Brownie points for her.

When no attack was forthcoming, she let out a pent-up breath and lowered her fists. With her wild gaze still darting around the room, returning over and over to him, she cautiously patted her neck, chest and stomach. Vivid color filled her cheeks as she jerked the edges of her blouse together.

"Where am I?" Her attention flew to the window, swept the room, landing on the door. She turned a scowl on him, suspicious. Ready to bolt. "Who are you? How did I get here?"

Calm. Well, *relatively* calm. Perfectly reasonable questions. Good. He could work with reasonable.

Then her palm skimmed her bruised jaw. Those beautiful eyes narrowed.

"How about we start with this," he coaxed, offering her the water bottle.

She considered the bottle in his hand and her scowl deepened. For heaven's sake, you'd think he'd offered her a snake. Then again, after what she'd been through tonight, he'd probably be apprehensive in her shoes as well.

Arching a brow, he held the bottle out between them and slowly opened it, so she could hear the plastic safety strip crack. Then, just as slowly, he tipped the bottle to his lips and poured a healthy splash of water into his mouth. Swallowing, he held the bottle out to her once more.

"It's safe. Go on."

Still cautious, she accepted the water in silence.

Lowering her feet slowly to the floor, she took a long guzzle, but her attention never left him. Confusion throbbed around her like an angry bruise on the air. "Where am I?"

"You're still in Ridgefield." He clenched his hands, fighting the urge to smooth his fingers over the length of her bare leg. Was it as smooth and soft as her cheek, as her neck? What would the tender inside of her thigh taste like? He forced a swallow. "Grove Street, just on the south end of town."

She studied him from the top of his damp, black hair to the tips of his scuffed combat boots. But she kept returning, over and over, to his eyes. Had she made the connection yet?

"Who are you?" Her brows drew together. "Have we met before? There's something about you that's—"

"I am Niklas." He weighed honesty against discretion. "We have never met before tonight."

Well, technically, that was the truth.

"How did I get here?" She glanced around again. "I don't remember." Her focus turned inward. "After work, I walked home through the park." Her forehead wrinkled in the most adorable way as she rambled disjointedly through the succession of events. "I heard chanting. I followed the sound. And then I saw—" She broke off, shaking her head as her words came faster and faster. "I ran, and this dark shadow. And then—" Eyes wide, she peered at him. "And then. Then that huge *m-monster*—"

He didn't want to give her time to dig herself further into the fear. Didn't ask to which monster she referred, Ronové or himself.

"You aren't crazy," Niklas soothed. "This night and all you witnessed was real."

Now she looked at him as if *he* were the crazy one. She glanced to the door again. He could all but see the wheels turning in her head. Could she make it before he caught her? Would he try to stop her?

"You've seen something you shouldn't have this night. Something not meant for human eyes."

"Uh-huh." She nodded in a placating sort of way. A weak smile pushed at her lips, thin and unconvincing.

A storm cloud of gray bled through her aura, darker, denser than before.

Heaving a sigh, he resisted the urge to roll his eyes. She might not be a screamer, but she had *runner* written all over her. That was just terrific. He had better things to do than chase her all over creation tonight.

Unobtrusively—at least, he imagined she *thought* she was doing it on the sly—her right foot slid back, angled, planted for traction.

And three, two, one...

Chapter Three

Niklas shimmered in front of the door a spare second before she got there. Her hand, stretching for the doorknob, brushed against his hip, perilously close to a certain rebellious part of his anatomy. A part that, until tonight, had been ruthlessly ignored. Until tonight— until *her*—Niklas had nearly convinced himself that his body no longer had *those* needs. Unfortunately, since he'd laid eyes upon her earlier, that part of him seemed to have taken on a mind of its own, gleefully mutinying against any semblance of control.

What a misguided fool he'd been.

With a stifled shriek, she jerked her hand away and backpedaled across the room.

"Woman, you must calm down." Holding his hands, palms out, in front of him, Niklas tried to moderate his voice, tried to soothe her into compliance. The walls of the apartment were paper-thin. If she screamed, would his neighbors investigate? Would they call the authorities? Damn, he could *really* use some help right now. "You must not become hysterical. We have much to discuss, and time is short."

"Don't tell me what I must and must not do." She backed away from him carefully, as if she expected him to pounce on her at any moment.

Though fear clouded her eyes and gray still saturated the air around her, her tone held sparks of defiance and courage. And he couldn't help but be just a little impressed.

"How? How did you do that?" She jabbed an unsteady finger toward the living area, though she never took her suspicious eyes from him. "Get from over there to over here so fast?"

"I can move quickly when I need to."

"Right," she said, disbelief etched all over her face. Somehow, in the middle of one of the most severe frowns he had ever seen, she managed to arch her brow. "How did I get here? Really?"

"I brought you here," he said. "I found you in the park. I, ah, I carried you back here."

When it looked as if she was about to press the issue, he held his hands up between them again to show her he meant no harm. "Look, you're not crazy. And neither am I. You must not doubt what you saw earlier. Your life, your soul, depends upon it."

"That's insane. What I saw c-couldn't have happened." Denial, but yellow seeped into the gray. Hope. Did she hope she hadn't lost her mind?

Or did she hope that by agreeing with him she might lull him into inattentiveness and then escape? He needed to convince her. But how?

"His name is Ronové, the demon you saw tonight."

"Demon?" she blurted, incredulous. "As in Lucifer's minions, escaped from Heaven and all that?"

He nodded. "Massive, ugly beast. Red with black Cryptoglyphs tattooed on his flesh, black claws, black eyes, breath like sulfur."

She blinked. Swallowed.

"And his minion, Dimiezlo," he added. "Creepy little sucker. 'Bout yea high, goat legs, horns, snake tongue. Groveling disposition."

Nodding, eyes glazing over, she dropped to the sofa.

"Woman," he took a cautious step closer, "you're not going to faint, are you?"

"Carly," she whispered. "My name is Carly. Carly Danner." She lifted a shaking hand and shoved at strands of hair that had fallen into her eyes. And then her fingertips dropped to the base of her throat, where they rubbed fretfully at a small red mark on her skin. "I'm a paralegal," she insisted, rambling to herself in a soft, dazed tone. "My life is routine. *Normal*. I like it that way." Was she trying to convince him, or reassure herself? "Things like this just don't happen. Not in the real world. Not in *Iowa*, for God's sake." Accusing brown eyes pierced him. "Not to me. This is *unbelievable*. Books. Movies. Not real life." Her fingertips rubbed absently at the base of her throat as she shook her head and lowered her gaze to her lap.

"They do happen," Niklas argued. "And what better place than a harmless town in an innocuous state? Who would think to look here, in *Iowa*, for rebellious demons bent on practicing forbidden rituals?" He returned to his seat on the coffee table. Her face was deathly pale. The colors swirling around her pulsed and changed so quickly his headache got worse just trying to track them. "You need to believe this is all real. You won't know when, you won't know where, or who. It might even be someone you already know. But he will get to you. If you leave this apartment without me, you will die."

That caught her attention. She looked at him once more. Alarm flashed.

His focus dipped to the scratch she kept poking at the base of her throat. It was red and inflamed. "Ronové won't stop until he has your soul."

"My soul," she croaked, cupping her throat, covering the mark.

Color continued to pulse and swirl around her. His head swam trying to keep up. And, strangely enough, weaving in and out of the fear whispered the faint tinges of—

Red?

The color of desire and attraction?

No. He couldn't be reading her right. Something must be affecting him, influencing his sight. His own attraction to her had somehow manipulated his power, making him see things that couldn't possibly be there.

"He's a Collector," Niklas explained, eager to focus on something, *anything* other than the strange anomaly occurring with his vision. At her curious murmur, he expounded, "Once a Collector gathers a soul, he offers it to Lucifer as a sacrifice. Every soul offered gains a Collector favor with the dark prince. The more souls he gathers, the higher his prestige in Lucifer's army. Ronové is a greedy demon. And, once he has a target, he's obsessed. He won't stop until he collects you." Niklas stood, crossed to the window. Gripping the window frame, he peered out into the night.

The thought of her falling into Ronové's hands left him cold and shaken. The need to keep her safe, to protect her, had become vital to him so quickly it made his already pounding head nearly spin right off his shoulders. Not a pleasant feeling at all. This desire for her was an animalistic drive, stronger than anything he'd ever experienced before. He didn't have any idea how to stop it. He scrunched his eyes closed. Grinding the heel of his palm to his throbbing temple, he pushed those disturbing thoughts aside. But it was hard. So hard to rationalize. So hard to think.

"How do you know all this about collecting souls for Lucifer?" Her voice was quiet, subdued, yet level enough to tell him she might be willing to give him the benefit of the doubt.

He was silent for several uncomfortable moments. Finally, he turned his head and met her doubtful stare. "Firsthand experience."

"Right." Nope, she wasn't buying it. She crossed her arms and narrowed her eyes. "If he won't stop until he has me, and he really is a demon," she all but choked on the word, "then how will I ever be safe from him? Isn't he like all powerful or something?"

"He's a demon, Carly, not God," Niklas stated flatly. "Yes, he has certain powers. But he has limitations too. All of u—all demons do. I'll keep you safe. You must trust me on this."

"Are you—" She broke off, drew a ragged breath. "Are you a demon hunter or something?"

"Or something," he replied with a self-deprecating smirk.

"For heaven's sake, will you please stop talking in riddles? If you expect me to listen to you, to stay with you, to trust you," she gritted out, "then you damned well better start giving me the truth, straight up. How will you stop him, Niklas? How can you keep him from getting to me?"

He turned to her. "I'll kill him."

His response gave her pause. She stared at him for

a long moment as a jumble of emotions flickered across her beautiful face.

"Demons," she repeated. She shook her head, frowning. "Can demons die? I thought they were already in Hell."

"Oh yes." Visions of countless battles filled his mind and he thought of all the demons he'd already slain. All his former brethren that he'd already sent to Oblivion. A cold void opened somewhere deep inside his chest, because Niklas knew he could just as easily have been the one to meet the unforgiving edge of a blade. "It's not easy, but they *can* die."

"What happens? When they die, what happens? Do they go back to Hell? Can they come back again? I mean, they already were there once, and they got out, right? Are they like recycled, or something?"

A hoarse, mirthless bark of laughter broke free. "No. When a demon dies, truly dies, he doesn't return to Hell. He doesn't resurrect. And he doesn't return to the Father. His soul is forsaken, and so he simply ceases to be. He is no more."

"You keep referring to demons as males. Are there no female demons...demonesses? Whatever you call them?"

"Yes, there are female demons. But they are extremely rare. Very few of the female angels sided with Lucifer at the time of the Great Fall. What can I say, he was a chauvinistic pig." Niklas shrugged. Lucifer really had been a jerk of the highest order. "And for reasons no one really knows, demon spawn rarely, if ever, turn out to be female."

"Demon spawn," she whispered, visibly struggling to assimilate all he'd told her.

"Can you not look beyond the limitations of your imagination?" He stared hard at her, eyes narrowed. Suddenly, inexplicably, he felt the anger swell inside his chest. He didn't have time for her disbelief. There was a very powerful demon gunning for her. One that would stop at nothing to collect her soul. And it was going to take every ounce of her cooperation for Niklas to keep her safe. "Do you not have faith?"

His temper sparked her own. Annoyance flashed in her beautiful brown eyes. "I do have faith. I do believe in God. But I just can't believe that—"

"No. No *buts*. Believe, or don't believe. There are no qualifications."

"All right, Yoda," she snapped.

Again, with the sarcasm. It was as if her temper were the trigger and sarcasm her bullets. She seemed to have a never-ending supply. When Xander snarked like that, it was just plain annoying. But when this bewitching pixie did it, it was adorable. And sexy as hell.

Shaking his head, aggravated, he worked hard to refocus on his lecture. "If you can believe in God, then can you not believe Lucifer is also real? Or angels and demons? Can one exist without the other?"

She remained silent, chewing on her lower lip.

"Can you not believe in what you *feel*?" Losing patience, Niklas crossed to her. He grabbed her by the wrist and drew her to her feet. Charging to the small bathroom, he dragged her along in his wake. After pushing her in front of the mirror, he impatiently tugged the collar of her shirt aside and, doing his level best to ignore the beguiling expanse of creamy flesh he'd just exposed, pointed at the angry, red scratch on her throat.

A scratch that had grown far worse in the short time that she'd been awake. "Can you not believe your own eyes?"

With a muffled cry, she pushed him aside and staggered into the living room. Sagging to the sofa, Carly raked her fingers through her hair. She wrung her hands together.

"Okay. Okay, I believe, all right? I know what I saw. I don't know how you came to be involved in all this. I don't know how you managed to save me. And I do appreciate your help. But I can't stay here forever, Niklas. I can't just hide."

The sound of his name upon her lips sent a tremor of pleasure shivering down his spine. He gritted his teeth against it. The muscle in his jaw ticked. Desire pooled like acid in his gut.

"I have to go back," she murmured. "I have a life I have to go back to. I can't just hide."

That took the wind from his sails, jabbing him with a hard jolt of something so dark and sinister, he clenched his fists in a bid for control. Again, the animalistic drive, only this time it urged him to seize. To ravish. To claim. The thought of her with another man, a boyfriend, or, God forbid, a husband—

Jealous fury shook him from the inside out. His vision blurred for a moment. His fangs began to stretch. His claws pushed longer. His muscles quivered. Sweet Christ, he was *changing*. Going demonic without conscious effort.

Her eyes widened, and she backed up a pace. "Niklas? Are you all right?"

Closing his eyes, he turned away and shuddered, dragging in one gulp of air after another. He could not change. He could not change. He could—*would*—would control this. He would. What was happening to him? Why was he reacting like this? What was it about this one small woman that had awakened these alien urges inside him? Damn, his head was killing him. Pressing clenched fists to his temples, he fought the pain.

"If you return to your family," he gritted out, "you will put them in danger. Ronové will stop at nothing. He'll hurt *anyone* to get to you."

"I have no family. I have no one," Carly whispered. The raw anguish in her voice raked at him, and he peered over his shoulder. Orange flared, like a flash of lightning. Pain. "My parents died when I was twelve. I lived with my uncle after that. He passed away last year. I have no one else." Sympathy swelled inside him, but she didn't give him any opportunity to express it. "But I do have a job," she added, lifting her jaw defiantly.

"No. If you go there, you'll die. Damn it, weren't you paying attention?" He rounded on her, nostrils flared in frustration and anger. "He will track you. He will send his minions after you. He will take great pleasure in torturing you, and he *will* kill you. He'll kill anyone you come in contact with. Do you want to die that way?"

"No." Barely audible, but acquiescence nonetheless. Carly stared at her hands for a moment. "How will you hunt this demon?"

"I have an associate coming to help out." His lips twisted wryly on the term. "He'll be here Thursday, so you just have to lay low until then."

Licking her lips, Carly nodded. She looked so tiny,

so utterly lost. Her blouse gaped as she rubbed at Ronové's scratch. Unbidden, his gaze dipped to the pale pink lace. Without a word, she tugged the edges of her shirt closed again. A becoming blush stained her cheeks.

He could have conjured a shirt for her. However, considering she didn't yet realize who he was, or rather *what* he was, he didn't think that wise. Not while he was still working on building her trust. Besides, he couldn't risk weakening himself further. He was in bad enough shape as it was. His head felt as if someone had buried an axe deep in his cranium.

"Here," he growled, unable to ease the edge desire had honed into his voice. He pulled his soft T-shirt over his head and tossed it to her. She caught the shirt with nimble fingers, and he turned his head away, so she could change. He didn't dare turn his bare back to her, or she'd have a whole new round of questions for him. Most likely beginning with, *How did you get those hideous scars?* The rustle of fabric grated on his nerves. And on his control.

"There was another demon, there in the circle with the others." Her muffled voice came to him from beneath the folds of his shirt. "He fought Ronové, killed some of his followers. He was bigger than Ronové, faster, more powerful. And his eyes were exactly like—" She broke off abruptly, the sound of movement stilled. A pregnant moment passed before the sound of movement resumed. "He spoke to me. Told me I was safe. Who was he, Niklas? Who was *that* demon?"

He flexed his fists at his sides. The moment of truth had come much faster than he'd hoped.

He'd wanted to build a rapport with her, build her

trust before he sprang that revelation on her. He turned to face her, preparing himself for what was to come, but his breath got tangled up in his throat. The sight of her wearing *his* T-shirt sent a jolt of raw lust straight to his loins.

Finally, for the first time in his life, he understood the ancient urges that reduced all men—be it the medieval knight, the conquering warrior, the bloodthirsty pirate, or the supposedly civilized modern man—into a primeval caveman obsessed with the need to claim a specific female for his own.

Clearing his throat, he forcefully redirected his thoughts. "Did you fear him? The demon that fought Ronové?"

Carly plucked at her lower lip with her thumb and forefinger. Her expression was a tangle of confusion. "Honestly? At first, yeah. He was bigger than Ronové, scarier. I mean, he singlehandedly fought and killed so many of Ronové's followers, not to mention battling Ronové himself, and he walked away without a scratch. But when he came to me—" She shook her head, lifting a helpless shoulder. "He said I was safe. And I *felt* safe, crazy as that sounds." Their eyes met, and she admitted, "I don't understand it. He *looked* just like the others. But he was *different*." Her voice trailed away as her frown deepened.

"Looks can be deceiving." Then again, a leopard was still a leopard, spots be damned. Niklas strode to the small cabinet above the sink. Pulling the door open, he peered at the contents of his cupboard. "Are you hungry? You're probably in shock. You should eat something." He shoved aside a partial package of chocolate chip cookies. A half-empty can of chips. A stale loaf of bread; he had nothing to go on it. He could conjure something inside the cabinet, and she wouldn't be able to see—

"Oh my God!"

"What?" He spun about, scanning the room for the cause of her distress. Had the ward stones failed? Had one of Ronové's minions managed to track them? Surely, he would have felt their presence. But her horrified stare was locked on...on *him*.

She bounded to her feet and closed the distance between them. The knowledge that she'd felt safe with him had filled him with such longing, with such unbridled hope, that all thought of his scars had momentarily fled him. She darted around until she stood behind him. He'd never allowed anyone at his back, not even Xander, and he was as close to a friend as Niklas had. Yet he found himself standing still, breath suspended, as he waited. Would she touch him? It would strain his control to the very breaking point. He should be praying with every last ounce of breath in his body that she stepped away.

Sweet Christ, please let her touch me.

The heat of her fingertips traced, feather soft, over his broad shoulders and down, angling toward his shoulder blades, hesitating. And then she touched them, the massive sweeps of puckered scar tissue marring his back. His breath left him in a tormented hiss. Her hands on his flesh had stunned him immobile, sending currents of fire coursing through his veins. He couldn't move, couldn't pull away. But her fingertips didn't stop at the edge of his scars. Her fingertips traced the line of his spine down, down, so slowly, as if she were memorizing the texture of his skin. His eyelids drifted closed of their own volition, and he quelled a shiver.

His body rigid with lust, he turned to face her.

"What happened to you?" Carly whispered, her eyes round, horrified. The rainbow of colors swirling around her shifted once more, stabbing at his vision, and his body went taut with a whole new emotion. He wouldn't take pity from her. Not from anyone. The loss of his wings had been a blow from which he still had yet to recover.

"Where did you get those scars?" She frowned. He could almost see the wheels turning in her quick mind, and in seconds, she gasped aloud. Her eyes widened, and she backed away until the sofa hit the back of her legs. Off balance in more ways than one, she plopped down and mumbled, "Wings?" She lifted a hand to cover her mouth. And then she met his steely stare. "You had wings—"

"Exactly." Though he tried with all his might, he couldn't keep the bitterness from his voice. Just as he couldn't strike it from his heart. "That's what happens when an angel falls. His wings are ripped from him." He could have bitten his tongue off as soon as the words left his mouth. Her face had turned pale. She looked as if she might become ill.

"How did you survive that, Niklas? Those scars are—"

"Are not up for discussion," he ground out, turning away. He could all but feel her gawking at the badges of his disgrace. He imagined her disgust, her horror...or worse, her pity. His patience was already stretched thin, so he changed the subject. "You're probably in shock. You need to get something in your system, something hot and sweet or—"

"Who was that other demon, Niklas?" Subdued. Determined.

Slowly, he closed the cabinet door. His honor would not permit him to lie to her. Releasing a resigned sigh, he abandoned the distraction of the cabinet and faced her. Preparing himself to shimmer in front of the door again, Niklas stared at her, long and hard.

"Me."

Chapter Four

"You?" Confusion, disbelief flooded her. What he claimed was too preposterous to be true. Wasn't it? She'd seen that great, black monster with her own eyes. That demon had looked *nothing* like the incredibly sexy man standing across the room from her.

Except for those eyes.

"Damn it," he muttered beneath his breath, glancing away. Then, as if firming his resolve, he faced her, pinned her in place with those mesmerizing eyes, and advanced on her, his stride purposeful. Intimidating.

So very much like the way that demon had stalked toward her.

Say something, anything *to break this tension*, she told herself. This was ridiculous. She couldn't have heard him correctly. Yet she leaned back, pressing against the cushions as cold dread seeped through her. "You're joking, right? This is all a prank. One really big, really screwed up prank."

But his scars—

Wings.

"Show me," she challenged, swallowing back the fear. He hadn't hurt her. Not yet anyway. And it just wasn't in her to cower. "If you're a demon, then show me. Change, or do whatever it is that you do."

"I'm not a circus performer," he snapped, halting

less than a foot from her.

She'd clearly offended him, but she wanted answers. She wanted the truth. "Look, if you can't—"

"I didn't say I *can't*. I said I'm not a circus performer. And no, before you push the issue, I will not change simply to satisfy your curiosity. Though it would probably be the most expedient way of convincing you. My head's already killing me. Changing back and forth would just make the headache that much worse right now." His expression, already grim, turned downright fearsome. "I wouldn't risk it anyway. When I go demonic, it's hard to come back. Difficult to remember why I decided to seek absolution in the first place. The temptation to stay demonic is nearly impossible to resist." He broke off abruptly, shaking his head and slashing a hand through the air, adamant. "No. Just no."

"Okay," she conceded. She may, or may not, have believed him at this point. But that didn't mean she was ready to tempt fate either, if what he said about his control was true.

Niklas sat down on the coffee table directly in front of her. Their knees brushed, and nerves fluttered low in the pit of her stomach. Despite his wild claims, the pull of him was magnetic. He flinched, rubbed his eyes, blinking hard at her as if suddenly having difficulty with his vision. Frowning, Niklas shook his head slightly and drew a deep breath, focusing on her with renewed intensity, dragging her into a mesmerized limbo. She literally felt herself sinking, unable, unwilling to break the connection.

"You must take everything I tell you as the truth," he insisted gruffly.

"Huh?" She shook herself free, feeling adrift in a sea of confusion. Centering her focus, she held her hands up. "Just wait a minute. You're trying to make me believe that *you* are a demon? Come on! Angel, yes, quite possibly. But one of those monsters in the park? No way."

"I *was* an angel. An Archangel, in fact, yes," he insisted. "What do you think happens to us when we fall, other than that we lose our wings? We become monsters, Carly. We become the nightmare." He stared at her with such intensity she couldn't find it in herself to doubt his words. "You must listen to me. You must take heed."

Unbelievable.

Okay, fine. She would listen. But that didn't necessarily mean she was going to believe everything he said. A fool she was not. Despite the fact he called to her on some level she had no way of comprehending, she didn't know him from Adam. She might still be naïve about some things, but she'd never been one to fall for the old *trust me* song and dance.

"What I'm about to tell you will be difficult for you to hear, but you must listen." He raked a hand through his hair, licked his lips. "You must listen, and you must believe that I won't hurt you."

She watched his mouth, and her mind wandered for a moment. Smooth, sensual lips surrounded by several days' growth of prickly black stubble. What would it feel like to have those lips on hers? What would it feel like to have that stubble scrape over her skin? Down the side of her neck. Across her chest.

A shiver went through her. She moistened her lower lip and caught it between her teeth.

Niklas's scowl deepened, and he blinked at her. His Adam's apple bobbed as he forced a swallow.

She let her attention wander to his neck, to the frantic movement of his pulse before sliding down over the defined muscles of his smooth chest and ridged abdomen. Would his skin be salty against her tongue? Hot?

Gasping, she jerked her alarmed gaze to his face. Heavens, she'd been all but eating the poor man alive with her eyes. Heat flooded her cheeks. A wanton, sensual hussy had somehow stolen inside her body. That just wasn't *her*.

Nevertheless, how could she not fantasize, just a little? Once the shock of waking in a strange apartment with an unfamiliar man had worn off, and she'd come to grips with what she'd witnessed in the park earlier, though she wasn't altogether certain she had just yet, she hadn't been able to push this uncomfortable attraction for him aside. Somehow, someway, her hormones had run away with her, leaving her drooling after this man, this potentially psychotic stranger.

What is wrong *with me?*

He leaned closer, resting his elbows on his knees. When he moved, his well-defined muscles flexed with the sensual grace of a natural-born predator. She should give him his shirt back. Then there wouldn't be quite so much of him to ogle. It was his fault, of course. She'd never been the kind of woman to ogle a man. Not until *he'd* come along, all shirtless and gorgeous. All that sexy bare skin. All those lean, rippling muscles that just went on and on and on and—

Oh, who was she trying to fool? She'd still have ogled.

Criminy, I've become an ogler!

She barely resisted the urge to fan herself. When had it gotten so hot in here?

Appalled by her own lack of self-restraint, she shifted uncomfortably on the sagging cushions. With great difficulty, she managed to look elsewhere. But that action had pitfalls as well. It forced her to focus on his words. Or rather, the sound of his voice.

A voice that moved over her, moved through her, like a lover's caress. Familiar. Eagerly anticipated. Drawing her attention right back to him. His hair was the silky blue-black of a raven's wing, waving around his head in a damp, wild tangle that made her fingers ache to smooth through the dark allure. The scent of him, spice and heat and raw sex, a scent she'd never before experienced, affected her as she imagined fine, aged whiskey might. Exquisite. Heady. Leaving her lightheaded and gasping for air.

Everything about Niklas was a sensual lure her body was hard-pressed to ignore.

"Are you listening to me?"

"I'm sorry, what?" She'd been watching his lips move, savoring the tenor of his voice, but she'd been so lost in her thoughts she hadn't really paid any attention to the actual words. She lifted her brows. Her study in innocence soon turned to a frown of confusion.

His expression was distinctly alarmed now. His hands gripped the edge of the coffee table on either side of his thighs. His knuckles were white.

"Did you hear anything I just said?" Nothing lover-like in his tone that time.

"I'm sorry," she stammered. "My mind wandered."

Niklas jerked his head away. He scowled at the far

wall. Glancing back from the corner of his eye, as if he might find something disturbing should he look directly at her, he skimmed the air around her. His scowl grew so frightening, she cringed. He turned his focus away again and shifted in his seat, looking decidedly uncomfortable.

"Son of a—" His hand swiped over his mouth, muting the rest. Fine dots of sweat had begun to bead his brow.

Alarmed, she sat there, unsure what to do. What was wrong with him? Why was he acting so erratically? Was he ill?

He lurched to his feet and swept a hand around to knead at the back of his neck. Niklas prowled to the window. He faced her, turned away, and then returned yet once more as he set to pacing between the door and the window. He was like a panther, powerful and unpredictable, prowling in a cage much too small for him.

"What's the matter?" she blurted. Her fingertips rubbed at the scratch on her throat again. The uncomfortable ache had slowly morphed into an outright, itchy burn. It took all her willpower not to use her nails.

"You haven't been listening to a word I just said," he accused.

"Jeez. I said I was sorry," she snapped, crossing her arms. Her temper sparked. "I've had a lot to cope with tonight. Cut me a little slack here."

And, on top of it all, now he expected her to believe *he* was a demon too. And not just any demon, but the nightmare that sent all the other little demons running in terror.

But the scars on his back, and his eerie eyes? How could she discount *that*?

Heaving a sigh, she folded her hands in her lap. "I'm sorry. Tell me again. I promise I'll listen." She probably would have been able to follow his explanation better, but a strange throbbing was slowly starting to build at the base of her skull. The pain was muffling her senses, making her feel as if her brain were slowly being wrapped in cotton.

Glowering, Niklas stopped pacing. He took two steps across the void, as if he meant to return to the coffee table, but then he seemed to change his mind. He pulled the single chair from the small dining table, and sat there instead, his ankle propped on his knee.

"You believe in Christian teachings? You know of Lucifer's betrayal and the Great Battle in which he and his followers were cast from Heaven?"

She nodded, her focus trained on his eyes. She wouldn't give in to the urge to stare at his mouth again. She'd never been so fascinated by a man's mouth before. Blinking, she absently massaged her temple. This strange attraction—hell, call it what it was, a crazy uncharacteristic obsession—was so far out of her experience she didn't know how to deal with it. Then again, she'd never had a headache come on so quickly either.

"When we were cast down, each of us was punished for our most heinous sin, or our most prideful vanity. We, every single one of us, had been gifted by God with a specialized gift. Something that would aid us in our missions for His Will. Each of us lost our gift. To compensate, Lucifer bestowed upon certain followers extra...powers."

Frowning, she leaned forward, bracing her elbows on her knees. "Like what?"

He considered his words for a moment. "While still an Archangel, Xander, the associate I mentioned earlier, possessed a voice that made all the other angels weep for the beauty of it. But there was more. His voice was so...so compelling, he could influence another's will, make them do his bidding without even trying. When he fell, his voice was taken from him, turned gravelly and harsh. So rough he rarely speaks at all now. But he gained other powers." He paused then, seeming to weigh his words before adding, "Well, he *used* to have other powers. Some of them have recently...changed."

"So, this Xander is now a demon? That's what you're telling me? That you both are demons."

Niklas nodded. "He is—*was* the Slayer, the right hand of Lucifer. It was his job to track down and kill any who rebelled against Lucifer's reign."

"But you're saying he no longer follows Lucifer, right?"

"That is correct."

"How many angels fell?"

His expression grim, he replied, "In the beginning, there were but a few small legions. Carefully kept track of, carefully managed. But the daughters of man drew us, a temptation our kind couldn't resist, and our numbers quickly multiplied. Wars broke out amongst us, battles for power and position. Alliances formed and dissolved, just as it is in the world of man. Now," Niklas heaved a weary sigh, looking suddenly tired, "there are too many to count."

Oh, *that* didn't sound good. Not at all.

"And how many are there like you? Demons

seeking redemption?"

"Five that we know of." He gave a small shrug. "Myself. The Slayer, ah, Xander. Gideon, Sebastian, and Mikhail. The five of us seek to atone for our sins. We protect the innocent from those loyal to Lucifer, and from those who've defected and are hiding on Earth's plane. From those who have escaped Hell but have no interest in returning to God's light. They live alone or in packs called nests. Those demons are treacherous and lethal. As powerful as the five of us are, even we've learned to tread carefully around some nests. Those rabid packs have loyalty to none but themselves."

Five seeking forgiveness.

Five against "too many to count".

"So Xander was the Slayer," she recited, brimming with curiosity despite the distracting headache and the burn at her throat. "What were the others? Gideon and Sebastian and Mikhail?"

Niklas was quiet for a long moment. Had she pressed too hard? Her curiosity often got the better of her, pushing her to delve where she ought not go. You'd think, after the way the situation in the park had panned out, she'd know better.

Obviously not.

He lowered his foot to the floor, leaned forward, and placed his elbows on his knees, mirroring her. "Gideon was the Demon of Temptation. Sebastian, the Demon of Vengeance. And Mikhail, the Demon of War."

"Demon of War?" She leaned forward, frowning. "You mean like one of the Four Horsemen of the Apocalypse?"

Niklas arched an eyebrow but kept his lips firmly sealed. His expression was inscrutable.

Silence stretched on, leaving her imagination to make of it what she would. Nervous now, she toyed with the thick, silver ring on the middle finger of her left hand. God help her, she was starting to believe him.

"So Temptation, Vengeance, War and Lucifer's own personal assassin. What about you? What were you the demon of?"

A muscle ticked in his jaw, but he held her gaze. "I was the left hand of Lucifer, the Bringer of Death. I was the Collector of Souls."

That pushed the breath from her lungs.

"So you were Death," she concluded. Another Apocalyptic figure. *Great. Just friggin' great.*

"I am called the Seer," he replied stiffly.

Hit a nerve there, did she?

"But you no longer follow Lucifer, either?" Even though she was nearly positive of the answer, she still needed confirmation.

"Correct."

Well, there was a plus.

Then her eyes narrowed.

Wait.

"You said Ronové was a Collector—"

And Niklas had, by his own admission, been a Collector too.

"Yes," he murmured, leaving her to draw what comparisons she would once more.

Chewing her lip, she twisted her ring, round and round and round. Carly peered around the room. Looked anywhere but at the man. *Demon*, she corrected. But even with that reminder, she still had trouble assimilating the facts. She needed her wits about her, and, when looking at him, she felt at a distinct disadvantage.

"Why?" She shook her head, leaning back in her seat, crossing her arms. "Why are you telling me all these things? I'm assuming this isn't exactly standard demon protocol, dumping your whole story out there on the first date, so to speak."

As soon as the words left her mouth, she felt the heat rise in her cheeks. Why would she say something like that? Man, this headache was really getting to her, dulling her wits.

His gaze became earnest. Piercing. "I'm telling you these things in hopes that it will save your life. You have to understand the world you live in. The real world. You have to understand that you are in grave danger. Right now, you, more than anyone else. Ronové will be coming for you." Why did he sound guilty about that? "It's my job to protect you now, and if you know the facts, understand the score, it just makes my job that much easier."

The midnight-black demon, if it really had been Niklas, might have *looked* like Ronové. But, as she'd thought previously, he had acted nothing at all like the beast who'd captured her and tied her to that tree. Then or now. Granted, he'd fought the other demon with vicious fury, killed those other twisted monsters with a complete lack of mercy, but he'd done so only in self-defense. They'd attacked him first.

And he'd saved her. Brought her here, kept her safe, just as he'd promised. He'd been careful and soothing with her. Gentle. Her eyes narrowed. Well, all but for that one moment when he'd punched her in the face.

With everything else, she'd nearly forgotten that. She fingered the tender ridge of her jaw. "You punched me," she accused.

Oh yeah. That was a whole lot of guilt in those blue eyes.

"Sorry about that," he offered, wincing just the slightest bit. "I could have tried mind control, but it doesn't always work. And sometimes...well, sometimes there can be lasting...side effects. I didn't want to take that chance."

She chewed that one over. Lasting side effects sounded a whole lot worse than a bruise. Lifting her chin, drawing herself up, she ordered in the most imperious tone she could muster, "Don't do it again."

He dipped his head in acquiescence, but humor and admiration sparkled in his eyes.

She might not be big on trusting strangers, but she was a firm believer in actions speaking louder than words. So far, his actions had gone a long way toward redeeming him, at least in her opinion.

That reminder gave her the courage to ignore any parallels she might draw between the two demons and the fortitude to continue her questioning.

"What about the others in the clearing?" She briskly rubbed her arms. Her skin was cold and clammy, though it felt like it had to be at least ninety degrees in the room. "What were they?"

"Those were also demons. A lower class of minions, easier to influence. Easier to control. Ronové has been gathering a legion of them."

Lacing his fingers over that wonderfully defined abdomen, Niklas leaned back and adopted the

51

expression of a patient teacher willing to answer any and all questions no matter how difficult or silly. She looked to his hands, and what they rested on. His muscles clenched tight. His knuckles turned white. She caught her attention dipping to— *No!* Not again. She jerked her guilty gaze back to his face. She would not strip the man, *demon*, whatever he was, with her eyes.

Niklas cleared his throat. When he continued, his voice was oddly hoarse. "While most are free to come and go, some demons—powerful demons that could potentially precipitate the end of the human race—are trapped within Hell's realm. In order for them to breach the barrier, they must be summoned. The ritual is called *Ritus Niger Noctis*. The Rite of Black Night."

"And that's what I saw? At the park? A summoning?"

Niklas nodded, solemn. "Whenever summoning a demon from Hell, a human sacrifice is required, a soul for the soulless," he stated without visible emotion. "View it as an exchange of sorts."

Then something else occurred to her. A frown darkened her brow. "So you were the Collector and Xander was the Slayer." She nibbled on her bottom lip, piecing together what she'd learned so far. "By profession, the both of you would be able to travel between Earth and Hell whenever you wanted, right?"

Niklas huffed out a short, exasperated breath and shook his head. "Do you always fly from one-line questioning to the next?"

"Usually, yes," she replied without dissembling. "Answer the question, please."

"Yes."

"Can you still travel between planes?"

"Yes, but we don't. If we returned to Hell, we'd be hunted by the entire population. Here, on Earth, we only have to worry about an occasional demon that stumbles across us, or the demons we hunt down ourselves."

"You said Lucifer gifted you each with powers?" At Niklas's grudging nod, she pressed, "What powers did he give Xander?"

Again, he paused. As if determining how much to reveal. At length, he carefully replied, "Xander can always tell whether someone is telling the truth or not."

She toyed with her ring again, twisting it, taking comfort in the warm, smooth silver. She knew she was being rude, firing so many questions at him, but curiosity was eating her alive.

He frowned at her hands. "Who gave you that ring?"

His sharp question caught her off guard. "It belonged to my mother. Why?"

If she hadn't been watching him so closely, she might have missed the infinitesimal way the bunched muscles in his broad shoulders relaxed. "You twist it when you are anxious or upset. It grounds you, calms you."

Uncomfortable with his observation, she tucked her hands into her lap and changed the subject. "What was your sin?"

"You ask a lot of questions, *tá'hiri*."

"My downfall, curiosity. I have so many questions, they just sort of spill out before my mind has a chance to censor." She gave a tiny shrug. "You want me to believe all this, then I need all the facts."

One corner of his mouth twitched upward. His eyes

glinted. Was that approval, admiration, or amusement?

"My sin was arrogance." He crossed his arms, probably unaware of how defensive the gesture might look to others. "And a lack of control over my carnal urges. My eyes were once a brilliant, sapphire blue. I spoke to others with my eyes, could influence others to my will with but a glance.

"But I saw only the physical beauty of others. I never took the time to look deeper. Never saw that others' worth lay not in the shape of their face, the shade of their hair, or the pleasure their bodies could give me, but below the surface, in the strength of their loyalty, the depth of the well of compassion in their soul, and the purity of the love in their heart."

She stared at him, fighting to hide her incredulity. The shade of blue might have changed, but he still held the power to speak with his eyes. At least, his eyes spoke to *her*. On a level that left her achy and breathless. Needy.

Compelling her to all kinds of carnal thoughts.

"So what's your power?" Carly asked, desperate to change the direction of her thoughts.

His warm gaze skimmed the length of her body, intimate as a physical caress, and her blood heated. Her heart pounded, just a little harder. He blinked. A puzzled expression crowded his brow.

"I see emotion."

"What do you mean, you *see* emotion?" She tensed, suddenly feeling exposed. "How? Is that like a psychic reading or something?"

Niklas lifted a brow. That single twitch of muscle combined with the wry twist of those magnificent, sensual lips spoke volumes.

"Sorry," she muttered, abashed.

"I see emotion like a swirl of color tinting the air around a person. An aura, if you will. Every emotion is a unique hue."

Her eyes widened. "You see this with *everyone*?"

Niklas nodded, clarifying, "Every human."

"So, like, anger is—"

"Black," he murmured, propping his ankle upon his knee again.

"And fear?"

"Gray."

"Sadness?"

"Blue."

"Blue, of course," she said, nodding.

"The depth of emotion determines the darkness of hue."

She licked her lips, shifting uncomfortably on the sofa. Her hands clenched in her lap until her ring bit into her flesh. Her throat felt suddenly dry, and tight. "Desire?"

He surveyed the air around her again. A bemused expression lit his face. He tilted his head slightly to the side, considering. And then, slowly, his lips curled on a smile, dangerous and wicked, making her heart skip a beat.

"Red," he murmured. He skimmed the air around her with more concentration, as if something was suddenly clicking into place for him. "Vivid. Pulsing." And then his eyes met hers. "Red."

At that very moment, she was positive that same vivid, pulsing red was creeping into her cheeks. The room became unbearably hot. Carly shot to her feet and hurried to the window. Her nails lightly scratched at the base of her throat. The burning itch seemed to be spreading, creeping into her chest, making it difficult to breathe.

Air. She needed air.

She struggled with the window. It wouldn't budge.

Before she could turn away in defeat, scalding heat suddenly scorched the length of her back. Long, well-muscled arms stretched on either side of her, lifting the stubborn window with little effort.

Gasping, she whirled around, coming nose to chest with Niklas. Instinctively, her hands braced against him, her palms connecting with his abdomen. The heat of his bare skin seared her. Tilting her head back, she stared up at him. As if drawn by some invisible force, his head slowly dipped. For a sliver of time, they stood immobile. Barely breathing.

Lips.

So.

Close.

"What does *tá'hiri* mean?" She could barely find her voice. Despite his wild claims, despite the very real possibility that he'd told her the truth about being a demon, her body continued to respond to him in a way it had never responded to another.

"*Tá'hiri*," he whispered, his warm breath fanning her lips, "means 'little lioness' in the language of my creation. I called you *tá'hiri* that first time in the park because I saw in you great courage and determination, an indestructible strength of spirit."

It didn't make any sense. Knowing what she knew, knowing *what* he was, she wanted him still. This was wrong. On so many levels, this was *wrong*. Yet she was helpless to resist. For once, just this one time, she wanted to experience life. She wanted to touch and taste. She needed to *feel*. She wanted to take the emotions she always kept bottled tightly up inside and just let them pour out.

Instinctively, Carly moistened her lip. Her fingertips curled into him, and she savored the bunch and ripple of solid muscle beneath velvet skin. The heat radiating from him, the raw desire glinting in his eyes, promised complete and utter possession. When he kissed her, there would be no holding back. He wasn't the kind that would tolerate temperate passions. Instead, he would demand absolute surrender with incendiary possession. She couldn't catch her breath. Her head swam.

Was this it, then? Would she finally learn what it felt like to be kissed senseless?

Chapter Five

Getting close to her probably wasn't the wisest choice, all things considered, but he crossed the floor without conscious decision on his part. He would just help her lift the window. At least, that was the excuse he used to justify his proximity. His arms, so unbearably empty and longing to feel her warmth, reached without his consent. His body, hungry for the soft press of her generous curves, leaned into her without his permission.

With a soft gasp, she whirled into his embrace, and he lost all power of reason. Lost himself in *her*. In the alluring scent that was so uniquely Carly. In the gentle curve of her lips. In the strength of spirit locked in her fragile body. In the warm, compelling brown of her eyes.

Her soft palms connected with his abdomen. Slid up, skimming his flesh, sending a shockwave of desire racing through his body. Everything else ceased to exist. Logic, caution had no place here.

Nothing held more importance than the imminent contact of their lips. The air around her throbbed violent red, like the dancing flames of hellfire licking away at his control, and he finally understood. The red tint to her emotions had not been his own desire reflected upon her, influencing his vision, but *her* desire.

Her need for *him*.

Well, this was one hell of a complication. Denying his need, his hunger was difficult enough. Knowing that she wanted him in equal measure was a heady aphrodisiac, leaving him alarmed and, God help him, elated. Certainly aroused beyond restraint and all good sense.

Niklas, known for his ruthless control and single-minded determination, was completely helpless, unable to resist this one tiny human female.

He had no business kissing her, no right to even think about it, and yet he lowered his head, his lips parting in anticipation. His breath caught in the back of his throat as that anticipation built to unbelievable proportions. The tip of her tongue darted across her lower lip, leaving behind a glistening invitation. Her eyelids drooped, and she leaned into him. Her fingertips curled into his bare shoulders, pulling him closer. No siren's summons could have been clearer. His hands moved to the curve of her hips, sliding up, slipping just beneath the hem of the soft T-shirt she wore. *His* T-shirt.

My woman. That dark, layered voice echoed in the back of his mind. Primal. Unyielding.

If he hadn't been so lost in his need for her, the unwavering, dangerous voice of his other self might have startled him with its unfamiliar tones of sheer possessiveness. As it was, it merely reinforced his hunger, encouraging him to take what she offered. To take what was his.

Take and demand more still, consequences be damned.

Her skin was so delicate, surpassing the finest silk. He stroked his fingers over the curve of her waist and the planes of her stomach, then curled them around the bottom of her rib cage and groaned from the sheer pleasure of having his hands on her at last. Niklas tilted his head until little more than a hairsbreadth separated their mouths. The very tip of his nose brushed hers. He drew her breath into himself, greedy. His focus locked on the lush, soft pink swell of her lower lip. Just a taste would be worth the risk of burning.

Without warning, her arms went limp, sliding down between them. Her knees gave out, and she collapsed against him, unconscious. His lips connected with the top of her head as the side of her face hit his chest.

Alarm swam through his veins. Selfish, bitter disappointment warred with concern.

So close, that layered voice mocked him.

He scooped her up in his arms, raced across the room and settled her upon the sofa once more. Her skin radiated heat more than what passion had kindled. She was burning up. Her cheeks flushed an unnatural rosy hue. Why hadn't he noticed, damn it? Why hadn't he been paying attention to the signs of fever burning bright in her eyes? Why hadn't it clicked, the way she'd kept rubbing and scratching at the wound Ronové had inflicted?

Tugging the collar of the T-shirt down, he swore again.

Ominous black streaks snaked out from the cut at the base of her throat, spreading rapidly across her inflamed flesh like grasping tendrils of death. And the scratch itself had turned a sickly, grayish color.

Demon venom.

He should have suspected. He should have

anticipated.

But he'd been so confused by her aura, so shocked and anxious over his own reaction to her, he'd let himself get distracted.

Niklas left her side long enough to dampen a cloth in the bathroom sink. He returned and placed it upon her forehead. Pushing her hair from her brow, he studied her. Her lips were rapidly taking on a bluish tint as the venom restricted oxygen saturation in her blood cells. Her face, now beaded with perspiration, had been leached of all color. And the air around her shimmered orange. Brilliant, pure orange. She was in pain.

A lot of pain.

His gut clenched.

There was no antidote for demon venom, and if he let it continue to invade her body at its current rate, she'd be dead in a matter of hours. If she had even that long. The only way to save her was to remove the poison from her system before it spread any further. Like snake venom, it had to be sucked out, quickly and efficiently.

Unfortunately, in human form, he would be susceptible to the toxin. While it wouldn't kill him, his human body continually regenerated and anything short of beheading would simply slow him down, demon venom would leave him weak. Vulnerable.

Transforming back into demonic form would be in *his* best interest. But that option, too, held peril. For one, should she suddenly wake up to find a massive, Cryptoglyph-covered demon sucking at her throat, there was no doubt she would struggle, attempt to fight him off. Not only could she harm herself further, but she could well trigger his demonic predatory instincts. He could kill her without realizing what he was doing until it was too late.

Then there was the physical attraction. He had a difficult enough time containing his desire, this unreasonable, nearly irresistible need to claim her, while in human form. In demonic form...

He shuddered at the thought. He had no idea if he would be able to harness those urges whatsoever. He had a bad feeling the temptation might be too great to resist. Bottom line, he couldn't trust himself in the demonic form. He had no choice.

Bracing himself for what he knew was about to be one of the most unpleasant experiences of his life, Niklas drew out the switchblade he habitually carried in his boot. Careful to keep the cut as shallow as possible, he drew the razor-sharp edge across her lethal wound. Blood welled, bubbling abnormally. After wiping the corrosive poisoned blood on the arm of the sofa, Niklas returned the blade to its hiding place. That small spot on the upholstery began to smoke and sizzle.

With gentle hands, he shifted Carly's body and slipped his arm beneath her shoulders. He lifted her until her head fell back, exposing her throat. He searched her face, pausing briefly on each lovely feature. He drew a deep breath, locking her image in his mind, telling himself he would remember to control himself. Closing his eyes, he lowered his mouth to the cut.

Niklas sealed his lips over the wound and sucked deeply. His brows snapped together, and he battled the urge to recoil. The first mouthful of infected blood seared his mouth like acid, triggering his gag reflex. He turned his head to the side and spat the venom on the floor. There it hissed and smoked, black and noxious, eating away at the carpet.

After sucking in a sharp breath, he returned to his task. And all the while he kept her face in his mind. Her eyes, so trusting, so innocent. Her lips, beckoning his. The sound of her voice. The feel of her soft hands upon his body.

God, how he wanted those hands all over him. The pure gold underlying all the other emotions that wrapped around her. Quite simply, she was hope. Pure. Innocent. Untarnished hope.

Carly moaned softly. The vibration against his lips caught his attention. He paused, glancing at her throat as he wiped his burning mouth against the back of his wrist. The black streaks had receded from her flesh. Her skin surrounding the wound was slightly more flushed, but at least a healthy pink once more. Her lips were once again lush, if still a little chalky. Her eyes no longer appeared sunken and hollow.

By contrast, his head throbbed like a bass drum. His arms and legs felt shaky now, his hands trembled. His stomach churned.

Her blood had lost the noxious tang, but the edges of the wound itself was still gray, the venom waiting to take a foothold on her system once more. He sealed his lips over the wound again and continued his ministrations. Over and over. A wave of dizziness assailed him. His vision blurred, the room darkened. And still he kept fighting for her life. He wouldn't yield. Wouldn't give her up.

She moaned again, stronger this time. He peered down at the wound. Woozy, he squinted. His vision swam. His head hurt so badly he could barely hold it upright. Blinking, he wiped his mouth against his wrist again. The skin on his wrist had blistered from the first swipe. The second sweep tore the blisters open, but he paid them no mind. Carly's wound was now pink. A small trickle of healthy, red blood trailed from the cut. No hint of venom remained.

Carefully, he lowered her to the sofa. With a trembling hand, he refolded the wet washcloth and sponged at her throat. Niklas squinted at the light fixture overhead. When had the dingy single bulb become so blindingly bright?

Carly stirred. Her eyes slowly drifted open. Fluttered. Focused.

"Did I—" She paused, clearing her throat. "Did I faint?"

"Yeah, you could say that." Hell's bells, his throat was sore.

"Wow," she murmured. "That takes kissing someone senseless to a whole new level."

He was puzzled for a moment. Then, despite the pain wracking his body, Niklas let a slow grin curl the edges of his lips. "You think you passed out because I kissed you?"

"Well, I—" She abruptly sat up, her frown deepening. "Didn't you—"

"*Tá'hiri*, when I do kiss you, you'll *know* it."

Color flooded her cheeks. "Then what happened?"

Sitting back on his heels, he braced a hand against the sofa beside her knee. The room spun. He frowned. He shook his head, and then winced as his brain ricocheted inside his skull. "When Ronové scratched you, he excreted venom into the cut."

Carly's hand flew to her throat. "It doesn't hurt

anymore. And my headache is gone."

"I sucked the venom out." He glanced to the floor beside him. The blackened edges of multiple burn holes continued to sizzle and smoke.

She followed his stare. Carly's eyes widened, and her mouth fell open. He offered her a small smile to show her he wasn't worried, though the way he felt right now, it probably looked more like a grimace.

She blinked owlishly at him, reached out to steady him.

Another wave of nausea swept over him. Her features distorted. Slowly, with a great deal of caution, he pushed to his feet. He stood there for a moment, willing the room to stop spinning.

"Are you all right?" She stood and moved forward. Her hand rested lightly on his arm, just above his elbow. "You're white as a sheet."

"It's the venom," he whispered hoarsely, wishing to high heaven she'd stop yelling. "I'm not feeling so well." He took one staggering step toward the bed, and then another. Who had filled his apartment with wet cement? He could barely force his legs to move. "Think I...need to..."

Lie down.

Had he spoken the words aloud? Or had the idea only reverberated off the inside of his battered skull?

He tried to find her in the kaleidoscope of colors swirling through the room. Shaking his head, he stretched out an arm, needing to hold on to something, anything. Just for a minute. Just to regain his bearings.

He found her, but the colors swirling around her, gray and purple, red and gold, blue and—

He couldn't focus anymore. The colors were too

much for him to handle right then. Her lips were moving, but he couldn't hear her. Scrunching his eyes closed, he pressed the heel of his hand hard against his forehead.

One foot in front of the other, he told himself. *Sleep.* He just needed to sleep it off. But something wasn't right. His body wasn't cooperating.

As if from a great distance, he heard her calling his name, like she'd been swept away to the end of a long, long tunnel. Fear, alarm saturated her voice. He needed to reassure her. Needed to tell her not to leave the apartment without him.

But darkness descended. Her soft body pressed along his side, warm and comforting.

And then he felt nothing.

****

"You have failed me." Stolas cracked his knuckles in annoyance.

Ronové went to one knee, crossing his arms, fists pressed to his shoulders. Head bowed, he replied, "Apologies, my lord." But then he peered up from beneath his lashes.

Unwise.

He'd not been granted permission.

"The Seer came," Ronové said, groveling. "He interrupted the ritual, my lord."

That unexpected bit of information caught Stolas's attention. Leashing his displeasure, he clarified, "Niklas?"

"There is but one Seer."

"Do you mock me?" Stolas queried softly. His initial reaction was to set Ronové's body aflame and then sit back to watch him burn. It would make for pleasurable entertainment while he dined. Or he could take Ronové's head as a centerpiece before dessert.

But experience stayed his hand. A dead demon was a useless demon.

Stolas watched as Ronové ducked his head lower and clenched his eyes closed.

Ah, the impudent minion had a lot to learn. Stolas smiled at the reaction as he reached for a jewel-encrusted, golden goblet on the table. He swirled the still warm blood gently around and around, careful not to slosh any over the rim. Swift retribution was over too quickly, the lesson not properly absorbed. Stolas had discovered through the ages that punishment was best served when least expected.

Dragging the anticipation out had more impact.

Leaning back in his seat, he set the goblet aside. The ruby liquid swirling inside the chalice captured the soft glow from the candelabra in the center of the long table. He watched the play of light and savored the smell of fear in the air. Ronové cowered for a few moments more before Stolas calmly speculated. "So, the Seer has finally come forth."

"Yes, my lord." Ronové pushed his luck further by lifting his head.

Stolas reminded himself that this ignorant boldness was exactly why he'd enlisted Ronové in the first place. Ronové had his uses. He was the muscle in this plot. At least until the summoning was successful. Then he would be nothing more than collateral damage. Unfortunately, the reminder didn't make his presence any more tolerable.

"The Seer attacked without warning, decimating the Earthbound legion I'd gathered. I barely escaped.

And Dimiezlo has located the scrolls. He is, even now, gaining entrance into the Guardian's lair. As soon as he procures the scrolls, he will bring them directly to me."

Ah, yes. The other integral part of his plan. The Scrolls of Prévnar. One of the four Sacred Relics necessary for his revolution to succeed. He already possessed the Sword of Kathnesh, rumored to be the one weapon destined to take Lucifer's head.

Of course, the Fallen had thwarted his plans thus far by stealing the Arc Stone away. But he wouldn't be denied. He would get the stone back, and he would sire the Chosen One.

As long as Lucifer didn't find out first.

"And if he is captured?"

"Not even Lucifer himself would be able to torture the truth from Dimiezlo," Ronové assured him.

"Overblown boasting does not reassure me, *grïzschreck'ta*," he hissed.

The insult struck its target. Ronové's nostrils flared, and the next breath he took was interminably deep. His body tensed, his knuckles bleached white. But he uttered not a sound.

At last, a shadow of wisdom.

"I make no false claim," Ronové vehemently denied. "Dimiezlo will take his own life before he'll allow himself to be captured."

"I don't need to tell you what will happen if you are discovered. If word of the conspiracy were to reach Lucifer..." Stolas dropped his napkin onto the table beside his plate. He rose from his seat, clasped his hands behind his back and slowly began to pace from one end of his hall to the other. Flickering firelight from torches mounted on the walls danced along the black marble beneath his feet. His hall, filled with riches, gleaming with proof of his prosperity, was little more than a gilded cage. A cage with no windows.

No point really, considering the view.

How long he had waited to feel sunshine on his flesh.

Niklas. Hmm.

The Seer was a complication he hadn't anticipated. He didn't like surprises.

Stolas flexed his fingers, clenched his fists. As royalty, his power in Hell was nearly absolute. Unfortunately, he had to rely on the likes of Ronové and his cohorts when it came to Earthbound matters. Still, this latest development posed interesting possibilities. He must take his time, weigh his options. All of them.

But what was that saying humans were so fond of?

Oh, yes. *Don't put all of your eggs in one basket.* He was rather fond of that phrase himself.

He'd already been working on that exact concept.

Folding his hands before him, he calmly returned to his seat. His cold stare came to rest on Ronové, and the demon quickly ducked his head, lowering his own gaze to the floor.

"I can track him, my lord," Ronové offered, his head bowed in meek submission. No doubt hoping to prolong his worthless life.

Stolas tapped his fingertips together, calmly considering Ronové from beneath one arched brow. No one had ever accused him of *not* playing with his food. "How?"

Licking his thick lips, Ronové glanced up again. "There was a woman."

"A *witness*?" He slapped the tabletop hard enough to make his silverware dance. "You left a witness *alive*?"

Fury bubbled anew. Ronové's idiocy knew no bounds.

No one could know of his preparations. *No one.* Not even a lowly human. If Lucifer so much as suspected—

He kept the urge to shudder firmly in check. His narrowed eyes must have eloquently expressed his growing anger, because Ronové rushed to explain.

"The Seer may have taken her, but I tasted her blood. I can track her. And through her, I can track the Seer."

Turning in any one of the five rebels would virtually guarantee unlimited power, but the loss of Niklas and Xander had been especially humiliating for Lucifer. As a result, he'd placed bounties on both of their heads so staggering even the highest echelon of demon royalty would gladly cut their own firstborn's throat to claim it. The whole situation had become a double-edged blade. Lucifer would handsomely reward any who captured a Fallen. And yet, because of those very same fallen, Lucifer would trust no one. Not even family.

Giving the Seer over to Lucifer would buy him time, lulling the Dark Prince into a false sense of security.

Yes, very good.

"I want the Seer brought before me. Alive."

Ronové's head shot up, his eyes wide and distinctly alarmed. His mouth gaped open. Niklas's reputation preceded him. He was a fierce fighter. Not as determined and methodical as Xander perhaps, nor as merciless and cruel as Mikhail. Neither was he as ruthless and cold-blooded as Sebastian, but formidable and deadly all the same. He'd more than earned his reputation. He was death.

Wisely, Ronové snapped his mouth closed and lowered his head in submission. Nodding briskly, he pounded his fists to his shoulders.

"As you wish, my lord."

"You will return to Earth, and you will gather a new Earthbound legion. I trust you've already disposed of the cowards." At Ronové's curt nod, Stolas went on, "At the next waxing crescent moon, you *will* summon me."

Stolas raised one hand, eyes narrowed in concentration. Power coursed through his body, erupting through the palm of his hand with a tingling burn. A terrible smile knifed across his face. Ronové's eyes rolled back in his head. He fell to his side on the black marble. Twitching, jolting spasms wracked Ronové's body. He gasped aloud, suffering too much agony to scream aloud.

Ronové's life force surged and ebbed, crawling up Stolas's arm and into his chest.

Oh, that feels good.

Almost too good to stop.

No, no, he had use for Ronové still.

Must stop.

Clenching a fist, he broke the connection and lowered his trembling hand to his lap. Taking a moment to steady himself after the rush of power, he drew in several deep breaths.

"Do you understand me, Ronové?" He kept his

voice soft, threatening. "I will not tolerate failure a second time."

Ronové struggled to his knees and braced the palms of his hands on the floor in a subservient position. Blood dripped from his nostrils, leaked from his ears and the corners of his eyes. "Yes, my lord," Ronové gasped. "I understand."

"Leave me."

Ronové pushed himself back until he sat on his heels. His shaking arms crossed over his chest, and though his body was still visibly tormented with pain, he pounded his fists to his shoulders in the proper show of fealty as he bowed his head. Stolas flicked his wrist in dismissal, and Ronové vanished.

"Admit Gusion now," he said to the Charocté Demon lurking in the shadows.

A moment later, the air near the end of the table distorted. A tall, handsome demon with long, blond hair and a lean physique appeared in human form. Crossing his forearms over his chest, he dropped to one knee and bowed his head, his greeting circumspect. Gusion's gaze remained judiciously on the floor.

"You may rise."

Gusion rose, lowering his hands to his sides. His focus still on the floor.

This one knows his place.

"You may look upon me, Gusion."

Gusion glanced up at last. His eyes were blue. Plain. Average.

Perfect.

"It has come to my attention that you regularly pass among humankind undetected."

Gusion shifted his weight to one foot, nodding. His

demeanor bespoke caution, and a certain amount of well-earned arrogance. "Yes, my lord."

Leaning back, propping his elbows on the armrests of his chair, Stolas steepled his fingers. "You are familiar with the United States?"

No emotion flickered over the demon's visage. "Yes, my lord."

"Tell me of this place they call Iowa."

"Small villages hardly worth razing. Cornfields and cows, sire," he said disdainfully. But then his lips slowly twisted on a wicked grin. "Ah, but the women... Farmer's daughters, I believe is the phrase used." Gusion drew a deep shuddering breath, his eyes glinting with unmistakable heat. He swallowed and licked his lips. "Delicious." As if recalling himself, he cleared his throat and schooled his features. "It has been many human decades since last I visited there. But I'm sure I could find my way around, my lord."

"Good, very good." Stolas lowered his hands to his lap and he assessed the demon before him. "I have a job for you."

Chapter Six

Panting, Carly plopped on the edge of the bed and stared at Niklas, wondering what to do next. It had taken all her strength to break his fall and he'd still gone down like a ton of bricks, nearly toppling her with him. She'd managed to rouse him long enough to help him up and onto the bed. At which point he'd grasped her wrist with surprising strength.

He'd blinked woozily, then peered hard at her, demanding, *"Don't...leave,"* before passing out once more.

Don't leave, indeed.

Every sane, reasonable fiber in her body urged her to run while the running was good. In fact, if she had an iota of common sense, she'd run straight to the nearest police station and turn him and all his psychotic friends in. He was hardly in any shape to stop her.

However, much as she tried to convince herself otherwise, she couldn't ignore the truth of the situation. She'd stumbled upon an honest to God demon ritual in the park. And this man—no, this *demon*—had saved her. She gingerly probed at the thin cut on her throat. It didn't hurt. It didn't even itch anymore.

Twice now, he'd saved her life.

She owed him. She couldn't just leave him here, not like this. Besides, what if he was telling the truth? What if her well-being, her very life, depended on

Niklas and his ability to protect her?

How could she help him? His skin was clammy and pale, his breathing shallow. Dark shadows circled his sunken eyes.

Okay. First things first.

She had to try to get him healthy again. Then she could figure out where to go from there. Carly went to the bathroom and opened the medicine cabinet. Over-the-counter pain killers. Not great, but it was better than nothing. A toothbrush and toothpaste. A razor. Shaving cream.

Nothing more, nothing less.

Lotta help here.

She knew basic first aid. *Venom.* She knew what to do in case of snakebite. Tourniquet, cut, suction. At least, that's what she'd learned…a long time ago. Had it changed? The problem was he'd *ingested* the venom, judging by his physical condition. There was no strike site to lance and drain. She was in over her head here. But somehow, she didn't think the poison control hotline would have a handy solution for demon venom. Dare she try to induce vomiting?

One wary glance at the blackened spots on the carpet curbed that idea quickly.

Lower his fever. That was logical and sounded as good a place to start as any. Shaking a couple Ibuprophen into the palm of her hand, she returned to the kitchenette.

Carly opened the fridge door and groaned aloud. Bottled water. A moldy hunk of cheese and a few other, equally questionable items.

This just wasn't going to cut it, not if he insisted that she stay here with him. She skimmed the rest of the apartment. No spare bedroom, no privacy. She wasn't prissy, wasn't spoiled or used to rich furnishings, but it didn't take a rocket scientist to figure out this arrangement wasn't going to work. After snagging one of the bottles of water, she closed the door, shaking her head.

"Niklas," she called softly as she returned to the bed. "Niklas, I need you to wake up."

Nothing. Not even an eyelid twitched.

She reached out to touch him. She paused, her hand hovering a few inches from his skin. He was radiating heat. Firming her resolve, she smoothed her hand down his arm. She could do this. She could keep this purely clinical.

She slid her fingertips over him and paused as she drew in a deep breath. His muscles, even relaxed as they were now, felt like granite beneath his smooth skin. She caught the edge of her lower lip between her teeth.

No, she had to be clinical. *Nurse to patient*, she reminded herself.

"Niklas, wake up. I need you to take this medicine."

He groaned, stirring. In a semiconscious state, he rolled to his side, and she helped him up onto one elbow. She pushed the pills past his chalky lips and held the bottle as he drank deeply. With another groan, he fell back on the bed, unconscious once more. Sweat glistened on his brow. His pallor worried her. Gray was not a good color, regardless of the species. At least, she didn't think so.

But what could she do? Call an ambulance? How would she explain poison by demon? For that matter, would a doctor be able to tell if there was something not quite right with *him*?

Carly silently debated her best course of action as she dug absently in her hip pocket and drew out a lip balm. She brushed his hair back and gently smoothed the ointment over his cracked lips.

If leaving meant risking falling into Ronové's hands again, it was probably best to stay put. Unless or until it became necessary to leave. Then? Well, she'd cross that bridge if and when she got to it.

Okay, I can do this. I can.

Rolling up her proverbial sleeves, Carly pushed to her feet. She returned to the kitchenette and rummaged in the drawers and cabinets. She found a plastic basin and a pile of tattered washcloths and set them aside. She opened drawers and doors, digging until she found what she was looking for. Pushing the crinkly packages of chips and cookies aside, she dug deeper. Five cans of soup. Well, there was a start. Coffee. Good, though the coffeepot didn't look as if it had seen the clean side of a soap bubble since coming out of its original packaging.

She could deal with this situation.

As long as she didn't give in to the terror clawing its way through her chest.

In short order, she had coffee brewing in a freshly scrubbed pot, a can of soup heating in the microwave and a basin full of tepid water sitting on the nightstand beside the bed. Standing back, she surveyed her patient.

His fever had spiked. His skin was drenched. He shivered and tossed restlessly, muttering in a language she couldn't understand. How long before the ibuprophen kicked in?

She sat on the bed beside him and began sponging

cool water over his broad chest, neck and face. And his arms. His wonderfully strong arms. The defined, whipcord strength of his body left her breathless.

Focus, Carly. Criminy, stop ogling him. The man is horribly ill!

Not an easy task as she found her gaze drawn repeatedly to his washboard abs and well-muscled chest. Shaking herself free of the visual trap of his body, she pushed and pulled until she managed to roll him onto his side. Maybe she ought to sponge his back with the cool water as well. Easier said than done. He was dead weight at this point, beyond rousing.

She froze, struck anew by the horror of the marks on his back.

They were the most hideous scars she'd ever seen. The sheer magnitude of the pain he must have experienced left her sick to her stomach.

Sinking back on her bottom, she reached out and gently traced one puckered ridge.

Wings.

As if aware of her caress, he arched his back into her touch. His skin was so hot. Recalling her purpose, she dipped a rag in the water and sponged it over his shoulders and down his back. She gently eased him to his back, her mind still preoccupied with his scars as she sponged his forehead. She searched his face.

He was handsome, no argument there.

Her own huge yawn caught her by surprise. Glancing at her watch, she blinked. Wow. No wonder she was dead on her feet. Niklas groaned, his body going rigid. His teeth clenched as his back arched off the bed. He strained there for a moment, trapped in the clutches of a seizure, his body taut. And then he collapsed against the mattress, limp, panting.

In that moment, it truly hit her. Exactly what he'd done for her. He'd taken this poison, this pain into himself. He's spared her this torture, and, in doing so, had willingly brought it upon himself. A tender ache settled into the middle of her chest, and she felt herself softening toward him. She dipped the cloth into the basin, wrung out the excess moisture, and laid it upon his brow.

****

Niklas came awake with a start. Oh, sweet Christ, he felt like death warmed over. He lifted his head from the pillow. The room spun. Groaning, he dropped his head, scrunched his eyes closed and prayed for the world to stop turning.

Or death. Right now, the way he felt, he'd welcome Oblivion with open arms.

It was then that he became aware of a foreign weight, soft and warm, draped over his chest and lower abdomen. Risking another bout with vertigo, he pried one eyelid open and peered at his chest. The sight of Carly's sleeping face shocked him. Dark lashes rested upon her pale cheeks. Her enticing lips were parted slightly. Her head rested in the hollow of his breastbone. Her aura was white, tinged by that golden glow only Carly seemed to possess. She was completely relaxed, her expression unguarded.

Niklas was stunned. She'd stayed with him.

The dark, layered voice inside him purred, shocking him speechless. Since when did he purr?

She stirred in her sleep, snuggling closer. Her hair fanned out behind her, tickling his stomach. The feel of it there, whisper soft against his skin, drove him crazy.

He should move. He needed to get up and call Xander. He should contact Asher, a renegade mercenary who'd recently escaped Lucifer's rule. Asher, like many of the other Earthbound demons, had decided that in the battle of good versus evil, the only side he intended to take was his own. Nevertheless, for the right price, Asher would sell any information, take on any job. If anyone knew whether Ronové had already begun the hunt for Carly, it would be Asher.

He needed to—

Carly moaned. A tiny crease formed between her brows. Her breathing deepened. Purple began to bleed into white.

Without realizing what he was doing, he lifted a hand and smoothed his trembling, weak fingers through her hair. Over and over. Wishing only to ease her fears. Wanting to be the one to offer her comfort. The crease between her brows disappeared and the purplish hue receded from the air around her.

An odd calm settled over him. Strange, he'd never offered comfort before, never tried to soothe another. And yet, soothing Carly felt natural. In fact, the longer he touched her, the longer he ran his fingers through her hair, the better *he* felt. And the feeling of her head resting so trustingly upon his chest...there was nothing like it.

Her arm twitched, slid. Her warm, soft hand settled on his abdomen, *low* on his abdomen. His eyes flew wide open. His breathing arrested. His fingers tightened in her hair. His entire body went rigid. Only a few short inches separated her hot palm from cupping him fully.

He was instantly, painfully aroused.

Part of him, that part of him that had worked

ceaselessly for redemption, prayed she'd wake up and withdraw her hand before he gave in to the impulse to thrust his erection against her. That part of him prayed for forgiveness for the urges coursing through his blood and the wicked thoughts filling his mind.

And wicked they were. The things he wanted to do with her, do to her...

The other part of him, the part that he'd fought so hard to restrain—the part that spoke in a layered voice and gleefully reveled in tormenting him with sin and temptation—savored the feel of her hand upon him. Two parts of the same whole.

Another wave of incapacitating vertigo washed over him. Then again, maybe it was the sudden redirection of his blood flow that made him lightheaded. His shaft felt as if it were growing thicker by the second, seemingly in tandem with the fact that logical, coherent thought slipped from his grasp like water through a sieve.

He was weak from the toxin, he reasoned.

If he didn't feed soon, he would become a danger to her. Still, he found himself in no hurry to move, no hurry to lose the unexpected intimacy he'd discovered in this novel experience.

Was this what it would feel like to have a woman of his own? Was this what it would be like, waking up with her every day of a mortal's life? Was this the solace God had offered Adam in creating Eve?

If he'd had a woman like Carly, would he have followed Lucifer?

Cold rationality finally settled upon him. Stupid question. He'd been an Archangel, not a man. A woman like Carly would never have been in the cards for him, regardless of whether he'd followed Lucifer or not.

But he *had* followed Lucifer. And he was damned.

The only thing he should want—no, the only thing he *did* want, he corrected himself—remained frustratingly out of his grasp.

Absolution.

Suddenly disgusted with himself and his useless train of thought, he purposefully shifted. Not his hips, as his body begged. But his shoulders. Moving until she blinked at him, drowsy and unfocused. And then she completely undid him. She closed her eyes and nuzzled her cheek against him, against his bare chest. A devastating wave of raw lust slammed into him. Damn it, if she didn't move soon, she stood the very real danger of being rolled beneath him, willing or not, and taken, over and over until they were both senseless.

Oh, sweet Christ, to be inside *her*—

Drawing a deep breath, she yawned wide.

Gasping, she bolted upright, wide-awake. A damp cloth rolled from her hand onto his shoulder.

"You're up!"

"Apparently," he remarked dryly. *In more ways than one.* Sweet Mary, he sounded like he'd had his vocal cords ripped out, shredded and then stuffed back down his throat.

I sound as bad as Xander.

"Here," she said, slipping an arm beneath his shoulders to help him up. An impish grin tilted the edges of her mouth as she offered him a sip of water and gave his own words back to him. "It's safe. Go on."

The tepid water slid down his parched throat. Ambrosia.

"Slowly." She pulled the bottle back before he was

done. "You've been really sick for," she checked her watch, "almost twenty-six hours."

Twenty-six—

Holy heaven, he'd been unconscious for *twenty-six hours*? Had the integrity of the ward stones been compromised while he was unconscious? Had she left the apartment?

He struggled to sit up. She pushed at his shoulders, urging him to lie back.

Weak as he was, he complied, for the moment. But still he pressed, "Did you leave the apartment?"

"What? No, I haven't even opened the door. But I'm going to have to soon. We're almost out of food."

Thank God for small favors.

Much as his body demanded he stay in bed, perhaps even tempt her to join him, he knew that was the last thing he could afford to do. In the ensuing battle of wills, Carly lost, but only because he was physically stronger than she was, even in his current, weakened state.

"What are you doing?" she demanded as he swung his legs over the side of the bed and set both feet on the floor. Once more the room spun. Gritting his teeth, he pushed through the weakness.

Holy Mother Mary! Where are my pants?

He could conjure another pair, but his head hurt so much. He'd probably just pass out again. Better to find the ones he already had, save his energy for something more important.

"I need to get out of here, Carly."

"You're in no condition to go anywhere," she argued.

She wasn't looking so healthy herself. Dark

shadows smudged the delicate skin below her eyes. He didn't need to read her aura to see how tired she was. Hell's bells, how long had she stayed awake taking care of him?

"Lie down and rest," he ordered, though his tone was softer now.

Niklas scanned the room, located his jeans folded neatly on the end of the coffee table. His boots were lined up on the floor at the end of the sofa. At least she'd left him in his boxers. Boxers that would soon start tenting if she didn't stop staring up at him with those sleepy, vulnerable, chocolate brown eyes.

His legs barely supported him as he crossed the room and pulled on his jeans. He plopped onto the sofa and tugged on his boots.

"You should try to eat a little something. I'll make some more soup for you. Just give me a few minutes to heat up a can. I think we have one left."

"More soup?"

"You had cans of soup in the back of your cupboard. I've been straining the broth and spoon-feeding the liquid to you. I was worried you might get dehydrated, and there was no telling how long you might remain unconscious." Embarrassment washed through the air around her. Color filled her cheeks. "You were running a really high fever. According to what I've read, the best thing was to push fluids and keep you as cool as possible." Her attention dipped briefly to his chest, and then shot across the room. The rush of blood in her cheeks heightened. Red bled through her aura. "With that in mind, keeping you cool and all, I took your jeans off, and I've been...ah, well—" She pointed at the damp cloth lying on his pillow.

She'd been spoon-feeding him. *And* she'd been giving him sponge baths. For twenty-six hours. *Sweet Mary!* No one had ever taken care of him before. Not for five minutes, let alone twenty-plus hours straight. No one had ever cared enough to bother. A strange warmth surged through his chest as he gazed upon her. He suddenly longed to pull her back into his arms. Longed to soothe her again.

But hunger was clawing at him. And not the hunger her soup would satisfy.

With a muffled curse, he summoned a shirt. Pain slashed through his skull, nearly brought him to his knees. She blinked, eyebrows shooting up as a new T-shirt appeared on his body.

"I have to go out," he repeated. "I won't be gone long. Lie down and get some rest. Do *not* open the door for *anyone*. Don't even respond if someone should happen to knock. There are wards around the apartment, protecting it from unwelcome visitors. As long as you don't cross the threshold, and you don't invite anyone in, you'll be fine."

Without waiting for a response, he shimmered from the apartment, his focus centered on a small section of alley behind a mall in a nearby town. Often frequented by pushers and strung out prostitutes, it was the best place he could think of to find what he needed at that moment.

The brush of warm air against his skin was his first sensation as he solidified beside a large green Dumpster. The next was the stomach-churning odor coming from the receptacle. Peering around the side of the garbage bin, he scouted out the alley. About thirty feet away, a dealer was "collecting" from one of his clients. Shades of red and green surrounded the dealer. Lust. Happiness. The hooker wore shades of blue and purple, despair and fear, liberally laced with streaks of black, disgust, anger. Hatred.

As soon as the dealer finished with her and stepped away, the hooker tugged her skirt down and thrust out her hand. The dealer dropped a tiny bag of white powder onto her palm. She quickly tucked it into her black leather bra before scurrying away. Niklas waited for her to turn the corner at the end of the block before he approached the dealer.

"Hey man," the dealer called.

Niklas nodded his head and eased closer.

"Whad'chu lookin' for, my man? You come to de right place. Ah hook you up, bro, you just tell ole Rodrigo whad'chu need." The Rs rolled so thickly from the guy's tongue, Niklas might have struggled to understand him, provided he actually cared what the man had to say.

Stepping closer, Rodrigo pulled the side of his trench coat aside, revealing rows upon rows of deep pockets brimming with tiny pouches and jumbles of gold and silver. The man was a walking pharmacy of illegal drugs and, apparently, a fence for stolen jewelry. The pusher also made sure he flashed the hunk of steel tucked into his waistband.

Like that gun would make a difference.

His actions justified, at least in his mind, Niklas raised his hand, slapping his palm to Rodrigo's chest. The dealer sucked in a sharp breath, his expression swiftly turning to a scowl as his body went rigid.

"Whad'a de hell, man. Get yo' fu—" His voice suddenly choked off, the sound garbling into a pained gasp. His eyes widened, and his aura bled brilliant orange. Rodrigo's knees gave out as his eyes rolled back in his head. He hung there, suspended from nothing more than the contact of Niklas's palm against his chest.

A tingling burn seared Niklas's skin as Rodrigo's life force began to seep into his hand and surge up his arm. At last, as Rodrigo's heart ceased to beat, as his lungs ceased to draw breath, Niklas dropped him to the pavement like the refuse he was. Knowing how useless it was to waste the effort over a man whose soul was as black as this one's had been, he muttered a brief prayer for all those affected by this man's greed instead.

Rubbing his hands together, warming his palms, he pushed plasma out, pouring it over the body. In a matter of second, flames engulfed the empty shell that used to be Rodrigo. Glancing one last time both ways down the alley, Niklas drew a deep breath and focused on the apartment.

Chapter Seven

Carly banged a palm against the window. She'd wiggled it, she'd pounded on it, and she'd pushed with all her might. But the window wouldn't budge. Stupid thing. She stomped to the sofa and sat down.

He didn't have a single book in the place. No magazines. Not so much as an old newspaper. No TV or radio either. She couldn't very well sit there twiddling her thumbs. This was ridiculous. She had a life, one she needed to get back to. Soon. Provided she hadn't been fired. She'd lost her phone in the park and, despite having an excess of time on her hands, she hadn't been able to crack the pass code on Niklas's phone. Then he'd done that vanishing thing and she hadn't even had a chance to tell him she needed to make a call.

And *that vanishing thing* he did had been the final straw in convincing her of his claims; his fantastic story was all true.

That, or she'd fallen down Alice's rabbit hole and might as well apply for permanent residency.

She wasn't one to sit idle. Digging through drawers, Carly located an old rag and set to rummaging beneath the sink for cleaning supplies. Her fallback. She was a bored cleaner. *Hmmm.* Come to think of it, she was a mad cleaner too. Peering into the dark abyss beneath the sink, she scowled. Not much there either. A bottle of dish detergent. A spray can of general disinfectant. A half-empty bottle of window cleaner. All had a thick coat of dust on them.

Wow, talk about a bachelor pad with the bare basics.

Shaking her head, she took out the window cleaner, her mind wandering to the travel guide she'd recently purchased. Blue liquid misted the window, and she set rag to glass. Paris. The Eiffel Tower. Bistros and sidewalk cafés. What would the city smell like? The scent of ammonia faded into the aroma of yeast and cinnamon. Fresh breads. Coffee.

She scrubbed until the rag had cleared away a squeaky, clean circle. And the Rhône Valley, recently named wine region of the year. What must *that* be like? Oh, how she'd like to visit all the great vineyards of the world. Italy, Spain—

"What are you doing?"

A strangled screech escaped her as she whirled around, clutching the rag to her chest as a meager shield, aiming the window cleaner at his chest like a gun, ready to fire.

Niklas. She dropped her chin to her chest as her shoulders sagged with relief.

Gathering her frayed nerves, she lowered the bottle and skirted him on the way to the kitchenette. Her hands trembled as she set her makeshift weapon on the counter. She'd almost shot him with window cleaner. Good grief. Just call her Rambo. Look out demons of the world. She was armed and dangerous.

"Cleaning. I was cleaning."

He was clearly baffled. "Why?"

Her earlier irritation returned. "Because you left

me here with nothing to do. Don't you own a TV? A magazine? A comic book, for Pete's sake?"

"I told you to rest."

"Pardon me if I don't sleep on command," she snapped.

Niklas stepped closer to the window, frowned and peered through it as if he'd never looked through a clean glass pane before.

"Where did you go?"

He turned to face her, and she got her first good look at him since his return. Her breath caught in the back of her throat. Chippendales' finest had nothing on him. He looked amazing. His face held no shadows, his skin was healthy and sun-kissed once more. His eyes were alert, his carriage strong and proud again.

He'd been gone less than an hour.

Not possible.

"What happened to you?" Unable to stop herself, she brushed her fingertips over his cheek. She searched his face for lingering signs of his illness. There weren't any. Not a single one.

He captured her wrist and pulled her hand away from his face. The muscle in his jaw leaped. "I've healed."

Turning, Niklas crossed to the bed and dropped to one knee. From beneath the bed, he pulled a large case and dropped it atop the mattress. Carly edged closer. Her wonder over his miraculous recovery was momentarily set aside as her curiosity over the case stirred. He clicked the latches open and lifted the lid.

Knives and daggers of various sizes were strapped to the inside of the lid. Some were bejeweled, others plain. Some had intricate scrollwork and symbols carved upon the blades. Others had handles inlaid with ivory, ebony and old bone.

He lifted a flat inner partition, presumably one that protected the knives from the rest of the case's contents. The case itself, perhaps a foot deep, was sectioned into five compartments with velvet-covered dividers.

One compartment held a hodgepodge of gold and silver jewelry. Delicate necklaces, thick chains, pendants, rings. A veritable pirate's treasure trove. The next partition contained a pile of small, velvet pouches that were tied with golden string. Dozens of tiny, corked bottles filled with multicolored liquids lined the third compartment. Parchment scrolls were stacked in the fourth compartment. And the last section was filled with rocks.

Rocks?

Bending closer, she peered hard at the last compartment, bracing one hand on his shoulder. No, not rocks. Crystals. Rough, unrefined crystals and stones.

Turning his head, he lifted a brow.

"Sorry," she muttered, swiping her hand back as heat swam up her neck and gushed into her cheeks.

She sat on the bed, tucked a foot beneath her and watched him paw through the pile of gold and silver. "What is all this stuff?"

"Souvenirs," he offered with a wry twist of his lips. "Ward stones, holy water, potions and powders. Ah, here they are." He extracted a long silver chain and a silver ring from the tangle. The ring looked like an heirloom; its center stone was a square-cut peridot, surrounded by small diamonds. An oval-cut garnet winked at her from a fragile-looking pendant suspended from the necklace. Its setting was a beautiful weave of silver filament dotted with slivers of diamonds, like something that might adorn an elven princess.

"Here." He held the pieces out to her. "Put these on. And don't take them off." His eyes met hers, his stare hard and insistent as he added, "*Ever.*"

She accepted them, bending to examine them more closely. "What are they?"

"They're guard stones." Niklas once again pawed through the pile of jewelry. He pulled out a thick signet ring inlaid with a strange, mottled, reddish-brown stone, and pushed it onto his pinkie.

"Is that what those big crystals in that compartment are? Guard stones?"

"No, those are ward stones."

Frowning, she held the dainty ring between her fingers, examined the stone, traced the edge with her forefinger. "What's the difference?"

After impatiently taking the ring from her, he grasped her left wrist and lifted her hand. Without ceremony, he shoved the ring onto her ring finger. "Don't take it off." He waved his finger at the necklace.

"Okay," she conceded, fastening the jewelry around her throat. *Touchy, touchy.* "What's the difference between ward stones and guard stones?"

"Ward stones protect a building or tract of land, preventing demons and evil spirits from entering or exiting a location. Guard stones protect the individual. The guard stone in that ring—peridot—protects against demons and evil. Diamonds and the garnet will protect against evil and during physical travel."

He dug with renewed vigor, finally extracting a bracelet.

Fearing a future as the Queen of Sheba, she held up a hand and exclaimed, "Look, I'm not really a jewelry kind of girl—"

"You are now," came his terse pronouncement.

Heaving a put-upon sigh, she held out her right wrist. After pushing it aside, he took her left wrist in hand, fastening the intricate clasp. She lifted her wrist to the light and studied the ring of small stones dangling from the pagan-looking bracelet. Despite her earlier complaint, she couldn't help but admire the craftsmanship. It really was beautiful.

"I've never seen these before. What are they?"

"Chrysoberyl to guard against possession, and brecciated jasper to protect during astral travel."

"Astral...are you serious?"

The glance he sent her spoke volumes. "Whatever you do, don't take that bracelet off. Or the ring. Or the necklace. The bracelet will prevent Ronové and his minions from shimmering with you."

"Shimmering?" She stared at him, frowning. *Shimmering?* The only thing she could connect the strange word to was... "Is that the vanishing thing you did earlier?"

"Yeah." One corner of his mouth edged upward. "That vanishing thing."

"What about you? Won't it prevent you from doing the same then?"

He wiggled the signet ring in front of her. The stone matched the ones on her bracelet. "They're cut from the same stone. The kindred stones will allow me to shimmer with you."

Silent, she examined the bracelet again. She'd read about the healing and protective properties of gems and stones. At the time, she hadn't really believed any of it valid. Now? Well, if Niklas said they worked, after all she'd recently witnessed, who was she to say otherwise?

Dropping her hands to her lap, she watched as he withdrew a scroll. Leaning forward, she squinted at the strange writing. She couldn't read a word. "What's that?"

Grudging amusement glinted in his eyes. "Didn't anyone ever warn you about curiosity killing the—"

"Cat," she finished for him, heaving a sigh. "Yeah, I've heard that one before. I figure by now, if I was that stupid cat, my nine lives would be about all used up." Her gaze zeroed in on the scroll once more. "What kind of writing is that?"

"Cryptoglyphs."

Frowning, she studied the strange symbols more closely. "I've seen those somewhere before."

"Ronové's tattoos. And mine, when I'm in demon form."

Her gaze flew to his face. "Do all demons have those marks?"

"No." He examined the scroll before replacing it and taking up another. "Only high-ranking generals in Lucifer's army—warriors who've proven themselves ferocious, merciless and cunning in battle—are gifted with Cryptoglyphs. The more legendary the warrior, the more magnificent his feats, the more intricate and extensive the Cryptoglyphs."

"So they're like Medals of Honor or Purple Hearts or something?"

"Something like that. They're like—" He glanced up, clearly searching for the right framework for his explanation. "Like the ancient Egyptians used hieroglyphs to tell the stories of their pharaohs, Cryptoglyphs tell the stories of revered demon warriors."

She fell silent for a short while, chewing on the inside of her lip as she recalled the plethora of Cryptoglyphs that had adorned Niklas's demonic body. He may not have followed Lucifer anymore, but when he had, he must have been among Lucifer's most elite generals.

With a tiny shiver, she turned her focus to something else. "Where did you get these scrolls?"

"They are pages torn from Lucifer's grimoire."

"Lucifer's grimoire? As in—"

"As in the book of dark magic Lucifer uses to create objects such as talismans and amulets, to perform magical spells, charms and divination, to summon or invoke entities such as angels, spirits and demons. Yada. Yada. That book."

After unrolling the crackling, aged parchment, Niklas studied the pictures and crude symbols scrawled across the page. He selected five of the ward stones and a black handled dagger, and then set aside the scroll. He strode to the center of the room and drew a large symbol on the floor with a piece of chalk. He then tucked the athamé in the waistband of his jeans before methodically placing the stones at strategic points all around him. When he finished this strange ritual, he checked the scroll one last time and then held his hands out. A frown tugged her brow, but she rose and went to him.

"Give me your hands. Now, look into my eyes and do not break the connection, do not even blink, no matter what. Do not interrupt." He squeezed her hands and gave her a warning look, and she snapped her mouth closed. "Save your questions for later."

"Fine." Pressing her lips together, she glared up at him.

Taking a deep breath, he locked his gaze onto hers. She couldn't have looked away even if the apartment suddenly went up in flames. He began to speak, his voice deeper, darker, layered.

"Mïachtra onto'on quïelletra baté en eschweïst," he chanted. His words spilled on and on, washing over her.

Everything outside the circle of stones dimmed as mist curled up from the floor inside the circle, swirling around them. All she could see was him. His eyes. They turned black. She didn't so much as blink. She couldn't. Power coursed through his hands into hers, tingling up her arms, tickling inside her chest.

She fell into his stare, numb and blind to all else. Pain pierced the skin on her palms, but she couldn't flinch, couldn't look away. Heat grew as his palms once again covered hers, grew until her skin must surely be blistered.

And still, she couldn't pull away.

The heat spread, coursing through her entire body.

"Ibentra talic manthras ocht." Her head swam. The cadence of her heartbeat filled her ears, or was it his heartbeat? The pulse of it throbbed around her, and yet inside her too. She couldn't be sure. *"Coré otháme aoté collas, tá'hiri."*

He finally broke the trance. The mist was gone, the room no longer shrouded in darkness, and yet the warmth lingered, pulsing in her every cell. An acute awareness of him. Intimate. Unsettling.

A sudden wave of weakness caught her by surprise. Her knees went out from beneath her. Niklas caught her against him, his arm slipping around her waist. He held her like that for a long moment, his gaze caressing her face, and then he swept her off her feet and lifted her high against his chest. Niklas stepped from the circle and lowered her gently to the bed. As he brushed the hair from her forehead, a disconcertingly tender expression softened his features.

When he pulled his hand back, she blinked and caught his wrist. Drying blood was smeared across his palm. A thin line of scarlet sliced across his palm, a once deep wound nearly healed. Holding her own palm up, she gasped, seeing the mirror image reflected upon her flesh.

"What did you do?"

His expression held unmistakable guilt before he turned away. Without a word, he gathered the stones from the floor and repacked the trunk, then returned it to its hiding place beneath the bed.

"Is that how you healed yourself while you were gone? With stones like these? With a spell or something?" Inexplicable, insidious fear swam into her blood.

"No, I—" He abruptly scanned the air around her, frowning. He shook his head, as though confused. Rocking back on his heels, he rubbed his eyes, and peered at her as if she'd grown two more heads.

"What? What's wrong?" Swinging her legs over the side of the bed, she pushed herself into a sitting position. "What?"

"I can't…" He shook his head, looking baffled and

more than a bit green around the gills. "I can't see you."

"What do you mean you can't see me?" Fear of a new kind surged through her. She lunged for him, grasped his face between her hands, and pulled him closer so she could peer into his eyes. They looked normal, not damaged in any way. He'd had a raging fever for so long. Fever could affect hearing. Perhaps it had affected his vision somehow. A delayed reaction of some kind. "Do you see anything at all? Is everything black, can you see any light? Are you able to—"

"No." He took hold of her wrists, though he didn't pull her hands from his face. "You don't understand. I can't see your aura anymore. There's no color. No color around you." His expression darkened, and then his eyes went wide. Horrified, his grip on her wrists tightened. "Are you okay? Do you feel strange?"

"I feel fine." She frowned, adding, "A little warm, maybe, but otherwise fine. Unless you count the bruises you're trying to give me."

His grip immediately eased, but his dark scowl remained. "Your emotions. You still have them, right? Emotions?"

What a ridiculous question. "Um, yeah?"

A long sigh shuddered from him. Only then did he release her. She could tell something was still bothering him, but he'd shut down.

"Niklas, you didn't answer me earlier. Did you use one of these spells to heal yourself?" A worrisome thought dug in and tendrils of unease spread. "You know, maybe that's not such a good idea, using those scrolls. Maybe that's what's affecting your vision, some aftereffects of whatever healing spell you—"

"That's not it."

"How can you be sure?"

"Because I didn't use a spell to heal myself." A muscle ticked in his jaw, and he turned away.

Her throat went dry.

"How did you get over your illness so quickly?" Unbidden, memories of that night in the park assailed her. "Those monsters in the park tore into that poor woman. They drank her blood."

Her stomach flipped over. Slowly, she lifted her hand and covered her mouth, eyes wide.

"No!" Turning to face her, he glowered. "I'm not like them. I don't drink blood. And I don't prey on the innocent."

"I didn't say—"

"You didn't have to," he snapped, clearly offended. "It's written all over your face."

"Then explain it to me," she demanded. Frustration poured over the room in waves.

"My kind are often called soul-feeders, *tá'hiri*." The moment the words left his mouth, he looked as if he wished he could recall them.

"I don't understand. What does 'soul-feeder' mean?"

"Different demons draw sustenance in different ways," he explained, thrusting his hands into his pockets.

"Sustenance? But you eat human food. Well, not humans as food, but food humans eat," she rambled. "I fed you. Soup. I fed you soup." Oh God, she was just making this worse.

"We eat more for satisfaction and to keep our human bodies strong than for actual sustenance. But we need more nourishment than your human food can provide." He watched her closely. She could tell he was gauging her reaction. "I and others of my kind are known as soul-feeders. We siphon the life essence from humans. I prefer to take mine from criminals and degenerates that would otherwise escape earthly punishment for their crimes."

Siphon? She frowned, waiting for him to go on.

"Their souls, Carly. I drain their souls from their bodies."

"And what happens to the human you drain?"

He gave her a hard stare.

Appalled, she took an involuntary step back. But he was the one who flinched, reacting as if she'd slapped him. He was silent, obviously waiting for her to speak, to denounce him in some way. To question him as she was normally inclined to do.

She walked to a straight-backed chair and sank into it. Words failed her. Utterly. She could only stare at the place on the floor where he'd formed the circle with the stones earlier. The place where he'd performed his magical woo-woo thingy with the words from the scroll and the unexplained mist. His chalk symbol had disappeared. When had that happened? No one had wiped it away.

Niklas stood there, silent and stoic. Waiting.

Some part of her felt as if she should say something. Bridge the yawning chasm that grew between them. But words failed her. Thought failed her. She could only sit there, stunned and speechless, trying desperately to wrap her head around all he'd said. Here he was, this man/demon before her, calmly telling her he was a killer. He'd been so gentle with her. He'd taken care of her. And she'd taken care of him. Had she saved him so he could murder humans? Did that make her an accomplice? Guilty by association?

An accessory after the fact? Or rather before?

He *siphoned the life essence from humans* to stay alive. She couldn't assimilate all this. She just couldn't.

After what seemed an eternity, Niklas muttered something about taking a shower. He disappeared into the bathroom and closed the door behind him with a soft click. Carly looked up, staring blindly at the door.

Confused, she spun her mother's ring. How could her life have come to this? Demons and angels. Spells and protective talismans. Rituals and sacrifices. Vampire-like creatures.

Soul-feeders.

The surreal impossibility of the situation overwhelmed her. Oh, she'd fallen down Alice's rabbit hole, all right. Straight into a nightmare that was not inhabited by talking animals and card-shaped soldiers, but by entities who were, beneath the thin veneer of attractive humanity, pagan, primeval monsters that reveled in torture and dealt in death.

She couldn't get her bearings. It was all she could do not to hyperventilate.

She had to leave. Not just the apartment, but the whole town. Yes, she needed to go. Now. She'd stop home long enough to pack a bag, and then she'd leave it all behind. With Uncle Jason gone, and likely her job as well, she had nothing to tie her there, not any longer.

She'd go somewhere else. She'd start over. Somewhere far, far away. Away from all this killing. Away from this dark magic she had no way of understanding, no way of fighting. Away from the irrational attraction she felt for Niklas.

Away from all this madness.

With a growing sense of desperation, she glanced at the bathroom door. The muted sound of running water whispered from within.

Carly slipped from the apartment.

****

"We've located the woman's abode, my lord. And we have learned who she is."

The minion was nearly prostrate with fear, as well he should be. For Ronové's sake, it was a good thing Stolas was Hellbound. And it was a good thing Ronové had sent this fool in his place.

Two Earth days.

Stolas was not a patient demon. Drumming his fingers on the arm of his chair, he reminded himself for the fifth time he could not kill this whelp, not until he had all the information first.

"She lives in Ridgefield, not far from the site selected for the summoning. Her name is Carly Nicole Danner. She is a twenty-six-year-old paralegal. Single. Her last remaining relative, her uncle, died of cancer last year. She——"

"I don't care about any of that," Stolas snarled. *Idiot!* "Have you eliminated her?"

The demon's already bowed head dipped lower. "Not yet, my lord."

"What?" He exploded from his chair. Fury boiled in his veins, crackled in the putrid air around him. "What do you mean, you haven't killed her?"

"The Danner woman has not returned to her abode since the night of the——" Wisely, the minion chose not to speak further of the failed summoning. "She has not returned to her place of employment either. It seems the

Seer has taken her into hiding."

Stolas paced across the hall, stopping here and there, examining a trinket, adjusting the placement of a trophy. And yet, inside he seethed. Tsking, he dusted a piece of ash from the head of a marble bust. Yet another reason he'd come to hate his gilded cage. The ash was pervasive.

He slowly made his way to an ancient broadsword hanging in a place of honor upon his wall as he considered the ramifications of this latest development. Why had Niklas taken the female with him? He'd already saved her. Why not just send her on her way?

Did she know something that the Seer might deem useful? Had she witnessed more than Ronové had claimed? Had she heard Ronové invoke his name? Could she somehow link him to Ronové, thereby threatening his plans? He lifted the sword from its brackets and ran his fingers over the ornate carvings on the sheath.

Did Niklas plan to use her somehow to get back into Lucifer's good graces? Use her as evidence of betrayal by Lucifer's own grandson?

"M-my lord," the demon stuttered. "We've stationed a small legion throughout the town, covering every point in which she might surface. The moment she comes out in the open, we'll take her out. My master also wished me to tell you Dimiezlo is within reach of his goal."

He coldly regarded the demon kneeling on his floor. His hands tightened on the hilt and the sheath. "And what do you know of Dimiezlo's goals?"

The minion's brow puckered. He blinked rapidly. "I-I know n-nothing, my lord. It is not m-my p-place to ask questions."

Such a pity this minion had been given to Ronové. Such a waste.

"Do you have further instruction for my master? A m-message you wish delivered, perhaps?"

"As a matter of fact, I do." The blade made not a whisper of sound as he withdrew it from its sheath, and little more than a gentle hiss as it swiftly arced through the air.

The demon's severed head bounced and rolled, leaving a trail of sizzling, black blood across his floor. Stolas dropped the sword and sheath onto the table and strode toward his bedchamber.

"Clean up this mess," he barked over his shoulder at the Charocté hovering in the corner. "And send the head to Ronové."

Chapter Eight

Carly took the bus across town, thanking the powers that be that she'd had enough spare change in her pockets to swing the fare. The whole way, she'd been a jumble of nerves, glancing over her shoulder, flinching at the slightest sound. Familiar, smiling faces greeted her. Niklas's warning rang in her ears.

You won't know when, you won't know where, or who. It might even be someone you already know. But he will get to you... If you leave this apartment without me, you will die.

She glanced up and down the street, feeling like a fugitive breaking in to her own home. Carly swiped up the key hidden beneath the frog-shaped flowerpot. Once inside, she went directly to the closet. After lifting a suitcase down, she hurried over, dropped it on the bed and unzipped it, then flipped the top open.

She couldn't handle this. She couldn't deal with this craziness. Panic choked her. Urgency made her hands shake as she filled the suitcase. Blindly, she grabbed and stuffed, grabbed and stuffed, and all the while she waged a bitter, silent argument with herself. This was ridiculous. How could she leave? How could she stay? She had to be losing her mind. Yet she'd seen those creatures, they'd touched her.

They. Were. Real.

Where would she go? Her hand paused, a wadded-up bra hanging from limp fingers.

Somewhere. She'd go somewhere. Anywhere, just as long as it wasn't Ridgefield.

Resolved, her mind raced ahead. She had to grab the family photo album, it was all she had left. And she needed her personal documents, social security card, driver's license, passport, though she'd never used it before. Maybe this was it. Maybe this was what she'd been waiting for. She had no more ties holding her there. No real reason to stay.

Just monsters hunting her, waiting to torture and kill her. Waiting to steal her soul.

And a sexy, self-proclaimed *soul-feeder* who set fire to her hormones.

Criminy!

Scotland. Spain. Jamaica. She'd keep moving. They'd never find her.

Scrambling through the house, she collected anything she thought she might need on her mad dash to disappear. She grabbed her purse from the hall table on the way by and rushed back inside her room, arms loaded. After dumping her haul into the suitcase, she used all her weight to hold the top down as she zipped it shut.

Hurry, hurry.

The suitcase bounced down the stairs behind her, heavy and awkward. Her apologetic gaze skimmed over the photos still hanging in the hall. Maybe she had a few minutes. She could just grab a few—

A solid wall of muscle suddenly appeared in her path. Screaming, she fell back on the steps. Strong hands grabbed her. Long, steely arms encircled her, crushing her against a rock-hard chest encased in a soft, white T-shirt. Niklas's scent, citrusy shampoo and sandalwood soap and all male, overwhelmed her.

"Sweet Christ, don't ever do that again!" Niklas took hold of her shoulders in a painful grip, shoving her back so he could glare down at her. His hair was still dripping wet. His lips were compressed in a tight line. Fury rolled from him in waves.

"Do you hear me? Don't you ever do something so stupid again!" He punctuated his displeasure with a little shake. "Are you *trying* to serve yourself up to Ronové on a silver platter? Do you *want* to be tortured? He could have—"

Once more he crushed her to him, foreign words tripped off his tongue in a rush. She didn't understand the words, but she understood that tone. His heart pounded furiously against her ear.

"Let me go." She pushed at his chest, struggling out of his arms.

He released her at last, eyeing the suitcase she retrieved with a frown. "Where do you think you're going?"

"I-I don't know." A sob rose up in her throat, slipping out before she could trap it. Heaving a shaky sigh, she tried again, shoving her way around him. "I don't know, but I'll find somewhere. I can't do this. I-I can't be a part of this insanity anymore. I need to—"

Cutting her comment off with a soft curse, Carly jerked the suitcase free when a wheel lodged against the doorframe. She sailed around the corner and made her way through the kitchen, heading for the back door. "I have to get out of here, leave town."

"You think that will solve your problem, Carly?" He dogged her heels. "You think Ronové's minions are bound to this town alone? They'll follow you. Wherever you go. Anywhere on Earth. They'll track you down. The hunt won't end just because you leave town. They won't stop, not until you're dead."

Staggering to a halt, she hung her head. His words beat against her like fists, leaving her bruised with realization, battered by defeat. Unchecked tears left tracks down her cheeks. She didn't have the strength for this. Slowly, she turned to face him, letting the suitcase drop to the floor. She didn't know what to do.

In a heartbeat, he was in front of her, his arms closing gently around her this time. Drawing her carefully, tenderly into a soothing embrace.

"Shhh," he murmured against the top of her head. "Shhh, *tá'hiri*. It's okay." He smoothed a hand through her hair. Comforting.

"No," she sobbed. Her arms hung limp at her sides. "Don't you understand? It's never going to be okay again."

He cupped her head with one hand, pressing her cheek to his chest. A warm, hard hand eased up and down her back. Slowly, her arms crept around his waist, and she leaned into him, accepting his comfort. But she couldn't seem to stop crying. Her nose was starting to get drippy too. She gave in to the urge to sniffle.

"Here." Anchoring an arm around her, he leaned slightly to the side and snatched a tissue from a box on the baker's rack beside them.

With her forehead pressed to his chest and his arms loosely encircling her, she dabbed at her puffy eyes, blew her nose. She hated crying. Her nose always got red and her face went all splotchy. Definitely *not* attractive. She tossed the tissue in the small trash can at the end of the counter and turned her head to rest her cheek against his chest again.

"Better?" His hands had begun rubbing slow circles over her shoulder blades, up her neck.

Nodding, drained, she plucked absently at his tear-drenched T-shirt.

"You will survive this, *tá'hiri*. I promise you." Niklas hooked a knuckle beneath her chin, lifting her face. "You are the strongest human I've ever met. If anyone can survive this, you can. But you're not alone. I won't let you be alone. You took care of me. You didn't have to, but you did. Now let me take care of you."

"I don't want your gratitude—"

"Gratitude has nothing to do with what I feel for you, God help me," he growled.

Without warning, he lowered his head, capturing her lips in a soft caress. His palm slid up to cup her cheek. His mouth moved back and forth across hers, light, insistent, coaxing a response from her. Her palms slid up over his chest, stretching upward until she cupped the back of his neck, sinking her fingers deep in his dark hair. Soft. Warm. And his body was so hard. With a murmur, she melted against him.

Innocently, hungrily, she accepted his kiss, wanting—needing—more. As if somehow sensing her acceptance, his tongue swept over her lower lip, slipping inside, tangling seductively with her own. Slow, but so incredibly sensual. His hand moved from her cheek around to clasp the back of her neck in a firm grip. The arm wrapped around her waist shifted, slid, until he cradled the curve of her bottom in his hand. The hard ridge of his erection pressed against her stomach.

With an involuntary moan, she arched into him, instinctively rubbing herself against him. Sparks ignited deep in her core. Gripping him tighter, she tilted her head, drawing him in deeper. Greedy. Insatiable. She let it all go. All the fantastic claims. All the unbelievable things she'd seen with her own two eyes. All of it. The only thing that existed was Niklas. Here in her arms. Solid. Real.

And just as hungry for her as she was for him.

With a harsh growl, chest heaving, Niklas suddenly set her away from him and quickly yanked his hands from her as if burned. He closed his eyes and dropped his chin to his chest. She gingerly touched her fingertips to her mouth, her eyes huge. It had never occurred to her that he—a demon—would or could possess such depths of passion and tenderness.

Or such control.

More control, apparently, than *she* possessed.

"We need to leave here." He sounded uneven. The glacier blue of his eyes glowed brightly in the dim room.

Okay, they weren't going to discuss what just happened.

That was perfectly fine with her. She wouldn't know what to say anyway.

"I just need to grab my suitcase—wait." Frowning, she tilted her head. "How did you find me? This house is still listed under my uncle's name. And the phone is unlisted."

"I used no phone book."

"Then how—"

"We don't have time for this."

"Make time," she snapped, planting her fists on her hips. Her head was still spinning from his kiss, but she wouldn't be denied. He was going to start being upfront with her, one hundred percent, right here, right now. No more holding back what he thought might upset her. "I'm not taking another step until you explain how you found me."

The muscle along his jaw leaped. "The ritual I performed back in the apartment, with the stones and the athamé? It was a binding ritual."

He held his hands up for her inspection. Long, thin, pale-pink scars ran across his palms. With a dawning sense of shock, she lifted her hands and examined the duplicate scars she bore. Dried blood still stained her skin. He'd cut himself, and her.

Her state of mind must have been way out there if she hadn't noticed *that*.

"The binding was to protect you, I swear." He took a step closer, but she backed away, thrusting a hand up to halt his advance. "If one of Ronové's minions manages to break through the ward stones, if they get their hands on you and the guard stones fail, I'll be able to find you. No matter where they might take you. No matter how far. Even into the bowels of Hell itself. I will find you."

"You bound me to you?" That just sounded so barbaric. So archaic.

So *intimate*.

"It was for your own protection," he insisted once more, scowling.

"You had no right!"

"I'm trying to keep you—"

"Safe, yes, I know. But you still had no right. You

didn't even discuss this with me."

His lips compressed. The lines around his mouth deepened. "It's done."

Carly crossed her arms. "How long before it wears off?" When his gaze slid away and her question went unanswered, apprehension tightened low in the pit of her stomach. "Spells wear off, right?"

"Normally, yes, they do."

Her shoulders slumped. She didn't like the way that sounded. Not one bit. "Why do I hear a *but* in there?"

Thrusting his hands into his pockets, he admitted, "I modified the spell slightly."

She stared at him with a growing sense of alarm.

Defiance glinted in his eyes. His chin went up. "The binding is permanent, *tá'hiri*. It cannot be undone. I will *always* be able to find you. Anywhere. Anytime. Anyplace."

"But why?" she wailed.

Raking his splayed hand through his hair, he stomped away, stomped back. His brows drew together. "I need to keep you safe," he finally admitted. Oh, he didn't sound happy about that at all, though she couldn't tell if it was the need itself that upset him, or simply being forced to admit it out loud.

Her sense of independence felt diminished. "But I thought that's what all this jewelry was for." She waved her bracelet-encircled wrist in the air. "Protection. So another demon couldn't flash—"

"Shimmer."

"*Shimmer* away with me."

"Jewelry can be taken from you. Integrity of guard stones can be compromised. I couldn't risk that. I had to protect you with the one thing that won't fail. *Me*."

She spun away, paced to the kitchen table and turned to face him. "You should have told me about this, Niklas. Before you took it upon yourself to make that decision for me. You go too far."

"I will not apologize. It was for your own good." He gritted his teeth, lifting his chin. Proud. Autocratic.

"So as long as you deem something *for my own good*, you're just going to go ahead and do it whether I agree or not, is that right?"

"As long as—"

"No." She cut him off with a slash of her hand through the air. Fury bubbled through her veins. "No more *as long as*." She jabbed a finger at him. "And no buts, ifs, or just in cases. No loopholes. You *will* consult with me *before* you do anything like this again. I may only be a human. You can consider me weak and beneath you if you want, I don't really care. But I'm no child. I make my own decisions. Do *you* understand *me*?"

Despite the lines of tension etching his handsome face, one corner of his mouth crept upward. "Yes, *tá'hiri*. I understand you, better than you understand yourself, I think. I do not consider you weak or beneath me. And consider you a child?" His scalding gaze raked over her, pausing long enough on her breasts to cause a warm rush of need to pool deep in the pit of her stomach. "Not by a long shot."

Flustered, she crossed her arms, shielding her breasts from his stare. "And no more spells," she added. "I won't tolerate it, Niklas."

He looked away, his frown fierce. Rubbing a hand over his mouth and chin, he rocked back on his heels.

"Swear it to me, Niklas," she demanded.

He peered hard at her now. "Why does it matter so much to you?"

She glared. "Because something happened. It had to have been the spell," she murmured to herself. Then, louder, she added, "When you appeared in the hallway a few minutes ago, when you initially hugged me and I realized it was you, I felt..." She shook her head, pausing, searching for the right words. "Swamped with relief. And when you kissed me, the feelings were so strong, so intense. The desire was stronger than anything I've ever—"

As she offered her explanation, his eyes slowly grew wider and wider, his eyebrows elevated.

"Has this happened before?" Carly lifted a hand, clutched the base of her throat. "This is a normal side effect, right?"

"Nothing about the binding spell would have changed your emotions or amplified them." He stared long and hard at her, like he was trying to read her mind, or her soul. He blinked, glanced down and away, as if searching for the answers inside himself. Then, suddenly, Niklas turned to her, his expression sucker-punched. Slowly, but with an unsettling, fatal conviction, he stated, "What you feel? Those emotions are your own, *tá'hiri*."

Her mouth fell open, and her eyes rounded.

Shaking his head, he raked both hands through his hair and paced away from her, pausing to peer out the window over the sink. He faced her and leaned back against the counter. He stared at her, but she didn't think he was actually seeing her. "The ritual," he whispered, apparently thinking aloud, "the ritual must have bound us more deeply than I anticipated."

"Ya think?" Oh, she wanted to punch something. Preferably him. Which was completely unlike her. She'd never resorted to physical violence before and had no intention of doing so now. How could he do this to her? How could he—

Before she realized what she was doing, she crossed the distance to him and smacked her palms against his chest, shoving him.

He blinked at her, incredulous. "What was that for?"

Beyond thought, beyond reason, she shoved him again. "Look what you did! 'I modified the spell slightly,'" she snidely mocked him, lowering her voice and puffing her chest out, throwing her shoulders back. Then she jabbed him with a pointed finger to the middle of his chest and snarled, "You don't mess with black magic and not expect it to backfire! I'm not magical, or paranormal, or whatever the hell it is that you are, and even *I* know that much." She stormed away, stormed back and drilled him in the center of the chest with her finger again. Dear Lord, she'd never been so angry in all her life. "Scrolls stolen from Lucifer. Seriously, Niklas? Did it not *once* occur to you that if you used them something *bad* might happen?"

"You have a temper," he wondered aloud. A grin spread across his tempting lips, which made her even angrier.

She tunneled her fingers in her hair and fisted them. "Everyone has a temper, you big jerk."

"Yeah, but with all that's happened to you so far, you've not lost your cool. Well, not until you tried to run away—"

"I have a long fuse," she barked. "So, sue me for not coming with a warning label."

"You get snotty when you're mad," he observed. If his grin stretched any wider his face might split. The big dumbass. "And you don't give me a headache anymore."

"*What?*" Carly hissed.

She gave *him* a headache? Of all the nerve.

"You—your aura—used to swirl with so many different colors that my head would pound trying to read you." His gaze swept the air around her and he actually sighed his pleasure aloud. "No more colors, no more headache."

"Well, yippee for you."

"You know, outwardly, you can appear so composed. But inside, you seethe with emotion. You keep them bottled so tightly. It's little wonder you don't explode more often."

"Keep grinning like that, bucko, and you're liable to see me *explode* all over this kitchen."

That sobered him. Mostly. Laughter still lurked in his eyes. Damn him.

Drilling her fingertips into her scalp and ruffling her hair, she went to the fridge. After pulling out a soda, she cracked it open and took a long drink. Carly set the can on the counter and, glowering, she began unloading the dishwasher and putting dishes away.

Niklas turned, rested a hip against the cabinets, and watched in silence. "Do you have some addiction to cleaning?"

"I need to think this through," she snapped, slapping a plate onto the stack in the cupboard. "I think better when my hands are busy." She shot him a dirty look, adding, "Be glad I'm putting them away and not throwing them at your head."

His amusement buffeted her like a warm caress. Her fingers clutched the plate in her hands so tightly, it was little wonder the thing didn't simply shatter. Now was not the time to be laughing at her. She opened her mouth to tell him so, but the air in her kitchen suddenly began to waver. Everywhere. Before her eyes, not one, not two, but six demons shimmered into view. The plate slipped from her suddenly limp fingers.

Niklas snapped to attention and threw himself in front of her, pushed her to the floor. She didn't even have time to scream. A red ball of energy burst against the cabinet, exactly where she'd stood only a second ago. Flames exploded across the wooden surface, dripping onto the countertop. A spray of glowing, red embers showered down on her, stinging her skin. She instinctively covered her head with her arms, curling into a tight ball. A bellow echoed throughout the room.

Niklas. Enraged.

Fear choked her. Peeking up from beneath her arm, she gasped. Niklas—the fully demonic Niklas—stood over her, a massive, protective shield between her and the six demons.

A bright ball of energy pulsed to life in his palm, a glowing ball of seething plasma. He hurled the plasma ball from his hand and a second later, the demon standing front and center exploded in a smoking ball of ash. Niklas took a glancing blow to the shoulder. Ducking, he fired off another shot, eliminating a short, stout demon with green horns and three eyes.

The remaining four fanned out across the confined space and came at him from all different angles. They slithered closer, their focus divided, warily on Niklas, greedily on her.

Worry began to engulf her. There were too many of them in too small of a space. If the fight became a physical contest of power, pitted against any of these demons, or even all of them at the same time, Niklas could win. But if three of them rushed him, kept him diverted, the last one might slip by and get to her.

By now, energy balls flew willy-nilly through her kitchen, igniting the curtains and the table. One of the chairs lay on its side, little more than splinters of kindling. The baker's rack had overturned. The intricate, wrought iron scrollwork was crushed and mangled like aluminum foil.

Pictures on the wall had tipped topsy-turvy, the protective glass shattered. Smoke filled the room as sporadic fires broke out. The ceramic flour canister on the counter exploded, and a cloud of white washed through the smoke.

Coughing, Carly pressed her spine into the corner of the cabinets. Niklas took another hit and staggered back. The back of his heel brushed her shin. Roaring, he let loose with two more plasma balls. The demon on the far left burst into a ball of flames and crashed through the doorway, falling into the hall. The carpet caught fire as he exploded into smoldering ash.

With their numbers rapidly dwindling, the demons must have realized their luck was about to turn. In unison, two of the demons launched themselves toward Niklas. The third made a dive for her, talon-tipped hands reaching.

Chapter Nine

Anticipating this strategy, Niklas dropped to the floor. He was already visualizing the apartment as he wrapped a hand around Carly's ankle. Off balance and injured, he had trouble controlling their arrival and the landing was hard, knocking the breath out of him. The moment they solidified, Carly's scream filled the apartment.

"*Tá'hiri*," he growled around a mouthful of fangs, his voice deeper and rougher than he'd intended.

He got no further in his warning, when, a split second later, the air beside him distorted. One of the assassins had followed his shimmer trail. Bracing himself, Niklas vaulted to his feet. The demon, a nasty little sucker with a wiry build and poison dripping from his fangs, took one look at Niklas before he lunged for Carly.

Niklas caught him in the midsection with a roundhouse kick. The demon crashed into the sofa, causing it to sag drunkenly in the middle. Niklas conjured an ebony-handled athamé in his right hand, beckoning the intruder forward with his left. Shaking off his surprise, the Ralsha demon sprang to his feet and eyed Niklas with newfound respect. And yet his fiery red eyes peered around the room, no doubt looking for leverage.

"You want her," Niklas snarled, "you have to go

through me."

The demon glanced one last time at Carly. She lifted her hand, nervously pushing the hair from her eyes. The demon finally noticed her bracelet, and his expression turned grim. Before Niklas could attack, the demon disappeared.

Swearing, Niklas lunged toward the distortion of air. But in those final, crucial moments before he followed the demon, Carly sucked in a sharp breath. Niklas skidded to a halt. His gut instinct was to leap into the void and follow the demon's shimmer trail, hopefully straight to Ronové. He could end Ronové now, and the threat the collector posed to his *tá'hiri*. But what if it had been a ruse, one designed to draw him away and leave Carly unprotected. Could he risk it?

He glanced over. When they'd returned to the apartment, she'd landed on the floor near the bed. She pushed up on one hip and, wincing, she cradled one arm to her chest. A sickening worry curled in his gut. Foreign. Baffling. Had one of those demons managed to hit her with a plasma ball? How badly had she been hurt?

She curled her long, bare legs beneath her and rubbed her shoulder, glancing around the room as if she expected demons to pour from the walls by the dozens.

Mine, the layered voice growled in the back of his mind. *Take. Mate. Claim!*

Lust rippled through his muscles, set fire to his bloodstream. His mouth watered. To have her small body beneath his, writhing as he ground his—

"Niklas?" She was staring up at him now, her face registering the alarm of a new threat.

He blinked. Shook his head. Started forward again. His hands slowly clenched, unclenched, clenched. He found himself hungering for her breasts, which pressed against *his* T-shirt. The faint outline of her bra enticed him as never before. Chest heaving now, he licked his lips.

"Niklas?" Carly scuttled backward until she came up against the bed. Her big, brown eyes were drenched with unmistakable fear. "You can change back now," she squeaked. "He's gone. The danger has passed."

He paused, tilted his head.

Why would he want to change back? This form held so much raw *power*. In *this* form, guilt did not stay his hand. Remorse did not keep him awake at night. If he stayed like this, he could better protect what belonged to him. *She* belonged to him, this tiny female. He'd already bound her to him. All he had left to do was to take her. He advanced. She recoiled.

Angered, he glared down at her. He'd battled for her. He'd won the right to claim her.

Why couldn't she understand?

"*Mershka*," he insisted in Demonic. And then, remembering she didn't speak Demonic, he growled in her human language, "Mine."

What little color she still had leached from her already pale face. Shaking her head vehemently, she scooted along the edge of the bed. "Niklas, you *must* change back. Remember your vow. You swore you'd protect me. Remember?"

He always protected what belonged to him. He knew, somewhere deep inside, that he was being irrational about this. Behaving far too primitively. But he couldn't seem to help himself. This wasn't like him.

Usually cold, calculating and methodical in demonic form, he couldn't seem to get his bearings. The battle, and Carly herself, had driven him beyond rational thought, turning him into an elemental beast focused solely on claiming his mate. He continued to advance. She continued to scramble away.

Why is she trying to get away from me?

His nostrils flared. His heavy breathing became a ragged rasp. She should be accepting him, eagerly welcoming his touch.

Why is she behaving this way?

Carly bit her lip and looked toward the door as if gauging the distance.

"Do not," he warned. Why would she want to run from him? He only wanted to protect her. Only wanted to claim what was already his. He'd been so lonely before. And now she was there.

Carly froze. Tilting her head, she blinked. And then her expression changed. Fearful. And yet determined. Without warning, she threw herself into his arms, pressing her cheek against his massive chest. Wrapping her arms around his waist. Holding him tight. Clinging.

"You're going to keep me safe. Remember?" Carly crooned. "You want to keep me safe. You don't want to hurt me, do you? But you might hurt me if you don't change back. You are too strong like this. Too big. You have to change back, Niklas. You'll hurt me. You have to change back. You have to keep me safe, remember?"

Safe. Yes. He would keep her safe. His *tá'hiri*. She was so tiny. So fragile. His arms went around her, protective and gentle, swallowing her up. He patted her hair, surprised to find that his hand virtually engulfed her head. Too big. He might crush her by accident. Too strong. If he flexed his arms, hugged her too tightly, he might break her. Ah, sweet Lord, he wanted to hold her tight. Touch her. Caress her. Closing his eyes, he willed the transformation.

Blinding pain slashed through his head. Gasping, he swayed in her arms. She held him tighter, stabilizing his weight. Searing burns lacerated his flesh. His shoulder, his back. He'd taken more hits than he'd realized.

Damn. Hurts. So bad.

He'd forgotten about the burns. He should have waited long enough for his demonic anatomy to absorb the burns before he'd changed back. Too late now.

His skull was being cleaved in two. Excruciating pain nearly bringing him to his knees.

But they had no time to waste.

"Have to...go," he rasped. He shifted her to the side and tucked her beneath his arm like a crutch. "Have to...leave...before assassin...returns...with backup. Ward stones...compromised..."

"We have to go back," she insisted.

"What?" He couldn't have heard her right. He must be in worse shape than he realized.

"We have to go back to my house. I need to get my suitcase. We have to go quickly, Niklas. Before the fire—"

"Gone...it's al...ready...gone..." He gasped, pressing the heel of his hand hard against his temple.

"No, we can still—"

"It's gone!" he bellowed, and then winced. Groaning. *Oh, God. It had never hurt this bad before.* "By now...the fire has probably...consumed the...whole house."

"Are you sure?" Her lower lip trembled. Tears filled her eyes. When he nodded, she lowered her head. She looked so defeated, he nearly promised the impossible.

No, her safety came first.

"I'm sorry, Carly." A fresh wave of pain slashed through his head, just behind his eyes.

She readjusted her hold on his waist and drew a deep breath. Resignation, resolve glinted in her expression. Even suffering from as much pain as he was, he couldn't help but admire her resilience. She'd just lost everything. Her home, her safety, her freedom. But she hadn't lost her spirit, her determination. God love her. If he wasn't in such rough shape and he wasn't worried about uninvited guests shimmering in at any moment, he'd have kissed her then and there.

"Where will we go now?"

"The trunk...can't leave...it behind." Damn it, just talking was draining him of precious strength. The thought of what was to come nearly put him on the floor. "Please...pull it...to me."

He braced his weight on the back of the chair and released Carly so she could do as he asked. Unable to help, he watched as she struggled to pull the trunk from under the bed and then drag it across the floor to his side. After tipping it on end, she shuffled it closer, so the handle was within easy reach for him.

"Come here." He motioned her back beneath his arm.

"Isn't there another way?"

"Not right now," he replied, conscious of the time they'd wasted lingering there talking. "Close your eyes. Remember, keep breathing...unless I tell you...not to."

"What?" Alarmed, she peered up at him. He offered her a pained grin, dropped an impulsive kiss on her lips, and then shimmered them to an alley behind a row of businesses.

"Oh God, I'm gonna be sick," she gasped.

"Told you...to close...your eyes." Every word ripped fresh pain through his skull. Wouldn't give in to it. Couldn't.

"You didn't give me time," she snapped.

"You know...I think I...like...this spunky...side...of you."

"You keep flashing—"

"Shimmering," he corrected, breathing through the pain.

"Shimmering me all over the place without warning like that again and you're likely to see all sorts of sides to me you're just gonna love." Carly peered around her. "Where are we?"

Strangely enough, they stood smack in the middle of the alley, with a deserted parking lot on one side and a small patch of manicured grass on the other. The ornamental lawn was butted up against what was obviously the rear entrance of a pet store, the grass lined with a decorative fence and a pristine sidewalk. There was even a bright fire hydrant for convenient use. It was a miniature doggie oasis.

"Algona. And before you ask, no, we're not staying." Every word was painful. Pulling her tighter against his side, he ordered, "Close your eyes."

This time he waited for her to comply before he shimmered them to their next location. She opened her eyes and glanced around. They'd landed in the middle of a sea of brilliant emerald rustling in the soft breeze.

"Where are we now?"

He made a point of dramatically peering all around them as well. "Looks like," he paused, breathing through a particularly sharp stab of pain, "a cornfield."

The pain was excruciating. But teasing her helped take his mind off it.

She blinked up at him, and then pinched his side, muttering, "Jerk."

He saw the half grin before she lowered her head. Despite the direness of their situation, he felt lighter, being able to banter with her like this. But she was so pale. "Closing your eyes helps, doesn't it?"

"Not really, but I think I'm starting to get used to it." She was quick to point out, "I don't like not knowing where we're going to end up. For all I know, your aim could be bad. You might drop us in a lake or something."

It was as if she somehow knew he needed this, needed her prodding and pricking him to keep him going. She gave him strength. Right now, she *was* his strength.

A strange warmth stole through him, catching him by surprise.

"I guess you're just…going to have to trust me." Suddenly that was unspeakably important to him, that she trust him.

She peered at him with a thoughtful frown. Finally, with absolute conviction, she said, "I do trust you, Niklas."

The warmth in his chest swelled until he had trouble breathing around it. Her expression softened, and she tilted her head, searching his face. He couldn't resist and leaned his head closer to hers. Her scent beckoned him.

"Put both arms around me now and hold tight," he whispered against her lips. She immediately complied, no questions asked, pleasing him to no end. He wished his hands were free to explore the texture of her skin. "We're going to shimmer very quickly now to a lot of places before we stop again."

"Why can't we just shimmer directly to wherever it is that we need to go? Or pick some random place so that they can't guess where you are going? Why do we have to make all these stops?"

"I have to be sure we aren't being followed. Every time we shimmer, we leave a shimmer trail, faint but there, nonetheless. After a few minutes, the trail dissipates, but if someone is following us, shimmering right behind us, they'd be able to follow." He scanned the area around them, extending his senses to be sure they hadn't already been followed. "Besides, I can only shimmer to places I've already been."

"But you shimmered into my house." Her eyes narrowed. "Have you been there—"

"No, I shimmered *to you*," he corrected.

"You shimmered blindly into a place you've never been? What if those other demons had been there before you came? You could have popped right into the middle of a trap."

"Shimmered," he corrected her. "Popped sounds so undignified." And then he turned serious. "You are the exception to the rule for me. Wherever you are, I will find you. I will always come for you," Niklas said forcefully. "I promised I'd keep you safe. My honor is all that keeps me from reverting back to what *they* are. Now…" He drew a deep, bracing breath. "Are you ready?"

She nodded.

"Close your eyes," he whispered, once more inexplicably pleased when she immediately and without question complied. He wanted to stand there and watch her all day, hold her for the rest of eternity and never let go. The feel of her arms around him was exquisite. He longed to kiss her senseless.

The blistered flesh on his shoulder, back and thigh sent a fresh wave of agony washing over him, making him dizzy. He wanted to give in to the pain and just pass out.

He needed to get them to their final destination as quickly as possible.

Niklas pressed her head against his chest, closed his own eyes, and centered his focus. The next series of stops were a complicated zigzag of motion, taking them from Des Moines to Atlanta, Reno to Chicago, Seattle to Miami, and a dozen places in between. He didn't have the energy to shimmer them any farther than the continental US. England, Spain, India, South Africa would have been better, would have pushed other demons beyond their limitations, but Niklas just didn't have the energy.

He was drained. He knew he couldn't go on much longer, and he couldn't risk passing out and leaving her defenseless. Needing a moment to gather the last reserves of his strength, he paused at the next stop, gasping for air.

"*Now* where are we?" Her eyes flew wide as she took in her surroundings.

"Not in Kansas anymore, Dorothy." Unable to help himself, he sagged against her.

"This looks like a whorehouse, Niklas," she hissed.

He didn't waste the breath to tease her. Didn't have any to waste. And so, he grinned wickedly down at her. Or as wickedly as he could, given the circumstances.

"A whorehouse? Seriously?"

"Didn't tell you," he wheezed, "to open your eyes."

She gaped at the tousled bed, the bordello wallpaper, and the red velvet drapes. A rainbow of slinky lingerie hung from chairs and dresser drawers, and off a decorative, trifold room divider with Asian symbols.

The glare she sent him could have seared the eyebrows off Lucifer himself.

Whoever had coined the phrase "still waters run deep" must have had Carly in mind. Anyone who took his precious *tá'hiri* at face value, as nothing more than a placid paralegal, was making a serious mistake. The word firecracker came to mind. He'd never understood that euphemism. Not until her.

The pain in his head was getting worse. He didn't know how much more he could take. Niklas shimmered them away before she could let loose the temper crackling in her eyes. They shimmered onto the steps of a beautiful church.

Gripping him tighter for a moment, she turned an unbecoming shade of green, blinked.

"Close your eyes," he reminded her.

"I think I prefer to see where we end up, thank you," she said primly.

Gritting his teeth, he finally took them to their last stop. He dropped the trunk and sagged. Carly braced herself against him and helped him to the nearest chair.

He'd brought her to an old farm place in southern

Minnesota, one of a dozen places his legion kept as a safe house. He didn't like to think that he might have compromised the place by leaving a shimmer trail leading here, Sebastian would kill him, but he couldn't think of anywhere else that would be safe for her.

"You look horrible."

"Thanks." Nausea gripped him by the back of the throat.

"What can I do?" She dropped to her knees in front of him. Her cool hands cupped his clammy cheeks. "How can I help?"

"In the…trunk."

Immediately, she dragged the trunk closer, popped the latches and lifted the lid.

"Purple pouch." Scrunching his eyes closed, he willed his stomach not to rebel. "Mix with water."

Without hesitating, her hand plunged into the compartment containing pouches. She drew out three.

"Dark one."

Dropping the two lavender-colored bags back into the trunk, she returned to his side. "How much?"

He swallowed. Considered. The normal dose would have been about a teaspoon. But the way he felt just now? "Half the bag."

"In a full glass of water?"

He nodded. The pain was overwhelming. He couldn't remember the last time he'd sustained so much damage, certainly none that he'd tried to heal while still in his human body.

Carly rushed to open cabinet doors, searching until she found the glasses. She took one down, filled the glass with tap water, and then located a spoon. After setting the glass on the table beside him, she began pouring the powder until he nodded to indicate she'd poured enough. She stirred, then handed the glass to him. The once clear liquid was now lime green and thick as sludge.

Niklas sucked in a shaky breath and downed the potion in one long guzzle.

Searing heat exploded in his gut, drenching his entire body. Panting, he set the glass aside, tipped his head back, closed his eyes and welcomed the burn. The potion would help. It wouldn't heal him like feeding would, but it would go a long way toward getting him back on his feet. He wouldn't tell her she'd just brewed more "dark magic." He didn't need the lecture right now.

Besides, Niklas couldn't count on God doling out any miracle healings.

Not for him anyway.

"What about ward stones?" She glanced back at the trunk. "Do I need to distribute them or something?"

"No," he replied, already feeling strength seeping into his muscles. "We've already placed ward stones all over the grounds."

"We? Oh, you mean you and your friends."

"Our legion, yes." His limbs no longer felt like rubber.

"So this is—"

"A safe house, one of many." He could feel his strength returning, sweeping through his system in wave after wave of heat. Even his splitting headache was receding. "Sebastian primarily uses this one whenever he's in the area, but it also serves as a meeting place when we all need to gather." He drew a deep breath, the first one since the battle that didn't set pain ricocheting through his body. "This farm's about fifty miles north of Ridgefield, just over the Iowa/Minnesota border. It's completely isolated. It suits our purposes."

"How long will we stay here?"

"As long as we need to." The thought of shimmering anywhere right now made him sick to his stomach all over again.

"What else can I do for you?" She twisted the thick silver ring on her middle finger.

Oh, the answers to that were endless, and very erotic.

"Rest, you're tired. Eat. The cupboards are kept stocked."

"What I really need right now is a shower."

"There are five bedrooms upstairs. Use the one on the left, first door. There's an adjoining bathroom. A change of clothing will be waiting on the bed for you."

"How can there be a—" She looked to his shirt, widening her eyes as if remembering. "Oh."

One corner of his lips lifted. "Remember, my talents are *handy*."

She looked as if she wanted to say something but doubted the wisdom of doing so. Silent, she turned to leave the kitchen. He snagged her wrist. The urge to touch her, to draw solace from the simple caress of her hair against his fingers, was far too strong to resist. The need to snuggle her against him and *feel* that she was safe took control of his body.

He shouldn't do this. Shouldn't give in.

But caring was beyond him at that point. His body had been ravaged, his control was in tatters. And he kept remembering how those assassins had looked at her.

With a deft tug and twist, he pulled her down in his lap. She gasped. Her hands landed on his shoulders. She blinked at him with wide, surprised eyes. Her lips parted, and her attention slid to his mouth. His fingertips coasted up her spine, urging her closer. Her breasts brushed tantalizingly across his chest.

Lifting his chin, he waited, eyes hooded. Breath suspended. Would she kiss him?

She met his silent challenge, slipping her arms around his neck. Carly lowered her head, brushed her lips across his. Light. Butterfly soft. Warm as sunshine. And then, by slow degrees, she melted against him.

Her tongue slid inside his mouth, tentative, questing, curious, sweet as honey. He let her explore, met her budding passions, just enough to keep her questing, but not so much that he scared her off.

Tremors of desire swept through him. Never had it been so difficult to restrain himself.

Niklas cradled her in his arms, gentle, possessive but careful not to press too hard or go too fast. Instead, he basked in the glow of her exploration. His heartbeat felt unusually thick, sluggish, echoed in his ears. His shaft grew painfully hard, but he resisted the urge to flex his hips against her, unwilling to do anything that might give her pause. Unwilling to do anything that might bring this sweet interlude to an end.

At length, drawing a shaky breath, she eased back in the cage of his arms, staring at him as if she couldn't believe her boldness. That minimal distance was suddenly too much for him to bear. He needed more of her. Needed the feel of her skin against his lips. Leaning forward, holding her still, he nipped kisses down the side of her neck. Resting his forehead against her jaw, he hugged her tight and held her for a moment, letting the scent of her seep through him, letting the feel of her in his arms imprint itself upon his soul.

When those minions had raided her house, when he'd been forced to throw her to the floor to keep her from being incinerated by that plasma ball, his heart had nearly stopped. Never before had he experienced such fear. Or such fury. The very memory of his helpless *tá'hiri* smack in the middle of a demon battle left him shaken. Too easily, one of those plasma balls could have ended her precious life.

For the first time since rescuing her from Ronové in the park, Niklas finally came face-to-face with the truth. Carly had quickly become more than just another innocent to him. Keeping her safe, keeping her by his side no matter the cost, had absolutely nothing to do with his mission to reclaim his immortal soul.

It had everything to do with his heart. Or maybe it was just that damned binding spell. Whatever it was, this obsession with her held him in an ironclad grip.

He would still lose her. Maybe not tomorrow to a demon attack. Maybe not next week. But *someday*. Years from now, a human illness, an accident, old age. Sooner or later she would die.

And he would go on living...if you could call what he did living.

True fear settled upon him. His arms flexed, tightening around her. He buried his nose against her flesh, then rested his cheek on her shoulder, his forehead pressed to her throat. His heart shuddered as her arms slipped more securely around him and drew him closer, cuddling him.

When—not *if*—but *when* he lost her, would he even care about his immortal soul anymore? Would he revert to the demon he once was? A creature without mercy or conscience?

No. Having found a woman like Carly, having his life touched by someone so innocent and pure, he doubted it was possible to return to what he once was. But would he care about returning to God's grace either? Somehow, unsettling as the realization was, that goal no longer held the appeal it once had. Would he continue to save the innocent? Would he continue to take out any demons stupid enough to cross his path?

Yes. Of course, he would.

But his priorities had subtly shifted. Without trying, probably without realizing it was even possible, she'd changed him, changed the very essence of who and what he was. He was no longer simply an Archangel cast from Heaven, looking for a way back. No longer a renegade demon escaped from Hell, doing his level best not to return there.

He'd become a desperate male willing to do anything to protect his female.

And with her death, he would finally be defeated. Not by Lucifer and all his hordes. Not by his ceaseless quest for redemption. Not by temptation and weakness. Not by his other, darker side. But by the loss of this one, precious human female, and the loss of the connection he shared with her.

Tilting her head, she rested her cheek against the top of his head. Unable to help himself, he nuzzled his face into the curve of her neck. Her fingers slipped through his hair. Tender. Soothing.

God help him, because he knew, deep in the pit of

his black soul, there would be no surviving the loss of her.

Chapter Ten

Carly wandered through the living room, taking in her surroundings as she made for the stairs. The kiss she'd just shared with Niklas, the precious moments she'd spent in his arms, weighed heavy on her mind. Yes, he'd made the first move, pulling her into his arms.

There was no way to wrap it up with a pretty bow. No way to point fingers and cast blame. *She'd* kissed *him*. Plain and simple.

And after that heart-fluttering kiss, he'd held her close, as if he couldn't bear to be parted from her. She couldn't find it in her to regret a second of it. No matter how badly it might complicate things.

The place was fully furnished. In the living room, a brown plaid sofa and loveseat combo with matching recliner flanked a fieldstone fireplace with a big screen TV hanging above the mantel. The base of the lamp on the end table was fashioned from some type of antler. The walls sported masculine, outdoorsy prints: pictures of hunting lodges and Labrador retrievers, lakeside cabins, and ducks in flight. Shaking her head, she stopped to peer through an open door into a den of sorts.

The masculine hunter motif had spilled into here as well, reflected in the artwork, the wallpaper, and the furniture. Books filled the bookshelves along one wall, so many of them, her head spun. The avid reader inside her gasped with joy. They were stacked haphazardly everywhere, both horizontal as well as vertical. Dog-eared. Tattered. Covers worn by time and use.

Her first instinct was to check the titles. Search for something to sink into. Her second was to organize.

She clamped down on those urges, reminding herself that she had priorities. Shower first. Food second. And then, God willing, rest. Later, provided some invading horde of demons didn't set up camp on their front step, she'd come back and wallow to her heart's content. Glancing around the room, she took in the heavy mahogany desk on one side of the room. A worn, navy armchair with a footrest in the opposite corner. A reading lamp.

Everything she needed.

Later, she reminded herself sternly. *Later.*

Carly slipped inside the bedroom Niklas had indicated. A huge bed with a plain tan comforter. Matching curtains. A glossy, cherry wood dresser set. The walls were utilitarian, white, unadorned. The carpet beige. Not a drop of color to be had.

And she found the clothing, just as he'd said she would, folded neatly on the foot of the bed for her inspection. A red, cotton, V-necked T-shirt and a red, cotton-and-lace bra and panties set. Blue jean shorts. He'd even thought of strappy leather sandals with large rhinestone decorations. At least she'd thought they were rhinestones, until she got a closer look. Shaking her head, she put them back on the floor. Nope. She didn't want to know.

Carly stepped into the bathroom. Spotless white tile. Black marble countertops. Gleaming silver fixtures. An array of soaps and shampoos, conditioners and lotions lined the counter. A stack of pristine, white, fluffy towels rested beside them.

Definitely handy.

A girl could get used to this kind of pampering. Now all she needed was a fruit basket and a mint on her pillow.

Mints, hmm.

Those little chocolate mints sounded good right about now. A handful of them sprinkled over chocolate ice cream had always been her one weakness. Well, until she'd met a certain sexy demon. She'd mentioned her weakness to Niklas down in the kitchen earlier when her stomach had growled. Her weakness for ice cream with mints, that was. Not her weakness for him.

Though she was pretty sure he'd probably already picked up on that one himself. Shower first, then she'd remind Niklas that she needed something to eat.

Finally relaxing for the first time in days, she selected shampoo, conditioner and soap. After setting the bottles on the ledge inside the shower, she frowned and picked up a large black bottle that was already there. Carly turned it in her hands and examined the label. Flipping the lid open, she sniffed.

Niklas.

Did this bedroom belong to him? That would certainly explain the Spartan décor and drab colors. No, not drab colors, she corrected herself. Calming colors. Soothing, neutral colors. Colors that wouldn't overwhelm his senses considering his *special gift.*

She took another sniff of his shower gel.

Warmth, need trickled in through her nostrils and saturated her body. Disconcerted, she set the bottle aside and stripped down, dropped her clothes into a ball beside the door, and stepped beneath the steaming spray, chiding herself. He was a demon, one who had been working ceaselessly to regain entrance to Heaven. An affair with her would hardly be on his to-do list.

And it shouldn't be on hers either.

But the memory of the kiss they'd shared buffeted her. Had it been merely an offer of comfort that had gotten out of hand? Had she read more into it than he'd intended?

A short while later, showered and refreshed, lathered in sweet-smelling lotion, Carly stepped from the bathroom. Her wet hair clung to her cheeks and neck, dripping onto her bare shoulders. Guessing Niklas would be growing impatient, she scrambled to dress. The last thing she needed was for him to come searching for her. The towel she wore offered little in the way of resistance or discouragement, to either of them.

She found Niklas sitting in the living room watching a Spanish news station. He'd also showered and was wearing a fresh pair of jeans. No shirt. She stepped closer, ready to tease him over his seeming preference to go shirtless. Until she caught sight of his burns.

Gasping, she hurried to his side. "Criminy, Niklas! Why didn't you say something?"

"I'll heal," he remarked, his attention torn between her and the news broadcaster. The announcer's face blinked off, though his voice continued to drone on as a grisly picture of a small village filled the screen. Rough wooden structures, now burned-out shells, smoked, charred black by fire.

Turning from the disturbing images, Carly examined the burns on Niklas's skin close up, horrified at the sheer damage his flesh had sustained. Stepping around him, she gasped again, staring at his back.

"Oh, Niklas. You should have told me. These should have been cleaned and treated before I worried about a shower."

Without waiting for a reply, she hurried back upstairs to the bathroom and rummaged for a first aid kit. Nothing. She hesitated for a moment, and then dashed into one of the other bedrooms and darted into its adjoining bath, feeling no guilt at all in her ruthless search. It was for Niklas, she justified. A few moments later, she returned, arms loaded with supplies. He watched her, impassive, motionless. She spread her supplies out on the glass-topped coffee table and sorted until she found burn salve.

Taking a seat on the sofa beside him, she briskly ordered, "Turn."

"This isn't necessary. The burns will heal quickly now that I've taken the...ah, the medicine."

"Medicine? You mean the green stuff I mixed for you? It wasn't some homeopathic remedy," she stated flatly. "That was more black magic woo-woo stuff, wasn't it?"

"I figured taking a 'don't ask don't tell' approach was safer."

Her lips thinned. "Turn," she insisted. "Humor me."

Heaving a sigh, he did as she asked, presenting her with his back. Carly gaped. Her anger over the use of potentially dangerous, evil magic was forgotten. In the short time it had taken her to retrieve the first aid kit, the blisters had already disappeared. While his skin was still an angry, raw red, it no longer looked quite so ghastly. She gingerly spread the salve over his wounds, nonetheless.

"Why did you have to burn the bodies in the park, when the demons in my house exploded and turned to ash?"

He held himself rigid beneath her ministrations, and her heart went out to him.

The pain these burns must be causing—

"The Earthbound legion in the park, they were possessions, Carly. Demon-possessed humans," he answered in controlled, even tones. "The ones in your house were demons sent straight from the bowels of Hell. True demons capable of shimmering, hurling plasma balls, and all the rest. Disposal methods are different depending on the...ah, circumstances."

"Why did we stop at so many churches when you were shimmering us here?" Careful to keep her touch light, she smoothed the ointment over his abused skin. Though his muscles were rigid, his skin twitched with every stroke of her fingers. It bothered her that he was in such obvious pain.

"You ask too many questions," Niklas snapped, and it became clear he hadn't liked that particular question at all.

"My questions haven't bothered you before, unless you're uncomfortable with the answer. Do you realize we popped—shimmered," she corrected before he could, "to seven different churches? But we never went inside a single one?"

He was silent so long she didn't think he would respond. She'd finished with his back and moved around to tend the wound on his shoulder.

"I need to call Xander. I haven't been able to get through to Sebastian or Gideon. From that news broadcast, something is going down in southern Mexico, and the others need to know—"

"You can change the subject, but here's something to think about," she interrupted, losing patience as she tossed the tube of ointment into the plastic case. "You ask an awful lot, but you give precious little in return."

"Just drop it—"

"No! You expect too much, Niklas."

He immediately bristled. Glancing down, he stared pointedly at the burns marring his flesh. "I think I've more than—"

"I'm not trying to belittle what you *have* given. I appreciate your protection. But I'm talking about all the rest. You've dumped all this on me, demons and angels. And I've rolled with the punches. Magic crystals and grimoires and mystical rituals. Demon battles in my damned kitchen, for God's sake!"

That brought waves of anger and sadness deeper than she'd thought possible. Pictures. Souvenirs. Memories. All gone. Her last connections to her parents and her uncle.

"I've taken it all in stride. Pretty damned well, if you ask me." She jabbed a finger at him. "I haven't wigged out yet. *Yet*, being the operative word there. You expect me to trust you. And I do, despite what common sense might dictate. But *you* won't trust *me*." Frustrated, she sat back on her heels and stared up at him, her hand resting on his knee. Softly, she pleaded, "Why?"

Why wouldn't he talk about the churches?

Why wouldn't he trust her?

He stared down at her. Silent. Giving nothing away.

"Fine. Keep your damned secrets." Heaving a disgusted sigh, she shook her head and pushed to her feet. Angry now, hurt for reasons she didn't care to examine, she threw the rest of the supplies back in the kit and slammed the lid closed. As she turned away, he grabbed her wrist.

"If you were a demon," he burst out, "would *you* risk entering God's house? Would you deliberately provoke His wrath?" He released her and turned to the fireplace. "I miss the tranquility. The gentle, easy silence. I miss sitting and looking upon his altar. I miss the scent of incense and beeswax candles. I miss contact with Him."

He was quiet for a moment, though he continued to hold her wrist in a loose grip. She could easily have broken his hold, but the despair, the utter loneliness etched in every line of his expression held her motionless. She just couldn't bring herself to turn her back on him.

"I do trust you, *tá'hiri*. If I didn't, I wouldn't have brought you here," he said quietly. "I would *never* have bound us together. Though I've probably damned you now as well. It was a selfish thing to do. I had no right to do it."

"Then why did you?"

He stared at her so long, she gave up hope that he might answer. "I could tell you it was the only way I could think of to keep you alive."

"Was it?"

Guilt was written all over his face now. "Maybe."

"Then why do you say it was a selfish thing to do?"

"Because I wanted the connection to you," he blurted. As if finally realizing what he'd admitted, he released her and stepped back. "Sometimes I wonder what the point in all of this is, this working for forgiveness. The things I've done..." He shook his head, a deep groove forming between his brows. "I'll never be able to make up for them."

His soft, hopeless words, and his unwilling admission, cooled her temper as little else could. Dropping to her knees before him, she ignored his impatient, embarrassed withdrawal and clasped his face between her hands. Forcing him to look at her, she stared long and hard into his glacier-blue eyes.

"You are a demon, Niklas," she said matter-of-factly. "But you are *not* evil." One hand slipped down to his chest to cover his heart. "Not anymore. Not here. Not where it matters."

He opened his mouth to protest, but she cut him off before he could utter a sound. "No, *you* listen for a change." With her hand still resting upon his chest, she held the pendant on her necklace up. "This pendant? It's supposed to protect me from evil, right? If that's so, if they truly work as you believe they will, then how could you be this close to me? How could you touch me if you were truly evil? I refuse to believe it, Niklas." Before he could repudiate her claim, she took his hand, pressed it to her chest, over her own heart. "I would feel it here."

Shocked by her own boldness, she let go of him. But his hand lingered on her chest. He stroked her collarbone, holding her trapped with that simple touch, barely able to breathe. His stare whispered over her lips, as substantial as a physical caress. And then his attention dipped, followed the lazy strokes of his fingertips.

Without warning, he wrapped his hand around the back of her neck and her lips were crushed beneath his. No gentle kiss, this. This was urgent. This was possession.

This demanded absolute submission.

His lips moved over hers, determined, tolerating nothing but surrender. Heat roared through her. Wave after wave of desire hit her, hard and fast. His hair, like damp silk, tangled around her fingers. His scalp was so warm.

She pressed closer. Couldn't get close enough. His hand slipped down until his hot palm cradled her breast. His thumb rubbed back and forth over her nipple, tormenting her with sensation. Moaning, she gripped him tighter. His tongue plunged into her mouth, over and over, sweeping against hers, drawing hers into his mouth. Suckling. Dueling. He changed the angle of the kiss. Deepening it until it spun out of control.

His arm snaked around her waist and he lifted her onto his lap, supporting her, pulling her closer. Frantic. Desperate. Need built. Hunger roared. Control snapped. Desire shattered his restraint. He gripped her knee, guiding it up and around his hip. Taking his lead, she straddled him, pinning his hips between her thighs. Writhing against him, Carly ground her aching core along the rigid arousal straining the confines of his jeans. Her body was no longer her own. Her will had been hijacked by raw, greedy lust.

His skin was so hot. Everywhere she touched, everywhere her fingertips skated. Every decadent inch of his naked flesh. His teeth snagged on her lower lip, gently nipping and tugging. And then his kisses, so incredibly possessive, branded the side of her throat. Searing. Torrid.

He splayed his hands and slid them up over her back. Niklas rolled his hips against her, increasing the friction. His ragged breath seared her skin. Oh, it felt delicious. He swirled his tongue over her neck, licking, suckling, lapping, dragging a delirious groan from her as she shivered.

Fast. This was happening too fast, but she couldn't control it, couldn't slow it down. Didn't want to. She'd been hollow. Empty inside. And he could fill her. Not just the ache in the most feminine part of her, but that other void deep inside her heart as well. The void that made her feel all alone, even in a room full of other people.

Hot, calloused palms swept against her skin. Her bare skin. Her shirt was suddenly gone. And her bra. Vanished into thin air. The startling realization hit her, made her surface from the dizzying desire long enough to question it. But then his hot mouth cruised along the slope of her collarbone, and she forgot all about clothing. He hooked his hands around her shoulders, pulling her back, holding her slightly off balance, supporting her weight on his forearms as he bent over her. Tongue swirling, he drew her nipple into his mouth.

Fire coursed through her veins. Need, as she'd never imagined existed. Too much. Her need. But his also.

Oh God, how could someone need *so badly?*

How could she contain it all?

How could she resist?

Nearly incoherent, she tugged at his hair. He obeyed, his lips devouring her neck on the way back to her mouth. Pulling her chest to chest, he claimed her lips again, greedy, devouring her. His muscles shifted, bunching and tensing. That was the only warning she got, and then she was flat on her back, pinned to the soft cushions as he loomed over her. She wiggled, locking her ankles over his flexed buttocks. The fabric of his jeans tormented her sensitive skin. His mouth never left hers.

The waist of her shorts had twisted, painfully cutting into her skin. And then they, too, were gone. Vanished. She was too aroused, too far gone to question it, not when it gave her exactly what she needed. Skin on bare skin. He skimmed along her side, curled his fingers around her hip, digging into her flesh as he gripped her bottom and ground her against him. The barrier of her panties swiftly became a nuisance, a thin strip of torment separating her flesh from his hands.

His hard chest, pressed to hers, rubbed, easing the awful ache in her breasts. His wicked touch slid up and over her thigh, slipping in between them. Questing, stroking fingers feathered over her. God, she wanted her panties gone. Now. Wanted his fingers deeper, inside her. Wanted *him* inside her.

He whispered something against the side of her throat. Deep, dark words. In the language he'd spoken in the chalk circle. In that layered voice that was his, and yet not. He nipped her skin. Blood rushed through her veins. Hot. Desperate. Her body was on fire. Couldn't he feel how she burned for him? His mouth returned to hers, and he repeated the words against her lips, his voice human again, but still she didn't understand. The only thing that mattered right now was the fierce need flaming inside her. Searing her from the inside out.

Did she have to beg?

His palm found her breast, distracting her for a moment. But then her legs met bare skin, and her attention instantly refocused. His jeans had disappeared. The soft cotton of his boxers teased her. He was doing this on purpose. Dragging it out. Layer by layer. *Damn him.*

Frantic, she tried to speak, willing to beg at this point, but his tongue thrust between her lips as his hips bucked against her. His engorged erection surged along her cleft, straining the thin fabric separating them. Her thoughts scattered like whispers of smoke on the wind as she gave herself up to his kiss.

Metallica's "Enter Sandman" ripped through the room, dark and pounding. Niklas tore his mouth from hers. His chest heaving, his grip painful, he stared into her eyes, greedy with hunger. He blinked. Once. Twice. His brow wrinkled with frustration, confusion.

And then, the slow widening of his eyes. The dawning shock.

The "oh, hell, what did I almost do" moment.

"Xander," he rasped, his voice hoarse with desperation. "Xander's calling. I have to—" He forced a swallow. Sucked in a shaky breath. "I need to—" His focus dipped to her mouth, went lower to where her naked breasts were crushed against his chest.

For a second, she thought he might say forget the phone. For a second, she prayed he would. She vibrated with hunger. Never had she wanted anything more than she wanted him right now.

With a stifled groan, Niklas sprang to his feet. The instant he did so, her clothing reappeared, and so did his. He snatched his phone from the coffee table and all but sprinted from the room. Her lips felt bruised. Her body was one big ache. Rubbing her arms, Carly sat up. Trembling. Cold.

And so very alone.

Chapter Eleven

Sweet Mary! Holy Mother of God, what have I done!

Struggling to regulate his breathing, he thumbed the phone on and pressed it to his ear. "Tell me you're on your way, Slayer."

"Negative," Xander rasped. "We found a Halfling. First generation. Kyanna's mother made contact before she died. And we found another nest."

"Where?"

"Thirty miles from the farm."

That revelation dampened some of the heat still searing Niklas's veins. "The apartment was compromised. We're at the farm right now," Niklas said. A nest, so close to the sanctuary he'd brought Carly to. Fury swamped him. "How many?"

"Twenty. Twenty-five." Small in terms of a Hellhound legion. Quite substantial in terms of an Earthbound nest. It just kept getting better and better. "Gusion was spotted at both nests, here as well as the one Sebastian is tracking in Mexico."

That explained the newscast and the burned-out village.

Dear Christ in Heaven, it was worse than he'd imagined. *What next?*

"Sent Gideon to you instead."

He should have known better than to tempt fate.

"Keep him. If you're dealing with a nest and a Halfling, you're gonna need him more than I do."

"Doubt it."

Damn it. He could hear the smirk in Xander's abrasive voice. Had he figured out Niklas's fears of giving in to temptation where Carly was concerned? *Fears?* Hell, he'd all but pinned her down and shoved his aching shaft deep in her hot, wet—

Swiping his shaking, sweating palm across his mouth, he tried to clear his head and dug deep for strength. Really deep.

"Did Mikhail find his target?" Niklas asked, desperate to get his mind off the woman he'd nearly ravished.

"No word. He's still off grid."

Better and better all the time.

Raking a hand through his hair, he paced from one end of the kitchen to the other. Christ Almighty, his blood was still boiling. Hoping to give his body a chance to cool off before he had to face Carly again, he sought to prolong the conversation. Discussing strategy seemed the best thing to divert his attention. "We need to meet. All five of us. Something serious is going down. There's just too much happening all at once, too much of an influx of demons, for this to be coincidence. This has Stolas written all over it."

"Probably." The silence stretched on.

Niklas had forgotten with whom he was speaking. Xander, master of the understatement and one-word responses.

He'd just been reminded.

"I'll call the others." Niklas heaved a defeated sigh. "Get here as soon as you can."

The phone went dead. Used to Xander's abrupt manners, Niklas thumbed in Gideon's number. Voice mail. *Great. Just frickin' great.* He ended the call without leaving a message and slapped the phone on the counter. Niklas braced both hands on the laminate surface and hung his head.

Breathe in. Breathe out. One breath at a time.

He had to get this under control. Had to cool his body down, somehow. Or else he might end up back in that living room yet, might find himself pinning her beneath him and—

AC/DC's "Thunderstruck" jolted him back into the moment. He snatched up the phone like the lifeline that it was.

"Gideon?"

"Nik, hear you need some help." Gideon's voice wafted over the phone line, husky and sensual. And for the first time in quite a while, Gideon sounded like himself...his *old* self, the one that could charm the knickers off a nun. Whatever wild ride the Demon of Temptation was on, his emotions were rolling right along beside him. Unpredictable seemed to be his middle name lately.

Niklas swore aloud. Just what he needed, *that* voice around his *tá'hiri*. Gideon hadn't even gotten there yet, and already Niklas felt the first stirrings of jealousy. Strung out, ready to explode, he couldn't remember having been aroused to this extent before. Ever. Couldn't remember ever having denied himself like this either, for that matter. And now, to throw Gideon into the mix? This situation just kept getting worse by the moment. How could he expose Carly to Gideon? Especially after he'd just left her as he had, sexually frustrated and confused. Vulnerable.

Oh, dear Lord!

Appalled by his unwarranted jealousy, he dragged a hand over his face. *What nex— No!* He wasn't stupid enough to ask *that* question again.

He made short work of bringing Gideon up to speed on his situation and informed him of the nest he'd uncovered in Ridgefield and its ties to the nest Sebastian had been tracking in Mexico. Most troubling of all, however, was the fact that Mikhail had yet to make contact.

Granted, Mikhail wasn't exactly the chatty sort either, but something just wasn't sitting right. He'd never remained in radio blackout this long.

A scream ricocheted through the phone line. What the hell was Gideon doing that was making so much noise?

Niklas heard shuffling. A thwack and a grunt. The scream strangled off. "Give me two hours"—a heavy thud and a soft curse—"better make that three." The sudden, familiar hiss and crackle of a plasma ball. The pop, whoosh of impact. "I'll come straight out to the farm as soon as I'm done here."

"Yeah. About that—"

The line went dead.

Damn it!

After leaving voicemails for Sebastian and Mikhail, he shoved his phone into his back pocket. Unhappy with the change in plans, worrying about two separate nests with common ties, something that had never happened before, Niklas returned to the living room.

Carly was gone.

A jolt of panic shot through him. Cold, clammy fear.

Before he had time to react, Carly appeared in the doorway of Sebastian's study, a book in her hand and a worried frown darkening her brow. "What's wrong?"

"Nothing," he muttered. *Nothing now*, he silently amended. She was safe.

And really mad. He didn't need to be able to see her aura to see how angry she was. The cold distance in her eyes, the drawn lines around her mouth, the rigid set of her shoulders and the scowl slashing her brow were pretty good indicators.

"There's been a change in plans. Xander's been detained. Gideon is coming instead." How could he caution her against Gideon's unintentional powers without coming off as a jealous ass?

"Temptation, correct?"

"Yes." He followed as she turned and strode back into the study without another word. "He'll be here in three hours."

"Fine." She said no more, giving him her back.

It was pure torture, standing in the same room as her. Being within grabbing distance, still aching for her. And, worse yet, knowing that he could have had her beneath him in the blink of an eye, naked, easing the burn of thwarted desire still coursing through him.

How could she put on such a calm front when turbulent need brewed inside him like this?

"Aren't you going to say something?"

"Why?" Carly called over her shoulder, stretching to tip the spine of a book down for closer inspection. She examined the book, leaving him to suffer in the icy distance growing between them.

It would be wise to let her have her way in this. But he just couldn't do it, hating the strain between them. "What do you mean, why?"

Slowly, she turned to face him. Her eyes were bright. Blotches of color rode high on her cheeks. Carly crossed her arms over those magnificent breasts he'd only minutes ago had his hands on. And his mouth. Sweet Lord, the things he wanted to do to her with his mouth—

"Why should I bother? What happened between us was obviously a mistake. You made it abundantly clear the last time we kissed that you had no wish to discuss it that time either. So what makes this time different?"

"Because this time I almost—" Breaking off on a soft curse, he strode to the window and stared blindly out at sun-drenched waves of emerald grasslands.

Clenching his fists at his sides, he grew angry himself. Conflicted. Everything seemed to be spinning out of control. Ever since he'd cut her loose from that tree, he'd been thinking things he shouldn't have been thinking. Wanting things he shouldn't have been wanting. Things he'd never get.

He wanted her. He'd been ready to throw everything else away. The last two hundred years of self-denial and sacrifice. His redemption. Her will.

When—*if*—she came to him he wanted it to be her decision as well. He didn't want her to regret choosing him. He didn't want her to feel like her hand had been forced due to gratitude or that she'd been coerced in order to keep his protection. He'd gone too fast earlier. Hadn't given her time to consider her options.

Shadows crept from the dark corners of his mind, planting the seeds of doubt, nurturing them with fear and self-loathing. Maybe Xander's phone call had been divine intervention. Maybe he wasn't meant to have this glimpse of Paradise. Maybe being with her was wrong. For both of them.

"No." She moved up behind him, her voice soft. So precious to him now. *Please God, don't let her touch me.* He was still too close to lose control. Still too confused. "*We* almost, Niklas. *We.*" The brush of air, her hand hovering over his shoulder, fell away on a sigh. "We're going to be stuck together for a while. Shouldn't we discuss this, talk about what almost happened? Shouldn't we figure out where we go from here?"

"*Nowhere.* We go *nowhere* from here," he growled out of pure instinct, spinning to glare down at her. "There should be nothing between us, Carly. Nothing. You are human. I'm demon. How can there be anything more between us?" Where were these words coming from? He didn't know, and neither could he stop them. It was as if all his fears were suddenly clamoring for release. "What happened was a mistake. One that can't happen again. I've already fallen once." His glare raked over her, and he hated himself for his weakness. "I *won't* fall again."

He didn't need to be able to read her aura. Every vivid emotion was stamped clearly on her beautiful face. Her pain was a tangible thing, bringing unshed tears to her eyes. Raking him with guilt. He'd never survive it.

He reached for her, his purpose, his fortitude, crumbling. He couldn't stay away from her. Who was he trying to fool? He didn't *want* to stay away.

But she darted back, just out of his grasp.

Clutching the book to her chest like a shield, she offered him a brittle smile. "Thank you for clearing that up. Now, if you'll excuse me, I believe I'll go read in my room."

She turned on her heel and strode regally from the room. Cursing, he shimmered into the barn a couple hundred yards from the house. Dust motes floated in the air, flashing in and out of the soft, golden beams of sunlight filtering through the cracks in the wall. Straw littered the floor, the sweet scent wafting around him as, with every step, he crushed it beneath his boots. The smell of horses lingered in the empty stalls. A swallow fluttered in the rafters overhead.

Damn it. He hadn't meant to lash out like that. She had done nothing to deserve his harsh treatment. Her temper had been his goal. Sparking her anger, inducing her to throw protective walls up. The good Lord knew *he* couldn't figure out how to push distance between them. And that was what he'd thought he needed at the time. Distance. Space.

Instead, he'd hurt her. He knew he had, could sense it even without his ability to read her aura. Creating a new vulnerability that hadn't been there before. The weight of bitter sorrow pressed on his chest. A hollow sensation filled the pit of his stomach.

Conjuring clothing for her had required little more than a blink of his eye. Meeting those simple needs hadn't fazed him. They were easily dealt with. It was this deeper pain he didn't know how to handle. This ache that shouldn't be physical—but was—had him off balance, uncertain how to respond.

He wanted, more than anything, to comfort her. And Heaven knew where *that* had come from. He

fought defensive instincts to shimmer away—
anywhere—just to put distance between them. Raking
splayed hands through his hair, he paced from one end
of the barn to the other. He kicked a bucket out of his
way. A pitchfork and a cracked harness went sailing
next. Violence simmered in the air around him. How he
wanted to punch something. He eyed the thick beams,
the wooden walls. The sturdy barn would come down
around him like a house of cards if he let loose. And
Sebastian would never let him hear the end of it.

An old tractor, rusted and dirty from years of
neglect, sat just behind the barn. Its weathered, rust-
brown nose peeked into view as he neared the open
back doors. In a blink, he stood beside it, glaring.
Before he realized what he was doing, he shot out a fist,
pounding metal. Pain slashed up his arm as skin split,
but the metal caved. He punched again. Another
satisfying shot of pain. Another dent.

Anger poured out of him. Metal crumbled and
twisted. Anger over the situation, fury over finding a
woman like Carly and not being able to claim her for
his own. Welds snapped. Iron screeched. Despair and
frustration. Billows of dust plumed. Clouds of rust
rained down upon him. Great chunks of the engine
collapsed beneath his enraged blows.

He'd worked so hard, denied himself and his dark
desires for so long. He'd saved so many innocents,
rescued them right and left from demon traps and ritual
sacrifices, too many to keep count of over the centuries.
He'd asked nothing in return, no payment, no favor, no
debt. He'd not even asked their names. And what had it
gotten him?

No closer to redemption, that's where!

Every day, sin called to him. Every night, loneliness weighed upon him, the heaviest penance he'd ever borne. Did he give in? Did he cave? Had he slipped, even once?

No!

Well, not until Carly.

But years had passed, nearly two hundred years. And he was no closer to God's grace than he had been the moment he'd sided with Lucifer. He continued to pound and smash, venting his rage, not stopping until the tractor was little more than an unrecognizable, mangled hunk of its former glory.

Fists torn and bloody, palms shredded, bones broken, he dropped down on the hard-packed, rocky soil and leaned his back against the rough barn wall. Shifted uncomfortably as the wood bit into one of his burns. Chest heaving, he dropped his forearm on his raised knee and stared out over the pasture. Wildflowers—buds of white and yellow, purples and blues and pinks—were sprinkled among the waving tufts of grass. Stretching skyward for one last moment of glory before the sun sank into the western horizon. He didn't know their names, but their scent wafted on the gentle breeze. Clean and crisp. Soothing. They, too, reminded him of Carly. So delicate and fragile looking. And yet hardy. Determined. Resilient.

In the distance, a hummingbird flitted from one flower to the next. Insects chirped. Birdsong trilled from the nearby grove, repeated some distance away. Late afternoon sunshine bathed the rolling hills in gilded tones.

The same warm tones that used to surround Carly.

Soft gold. *Hope.*

Of all the things he'd given up, all the things he'd sacrificed over the last Earthbound centuries of his life, he missed seeing that color surrounding Carly the most. She was the first thing, the only thing, he'd felt truly connected to since his fall. And that had been before the binding. But the connection he'd gotten in return through the binding ritual, this magnetic awareness, this sense of connection, he wouldn't give it up for anything. Not even to mitigate the guilt he felt. He couldn't have sentenced her to Oblivion, or Hell, with his binding ritual. She was too good. A blinding light.

He couldn't bear to think of that light tarnished or lost. Not because of him.

In such a short bit of a time, she'd come to mean a great deal to him. He had some heavy choices ahead of him. Choices more important than what to do about the nests. Choices with far more impact on his future than how to capture Ronové.

Through her, he could have the chance to truly live, even if only for a short time. Someday she would leave him, die as all humans did. If he allowed this connection to grow, the loss of her would be unbearable. Devastating. A blow from which he might never recover. He'd been down this road, considered these risks when they'd first arrived at the farm. He'd been too afraid to face them head on then, and he'd pushed the decision away.

Now he faced it. Tore it apart and considered the pain, and the joy. Yes, she would die. But until that day, he could protect her, and cherish her, and—

Did he dare?

Did he dare *not*?

What he was certain of was that he couldn't face

her until he'd made up his mind. It wasn't fair, not to him and especially not to her, to keep her on a yo-yo, wanting her, needing her, only to lash out and push her away.

His looked upward. Puffy, white, cotton-candy clouds hung in the sky. They didn't appear to be going anywhere anytime soon.

And neither did he.

****

Carly woke to the scent of pasta and garlic bread. Her stomach rumbled. A soft, warm blanket shifted, slipping from her shoulder as she sat up, yawning. Odd, she didn't remember covering up before she'd fallen asleep.

Blinking, stretching, she glanced around the dim room. A covered, silver tray sat on one of the dressers. Pushing the blanket aside, she got up, stretched and approached the dresser. Lifting the lid, she stared down in wonder. A thick square of lasagna, oozing melted cheese and garnished with a sprig of parsley, filled one silver-rimmed plate. A small dish of green beans with tiny bits of bacon. A thick hunk of buttery garlic bread. A large mug of steaming, creamy coffee. "I thought you might be hungry when you woke up."

Stifling a screech, she fumbled the silver cover, catching it in the nick of time.

"Don't do that," she scolded, peering into the darkened corner of the room. Niklas sat in an armchair, one that hadn't been there before. He reclined negligently, his fingers laced over his middle, elbows braced on the padded chair arms, ankle propped on his knee. How long had he been there?

He peered hard at her, steady, determined.

Unsettling.

"I'm sorry. I didn't mean to startle you."

Frowning, she replaced the cover on the tray. "You didn't have to…"

"Conjure," he supplied.

"Conjure a meal for me. I'm perfectly capable of cooking for myself. And for you too." A tiny frown creased her brow. There was something…*off* about him.

Toying with the ring he'd given her, she wandered back to the bed, perched on the edge. One corner of his mouth rose slowly as he watched the nervous movement of her hands.

The tray vanished from the dresser and reappeared in the center of the bed. "Please, eat."

She glowered suspiciously, drawing a breath. There was something different about the way he was looking at her. Something different in the way he was acting. If anything, he was being even more solicitous than normal. Charming, even.

He said no more, simply waited her out.

She tried to relax, but it was no use with him looking at her like that. So serious. So possessive. Gah, her imagination was running away with her. Maybe she was more tired than she'd thought. Maybe she really was having wild hallucinations after all. Giving a small shrug, she scooted back on the bed. As far as hallucinations went, she could do far worse than a sexy man who devoured her with his eyes and a platter full of aromatic, mouthwatering food. She crossed her legs and pulled the tray in front of her. The silver cover disappeared.

Arching a brow, she stared pointedly at him.

"Sorry," he said, shooting her guilty smile.

Carly dug into the meal. She was hungrier than she'd thought. Once the first hunger pangs wore off, though, she grew uncomfortable beneath his unwavering attention. "Aren't you going to eat?"

He seemed to weigh his words. "I'm not really hungry anymore."

What did that mean? Had he already eaten then? And then another thought occurred to her, making her faintly sick to her stomach. Had he gone somewhere while she slept? Had he drained the soul from some criminal, as he'd done before? Had he—

Niklas leaned forward, a frown flashing across his brow. "What's wrong? Is there something else you'd rather have?"

"No." She gently set the fork down and pushed the tray aside. "I'm fine," she lied. "I'm just full."

His lips pursed, but he didn't challenge her. The tray disappeared.

Handy.

"Gideon should be here shortly." He leaned back, lacing his fingers again. "The others are coming as well."

"Others?" The thought of a house full of demons was disconcerting, to say the least.

"There have been some new developments. We've discovered a nest about thirty miles from here."

"A nest?" She frowned. Why did that sound ominous, like a slithering pit filled with poisonous snakes?

"A nest is a den, if you will. A gathering of Earthbound demons. It's pretty uncommon for demons to cohabitate. Too volatile, usually. Most demons kill each other off before a nest can successfully be established."

"Then why—"

"We don't know yet, but we've reason to believe there are ties between the nest here and the one Sebastian's been tracking in Mexico."

"Why is Sebastian tracking a nest?"

"It's what we do, *tá'hiri*. When a nest flagrantly attacks human settlements, when they begin slaughtering humans with little or no regard for consequences, we step in. We track them down. We eliminate them."

She recalled then the newsreel he'd been watching earlier. Before they'd almost—

"Why do you think the nests are tied together?" She reached back and drew the blanket around her, suddenly chilled. A strange, almost tender expression softened his features. "Niklas?"

He let a long breath seep out slowly. "Two of the same individuals have been seen shimmering into both locations. Gusion—he has ties to some of the highest-ranking royalty of Demonarchy. And now we've discovered Glasya is also involved. He's particularly dangerous. He can, for lack of a better word, manipulate the hearts and minds of friends and foes, causing love or hatred between them as he wills it. I've also received word from Asher, a mercenary I've gotten reliable information from in the past, that the scrolls have been located. We can't lose another of the relics. The Sword of Kathnesh has already been stolen, its Guardian killed."

"The Sword of Kathnesh?"

"It's demon lore. The only way to kill an upper level demon is by beheading. The Sword of Kathnesh is rumored to be the only blade that can take Lucifer's head. It's reported to be made of Quïnï, a composite of cursed metals infused with Ralsha poison. A very rare material, rare but extremely lethal. But no demon is powerful enough to stand against Lucifer alone, even with the sword. He must possess all four of the Sacred Relics."

"If these relics are so dangerous, why didn't Lucifer have them destroyed?"

"They were created in secret and hidden away before he could order them destroyed, or before he could destroy them himself. The lore tells of sacred Guardians who, by right of birth, hide the ancient relics away and protect them with their lives."

"So, there's the sword, which the other team already has. What are the other relics?"

"The Arc Stone, which will make its bearer impervious to physical harm. We've already recovered the stone, thanks to Xander. And then there are the Scrolls of Prévnar. Printed on the scrolls, supposedly, is an incantation powerful enough, compelling enough to make the one who reads it aloud resistant to Lucifer's control, and wise to any deceptions Lucifer might throw his way."

"And the fourth relic?"

Niklas drew his palm along the side of his face, and then dropped his hands into his lap. "The Prophesy says it's a person. A being. The child of demon and angel and man, all three. A hybrid species."

"I didn't realize that angels were allowed to…" She trailed off, cleared her throat. "You know."

"They aren't. Not since the Great Battle. That's why this prophecy seemed so unlikely. We've recently found out just how wrong we were about that though."

Carly sat for a long moment, considering his words, and the intent behind them. He was giving her a lot of information. And she wasn't having to pull teeth for every greedy little bit. "Why are you telling me all this?"

"You have a right to know."

And this is your way of showing me that you trust me, she silently added. Maybe there was hope after all. He stood, held his hand out to her.

"I could use some fresh air. Come with me."

Carly glanced out the window. She'd learned to fear the shadows. "Are you sure that's a good idea?"

"I'll keep you safe." A warm, languid smile spread over his face, stealing her breath. "Trust me."

Chapter Twelve

She watched that slow smile curve his lips and fought the urge to melt into a puddle. Or throw herself at him. Surely, Lucifer must have given Niklas the wrong title. With a smile that devastating, not to mention the way he kissed, surely Niklas should have been the Demon of Temptation.

Standing, she slipped her hand into his and let him take the lead. She expected him to drop her hand as soon as they left the room. Or surely as soon as they left the house. But he held on, showing no signs of relinquishing her hand any time soon. It was hard not to be affected by his touch.

Cool night air kissed her skin. She barely had time to shiver. In the blink of an eye, her shorts and T-shirt were gone, replaced with jeans and a thick sweatshirt. Sneakers and warm socks in lieu of sandals.

"Thank you," she murmured.

He gently squeezed her hand in reply.

They wandered down the back steps. Moonlight cast a silver glow over the yard. Crisp, clean air filled her lungs. And, as scents often do, they brought back memories. Bittersweet. Precious.

"I grew up on a farm much like this one," she began, aware that—though he did not look directly at her—she now had his undivided attention. The pain of remembering was sharp. But so was the pride. And the love. "My parents owned a farm. We had an old hound dog named Beauford. My dad used to cuss that dog, said we should have named him useless instead." She smiled over the memory. "But Beauford stuck to my dad's heels like glue, and Dad always had a treat in his pocket."

They walked in silence as they drifted across the yard and down the hill. The grass in the meadow swirled around them, knee-high. The night was surreal. Maybe that was why it was so easy to open up and share this piece of herself with him.

Then again, maybe it was Niklas himself.

She hadn't let herself think about those things in a long time. But now she let the memories come, telling Niklas of her life before her parents' deaths. How easily it all came back to her now. Funny how time had a way of sharpening some memories, dulling others.

Eventually, he asked, "You don't have any brothers or sisters?"

"No, I was an only child."

"But you were happy." Statement not question.

"I was happy." She drew a deep breath. "Even after the accident...after my parents were gone, my uncle made sure I was happy. I mean, obviously I grieved for my parents, but he did the best he could to make sure I knew I was still loved. He worked hard to give me a normal life. I never wanted for anything. But more than that, he was always there, rooting for me, cheering me on. I had a normal, well-adjusted life. Friends. A solid education.

"But Uncle Jason had a lot to deal with," Carly said. "Shortly after I went to live with him, he found out that he had cancer. He underwent chemo. It was a

169

long, difficult treatment, but the cancer went into remission. He'd buried his parents, his sister and brother-in-law. And he beat the cancer. Held it back for so long. Uncle Jason was a survivor."

Drawing a deep breath, she bent to snap the stem of a drooping daisy. Swirling it between her fingers, she stared ahead, over the rolling meadow bathed in shadow and moonlight.

"We eventually had to sell the farm. It was just too much for him to handle alone, and renting the land out wasn't practical anymore," she pushed on. "It was a hard decision, but we made it together."

"That's a big decision to have to face at any age."

"Uncle Jason didn't want to take my inheritance away from me. My dad was a third-generation farmer on that land. I know if I'd told him I wanted to keep it, he'd have found a way. But I didn't want to be a farmer, and neither did he." She offered him a rueful smile. "Uncle Jason always encouraged me to do what made me happy. 'Life is too short to make miserable choices,' he used to say. 'Do it right the first time. Then you don't have to live with regrets.'"

"It sounds like he was an amazing man."

"He was the strongest man I know."

"You miss him."

"Every day." No two words had ever been spoken with more emotion. She battled the tears back, swallowed the lump in her throat.

"You've lost so much. Your parents. Your uncle. The home you once believed your birthright. How do you carry on and not just cave beneath the weight?"

Lines dug deep grooves between his eyebrows as he frowned down at her. The expression on his face, the look in his eyes gave her the impression that he truly didn't understand, but he was trying to.

Carly took a moment, chewed on the edge of her lip as she considered his question. No words could adequately describe the holes that were left in you after the death of a loved one.

The ache of not being able to share the comfort of mundane events of everyday life. Or the frantic need to relate some extraordinary bit of news, only to realize that person wasn't there to pick up the phone. That nearly paralyzing, desperate obsession to see them, hold them, talk with them, just one more time.

Or, worse still, how did you describe that stunning moment when your throat burns with unshed tears and you just can't breathe past the tightness in your chest, when you truly, completely realized "just one more time" will never happen?

Time softened the edges of the pain, but the holes never really disappeared.

"I carry on," she finally offered, her voice hoarse, "because that's what they would want me to do. I carry on because there's nothing else *to* do. Uncle Jason was a survivor. I could do nothing else, *be* nothing less than that. For him. For my parents. For me."

He rubbed the back of his neck. "I'm used to seeing other's emotions through the swirl of color in their aura. Those emotions have never bothered me before. I've always been able to easily read human intention, human motivation by that swirl of colors. But your emotions were such a blur. I must admit, I had trouble processing it all."

"So you said." She glanced sideways at him, her lips twisted in a rueful smile. "No more headaches caused by yours truly, right? At least this connection between us has one perk." She shoved her free hand deep in her pocket while she studied the flow and ebb of the tall grass as it swayed around them.

Niklas stopped, tugging her around to face him. He traced the curve of her cheek with just the tips of his fingers as though she were made of glass. As though she were...precious. "I'd never before considered such a connection with anyone. I've never felt the need. But with you—" He broke off, shaking his head.

She stared at him for what felt like forever. When she didn't think he would go on, when she started to turn away, he captured her chin in a gentle but firm grasp. "With you," he finally said, a determined glint in his pale blue eyes, "I will *never* regret the connection, however unsettling it might be at times not knowing what you're thinking or how you're feeling."

Without warning, his lips lowered to hers. Soft. Sweet. Brief.

Pulling back, he slipped his fingers through her hair, brushing it away from her face. "The connection we share has come to mean a great deal to me. Knowing I'll always be able to find you. Always be able to keep you safe. It gives me..." He tilted his head, considering. "It gives me peace."

She parted her lips to speak but couldn't find the words. She had no right to lay any kind of claim on him. No right to let herself soften toward him.

Curiosity got the better of her, as it usually did. All this talk of her uncle and her parents got her thinking.

"Tell me what it was like, Heaven. Do you miss it—wait, strike that. Obviously, you miss it, or you wouldn't be trying so hard to go back. After you fell, how long did it take for you to decide you wanted to return?"

"Hmm, that's not an easy answer."

"I understand if that's too personal of a question—"

"No, that's not it. You see, time passes differently in Heaven than it does on Earth. It's the same with Hell. A few minutes in Heaven can be days on Earth. A few hours on Earth can be weeks in Hell."

She weighed his words, rolling the concept around in her head for a while. Baffling. "What's Heaven like?"

"Peaceful. Calm. Soothing." He glanced at her. A tiny crease formed between his brows. And then, just as suddenly, his lips curved on that slow grin again, and his expression transformed. Her heart skipped a beat. "A lot like the way I feel when I'm with you. That is, when I'm not kissing you. That's anything but calming," he teased.

Ducking her head, she worked to contain the smile his comment provoked. It was a good thing twilight had finally caught up with them. The dim light helped her hide cheeks she was positive must be as red as an apple. But he wasn't having any of it. He squeezed her hand gently and gave her a shoulder bump until she finally looked up at him.

His grin made it difficult to concentrate on the conversation. Clearing her throat, she pressed, "Is that it? Calm? Peaceful and soothing? It's calm in this meadow. It's peaceful by that stream over there. The sounds of night all around us can be considered soothing. I want to know what *Heaven* is like, Niklas. Does everyone walk around with haloes, wings, and little golden harps? Is everything white? Are the streets paved with gold?"

His lips twitched. "It's a different experience for everyone."

She gave his hand an impatient squeeze.

Relenting, he drew her to a halt. He looked toward the stars as he seemed to search for the right words. "Heaven is subjective. What one cherishes in life, one often finds in Heaven. If family is vital to you here on earth, being reunited with lost loved ones is often a comforting reception. If sitting beside a calm lake, surrounded by nature's beauty is soothing, then this is what you shall find. God is in all things. He is everywhere." His fingers feathered through her hair, skimmed along the curve of her jaw. "But Heaven, *tá'hiri*, can be found in many places." He turned to her. His thumb traced her bottom lip. His expression was solemn. His tone was pensive. "Sometimes you find it where you least expect."

Disconcerted, Carly forced herself to look away as she took an unsteady step back.

His hand fell to his side. The loss of his touch was unnerving.

"Subjective," he reiterated, allowing her the space she so suddenly needed. "But through it all, God's love and grace are the ultimate reward."

Nodding, she resumed walking. His hand found hers again and their fingers laced. It felt natural.

He spoke so easily of Heaven. And she could see how much he missed it. And yet, tonight there was a new emotion flitting through his gaze. Complex. Elemental. Though she struggled to isolate it and pick it apart until she understood it, her own emotions were just too tangled and volatile to sort through.

He'd slipped inside her defenses, getting closer to her than she'd allowed anyone since her uncle had passed away. She'd had boyfriends, but she'd never *felt* for them what she felt for Niklas. They'd never touched her, body or soul, the way Niklas had. With such longing. With such desperate need.

And everything Niklas had worked to accomplish and worried over and bled for, since before she'd been born, he'd done with the specific goal of returning to Heaven and God's grace. He'd come so far from his fall, probably further than she could ever imagine.

What would it be like to have someone love her, cherish her with that depth of commitment? With that level of devotion? To have someone who would do anything, whatever it took, to never leave her side?

Suddenly she wanted to cry. She shouldn't have come out with him. She needed to think, and she couldn't do that with him so close, much less touching her. Disheartened, she tugged her hand from his and, ignoring the frown abruptly darkening his face, paced toward where the stream cut a path through the grove.

She didn't get far. Niklas caught her wrist, urging her around to face him.

"What happened?" he asked. "Why did you pull away?"

"Nothing happened." She tried to withdraw again, but he kept her wrist shackled.

"Do you know that when you lie, you get a little twinge in the corner of your eye?"

She huffed. Could she keep nothing from him?

He captured her chin in his free hand, forcing her to face him. "Something *is* troubling you, and I want to know what it is."

She didn't know where they came from, but tears suddenly welled in her eyes. She would lose him.

No, that wasn't completely honest either. He'd never really been hers at all, had he? Sadness engulfed her. Raw. Hollowing. Almost as painful as the moment the doctor had checked Jason's vitals, then turned to her and gently told her that her uncle was gone.

Alarm flared in his eyes. He looked so serious. So determined. As if he'd battle her demons, slay her dragons, if she but pointed him in the right direction. His reaction surprised her. Shaking her head, she tried to slip away once more, but he wouldn't let her go. He searched her face for one long moment, and then cupped the back of her neck, holding her in place as he moved closer.

His lips settled over hers in a soft, coaxing caress. Light as air. Warm as the summer breeze. Achingly sweet. Carly let her hands slip upward, gliding over his shoulders, easing around his neck. She knew this was wrong, knew there could be no future between them. When this mess was over, Niklas would go on his way, and, eventually, he'd return to Heaven. She was only setting herself up for heartache. But she couldn't resist, needing this moment between them.

It would have to last her a lifetime.

His kiss was tender. One meant to offer comfort. She could only pray he drew as much solace from her as he gave. He deliberately kept the contact light, and for that she was grateful. The wild abandon of earlier was beyond her realm of experience, overwhelming, and, as such, she still didn't know what to make of the whole thing.

Niklas stiffened, abruptly tearing his lips from hers. Dazed, she stared up at him, still trapped in a skillfully spun web of sensation. His arms tightened. He peered around the grove, his expression fierce. His mood swiftly shifted from that of a would-be lover offering comfort to that of a predatory beast defending its territory.

He laid a finger against her lips, a universal demand for silence, and tugged her behind him, shielding her with his body. Still holding her wrist, he led her forward, not toward the house as she'd expected, but deeper into the heart of the woods. Silent. Stealthy. Following his lead, she carefully picked her way over twigs and rocks.

Niklas paused beside an ancient oak, its gnarled trunk broad enough to conceal them both. He motioned her to remain silent and to stay put before he dropped a brief kiss to her forehead and crept away. Carly watched in mute confusion as Niklas darted behind another tree some distance away. The shadows made it nearly impossible to see him now. A few moments later, four men approached.

Curiosity stirred, she held her breath and peeped around the edge of the tree. Masculine voices wafted to her on the wind.

"I tell you, I got as far as this stream, and I could go no farther," the short, balding gnome of a man grunted.

"It's all in yer bloody 'ead, ya bloomin' fool," the burly brute snarled. "Why in the name of Lucifer would there be ward stones way out 'ere where there be nothin' to protect?"

Ward stones.

Not men. Demons!

What were *they* doing out here? Were these demons from the nest Niklas had told her about?

"There's ward stones, I'm telling you, you great, dim-witted ass!" The gnome hopped to the side as the brute took an unsuccessful swing at him.

"Would you two knock it off? It's bad enough I have to traipse out here in the middle of no-freakin'-where. I'll be damned if I'm gonna listen to you two squabble like a couple *nrécnitgha'ta*. I'd rather fry both your asses and go find someone more interesting to do." This from an average-looking Joe with short brown hair and pale, pale skin.

A tall, gangly man with long blond hair stepped between the gnome and the brute. He looked more like a rock star than kith and kin to the demons with him. A plasma ball materialized in the palm of his hand and hung suspended there, crackling and hissing, more effective than any possible verbal threat.

The gnome and the brute immediately backed down, bowing their heads deferentially. Joe snapped his mouth closed and, eyes slightly widened, took a hasty step back. The plasma ball dissolved, and the rock star lowered his hand to his side.

"Where?"

He was attractive, almost as attractive as Niklas. Almost. But his demeanor reeked of vicious brutality, and his voice—

Frost came to mind. A hard, killing frost.

"Here." The gnome pointed. "Just over the stream by that oak yonder."

Carly tensed. Surely not.

Through the shadows, she saw Niklas lean forward

menacingly. His hand lifted, and he held a finger to his lips, motioning her to be silent.

Great. The oak she was hiding behind. Didn't that just figure? Unpleasant memories assailed her of the last time she'd been in the darkened woods, a tree pressed to her back, and a pack of demon's swarming her.

Pressing her spine against the rough bark, Carly gauged the distance to the barn. Up the hill and over hundreds of yards of wide-open meadow. Too far. She'd never make it, certainly not undetected. Twigs snapped. Water sloshed.

"I feel it," Average Joe said. "It's getting difficult to move beyond the stream. What the hell is this?"

Rustling, scratching. A sharply indrawn breath. A muted curse.

"See. Ward stones, just as I said," Gnome gloated.

"That's not all." Average Joe called. "Can't you feel it? Chrysoberyl and jasper, brecciated jasper. You can feel them too, can't you? That stuff makes my skin crawl."

Carly fingered the jewelry Niklas had given her.

"I can feel them," the gnome confirmed. "But they weren't there before."

Movement from the far edge of her peripheral vision snared her attention. What was Niklas doing?

Oh, no!

There were too many, and he was all alone. No, he couldn't be considering—

With a startling yell, he sprang from behind a tree, plasma ball pulsing in the palm of his hand. Niklas hurled the plasma ball at the gnome, striking before the intruders had time to react. The gnome instantly burst into a fiery ball of ash. Launching a second plasma ball, Niklas dove for cover. He missed the tall, blond demon by less than a foot. The remaining three demons vanished, only to reappear in different locations. Plasma balls hurtled through the night like comet tails, streaking this way and that. Exploding. Splintering trees like toothpicks.

Nearly paralyzed with fear, Carly crouched down, searching desperately for Niklas. She could barely breathe for the fear crowding through her. Three against one. He'd gone up against worse odds than this. But that didn't reassure her. All it would take was one lucky shot.

And something about that blond demon made her incredibly nervous. He was...different. Even more dangerous than Ronové had been.

She caught sight of Niklas crouching behind a maple, just the outline of him. A plasma ball exploded close to him, so close the sleeve of his shirt ignited. She gasped, blinked, and he was gone. No, no, there he was on the other side of the stream. The side with no ward stones. He limped, staggered, stumbled behind a tree. Her heart lurched, dropping to her boots. He'd been hit. She rose to her feet, prepared to charge to his side. Little good that would do either of them. But instinct had her in a death grip.

Oh, oh God, no.

The brute followed, as did Average Joe. The rock star reappeared, vanished, reappeared, popping in here, firing, popping out, popping in there, firing, popping out. Carly twisted this way and that, struggling desperately to keep a visual on all of them. Frantic, she gripped her hands together and prayed as she'd never prayed before.

Please, God, please don't let Niklas get hurt. I know you're not real happy with him right now. Haven't been happy with him for a while, in fact. But he's trying so hard. Let him live, God. Let him have his second chance. Please, God, please.

The demons closed in on Niklas from different sides, plasma balls palmed and ready to release. Niklas popped—*shimmered*, he *shimmered*—behind the brute. A moment later, the brute went down in flames and ash.

The crackle of a twig directly in front of Carly snapped her head around and up. Average Joe blinked down at her, his eyes wide with surprise. A sinister grin slowly knifed across his face. Panic, horror congealed in her gut. For a split second, she couldn't move, couldn't utter a sound. And then Joe reached for her. Terror gurgled in the back of her throat.

Joe's fingers were within inches of Carly's arm when he suddenly drew back with a hiss, as if she were made of fire and he'd singed his fingers. He glowered down at her and at the bracelet she wore.

The guard stones are working.

Niklas shimmered behind Joe and wrapped an arm around his forehead. In that same instant, he slashed a wicked-looking blade across Joe's throat, so deep, so forcefully he completely severed Joe's head from his body. Carly flinched, her eyes scrunching closed as she whipped her head to the side. Hot demon blood splashed over her, splattering her face and neck, drenching through her shirt.

Gagging, Carly dragged her forearm over her face.

By the time she opened her eyes again, Joe's body was nothing more than a smoldering pile of ash at

Niklas's feet. Niklas stepped closer to her, his clothing singed and splattered with demon blood. He held his hand out to her. Trembling, she placed her hand in his.

Niklas drew her to her feet and pulled her against him, tucking her under his arm. He turned warily, scanning the area. The night had gone unnaturally silent around them. As if waiting. Waiting for the next wave of violence to strike.

"Where—"

"Shhh," he cautioned.

The crackle and hiss of a plasma ball was all the warning they had. Niklas took her down with him as he dove to the ground. He rolled at the last moment, cushioning her fall with his body. He kept rolling, shielding her. Another crackle, hiss. He jerked, arching against her. Panting, he wrapped his body around her and kept rolling until they'd reached another large tree. Pushing to his feet, grimacing in pain, Niklas kept her pinned between his broad, wounded back and the tree.

"Gusion," he hissed.

The rock star, she surmised. Carly peeked over his shoulder, careful not to touch the raw blisters and newly charred flesh of his back. The blond demon stepped out from behind tree cover. Out into the wide open. Smug. Arrogant. He balanced a sizzling plasma ball in each hand. His stance challenged Niklas.

"So, this is where you've been hiding, Seer." His focus strayed over Niklas's shoulder, and he leered at Carly. "Can't say as I blame you. I think I'd go to ground for a while too, if I had a piece of tail like that."

Niklas's muscles tightened beneath her hands. He said something in that dark, layered voice. Guttural sounds she couldn't identify. A plasma ball erupted in his hand.

"Aw, now, no need to be nasty," Gusion said. "I take it that means you don't want to share."

Niklas hurled the plasma ball at the blond demon, but Gusion nimbly shimmered a few steps to the side. He hurled his own plasma ball. Niklas flicked a plasma ball up, and the two collided in midair, raining sparks and embers down like fireworks. An impasse.

Gusion eyed the ground speculatively. He took a step forward, and then another. And another. And then he froze, a pained, sickened expression twisting his handsome features. Taking a hasty step backward, he snarled, scowling at the ground.

"You can't hide behind ward stones forever, Seer." His scowl morphed into a smile. A terrible smile that sent chills darting though Carly's bloodstream. "That's all right. I can wait." His gaze drifted to Carly again. He licked his lips, making Carly's skin crawl. "After all, they say anticipation is half the fun."

Chapter Thirteen

Niklas waited several moments longer, every cell in his body trained on the area around him, sifting and searching, until he was certain Gusion was truly gone. The other demon might not be able to cross the ward stones, but a plasma ball could. Carly's fear was a tangible thing, sitting hard and cold in the pit of his stomach. Niklas turned, lifting a hand to Carly, beseeching. Needing the contact as much for himself as for her. Some of those plasma balls had exploded so close to her, he'd thought his heart might leap from his chest.

Carly launched herself into his arms, trembling, burying her face against his neck. She wrapped herself tight around him. Sobs wracked her small body. He ran his hands up and down her back. She felt so right pressed against him, seeking comfort and protection.

"I was so scared they'd hurt you, Niklas." An anguished sob tore from her throat.

She'd been afraid. For him.

A strange stillness slipped through him.

Touched beyond words, he cradled her to him. His precious, brave *tá'hiri*. He smoothed a hand over her hair, down her back. Her hair was damp with demon blood. Her clothing. Her skin. Violence had touched her, and he couldn't stand it.

For a moment, he wavered. He'd been so certain,

sitting there beside the mangled remains of the ancient tractor, that this—*they*—were meant to be. He'd convinced himself that maybe he'd earned her. That God had seen fit to give him this small bit of Heaven. A reward for his steadfast devotion.

But even now, that tainted voice—the darkest part of his soul—laughed at him. His crimes were too heinous for him to ever believe he'd be forgiven. He'd earned nothing. He *deserved* nothing. Not absolution. Not a reprieve from his eternal punishment. Certainly not a reward as precious as Carly. He'd been wrong to think he could keep her. He slid his hands to her shoulders, gripped her upper arms, preparing himself to push her away. Just the idea, though, caused a physical pain deep in his chest.

Clinging tightly to him, she whispered, "I don't know what I would have done if I'd lost you."

The ache was too much. He couldn't bear it. He'd been alone far too long. She was here now. With him. And he wasn't going to let her go. Shimmering them directly inside the bathroom adjoining his room—now hers—he pressed his lips to her temple and murmured, "Shhh. It's going to be all right. You're safe." She trembled in his arms, shaking her head, and he amended, "We're both safe. *Both* of us. Let me help you. Let me take care of you."

Niklas turned the water in the shower on. He held her, petted her, whispering nonsensical sounds as the steam built.

She was so cold she trembled with it. Chilled from the inside out. "We need to get you out of—" No, reminding her she was covered in demon blood probably wasn't a good idea. "We need to get you into the shower, Carly. You're starting to go into shock."

Pulling her into the huge, tiled shower, he soothed her with words and hands. Once he had her tucked safely beneath the warm spray of water, he vanished her shirt and jeans. When he'd conjured the crimson undergarments earlier, he hadn't been able to stop himself from imagining her, fantasizing about her, in them. At the time, the erotic pictures his mind had produced had tortured him. But the red lace and cotton looked so garish now. Blood coated her pale skin. He'd never put her in red again.

Water sluiced over her, rinsing the blood away, pooling at their feet in a pink puddle on the white tile. His shirt and jeans clung to him uncomfortably. Glancing down, he noticed for the first time that his own clothing was stained red too.

He vanished his shirt, boots and socks, and briefly considered getting rid of the jeans as well. Then he glanced back at Carly, standing beneath the spray, wearing nothing more than panties and a stained bra. She shook, looking bedraggled. Overwhelmed. Her eyes were huge, her skin so, so pale.

Shock. She was in shock, he reminded himself. Now was not the time for desire and seduction.

Yet, desire her he did.

No, best not to push his control too far.

Conjuring a clean pair of jeans, jeans that quickly became soaked and uncomfortable, he reached for the bar of soap lying on the ledge. He quickly built up a thick lather in a washcloth and set the bar of soap aside. She might well be mad when she realized he'd stripped her and showered her, but he needed to do what he could to wash the horrors of the night away for her.

For them both.

Then again, maybe she wouldn't be too upset. He'd given up on guessing her reactions. She continued to surprise him.

"I'm going to wash you now, sweetheart. But I need to remove the rest of your clothes. Is that all right?"

She didn't move, didn't speak. Didn't so much as blink.

Bracing himself, he vanished her bra and panties. It was worse than he'd imagined, the raging lust clamoring through his body. A violent jolt ratcheted his system so tightly he thought he'd explode. She was perfection. Nothing else could compare.

But she wasn't anywhere ready for passion. She was nearly catatonic, sweet Christ. Hot on the heels of lust, an unexpected wave of tenderness rolled through him, going a long way toward steadying his hand. With gentle strokes, he eased the washcloth over her. Wiping away the blood, leaving rich lather in its wake. Her skin was so soft, so silky smooth. He traced her collarbone, washing her arm from shoulder to wrist. He cleaned each finger, scrubbing her nails, buffing her palms before rinsing the soap away. Then, unable to help himself, he pressed quiet kisses to each fingertip. He repeated the process with the other arm.

And Carly stood still beneath his tender ministrations, pliant as a half-sleeping child.

He worked his way down her torso, torturing himself with the weight and perfection of her breasts, the soft skin of her stomach, the gentle flare of her hips, the alluring mound of her womanhood. His throat wasteland dry now, he knelt before her. Water slid over her body, splashing on him. He built lather in the washcloth again and eased it along the mile or so of her trim legs. He lifted her foot and braced it on his knee.

When the washcloth passed over the arch of her foot, she shivered and jerked. She dropped her hand onto his shoulder. Response at last. But he didn't dare look up at her, didn't dare risk lingering upon her nakedness for too long. It might be more than his frayed control could handle.

When she was ready—tomorrow, or the next day, perhaps—he'd spend hours kissing and tasting every delectable inch of her. But for now, he concentrated on easing one foot to the floor and lifting the other. Again, she jerked.

Her sobs had long since ceased. Her breathing shuddered in and out.

Niklas gently grasped her hips and turned her until she faced the spray. He carefully washed his way back up her body, pausing to drop an impetuous kiss on the irresistible indentations at the small of her back. Once he'd finished washing her back, he set the washcloth aside and began working the knots from her muscles as the water rushed over her, sliding the soap away. Heavens, how he longed to let his hands roam. Let his lips follow.

But he just couldn't. Not now. She was too vulnerable, and it broke something inside him to see her like this.

When she was all but boneless, he lifted the bottle of shampoo and squirted a generous amount into his palm. He carefully massaged her scalp, working the lather to the tips of her hair. After turning her again, he tilted her head back, slow and easy, and rinsed the lather from her hair.

He grabbed the washcloth once more and made short work of lathering and washing his own face, neck, chest and arms. He moved her gently to the side, rinsed the soap off and picked up the bottle of conditioner before guiding her back beneath the water. Keeping his touch light and gentle, he eased the cream into her hair. As he tilted her head back for one last rinse, her hands finally came up between them. He glanced at her face. Her expression stunned him.

He'd been so focused on taking this one step at a time, deliberately thinking of the shower in a cold, clinical light, that he'd missed all those little hints that she was coming out of her stupor.

Without a word, she skimmed her hands up over his chest, sliding through the rich lather. Sensual. Seductive beyond anything he'd ever experienced. Her splayed fingers sank into his wet hair, and she cupped his scalp, pulling his head down. She gave a small murmur before sealing her lips over his. His jaw went lax. Her questing tongue, hot and so incredibly sweet, swept past his lips and plunged inside. He was stunned by her aggression. Blood surged to his groin, painfully. His eyes flew wide open, only to flutter closed when she angled her head to the side and deepened the kiss with voracious intent. His hands settled on the curve of her hips. He'd intended to push her away, keep her at arm's length at the very least.

He shouldn't be doing this, shouldn't be giving in to the furnace of desire searing the blood in his veins. But just then, with her lips moving so wantonly beneath his, with her body slipping and sliding along his, he couldn't quite remember why.

All he knew was that he wanted her more than he wanted his next breath.

His grip on her hips tightened. His hold on control slipped.

Her body—her very naked, very slippery body—pushed against his. Dear God, the feel of her wet breasts sliding against his chest. He shuddered. Groaned aloud. He'd never felt anything so erotic.

She shoved him back until tile pressed against his skin. The smooth surface abraded the burns on his flesh, but she was a fireball in his arms, demanding and so very vibrant. Bells and whistles began going off in his head, but the texture of her bare skin, the rough tangle of her tongue against his, drove thoughts of self-restraint from his befuddled brain.

She brought her knee up and hooked it over his hip. His fingers found their way to her thigh, gripping, sliding, squeezing, lifting her higher still. His hand pushed along the length of her silken thigh. His palm claimed her bottom, his fingers closed possessively, squeezing, kneading. The heat of her, so close, oh sweet Mary.

In a heartbeat, he grabbed control of the kiss. Greedy. Refusing to be denied. But Carly wasn't about to meekly surrender. She fought back, gripping his hair in her small fists, mashing her mouth to his, waging a silent, sensual war for domination. Blood rushed in his ears. His heart slammed in violent rhythm. His knees actually shook.

But he was bigger. And she'd stirred something dark and dangerous deep inside him. Something he'd only experienced when in demonic form. Something he'd never before tried to contain. Twisting, he shoved her up against the shower wall. Upon impact, her breath left her in a whoosh and a soft grunt. But just that fast, her lips were back, demanding, her tongue thrusting, tangling. His hips surged against her, grinding, pumping. She lifted both legs, locked them around his waist. Another split second and he would have conjured the rest of his clothing gone and sunk his shaft deep inside her scalding heat, but her nails raked across his back, across the burns and blisters from Gusion's plasma ball.

Blinding pain rocketed through him. He ripped his mouth from hers and sucked in a sharp breath, gritting his teeth. The burns—burns and blisters on top of already abused flesh—were still too fresh for such rough treatment. Instinctively, he captured her wrists, forcing them against the wall on either side of her head. His chest heaved against her, great, rasping gasps for air. His blood boiled. His cock was so hard inside his pants, it was little wonder the seams hadn't split.

He stared at her upturned face.

Holy Mother Mary, what am I doing?

He couldn't believe he was about to say this, but—"Stop."

She tightened her legs, squeezing him, rubbing against him. Moaned, low and deep. His throat nearly closed in response. His heart shuddered.

"Carly, stop. Sweet Christ, you're killing me."

"I don't want to stop, Niklas. I'm so numb. Make me feel. Please, just make me—"

With a harsh oath, he pried her legs from around his waist and jerked himself from her grasp. Taking a big step back, he left her propped against the shower wall. Her breasts rose and fell on deep gulps of air, driving him crazy.

"No," he barked. "You're in shock, *tá'hiri*. You would regret this tomorrow."

"Don't tell me what I'll feel." She shoved herself off the wall, but she swayed on her feet. Anger sizzled in her tone. "Did you see that blond demon? See the way he looked at me?"

Oh, he'd seen the way Gusion had leered at her. And Niklas had nearly taken the bait, so livid had he been.

"It was like Ronové all over again. Only worse. Just a look from him and I felt dirty. I want to *feel* right now, Niklas. You make me feel clean and whole—" She broke off on a sob. "I want to put it all out of my mind. They want me dead, Niklas. But I'm not dead yet. I want to feel alive."

She reached for him, but he caught her wrists, pushing her back. "No, damn it. You're in shock—"

The moment he let go of her wrists, she reached for him again. "I don't care—"

"I do." Angry now himself, he captured her wrists again, squeezed, pulling their joined hands down between them like a shield. Niklas transferred possession of her wrists to one hand, shut off the water and conjured a thick white robe, one that covered her from neck to knee. "When we come together, Carly— *when, not if*—it won't be because I took advantage of you."

"I want this—"

"If you truly want this now, then you'll still want it tomorrow," he bit out. "For tonight, let me be noble."

Conjuring dry clothing for himself, he scooped her up and carried her to the bed. He smoothed the wet hair from her brow, ignoring the burning emotion in her deep brown eyes, and pulled the thick, soft blanket up over her to tuck her in. After dropping a tender kiss on her forehead, he stood and crossed to the door.

One last, longing-filled glance over his shoulder assured him that she was still aroused, and mad as hell at him. Shooting a glance at the dresser and closet, he vanished half the clothing already there, spare clothing he'd left behind for those occasions when he'd been too exhausted and in too much pain to conjure clothing for himself, before filling them with a wide assortment of clothing for her. He couldn't keep conjuring one outfit at a time. She was too independent to continue to let him dress her every day.

And he sure as certain couldn't spend another day visualizing each article slipping over her enthralling curves.

Heaving a deep sigh, he pulled the door closed softly behind him. Niklas leaned against the wood, propped his forehead against the cool surface and closed his eyes. Reaching down, he readjusted the fit of his jeans around his still-swollen shaft.

Of one thing, he had little doubt.

Being noble was going to be the death of him.

Pushing away from the door, he grimaced. He needed to start searching for Ronové. He couldn't put any of this off any longer. Carly would be safe enough there in the house with the ward stones and the guard stones for a short time. Conjuring black camo pants, a black T-shirt and combat boots, Niklas centered his focus on a seedy little bar about twenty miles away that was a known hangout for his kind and shimmered himself there.

Grim-faced, he kept his chin down, propped an elbow against the bar and scanned the crowd. *Purgatory.* He chuckled mirthlessly at the irony of the bar's name. He rapped on the bar to draw the barkeep's attention, ordered a drink and then sat back.

He didn't have long to wait.

****

Carly flipped a piece of French toast in the sizzling skillet. Heat seared her cheeks every time she thought of last night and her behavior in the shower.

How humiliating!

And then, for him to deny her, for him to turn her away on the pretense of being noble?

In the bright light of the morning after, she'd begun to second-guess everything. What was wrong with her? What had she done to drive him away? Never mind the fact that she'd already made up her mind to be noble herself and keep a healthy distance from him for the sake of his salvation. She wouldn't come between him and his faith.

But still, the cold slap in the face stung. Waking up alone this morning hadn't helped matters. Oh, he'd filled the closet and dresser with a brand new wardrobe that would turn any woman's head. Pants and dresses, shorts and shirts. Unmentionables by the dozens. Though she'd have to have a little talk with him about those unmentionables. While, yes, a woman liked to wear sexy silk and lace once in a while, she also needed something a little more...*comfortable.*

And the shoes.

My word, the shoes!

But what had surprised her had been the fact that the other half of the dresser, and the other half of the closet, had been filled with male clothing. Niklas's clothing.

Seeing their clothing side by side like that... Well, it had done strange things to her insides. It was just so intimate. So cozy. So wonderfully pleasant. A brief respite in an otherwise crappy morning.

Oh, yes. He'd also left a note. How could she forget *the note*?

Tá'hiri,

Back soon. Don't leave the house.

N

Wonderful. She jabbed at her breakfast with a fork, her mood turning sour once again. Well, that was all well and good, wasn't it? *Don't leave the house.* He'd left her here, holed up like some escaped convict, while *he* got to go out, gallivanting all over God-only-knew-where.

He'd have a conniption if she left a stingy note like that for him.

And could anyone blame her for being a bit prickly? She'd gone for an innocent walk and somehow ended up smack in the middle of another demon battle. And *then* she'd thrown herself at Niklas. Shamelessly. Thoughtlessly.

Unsuccessfully.

He'd shot her down, of course.

And he'd walked out. As if her offer had meant nothing. As if he'd had so many women throw themselves at him that he'd become inured.

No, she corrected. As if he was a demon trying to earn back his maker's favor. A demon holding himself to a higher cause.

And how could she be mad at him when foregoing

physical intimacy was the very thing she'd already decided was the right choice? Carly unhappily flopped the slices of French toast onto a plate beside a couple slices of bacon and flipped the burner off.

"That smells delicious," a dark, sensual voice, coated with a sensual Southern accent, murmured from behind her.

Her plate clattered to the counter as she whirled around, brandishing a spatula like a sword.

His eyes were the first thing she noted. Amber. Striking. Hypnotic. And then his face. Smooth shaven, strong jaw. Flawless. His lips were alluring, to say the very least. His hair was a wild, tawny color. A longish, curling mass of gold, calling to mind midnight fantasies and disheveled, sexual satisfaction. His pose was relaxed, careless. He was tall. But not too tall. Muscular, but not bulky.

Any—*every*—woman's fantasy come to life.

And the come-hither grin he sent her positively dripped seduction at its finest.

"Niklas!" she screamed, panic ripping through her.

Before she'd finished the last syllable of his name, he appeared in front of her. Facing the intruder, brandishing a sizzling plasma ball in his hand, Niklas tensed for combat. The intruder didn't so much as flinch.

Straightening, Niklas let the plasma ball evaporate in his palm. "You were supposed to be here last night," he snapped.

The devastatingly handsome man—demon, Carly corrected herself—the handsome *demon* leaned a hip against the counter, ignoring Niklas's rebuke. He considered Niklas for a long minute before turning his amber gaze to Carly. She supposed he meant to appear respectful. But that face of his—and those eyes, fashioned of pure sin—just made the effect all the more seductive.

"I'm sorry to've startled you, ma'am." He dipped his head. His tone was circumspect.

Realizing she still gripped the spatula, she set it aside with a trembling hand. Sooner or later she would get used to all these demons popping—*shimmering*, she silently corrected—*shimmering* in and out willy-nilly. And the seemingly inevitable demon battles. She would. Sooner or later.

Maybe.

Carly offered him a tentative smile. "I'm sorry for screaming. And for threatening you"—she glanced down at her hand, then back at him—"with a spatula."

His grin widened. The corners of his eyes crinkled in amusement. "No harm done, darlin'."

"Well, aren't you in a chipper mood?" Niklas remarked, eyeing the newcomer suspiciously. Almost as if Niklas expected him to suddenly sprout horns and go nuclear.

Lifting a tawny brow at Niklas, the newcomer didn't respond.

Heaving a sigh, Niklas turned so he faced them both. "Carly, this is Gideon, the Demon of Temptation. Gideon, this is Carly Danner."

"Former," Gideon reminded Niklas, his tone put upon. "Former Demon of Temptation." Turning his gaze to Carly, he drawled, "Pleasure to meet you, my dear."

"It's nice to meet you." She held her hand out as she crossed the short distance between them.

He eyed her hand longingly, though he made no move to take it, which seemed genuinely out of character, what with his Southern gentleman persona and all. Puzzled, she dropped her hand and frowned curiously up at him.

"Please, don't be offended. It certainly isn't anything to do with you." Straightening away from the counter, he slowly reached for her. Beside her, Niklas stiffened but made no move to stop him. Gideon's long-fingered hand stopped an inch from her cheek, cupped slightly as if he meant to caress her skin. And then his hand passed right through her head. She shivered as a chilly sensation entered one cheek, then swam through her head before it exited through the other side of her face.

Gasping, she staggered back a step, eyes wide.

"I see," she whispered. Though she didn't. Not quite. Then, turning to Niklas, she asked, "Is this like your vision thing? The gift and the curse?"

Nodding, he tersely replied, "Gideon can no longer physically touch another."

"Oh," she breathed. How sad for him. How lonely. "Is it all right if I call you Gideon?"

The full force of his smile returned. "You can call me whatever you like, darlin'. I'll answer to just about anything. In fact"—his warm amber gaze slid down her body, back up—"I've even been known to answer to 'oh my God' a time or two." Gideon's grin was cocky, irreverent. He garnished it with a wicked wink. "Of course, if I could manage to talk you out of some of that French toast, and it tastes half as good as it looks, I might be willing to relinquish that particular title to you, darlin'. At least for a little while anyway."

She should have found him offensive and crude, despite the Southern charm liberally slathered over every word, every glance. But she didn't.

In fact, she found she quite liked him. Though Niklas continued to stare at him as if there was something...wrong with him.

Gideon's banter was light and teasing. In a world where everything had become dark and sinister, he was a welcome beam of sunshine. A smile—a genuine, honest-to-goodness smile—formed before she gave it another thought. She really shouldn't play along with him. But she couldn't seem to resist. "It just so happens I have plenty of ingredients. More than enough to share. Pull up a chair, *sunshine*."

Gideon let out a loud hoot of laughter. Carly's smile widened. Niklas's scowl darkened. Chuckling, Gideon took a seat at the table. Niklas jerked his chair out and plopped down. Watching the two of them, Carly fought not to laugh. Night and day, she mused. So intense and thoughtful, the one. And the other, a devil-may-care rogue through and through. She moved from the fridge to the counter and then to the stove while the two of them discussed these nests Xander and the others had uncovered.

"Gusion *and* Glasya." A tall coffee cup appeared in Gideon's hand. The scent of caramel and coffee filled the air. He took a long drink, sighed and set the cup back down. Despite Niklas's habit of conjuring and vanishing things, Carly still did a double take. "You think they know where the sword is?"

"It's kind of hard to assume otherwise. The timing's too close to ignore. And there's just too much of an influx of demons in this region for them *not* to be tied together somehow."

"And rumors of the scrolls have surfaced, huh?" Gideon traced the logo on the side of the cup perfectly, though he never once so much as glanced at it. "Now that we've found the Arc Stone, I'd say the playing field is about even. Have you heard anything about the other two relics?"

"Not yet."

Carly set a heaping platter of golden French toast on the table in front of them. Before she could return to the cabinet for plates and silverware, place settings for three suddenly appeared on the table. And, in the blink of the eye, Gideon disappeared from his chair, only to reappear behind hers. With dashing flair, he pulled the chair out and waited for her to take her seat.

"Oh," she exclaimed, startled. "Ah, thank you."

Sinking into the chair, she smiled up at Gideon. He returned the smile, then shimmered onto his own seat once more. Niklas's scowl became downright thunderous.

Why is he being so surly?

The answer hit her fast and hard. Stunning her into staring, openmouthed, at him.

He's jealous!

No, surely not.

But the thought wouldn't leave her. Could Niklas truly be jealous, worried that she might find Gideon irresistible, despite the fact she obviously couldn't touch him or him her?

Niklas's face turned red as he faced her, eyes slowly narrowing. Snapping her mouth closed, she turned her gaze to the platter of French toast.

He is *jealous. Wonder of all wonders. Huh.*

Seeking to fill the sudden silence, she glanced around the tabletop. "I'm sorry, but I didn't have any more bac—"

A plate piled high with crisp bacon appeared before her.

Clearing her throat, she questioned Niklas, "Should I make coffee, or shall I just place my order for that as well?"

A big mug of it appeared next to her plate. A hint of creamer and two scoops of sugar, just the way she always drank it. He'd been paying attention.

The corner of Niklas's mouth lifted in a smug grin.

The next hour passed in a befuddled daze for Carly. Gideon dazzled her with Southern charm and impeccable manners.

And just like that, her every tiny little desire suddenly came into reality. A sweater because her arms had grown chilly. A second helping of French toast appeared on her plate before she could reach for it. Another slice of bacon. The coffee cup refilled itself.

Gideon paid lavish compliments, flirting shamelessly.

And soon the dirty pans and dishes suddenly vanished, and the counters sparkled. It was as if they were having a silent, willful contest to see who could impress her more.

Her heart melted just a little. She thanked Gideon, then turned to do the same for Niklas. His smoldering gaze caught her, though, and the words died on her tongue. He'd looked at her like that—just *exactly* like that—in the shower. Heat flooded her cheeks.

Gideon, obviously puzzled, looked back and forth between them. Could he feel the sudden tension in the air? How could he not? It was so thick, Carly could hardly breathe with it.

She lowered her eyes and shivered, remembering how it felt to be pressed between Niklas and the shower as he used his mouth and body to wrest control of the kiss from her. Sparks of heat cascaded through her. She shifted uncomfortably in her seat.

Niklas suddenly stiffened. He watched her teeth nibble nervously at her lower lip. Oh yes. That was most definitely *the look*. The one he always gave her just before he kissed her.

Lost in his glacier-blue eyes, Carly almost missed the blur of motion behind him.

Almost.

The demon was tall and rangy. Shadow stubble covered his jaw. His dark hair was cropped close in a buzz cut. His eyes were a flat, emotionless gray. Drawing a startled breath, Carly squeezed Niklas's arm in warning as she gaped at the man—the demon— behind him. Why weren't they reacting? Why hadn't Gideon leaped up? Why hadn't Niklas moved to protect her?

"Xander." Niklas greeted the demon without looking behind him.

"Don't have long," Xander rasped.

A second demon shimmered—*yes!* She got it right this time—into the kitchen beside the first. This one had a handsome face and short, tousled blond hair. He looked more like a Viking warrior than a demon. He wore black from head to toe.

"Sebastian." Again without looking over his shoulder.

"Dude," Sebastian replied, then his attention

snagged on Carly. His tone changed. "Well, hello, gorgeous."

"Off limits," Niklas snarled.

Sebastian gave a good-sport shrug, flipped his black trench coat out of the way, and hopped up to sit on the counter.

"Sebastian, Xander, this is Carly." Gideon made the introductions. Sebastian nodded, his assessing, appreciative look lingering. Xander glanced at her, and then moved on, a seen-one-seen-'em-all glance.

"Any word from Mikhail?" Niklas asked as Xander took the seat opposite Carly.

Shaking his head, Xander conjured a can of soda and tipped it to his lips.

"Gusion is here," Niklas informed Xander and Sebastian.

Xander showed remarkably little emotion as he lowered the can to the table.

"Really?" Sebastian's eyes narrowed, his expression turned predatory. His face might inspire erotic fantasies, but something in his tone warned her that he was a prime example of not judging a book by its cover.

Niklas made short work of filling the three demons in on their late-night visitors, ending with, "I left Mikhail a message." He leaned back in his chair. "Once he gets here, we can figure out a game plan where the relics are concerned. I think we're all in agreement that finding the scrolls and the Chosen One needs to take top priority now. Even over the nests."

The others all nodded.

But the reminder that yet another demon would soon appear brought a valid point to Carly's mind.

"Wait a minute," she said. "I'm confused. Why do the ward stones keep the others away, but you guys"—she glanced around at the four of them—"you can all come and go as you please, right? In the grove last night, one of the demons said he could feel the chrysoberyl." She held up her wrist, flashing the bracelet Niklas had given her. "And the brecciated jasper. He said they made his skin crawl. Why don't these things affect you?"

Niklas lifted the ring on his finger. Xander pulled a slim silver chain from beneath the collar of his shirt. Gideon tapped the flashy watch on his wrist. Sebastian flicked a finger against the stud in his ear. All contained smaller versions of the same stones in her bracelet.

"You could say we've built up a tolerance," Gideon said.

"That, and these were all cut from the same stone," Sebastian added.

"So, it's possible that other demons could learn to tolerate these stones?"

"Maybe after years of exposure," Gideon said.

"Centuries," Xander rasped.

Carly tried hard not to stare. Oh, the poor man's—*demon's*—voice. It hurt her own throat to hear him speak.

She tried to take comfort in their reassurances. But she'd seen what Gusion and his demons could do. Though Niklas had successfully fended four of them off, he'd had to work for it. The thought that one of them could shimmer onto the farm, shimmer inside this house—

Chills swept through her. She rubbed her hands briskly up and down her arms. Niklas glanced sharply at her, questioning her with his eyes.

Carly tried to reassure him with a sunny smile. By the expression on his face, she failed miserably.

Chapter Fourteen

Shadows clung to the corners of the Great Hall. Like a cancer, those shadows bided their time, hungry to completely engulf the room, beaten back by the garish red firelight flickering over gaudy gold floor and walls. Stolas strode toward the massive black doors, fury seething through him, a living thing. Fury he was careful to hide. The Scathé Demon, Lucifer's personal guard, stared him down with suspicious eyes.

Treading lightly past the Scathé, he held his chin up, working hard to keep his heart from racing with fear, despite his anger. The Scathé, though tall and deceptively weak-looking to the point of ghoulishness, were fierce warriors, lightning fast and trained in all the deadly arts, possessing incomparable skill with a blade and unswerving loyalty to Lucifer.

The massive doors swung slowly open, allowing him escape from Lucifer's hall. Oh, how he hated these obligatory appearances at court. Condescension hung heavy on the sulfur-laced air. Just one more way for good old Granddad to force his followers to worship at his cloven hooves. Like a medieval king, Lucifer had sat on his skeletal throne, demanding homage. Homage levied in the form of human souls. A great number of them.

And to be treated no better than a common servant in front of all those demon hordes, despite his blood ties, was degrading. Insulting.

Unforgivable.

Stolas's claws curled, digging into his palms, drawing black, sizzling blood. The bastard would get his due, all right. God might not see fit to send Lucifer's rotten ass into Oblivion, but *he* would take immense pleasure in doing so, and not think twice about it.

A glimmer of satisfaction swelled. He had the Sword of Kathnesh. Ronové—or, rather, his minion, Dimiezlo—had been useful after all. *And* Dimiezlo had managed to stir rumors of the scrolls, false rumors. Rumors that would send the Fallen scurrying all over the globe while his own minions would close in on the true Guardian. After all this time, things were finally falling into place.

Now, as soon as Gusion tied up the final loose end, Stolas would be in a better position to set the next phase of his plan into motion. Thoughts of the human female, though, left a troubled frown on his face as he shimmered to his own hall. The assassins he'd sent after her thus far had all failed to locate her. The Seer continued to protect her with such ferocity that he now had difficulty finding assassins willing to go up against him. Had Niklas formed an attachment to her? Could he, at last, have found the great Seer's Achilles' heel?

He vanished his ceremonial robes, then conjured something more comfortable to wear. He longed to shimmer to the wasteland at the far eastern borders of Hell where he'd secreted the Sword of Kathnesh away, was greedy to examine the relic for himself. But he wouldn't risk it, such a foolish chance when he had his goal well within sight. Instead, he paced to the long table, skimming over the latest cache of offerings one of his legions had brought back from a world he longed to experience for himself. Curious items.

He picked up a small, slim, white device with a long cord dangling from one end. This particular piece never ceased to amaze him. Pushing buttons, he frowned as the strange sounds buzzed from the tiny round bumps at the end of the cord. Lifting one of the bumps to his pointed ear, he growled approval. Sound poured forth. Loud. Driving. Pounding.

Fabulous.

He examined the cover. What a wonderful invention. His lips edged into as close as he'd ever come to a smile as he held the bump closer to his ear.

Absolutely astounding!

After setting the music-maker aside, he reached for another discovery. Narrow, gray, contoured. It fit comfortably in his palm. Covered with dozens of tiny buttons, it immediately intrigued him, particularly after the pleasant surprise of the music-maker. Using his thumb, as seemed natural, he depressed button after button. Nothing happened. Frowning, he shook the worthless device. Held it to his ear. Nothing. Turning it round in his hand, he peered more closely at it. Small letters were printed on the bottom. Worn and illegible. Not nearly as clever as the music-maker. How disappointing. Unable to make the gray device do anything useful or interesting, he tossed it aside and reached for another item.

He pushed through the pile and examined a small ring. Many oddly shaped hunks of silver with jagged edges running along one side dangled from the ring. He ran the edge of one metallic piece along the pad of his thumb. Too dull to cut, the metallic pieces would be useless as a knife. He shook it and the metal pieces tinkled. But that seemed to be about all they were good for. He tossed them aside with a shrug, sifted and sorted.

What a strange looking weapon!

He picked up another curiosity, and turned the object this way and that, examining it with great interest. The handle was comfortable, with an odd, rubbery grip. The instrument was circular, with a flat guard that separated the blade from the handle. He flicked it with his thumb claw, and the blade spun, glinting in the firelight. Interesting. He rolled the device across his forearm. Too dull to slice through flesh, though. But the edge could easily be honed. Pleased, he set it aside for later consideration and reached for a small, roundish vessel. The top portion was white, molded to resemble pictures he'd seen of those things called…ah, yes, *flower*. The bottom half was clear and appeared to be filled with a liquid of some type. Two copper-colored prongs protruded from the back.

He pressed on the prongs, but they didn't move. He shook it. It made a soft, sloshing sound. He noticed some of the liquid had leaked down the side. He licked it and cringed.

Ack. Awful.

But an unexpected, pleasing scent caught his attention. Holding the bottle close to his nose, he inhaled. Again, deeper. Light. Sweet. Quite enjoyable.

Now this! This is incredible.

This was something he could surround himself with, a scent he would happily breathe in for the rest of eternity. Perhaps he should offer a special reward for those who brought more of these back. These and the music-makers. He looked for a name on the scented object. Everything in the wonderfully modern world of man now had a name on it. Ah, there it was, how clever.

A small sound echoed from the far end of the room. The delicate clearing of a throat.

Turning, he appraised the small Charocté slave. Eyes downcast, head bowed. On bended knee. Ah, another perfect subject. Charocté Demons made such ideal servants. Obedient. Loyal. Submissive. Spiritless.

"Yes?"

"Gusion is waiting, my master."

Finally. "Send him in."

"Yes, my lord."

Rising, eyes still trained on the floor, the Charocté backed from the room.

A moment later, Gusion shimmered into his inner sanctum.

"Rise," Stolas commanded, eyeing the demon with growing displeasure. "You seem to be missing something, Gusion."

"My lord?"

"The woman's head," he supplied, impatient. "I don't see it."

"She is still in possession of her head, my lord." Gusion lowered his own head, wordlessly acknowledging his failure. "The Seer guards her most ferociously."

"I've ascertained that for myself by the number of your kind that he's exterminated."

Gusion continued to keep his eyes downcast. "If I may speak freely, my lord?"

"Go on."

"I believe I know where the Seer has secreted the woman away. There is a farm, a single, isolated dwelling located in rural Minnesota, a portion of the Midwest in the United States. I believe he's using this farm as a base of sorts. The nest Glasya set up near there, some of the demons were out scouting for entertainment. They stumbled upon an area of land that was heavily protected with ward stones. Curious, suspicious, I returned with them. We ran into the Seer. The woman was with him. A Scavenger Demon got close enough to reach for her. But the Seer has given her guard stones. A lot of them. Powerful stones. Peridot, brecciated jasper, and chrysoberyl. Before the Scavenger could react, the Seer shimmered behind him and beheaded him. He appears fiercely protective of her."

Stolas rubbed his hand over his coarse beard. Considered. Plotted.

"She is a fairly pretty little thing," Gusion added; a hint of lust gleamed in his eye for a moment, and then was carefully hidden. "I deliberately provoked him, but he wouldn't leave her side. I could tell I got under his skin. But he didn't attack. He was acting quite out of character. *Very* protective. If I might make an unsolicited observation, my lord?" He paused, waiting until he'd received a grunt of permission. "I believe he's grown unusually attached to the human female. Her...*death* would cause him great torment." Again, that lustful gleam flickered on his face, making Stolas wonder just exactly how *fairly pretty* this female was.

Tilting his head, Stolas clasped his hands behind his back and began to pace. Gusion's comments were enlightening. Certainly worth taking under advisement. If Niklas had indeed grown attached to the woman, she could be used as leverage. It was impossible, at this point, to guess whether or not she knew anything that might endanger his plot. Still, turning the Seer over to Lucifer? That would certainly buy him the time he needed to procure the other relics.

"Continue to hunt for the female and the Seer." He picked up the pleasantly scented object again. Sniffed. Savored. "But I want them, alive. Spread the word. She's not to be killed. I want the honors for myself."

Lines of disappointment bracketed Gusion's mouth.

"Yes, my lord." Gusion bowed his head, crossed his arms, thumped his fists to his shoulders and vanished.

****

What was he doing here? This was crazy. Hell, *he* was crazy. Leaving Carly in Gideon's care had probably been one of the biggest mistakes of his life. And that was really saying something, all things considered. Granted, Gideon was behaving more like his old, charming self. Niklas still hadn't figured out why. But he would. Eventually. Still he couldn't make himself go back to the farm. Not just yet. He needed a moment to himself. A moment to process everything. A moment to make absolutely certain that the decision he'd come to had been the right choice. Like Xander, he was a brooder. Why he'd chosen this particular place to come to brood? Well, that was probably yet one more reason for his *crazy* self-diagnosis.

He hoisted himself up on top of the white, pitted, weatherworn slab, and scooted back, letting his legs dangle. A small pebble poked the back of his thigh. He swiped up the small stone and absently rolled it between thumb and forefinger, smoothing it, spinning it as his gaze wandered over the small graveyard. Spanish moss dripped from the ancient, gnarled trees overhead. A rusted, waist-high fence surrounded the small cemetery. And inside that wrought iron fence, a couple dozen decrepit, sun-bleached headstones thrust up from the ground at haphazard angles. Some were pitted and missing chunks. Some had been worn smooth by wind and rain so that names, dates and epitaphs were no longer legible. All were coated on one side with the spongy growth that thrived in the humid heat of the bayous.

In the distance, just up the hill, a loose shutter slapped against worn clapboard. Glancing over, he noted the cross on the steeple had begun to list to the side. The little country church sat empty. Its pews collecting layer upon layer of dust and dirt. Its altar barren. Forgotten. Just like this tiny section of burial ground. But, unlike that church, this graveyard was unconsecrated ground. Thieves, adulterers, murderers were buried here. Those who would never look upon the gates of Heaven. The Unforgiven.

The fallen.

Maybe that was why he was so comfortable here. He fit right in.

He'd stumbled upon this church a long, long time ago. Back in the early days when he'd first begun to doubt his choice to follow Lucifer. He'd wandered close to the church, actually had the audacity—the nerve—to peer inside. He'd even risked rubbing his sleeve to the window to clear a spot to see better. Of course, when thunder had rumbled warningly in the distance, and a shot of lightning had cracked through the air some miles away, he'd been quick enough to step back. Put a bit of respectful distance between himself and hallowed ground. He always returned there, though, it seemed. Whenever something was troubling him.

Whenever he felt in danger of losing his way.

He'd come there a lot in the last few decades.

He hadn't even realized this was his destination tonight. Not until he'd arrived a few minutes ago. Was his subconscious trying to tell him something? Maybe. Just when it seemed he'd figured everything out, been so sure that keeping Carly was the right thing to do, he'd started second-guessing himself. Second-guessing everything he'd fought for and bled for, everything he believed in.

Would God ever forgive him for all his trespasses? Niklas's betrayal had been so deep. He'd almost convinced himself centuries ago that his God was loving and forgiving. All you had to do was repent and ask forgiveness.

But he'd been asking for so long, asking with no signs of an answer, that he'd begun to dwell on all the stories of a wrathful, vengeful God. Stories that filled the Bible. From Eve's curse to the Great Flood. Lot's wife whom He'd turned to a pillar of salt simply because she'd not followed his command and looked back. The Lord had rained down upon Sodom and Gomorrah brimstone and fire for their sins. On and on the stories went. And yet, Niklas held within him some small kernel of hope. Hope that his transgressions could be forgiven. Hope that he had not been cast out eternally. Hope that he would one day find peace.

Heaving a deep sigh, he called to mind the image of Carly's face. There was something special there. Something special about her. Why would God let one such as him guard and protect one such as her without reason, without a plan? He could no longer view her as a test. He'd done that already. Too often. Viewed every innocent he'd ever saved as a test.

He'd passed all those tests. At least, as far as he could tell. And still he'd not earned redemption. Pinching the bridge of his nose, he frowned. If he kept Carly as he wanted, if he selfishly took what he craved most, would it only prove he didn't deserve forgiveness?

Hanging his head, he braced his palms against the rough edge of the stone and drew a deep breath. One thing was for certain. He couldn't keep going like this. Doubting himself. Doubting his judgment. His gaze lifted, settled upon the broken church. How he longed to go inside. Longed to lay his burden upon God's altar. Longed to absorb the tranquility, the peace of knowing that when he walked through those doors, his soul would be clean once more. Clean enough to deserve the woman who was fast stealing his heart.

****

"Can I make you some lunch, Gideon? Are you hungry?"

"Darlin', you'll make us all fat and lazy." A customary cup of coffee appeared in his hand as he leaned his hip negligently against the counter.

She blinked but kept on smiling. It was getting easier.

"No, you don't need to cook for me. You don't

even need to cook for yourself." He leaned close and did a poor imitation of a stage whisper. "I can conjure anything you want." He settled back, wiggled a limber eyebrow and offered her a bawdy smile. "Anything at all, sugar."

Laughing, she shook her head. He set his cup aside and pulled the chair from the table for her, and she sat. He took the seat across from her. His cup disappeared from the counter and reappeared in his hand.

This time she didn't even blink.

"Actually, one of those looks pretty nice." She nodded to the coffee. The words had barely left her mouth when a cup appeared on the table in front of her.

"Thanks." She took a cautious sip. Hot. Sweet. Creamy. Sublime. "You really are good."

"Not quite as good as Niklas, though." Gideon raised a speculative eyebrow.

"What do you mean?" She tilted her head, running a finger up and down the side of the cup in studied innocence.

"This morning at breakfast. Niklas conjured stuff right and left, almost before you could even ask for it. Now, I know Niklas—have known him quite a while, mind you"—he leaned back, draping an arm over the back of his chair—"and I've never seen him so..." He narrowed his golden eyes, tilted his head as if searching for the right word. "So *obsessed* over anyone's comfort as he is yours."

Feeling suddenly awkward, she lifted the coffee to her lips, delaying her reply while she thought of an appropriate response. To her embarrassment, she couldn't come up with anything better than, "Oh?"

"Now why is it he's suddenly concerned himself

with your every comfort?"

"Why didn't you ask *him* these questions?"

"Tried to. I was met with the usual tight-lipped Niklas stare." Gideon paused, gave her a mocking rendition of Niklas's infamous stare, and then took a sip of coffee. "Besides, you're right here."

"And I can't shimmer off in a fit of temper?"

Chuckling, he set the cup down. "There is that."

"I think I'll plead the fifth." At his puzzled frown, she said, "You're going to have to wait for Niklas."

"Darlin', I'll be old and decrepit before he gets around to explaining himself to anyone."

She lifted an impish eyebrow. "And that'd be different from now how?"

Tossing his head back, he gave himself over to a good belly laugh. "I bet you give Niklas fits."

"On occasion," she said with a small grin.

"What will you do when this is all over?"

"Provided I live through it?" She smiled, but then heaved a deep sigh, traced the rim of her cup. "Go back to work, I suppose. I used Niklas's phone last night and called my boss. I pleaded a family emergency and bought myself a week. Maybe two."

"He must be pretty understanding, giving you that much time off on such short notice."

"Understanding?" She laughed, shook her head. "Scrooge himself could take lessons from Mr. Tate. No, I'm just good at what I do. He knows that. He also knows he'll never get anyone else with the scarecrow salary he pays."

Gideon frowned, studying her over the rim of his cup. "Why do you stay when this job obviously makes you unhappy?"

"Good question." She took a long sip, set the cup down, then turned it in slow circles. "I wanted to make a difference. Sounds naïve and clichéd, I know. But I did. I wanted to help people. I thought this was a good way to do it. Unfortunately, my boss and I disagree on the type of people we should be helping. Conner, Tate and McGaffney was the only law firm hiring at the time in this area. And I didn't want to go away, I couldn't leave Uncle Jason after he got sick again. I guess I let myself get stuck in a rut."

"Sounds like you're ready to break out of that rut."

One corner of her mouth curled up on a rueful smile. "You know, standing up to Tate was surprisingly easy. Maybe all these demon battles are starting to toughen me up. They certainly have a way of putting things into a new perspective."

"Oh, I think you were probably tough enough all ready." Chuckling, he nodded approval. At length, he leaned back in his chair and watched her sip her coffee, a curious light in his eyes. As if she were some fascinating puzzle he couldn't quite figure out. "You know, you're surprisingly okay with all this curse-of-the-damned stuff."

"I was raised to be open-minded. I have faith, and I have a good imagination. What can I say?" She took a deeper drink of coffee, then set the cup down in favor of twisting the peridot ring on her finger.

"You could tell me how you hooked up with one of the meanest, most dangerous demons Hell has ever produced."

And so, she told him the story of how she'd stumbled upon a demon ritual in the city park. How she'd come to be tied to a tree, and how Niklas had, apparently, rescued her. She hadn't realized she'd allowed emotion to slip into her voice, until Gideon peered at her with a soft, pitying expression.

"And you fell in love with him," he said softly.

"No!" she burst out. But his gaze said he knew better, and she reluctantly admitted aloud, "I've come to care for him. I'm a fool." She held a hand up, forestalling any sympathy or words of caution he might be ready to offer. "I know, I know. He's a demon. I'm human. There are a hundred and one reasons why it would never..." Her fingers fumbled the coffee cup.

She made a second quick grab, but he'd grabbed too. Their hands clasped the cup at the same time, rescuing it from spilling. His hand passed right through hers. A whisper of cold, and then he withdrew. Her gaze flew to his, met. He looked away first.

But not before she saw the pain, the longing, the despair.

Her heart went out to him. "How long?"

He turned back to her, the question in his eyes.

"How long has it been since you last were able to touch someone?"

"The entire time I've been Earthbound." At her confused frown, he elaborated. "That curse was one last parting jab from good old Lucy right before I escaped. A punishment, if you will."

"And Niklas summoned you around the same time he escaped Hell?"

Gideon nodded. "Almost two centuries now."

Two hundred years. Wow.

She kept her sympathy to herself, knew it would be as useless and unwanted as any he might offer her. But empathy was too strong in her nature to not reply at all.

"I'd give you a hug if I could."

And she meant it. From the bottom of her heart.

He blinked at her, clearly surprised. A wide smile slowly split his face, and for once, there was no teasing seduction. Only a warm offer of friendship. "I'm beginning to see what draws Niklas to you."

She stared at him, long and hard. Then she quietly said, "I won't try to keep him, Gideon. I don't want you to worry over that. I know it would never work. I'll grow old. I'll die. And he won't. I would never ask him to watch that. And I'd never dream of asking him to choose between me and everything he's been working so hard for." She lowered her grief-filled gaze to her hands, surprised to find herself twisting the ring Niklas had given her instead of her mother's ring, as was usual when she sought comfort. Lifting her gaze to Gideon, the demon she presumed to call friend, Carly vowed softly, "I care about him enough that, when the time comes, I'll let him go."

Gideon reached out and laid his cupped hands on top of hers. Hovered them there. A cold whisper of air was the only thing she felt, but the warmth of his gesture went clear to her heart. In his eyes, she found understanding, respect and unspoken sympathy. But no pity.

"Appease my curiosity?"

He shot her a lopsided grin as he withdrew his hands. "Maybe. Depends on the question."

"Ever since you showed up here, Niklas has been giving you strange looks. Like he'd been expecting one person, but somebody else showed up...in your body. What's up with that?"

Gideon leaned back and seemed to weigh his

response. He considered her for a long moment before finally speaking. "Two hundred years is an awfully long time to go without...without touching someone," he began. "After a while, it begins to weigh on a body. I'm sure you can understand, I got to be a bit...surly."

Frowning, she nodded agreement. His punishment did seem unusually cruel.

"Well, darlin'," he drawled, looking for all the world as if he were a little kid about to share a precious secret. "I think I just may have found a loophole."

"Oh Gideon! That's wonderful."

"It's only a maybe, mind you. And I haven't got all the why-fors and what-nots figured out yet. But I'm workin' on it." He rubbed that emblem on his coffee cup once more, his expression as serious as she'd ever seen it. Serious, and filled with shining hope. Hope she suspected he hadn't felt in a very, very long time.

"Hope can be a very powerful thing," Carly observed solemnly, suddenly and unaccountably worried for her new friend. Sometimes when things didn't work out the way one expected, the loss of that hope was crueler than the curse could ever be.

He laughed, clearly surprised. "Yes, it can, darlin'. Yes, it surely can."

"Fair enough." Smiling, not wanting to ruin his mood, she drained the last of her coffee and set the cup aside. "So, what do we do while we wait for the others to get back?"

He thought for a moment, and then asked, "Chess, anyone?"

She grinned. In short order, she snared the chess set she'd seen in Sebastian's den and set the board up on the kitchen table. That was how Niklas found them two hours later when he returned from wherever it was that he'd shimmered to. They were laughing companionably as they battled head to head for the title of chess champion.

She turned in her seat to greet him, but the glower on his face threatened the good mood Gideon had worked so hard to cultivate. Dark shadows smudged Niklas's eyes. His wounds had healed, and his face was no longer drawn with pain. He'd fed, she surmised; a chill swept over her, and her smile slowly died. This was something else she'd have to learn how to deal with, adjust her thinking to accept. Niklas needed to do this horrible, revolting thing to survive. Regardless of whether or not his victims were evil, regardless of whether or not they deserved to die this way, losing their very souls, they were still human.

Human…like her.

"Well, glad to see you two have gotten so cozy." He tossed a black duffel bag to the floor. He scowled at Gideon. "Don't you have something more important to do than sit here playing games?"

"If I might remind you, you were the one that demanded I stay here to watch over her while you were gone."

"I said watch over her, not flirt with her and be her cheap entertainment."

"And that's my cue." Gideon pushed to his feet and offered Carly a deep bow. "I concede the field, my dear." He took one long look at Niklas, then shot a sympathetic grin her way. "I'd ask if your shots are up to date, but mankind hasn't formulated a strain for demon rabies yet."

"His bark is worse than his bite," she assured

Gideon with a negligent shrug. "Besides, I've been known to bite back."

Gideon's brows lifted at that and he chuckled. "Well, then, on that intriguing note, I'll be off. Demons to slay and all that. I'll be seein' you later, darlin'."

He shimmered from the room, leaving her to face Niklas's disagreeable disposition alone.

Carly crossed her arms. "Can I make you something to eat?"

"If I want something, I'll conjure it." As if to prove his point, a can of soda appeared in his hand. "You can save playing house for Gideon."

"We weren't *playing house*. And you didn't have to be so rude to him, you know," she scolded.

He snarled, plunked down and shoved the chessboard roughly aside. Kings and queens rolled. Pawns and bishops clattered to the floor.

"What is your problem?" She squared off against him, gripping the back of the chair.

"My problem just left. Or at least half of it did."

"What's that supposed to mean?"

"It means I've barely been gone for a few hours, and here you two sit, chumming it up like besties."

"You're jealous." Baffled, she rocked back on her heels, frowning. "Don't you know that there's nothing for you to be—"

"I am not," he scoffed, pushing to his feet. He strode from the room, leaving a full can of soda on the table and scattered chess pieces littering the floor.

"Don't walk away from me," she snapped, racing after him. "And you're certainly *acting* jealous." She glared at his back while he stomped through the living room, heading for the den. "Damn it, I'm talking to you." Overcome with frustration, she snatched up a throw pillow from the couch, threw it at him with all her might and hit him square in the back of the head.

He whirled around, his mouth hanging open, incredulous.

Striding right up to him, utterly fearless, she smacked his chest and demanded, "Did I *look* like I was putting the moves on him? Do I look like I wanted him?"

"No, right now you just look pissed off."

"I meant before, when you came back and Gideon was still here. Did I honestly look like I was flirting with him? Was I all"—she waved wildly—"all hot and bothered when he was here?" She smacked his chest again, snarling, "No! *I was not.*" But she wasn't through. She didn't want to have to repeat this scene every time he left her there with one of the others either. "Do I act all hot and bothered by Xander, or Sebastian? No and no. So, don't start accusing me of lusting after one of your buddies, you big, blind, hard-headed jackass. I don't feel desire for any of them."

"Only me," he whispered, staring down at her with a strange, bemused light shining in his eyes.

"What?" That put her back on her heels. Frowning, she took an uneasy step back.

"I said 'only me.'" He edged closer, following her, making her feel as if the tables had suddenly turned. Making her feel like prey in the sights of a dangerous predator. "Your body only goes haywire whenever *I* get close to you, when *I* touch you. And when I kiss you—" He broke off, sucking in a sharp breath of understanding. His whole demeanor changed. Before he seemed angry and jealous. Hurt. Now, he seemed, intrigued. Hopeful. "In fact, unless I'm mistaken, right now, you're getting a bit, ah, 'hot and bothered', wasn't it?"

"The only desire I have right now," she fired back, eager to divert the focus, "is the desire to hit you over the head with a few of Sebastian's books." She turned on her heel and beat a hasty retreat toward the kitchen.

Niklas shimmered across the living room, directly in her path. Dodging him, she veered around the sofa and toward the stairs.

"Ah-ah," he crooned, wagging a finger as he once again shimmered into her path, "not so fast." Before she could evade, he caged her in his arms. "You want me to face facts. Fine, I'll admit that you don't want any of the others. I've been letting my jealousy get in the way of seeing the truth. A mistake I won't be making again. And I'll also admit, and you will too, here and now, that you want me." His eyelids lowered until he gazed at her with sensual intent. "*Only me.*"

Her eyes flared wide. This was not what she'd intended when she'd chased him from the kitchen. Oh, she wanted him all right. Wanted the hell out of him, no pun intended. But one of them had to consider his salvation, his return to Heaven. And the loneliness she was sure to face once more in the very near future.

And it sure didn't appear to be him, by the look in his eye.

Why did he have to give her *that* look again? She couldn't resist *that* look. Oh, she was in trouble.

Deep, deep trouble, was her last coherent thought before he seized her lips.

He didn't give her time to object. Didn't give her time to call to mind the many reasons she shouldn't be doing this. He simply moved in, staking his claim. His heat surrounded her, caged her, seduced her. His hands eased over her, rubbing, gripping, molding her against his body. His long, lean, *hard* body. The evidence of his arousal pressed to her stomach. He shifted his hips, rubbing the rock-hard bulge in his pants against her.

Moaning softly into his mouth, she twined her arms around his neck and laced her fingers in his hair, pressing closer still. He'd firmly assumed the role of aggressor, laying siege to her defenses, decimating any good intentions about forgiveness and salvation she might have clung to.

Without warning, he shimmered them to her bedroom. *His* bedroom. She'd lost her clothing somewhere along the way. One moment, she'd been wearing the cheerful sundress and sandals she'd found among her new wardrobe. The next moment, she wore nothing more than a scandalous, lacy bra and a scrap of lace that, only to an optimist, might pass for panties. In fact, all the bras and panties in her drawer had been nearly exact replicas of this set, just in different colors. Heat had filled her cheeks this morning as she'd dressed herself, thinking that he'd conjured them for her.

He pulled back to look at her. His expression turned her knees to water. Heat filled her cheeks now as it was more than obvious he approved.

Slowly, he took her hand, lifted it and kissed each of her fingertips, then her palm. His shirt vanished, leaving her with a mouthwatering vista of deeply tanned skin and sculpted muscles. Niklas pressed her hand to his heart and held it there. His expression was so intense, she had trouble focusing on anything else.

He drew a deep breath, his chest rising beneath her hand.

That momentary break was just long enough for sanity to return. Suddenly, doubt assailed her. How could she make love with him? How could she hold him back, how could she come between him and his chance at forgiveness? How could she—

As if sensing her doubts—fearing them—he dipped his head and captured her lips, ensnaring her once more, not giving her a moment longer to examine her thoughts too closely. His hands skated up the sides of her body, pulling her closer. Giving herself over to the overwhelming need, both his and hers, she wrapped her arms around him and kissed him back with wild abandon. She might end up all alone again after this was over. But she had right now, this moment, with this man. She'd be a fool not to give herself this moment to carry with her.

The way he kissed her, the way he held her.

This time, there would be no stopping. No pulling back, no pulling away.

She slid her hands down his chest and a shiver of need swept through her at the warmth of his bare skin. She grasped the waistband of his jeans.

"Please," she panted against his lips, before he could deny her the pleasure. "Let me."

He cupped her cheeks, angled his head and kissed her with renewed urgency. But he didn't vanish his jeans, bowing to her wishes. Her fingers skimmed the velvety skin of his abdomen. His muscles contracted. *Ticklish*, a tiny corner of her mind registered, even as she tugged at the button, manipulated the zipper. Her hands slipped into the sagging waistband, and then beneath his boxers, sinking to cup his taut buttocks.

Groaning, he vanished his clothing. His mouth, hot and greedy, branded the side of her neck. His movements lost their smooth grace. He was rough now, driven by primal urges.

"You were supposed to let me do that," she protested, breathless as his lips left a hot trail from the corner of her mouth to suckle at her earlobe.

"Next time," he growled. His hands gripped her hips as he thrust his scalding, engorged, naked erection against her lace-covered womanhood. "I've already waited an eternity for you," he rasped between stinging nips and lavish suckling. "I can't wait any longer."

He lifted her in his strong arms, settled her on the bed, then crawled over her, covering her with his body. The look in his eyes seared her. Her nipples puckered in response. Her body ached. His erection pulsed between them, thick and demanding, begging for her attention. Unable to resist, she slid her hand down his ribs, over his hip, down and then back up the length of his thigh, marveling at the texture of his hot skin.

As she neared his erection, his breath arrested and the muscles in his abdomen flexed. Carly looked at his face, pleased with his stunned expression. An amazing sense of power enveloped her. She sifted her fingers lightly through the dark, wiry hair surrounding his manhood, and she studied his expression closely.

He held completely still. And he watched her. Oh, how he watched her.

He liked how she touched him. The sense of anticipation, the torment. She saw that easily enough.

She caught the edge of her lower lip between her teeth and, with just the tips of her fingers, she traced his erection from base to tip. His skin was soft as silk. And, beneath the silk, rock solid. Throbbing. Thick. So very, very hot. Her fingers traced him, skimming the head of his arousal. Palming it, she slowly closed her fingers around him and stroked him tip to base.

His eyes all but rolled back in his head. Smiling, she pushed farther up on the bed, licking her lips. Her mouth watered. How would he taste?

Carly pushed at his chest, forcing him onto his back, and then leaned over him, her intent more than obvious. His chest expanded on a sharp breath. And then he froze in anticipation. Her lips grazed the very tip of him. A raw oath exploded from his lips. Before she could taste him fully, before she could draw him into her mouth, he let out a harsh growl and twisted, shoving her back on the bed. He towered over her, his expression fierce. His lips found hers. His tongue plunged. Ravenous. His body pinned hers. His hands were no longer gentle. Her bra was gone. And her panties. She couldn't remember the exact moment they disappeared. Then again, maybe he'd simply shredded them in his haste to touch her bare flesh. What she did remember was the exact moment his mouth sealed over her nipple and he drew it deeply into his mouth. His fingertips feathered over her stomach, dipped lower, seeking.

Finding.

Oh!

His fingers slicked, smoothed, played, setting fire to her blood.

Gasping, she writhed beneath him. Mindless. She pulled at him, gripped him, scored his shoulders with her nails. Labored breathing became ragged pants as her hips mindlessly followed his fingers.

"Please, Niklas—"

His fingers slid through her curls, circled, slow, languid, so at odds with the frantic pull of his mouth at her breast. She'd thought she'd been on fire before. She'd had no idea what it meant to burn.

Now she did.

His lips left her breast, sought the other, and still he continued to circle her, deliberate, unhurried. He trailed nibbling kisses over her stomach, across her hip. He devoured her with his mouth, greedy and hungry, and yet continued to torment her with the slow pace of his hand. His finger would slip closer, so close to sinking into her, only to draw back.

Carly squirmed on the bed. Thrashing. Moaning. His mouth slid up her thigh, meandering, leaving a trail of fire in its wake. Closer. Closer.

She gasped aloud, nearly came off the bed altogether, when his mouth finally found her core. Oh, dear Lord, burning never felt so good.

He played his lips, his tongue, his teeth over her. And—God, yes—he finally eased his finger inside, circling, plunging. Dragging her closer to the edge. The pressure increased as he slid a second finger inside her, sinking deeper still. And then a third, stretching her, preparing her.

She was frantic now, sobbing his name.

He twisted his wrist, changing the angle of his strokes, deepened the intimate kiss, finding just the right spot, applying just the right amount of pressure, sending her screaming into a spiral of sheer ecstasy.

Niklas didn't stop there. He continued to lavish kiss after kiss on her, savoring the flavor of her nectar on his tongue. Never had he been so in tune with a woman's body. Never had a woman's pleasure mattered so much or affected him so strongly. This was his *tá'hiri*. His Carly. His female.

His *mate*.

Her release had been so powerful, it had taken every ounce of his control not to spend himself against her calf. But he wouldn't. He'd waited too long. When he finally found his release, it would be inside her body. He would give her every last ounce of his seed.

He allowed her less than a moment of respite, time he desperately needed himself, before stroking passion into her body again with his fingers, with his mouth.

When she was writhing once more, clutching at him and tugging at his hair, once he realized that if she found orgasm again he likely would as well, whether he was ready or not, whether he was *inside* her or not, Niklas slowly slid his fingers from her hot, drenched flesh. Her disappointed groan, the way she arched toward him, brought a feral smile to his lips.

Crawling up her body, he sampled her skin, savoring the light, musky sheen of sweat he'd wrung from her. Her lips clung to his, her tongue thrust against his, tangled, suckled his as he settled his large frame over her. Even lost in passion as he was, nearly wild with it, he braced most of his weight on his elbows, ever cognizant of the difference in their size, aware of how easily he might injure her.

He slipped between her legs, used his knees to widen the cradle of her thighs, struggling to hold himself back, determined to take it slowly. Now that he had her naked and writhing beneath him, part of him was eager to draw the moment out. He suddenly didn't want to rush, not this first time with his Carly. But she was so impatient, had been so tight on his fingers, urging him on, begging for his touch, straining his control. And he'd gone without release for so long. His body and his mind had never been so at odds. Make the moment last, just a little longer? Or plunge and ravish?

"Slow down," he ground out between clenched teeth, the admonishment as much for himself as for her.

"Faster," she argued, wrapping her legs around his waist, squeezing him, lifting herself like an offering. "Please, Niklas, I need you now. Slow can come later. I can't wait."

The head of his shaft skated across her core. She was ready for him. Oh, so wet. And so unbelievably hot. He shuddered, then every muscle in his body went rigid. The darker side of his nature took over completely, snapping his restraint like a single strand of thread.

Take. Claim. Now!

He grabbed hold of her knees, shoved them up and plunged inside her, all the way to the hilt in one fast, delirious stroke. She screamed in his ear, raked her nails across his shoulders. He gasped, staring down into her eyes, frozen, stunned by the brutality of that first thrust. Every one of his senses overloaded. Carly thrashed her head, arched her back, and clenched him tight, all the while crying out for more. His lack of control had somehow heightened her arousal.

Her eyes had glazed over. Her chest rose and fell in quick little pants. She whimpered, pleading for more. He'd never witnessed anything so sensual, so utterly erotic in his long, long life.

Her muscles contracted around him, once, twice—

God help him, she was doing it on purpose—and stars exploded before his eyes. Throwing his head back, he lost control of his body. He began pumping, his back arching. He slammed himself inside her, each thrust a precious ecstasy, a divine agony. Over and over. Deeper. Harder.

And she was right there with him, moving, holding him tight, demanding more. Somewhere in the dark recesses of his mind, he felt the connection—the bond between them—strengthen and intensify. What once had been important to him, if for no other reason than the binding ceremony they'd shared, suddenly became unreservedly vital to his existence.

Absolute.

He would possess her. He would keep her, no matter the cost. She was meant to belong to him and him alone. Unequivocally. Eternally.

He slipped a hand beneath her hips, squeezing her bottom, pulling her even higher to meet his thrusts. Her fingers tangled almost painfully in his hair, drawing his head down. Her lips sought his. Time stood still as their bodies melded, moving as one.

He grappled desperately for some semblance of control. Scrabbled tooth and nail for it. But restraint, control eluded him. Her orgasm was, even now, coiling inside her. He could feel it. Tightening her sheath upon him with every thrust. He could *feel* it. At the first violent spasm of her release, he threw his head back and roared. His own release was shattering, exploding from him in wave after wave of mind-numbing pleasure. More powerful than any he'd ever experienced. He arched and jerked as he poured himself into her. Deep inside her. Thrusting to go deeper still.

The world ceased to spin. Time stood still.

And then the gentle fall.

Bracing his weight on trembling arms, he stared down at her in awe, relishing the lingering shockwaves of passion. Every muscle in his body had turned to jelly. And yet, he was invincible. Carly's expression was dreamy. Her eyes were heavy with sated desire, her lips swollen from his kisses.

Still hard inside her, he shifted his weight, moving his arms until he captured her hands. Lacing his fingers through hers on either side of her head, he feathered gentle kisses over her brow, across her cheeks, along her lips.

And he started to move once more. Slowly, as if he had the rest of eternity to love her and intended to use every moment of that time doing exactly that. Lengthy, deep thrusts that left her blinking up at him in dazed confusion.

"I-I thought you already—"

"I did," he confirmed, smiling at her. His hips continued the gentle, deep roll.

"But you're still—"

"I am," he gloated, surging his hips a little deeper. Measured and easy.

Her breath caught in her throat. Her eyes widened. "Are we going to—"

"Oh yes, *tá'hiri*." He dropped teasing, nibbling kisses to her lips as his hips continued their determined, languid rhythm. "We are. Again." He nipped her lower lip. "And again." He nibbled her chin. "And again." Her hips began to pick up his rhythm. Her eyes began to darken with passion once more. He sprinkled kisses along her jaw as he rocked inside her. He thrust deeper, his lips tugged at her earlobe.

And then he whispered against her ear, "All. Night. Long."

Chapter Fifteen

Carly woke to the soft strokes of Niklas's fingers over her breasts and stomach. His warm lips and wicked tongue toyed with the pulse beating at the base of her throat. Yawning, she stretched, feeling decadently sensual. She was boneless. A mass of sated, languid pleasure.

"Good morning," he purred against her skin.

And then, before any niggling kernel of awkwardness could germinate, his lips found hers, teasing away her shyness, and his hand slipped between her thighs, stirring her passions. Again.

"Good, *oh*, morning." She sighed when he let her up for air. He nibbled at her earlobe. How could he set her body aflame so quickly? Somewhere in the wee hours of the morning, she'd lost track of the number of times they'd come together. She now knew his body better, perhaps, than she knew her own.

She was positive he'd mapped out and staked claim to every inch of hers.

"Sweet Christ, I can't get enough of you," he murmured as he moved over her, positioning himself at her core. His kisses deepened, drugging her mindless, as he slowly filled her. "I could happily spend the rest of eternity inside you," he growled against her lips, thrusting into her.

Niklas captured her cries of pleasure and ruthlessly

pushed her up one peak after the next, until she clung to him in helpless surrender and sobbed his name. Only then did he let go and hurtle them both over the jagged cliffs of release.

Luxuriously sated, she wrapped her arms around him, cuddling him close when he dropped his head to the curve of her shoulder. His big chest heaved against hers. A sheen of sweat slicked them both.

"You know, you might have warned me," she murmured against his hair.

"About what?" he asked, his voice heavy. She wasn't the only one who hadn't managed much sleep last night.

"That demons are insatiable in bed." She gasped as he dragged a calloused palm over her sensitized nipple.

At last, he lifted his head and grinned at her, unrepentant. "Oh, but I did. Don't you remember? I believe I said, 'Again. And again. And again.'"

Giggling, she batted his shoulder.

The kiss he gave her then was incredibly tender. When he released her lips, she smiled up at him and traced the line of his jaw with the tip of her finger.

"So, what's on the agenda for today?"

"Today, hmm. Gideon is following up with the coroner's office in the next county over. A warehouse was discovered with over a dozen—" He broke off, seeing the expression of horror that must surely have been etched upon her face. Clearing his throat, he hurried on. "Xander's going to be shadowing the nest, trying to find out whatever he can about what's going on there."

"And Sebastian?"

"He's going to work on the location of the scrolls

and, hopefully, pick up a lead on the Chosen One as well. But everything seems to change from one moment to the next here at Demons'R Us, so who knows what will happen by the end of the day."

Already, she could feel the warm comfort of this morning slipping through her fingers. "And what are we going to do? Work on a trap for Ronové? You know, I was thinking about that yesterday. I think, if we could lure him out into the open, maybe use me as bait—"

"That's not even an option, so get it out of your head right now," he admonished, his body gone suddenly stiff.

"But—"

"No! I will not allow you to place yourself in danger." Softening his expression, he dropped a peck to her lips, adding, "Besides, I already have plans for the day."

Before she could ask what his plans were, she found herself standing in the tiled shower under a hot spray of water. Niklas reached over her head and snagged the shampoo bottle. Within minutes, they were both covered in rich, fragrant lather, writhing against the shower wall, their bodies locked in a sinuous embrace.

A long while later, after a cozy breakfast in the kitchen, one that Carly had insisted on making herself, Niklas took her by the hand and led her from the house.

"What about those other demons?" she asked, eyeing the far edges of the tree line where they'd been attacked.

"It is safe. Trust me, I would never allow you to be put in danger," he said, his words warming away the sudden chill of worry. "We've reinforced the property boundaries with special stones and wards from Kyanna, Xander's woman."

"She sounds very powerful."

"She is. Far more than she ever realized, I think." He gave her a wolfish smile. "Xander is very protective of her. He doesn't like to let her out of his sight for long and is a real bear when it comes to her safety. Once we have eliminated the nest near here, I'm sure you'll have the chance to meet her."

She wondered that he didn't see the parallels between himself and his friend.

They wandered over the farm, poking into this and that, hand in hand. They explored the hayloft in the old barn, and the machine shed, and the overrun area fenced off for a garden. And they talked. Well, mostly she talked, and he listened.

"My mother used to have a huge garden much like this one," she told him as she bent to pluck a wild strawberry. "She worked out there for hours and hours on end, but she loved every minute of it. We'd can most of the produce. And she'd make jellies and jams with the fruit."

"You miss it."

"Yes," she replied simply. And, for once, when she spoke of her mother, there was no pain. Only a fond smile.

As if sensing she'd turned an important corner, Niklas became the insatiable inquisitor. By the time the sun peaked, he'd managed to pry all manner of information from her. Every highlight of her life had been laid bare for him like an open book. From her first lost tooth and the first time she'd ridden a bike, to her first kiss.

They meandered across the meadow, where Carly stopped in her tracks and blinked. There in the middle of an ocean of wildflowers lay a plaid blanket and a basket. She glanced to Niklas. He smiled, slow and easy. He'd been doing a lot of that today, she realized. Smiling. Effortless. Unburdened.

"A picnic?"

"If you'd rather, we can go back to the house." He gave a small shrug.

"No, this is wonderful. Perfect." She turned into him, cupped his cheeks and pulled his head down to offer him a tender kiss. Her fingertips caressed his face as she gazed into his eyes and whispered, "Thank you."

He tugged her down beside him, settled on the blanket, and laid a feast before her, smiling as she delighted over each dish. He fed her grapes and chocolate-dipped strawberries. They spoke of places she'd like to see. And places he'd already been. They drank champagne.

Carly caught him watching her. Again. His stare was so intense, so full of awe that heat filled her cheeks, and she dipped her head. "What?"

Without a word, his expression unchanged, he took the glass from her hand and set it aside. He lifted her hand and pressed light kisses over her knuckles. By the time he nibbled at the inside of her wrist, she was breathless...and naked.

Beneath the cotton-candy clouds and the baby-blue skies, with the rustle of grass and the scent of wildflowers surrounding them, he gently pushed her back and leaned over her, blocking out the sun. Niklas took her on a sensuous journey, savoring every curve, mound, and valley of her body, leaving no inch of her untouched, unkissed, unloved. Her heart trembled at the lavish tenderness he poured into each kiss, every caress.

He didn't speak. No words were necessary between them.

But the way he looked at her...

With such heat in his gaze. Such longing and hunger. As if she was something precious. Something he couldn't live without.

His wonderfully skillful lips wrung sighs from her as he sampled her flesh. The tender skin on the inside of her elbow. The ticklish spot at the base of her spine. The sensitive place at the nape of her neck that sent shivers quivering through her entire body. The curve of her knee. The inside of her thigh. He nuzzled against her belly. He paid homage to her breasts until they were heavy and so sensitive that the mere brush of his breath across their turgid nipples made her arch her back and whimper.

Niklas trailed kisses, alternating between playful and sensual, over her entire body. And when his mouth took her, possessing her deeply and thoroughly, she cried his name and trembled.

Only once she was sated and dreamy did he turn her over on her stomach and pull her up on her knees. He played the head of his erection along her still pulsing, slick cleft. Carly moaned aloud, instinctively arching her back, tilting her hips in invitation. In plea. Groaning, the first sound he'd made since beginning this erotic foray, he took his thick erection in hand and slowly fed it inside her from behind, filling her, pushing deeper and deeper, sinking all the way to the hilt deep inside her womanhood until she gasped aloud, fisting her hands in the soft blanket. The pressure was enormous. Hot. Pulsing.

He flexed, making his shaft jerk inside her sheath. Moaning, she tried to swivel her hips, but he grasped them firmly, holding her still. Holding her completely at his mercy. She couldn't see his face like this, but she could feel the conflict in him, feel him fiercely grappling for control, and it heightened her arousal.

His fingers tightened on her hips. And then he moved.

A slow rotation of his pelvis. Grinding himself inside her, as if seeking to gain every last bit of contact he could get. Reaching below her, he splayed his hand on her chest and drew her up until her back pressed against him.

Now she was truly helpless, knees spread, fingers gripping the sides of his thighs, relying solely on Niklas for balance. He wrapped one arm around her waist, low across her hips. The other rode high across her rib cage, just beneath her breasts. He tucked his chin into the curve of her shoulder, nuzzled her and purred.

Gilded sunshine poured over her naked flesh, warming her front as Niklas seared her backside. Drawing a deep, appreciative breath, she smiled. Happy as she'd never been before. All around her, colors exploded. More vibrant, more real than she'd ever seen them. The verdant grasses. The lush trees. The cheerful hues of the wildflowers. She'd never walk through another meadow without thinking of Niklas and this exact moment in time.

His chin nudged the side of her face until she turned her head. And still he didn't speak. His lips captured hers, and he ravished her mouth as his hips began to flex and rotate. His shaft withdrew, almost to the tip, only to return, caressing her tight sheath, made all the tighter by the position he held her in.

She sank her fingers deep in his hair. The arm at her waist shifted. His big, calloused hand slid across her belly and down between her legs. She expected him to touch her, to caress the nub of her womanhood to send her careening into the beyond. But he didn't do that. Instead, his fingers spread at her entrance, parting her, *feeling* where his shaft drove in and out of her over and over—*feeling* where they were joined, as his palm cupped her, massaging her at last.

He didn't simply make love to her with his hands and his mouth, with his entire body. Niklas *worshipped* her. She knew she'd never be the same again, and it was all because of this incredible, sensual, multilayered demon.

Her body took over, driving thought from her brain. Her senses revolved around Niklas as he continued to hold her mouth captive, and the touch of his hands, the caress of his body around and inside hers.

And when he finally allowed her release, when he finally granted her a shattering, soul-branding orgasm, Carly cried softly, and he drank her whimpers in. Only then did his body go rigid behind her. His arms tightened around her, almost—but not quite—to the point of pain. And he groaned into her mouth as his shaft jerked and pulsed, pouring searing heat deep inside her.

Niklas drew her down on the blanket with him. Still buried inside her, he cradled her in his trembling arms and wrapped his body around her. Weak, gasping, she closed her eyes and savored the moment.

For a time, she forgot about Ronové and the threat hanging over her head. She forgot about the relics Niklas and his friends needed to find so that some rebellious demon couldn't overthrow Lucifer and overrun the world. She even put aside her worries over the troubling way Niklas seemed to have lost his focus on returning to Heaven.

She only thought of this wonderfully romantic, whimsical side to an otherwise serious and purpose-driven Niklas. He'd tucked a daisy in her hair. And though he'd refused to read poetry to her or debase himself in any other equally sappy form of courtship, he'd made love to her with an aching tenderness and then tucked her against him, holding her as if he'd never let her go. They lay on the soft blanket in the middle of the meadow and watched the clouds drift by. Niklas rubbed his cheek against her hair, trailed his fingertips over her belly and pressed kisses along her brow.

The afternoon was better than any fantasy.

****

"Have you ever met this Asher guy?"

"Demon," Gideon corrected with a benevolent smile. "Asher is a demon mercenary, darlin', not just your average snitch off the streets."

Wringing her hands together, Carly paced the length of the living room. Niklas had left her in Gideon's care once more, although this time with a smug smile on his lips and nary an ounce of jealousy in his kiss.

She glanced at her watch. Almost six hours. What was taking him so long?

Had he walked into a trap? Oh, dear God.

"You don't think this Asher might have lured him into a trap—"

"Darlin', Niklas knows what he's doing." He stretched his long legs out in front of him, propped his booted feet on the coffee table and crossed his arms behind his head on the back of the sofa. "Now, why don't you come over and sit down. Watch some TV, try to take your mind off Niklas and just relax for a spell."

Why bother? She was too restless and worried. Relaxing wasn't even on her radar. For the hundredth time, she glanced out the window, peering unappreciatively at the magnificent streaks of magenta and orange snaking across the evening sky. Where was he?

Gideon belted out a hoot of rich laughter, his sparkling amber eyes glued to the TV hanging above the mantel. "Lord, I love this show." He chuckled once he got his breath back.

She glanced absently at the screen. Another sitcom. Gideon had been watching them all evening. He seemed to be trying to meet a lifetime quota of comedy all in one evening.

He laughed again uproariously. Though she'd missed the joke, the voices from the TV having been reduced to nothing more than background noise for her, she caught a glint of moisture in his eyes. He held his side as his laughter died to chuckles once more.

Adorable dimples. Dancing, amber eyes. A grin that could tempt the habit off a nun. The man was the very definition of sex. But to her, Gideon was nothing more than a sympathetic friend. Brilliant, utterly ruthless when it came to chess. Granted, he'd had a few more centuries to practice than she'd had, but still. He was a strategist to the bone. She'd never seen him in his *other* state, and, perhaps because of that exact reason, she often had trouble reconciling the fact that he wasn't human.

Gideon let out another roar of laughter.

He was, apparently, also a demon with a serious sitcom addiction.

Carly recognized a kindred spirit in Gideon. Well read. Insatiably curious. But always on the outside looking in. Besides, it was difficult *not* to like Gideon, at least if you were a woman. She supposed, however, it might be easy for other men to be jealous of him. Regardless of whether or not he claimed the title, Gideon simply was temptation incarnate. Every woman's sexual fantasy come to life. Every man's worst ego killer. It didn't seem to be a conscious effort on his part.

Gideon existed, and, therefore, temptation he was.

She was just glad Niklas now understood where her heart lay—or rather, where her desires lay, she corrected herself. Frustrated, she nibbled on a thumbnail. Why was it so hard for her to remember that what she had with Niklas was only temporary? Why couldn't she stop herself from wanting *more* with him?

Because of afternoons like the one they'd just shared. She harrumphed. How could *any* woman not want *more* of a man like that?

Desire and Niklas went hand in hand.

Where is he?

She glanced at her watch, rubbed her hands up and down her arms and continued to pace.

"Are you chilly, darlin'?" Gideon glanced over, an inquisitive frown wrinkling his handsome brow. "Do you want a sweater?" He lifted a hand and pointed at the fireplace. "Would you prefer I start a fire?"

"No, thank you. I'm fine," she replied absently. "Isn't there some way for us to call him? How would we know if he needs help, or if—"

"If Niklas ran into trouble, the last place he'd want you was there with him. I happen to like my skin just where it is." He fluffed a pillow and patted the cushion beside him. "You're going to worry yourself sick. Come sit down now. He'll be back before you know it."

Heaving a reluctant sigh, Carly finally conceded, dropping down beside him. "Take my mind off my worries? Tell me about this loophole."

He regarded her for a long moment, licking his lips as hope gleamed in his bright amber eyes. "I think I found a way around the curse. There's a legend about an ancient Mayan amulet. No guarantees, but it's worth a shot."

"Why aren't you out there looking for it right now?"

He offered a meaningful grin. "My being able to overcome this curse would be rather pointless if there isn't anyone left to touch, now wouldn't it? Relics first, then the amulet."

How selfless. She didn't know if she'd have that kind of fortitude. Instinctively, she reached for his shoulder, remembered at the last minute, and let her hand drop to the couch behind him. She was his friend. She wanted this so badly for him. But she was also a realist. She didn't want to see him hurt.

"What happens if there is no amulet? Or if it doesn't work?" She'd no more than tucked her feet beneath her and settled onto the sofa than the air near the fireplace began to distort, cutting short Gideon's reply. For a moment, hope soared. But then she sagged back against the cushion in disappointment.

Xander glanced at the two of them, flicked his gaze to the TV and then arched a brow at Gideon.

Gideon shrugged, lifting his hands up in an it's-a-dirty-job-but-somebody's-gotta-do-it motion.

Xander glanced around the room. Lifted both eyebrows.

"Sebastian and Niklas left to meet up with Asher," Gideon replied. "He got some intel on Stolas, and a possible location for Gusion."

"You got babysitting duty?" His tone and choice of words were laced with insult for both her and Gideon.

Carly stiffened, though she knew Xander's allegation of babysitting was essentially true. Niklas may have appointed himself her protector, but he couldn't be with her 24/7. He had leads to follow, as did the others. And, much as she hated to think about it, he had to feed. He would weaken if he didn't.

And yet, he refused to leave her alone, not while Ronové and his minions were gunning for her. And now this Gusion guy. Though she knew better than to let Xander's snarky attitude get under her skin, the way he'd phrased his question struck a nerve. She might feel sorry for him because of his voice, but sympathy only stretched so far.

Taking Xander's bad attitude in stride, Gideon showed no outward sign of reaction. "Aren't you supposed to be out killing something?"

Then again, maybe not.

"Movement at the nest," Xander reported. "A gathering."

That caught Gideon's attention. Dropping his feet to the floor, he sat up. "You think they're gearing up for something?"

Xander crossed his arms and shot Gideon a bland look.

Why did she have such trouble remembering that the others in the group were demons, and yet she had no trouble pinpointing Xander as a citizen of Hell? Maybe the old adage was true, it was all in the attitude. Carly might not have had much experience with the cryptic demon, but she was fast becoming used to his abbreviated, blunt, sarcastic comments and *non*verbal communications.

"Something *immediate*," Gideon clarified.

Xander gave a curt nod.

Gideon swore, pushing to his feet. Suddenly he wasn't just a friendly shoulder anymore, no longer simply a companion to pass the time with. He was dangerous. He was focused. He was lethal.

So this was her first glimpse at the darker side of Gideon.

It gave her chills.

"Do you think we could slip inside? Get in a position to hear their plans?" Cold intent dripped from his words. Gideon the strategist.

Xander seemed to be giving his questions a great deal of thought. Finally, he offered a small nod. His grin was slow...and frightening. Energy pulsed in the room.

Gideon approached Xander. "I've not been to the nest. I'll have to follow you there." Then he paused. "Damn it, I almost forgot—"

"Go," she urged. "This is important, isn't it? Just

go."

Gideon shot a telling look at Xander. Shaking his head, Gideon stepped back. "I can't leave you here alone. Dealing with one of Lucy's temper tantrums would be safer than what Niklas would do to me."

"Lucy? Oh, Lucifer." She answered her own question. "But—"

"Trust me on this," Gideon assured her. "Niklas would start by cutting off body parts...parts I hope to someday use again, God willing. He'd take his time filleting me, and then he'd drag my innards out through a tiny hole he cut in my gut. Which would be especially cruel." At Carly's confused frown, he clarified, "Sugar, I am, for all intents and purposes, immortal. I wouldn't die."

Carly clutched her throat as she considered Gideon's dire predictions.

"Darlin', believe me, if I left you unprotected, Niklas would have no problem extracting several pounds of flesh. And I have no interest in enrolling in the Seer's specialized weight loss program."

"He's right," Xander grated, clearly annoyed.

"Like you'd leave Kyanna if she were in imminent danger," Gideon snapped.

A muscle in Xander's check clenched, and he nodded, conceding Gideon his point.

Carly glanced between the two demons, very conscious of the fact that the only thing standing between them and what could be a vital mission was her and their deference to Niklas's wishes where she was concerned. "Then take me with you."

Xander and Gideon stared at her as if she'd suggested inviting Lucifer himself over for supper.

"I'm serious. Take me with you." She pushed to her feet, facing off against Gideon and Xander, two of the most formidable males she'd ever met. "I'll do exactly as you say. I'll stay out of the way. You'll get the information you need. And Niklas can't object. I won't be left alone."

"You don't think he'd object to us taking you into the middle of a nest?" Gideon peered at her in disbelief. Xander appraised her with a hint of grudging approval.

"Think about it," she said, rushing on. "The last place Ronové would think to look for me would be in the middle of a nest. I'll be with you the whole time. I'll be perfectly safe. That is, unless you doubt your ability to protect me?"

"Oh, don't think I'm falling for that, darlin'."

She could see it all over his face. Gideon wasn't going to budge. Not without help. Much as Xander intimidated her, she ignored Gideon completely and tried her best to reason with the forbidding male with the cold, calculating eyes. "Take me along. You know it makes sense."

"Niklas would kill us!" Gideon squawked, incredulous. "You know that, right? Don't even think about it."

Her nerves were a jangled mess. She didn't believe they'd even consider her request, let alone approve it. But she was just as determined that they go.

Xander grimaced. "He's right. Besides, they'd feel the guard stones you wear."

"Fine. But you two *have* to go. What if this mastermind has something big in the works? What if he already found another relic?" This was too important to them. And to Niklas too. She'd use whatever incentive she could to get them to go, but she hoped to high heaven Xander understood what she was planning. "Just go. I'll be fine."

Xander moved his head to the side, as if something unpleasant had just crawled down his spine, and he narrowed his eyes at her. Behind her back, out of Gideon's angry stare, she fiddled with the bracelet and ring Niklas had given her, slipping them off. She couldn't go into the nest with them on, just as Xander had stated. The other demons would know she was there the moment she arrived. When Gideon turned to face Xander, the better to argue his point, Carly reached up and quickly removed the necklace. With her first healthy dose of apprehension, she reluctantly dropped the jewelry on the sofa.

Smiling nervously, she addressed them once more, her meaningful gaze locked on Xander now. "You really should go. *Now*."

A tiny groove formed in Xander's cheek and that brief glint of admiration flickered in his otherwise stony stare.

"Stay inside," Gideon ordered. "Don't leave the house. We'll be right back."

For a moment, she thought Xander hadn't understood, or that he'd understood and chose to ignore her unspoken request and leave her behind. But at the last possible moment, just as he and Gideon began to fade, Xander smiled that frightening smile of his and thrust his hand out to her.

Grateful, worried about what she was getting herself into, she leaped forward and grabbed on.

Chapter Sixteen

The minute the room around her began to distort, Carly squeezed her eyes closed and sucked in a deep breath. Xander's large, strong hand closed like a steel manacle over hers, anchoring her. The bottom of her stomach dropped away for a moment and her head went a little light, like the first drop on a mile-high roller coaster. Her muscles turned to jelly, and then surged with renewed strength as the ground returned to support her. An earthy, musty scent assailed her a split second before she opened her eyes.

Dark, nearly impossible to see. Xander tightened his grip for a moment. She supposed she could view the contact as an unspoken form of comfort. Then again, considering this was Xander, it was likely nothing more than a muscle spasm. He released her so quickly she couldn't help but feel a little insulted.

Then that big, calloused hand clamped roughly over her mouth.

"Shhh," Xander breathed into her ear.

Nodding, she stood still, waiting for the rest of her senses to come back online. Slowly, gray silhouettes began to take shape. Tools. Small machinery parts. A lawn mower. Gardening tools. Bare stud walls. Dust. Cobwebs. Dirt floor.

They were in a shed of some kind. Xander released her and moved silently toward the door. Where was

Gideon? With a great deal of caution, Xander lifted the old iron handle and eased the door open just the tiniest bit. No light seeped through the crack. Night had descended completely outside.

"Are we on another farm?" Carly eased closer, trying to peer over Xander's shoulder.

"Shhh."

"What in the name of ever loving hell do you think you're doing?" Gideon exploded from the shadows behind her.

"Shhh," Xander hissed.

"For the record," Gideon whispered, "when Niklas finds out we brought her to a nest, and he's using our entrails as Fourth of July decorations—you know, the painful bit before he skins us alive and takes our heads—don't say I didn't warn you."

Glancing over her shoulder, she offered Gideon an apologetic smile.

"It's a little late for that," he snapped. He made a visible effort to glower direfully at her. But then he softened, adding, "Oh, hell. I'll forgive you anyway. Eventually. Maybe. If Niklas decides not to use my balls for a necklace."

"Shhh." Xander snarled something beneath his breath, something insulting and liberally laced with enough swear words to make a biker blush.

She edged around Xander, leaned closer to the opening and squinted out into the night. A light cast a dim golden glow on the yard some distance away. An old farmhouse sat on a gentle rise. White, two-story. Weathered slate siding. No decorative landscaping, no ornamentation of any kind. A straggling bush sprouted up along the house's foundation near a waterspout. A spindly TV antenna clung to the side of the house, reaching up into the night sky like a skeleton's rib cage. All the windows on the bottom floor glowed.

Carly pushed a stray strand of hair from her face as she peered hard at the ground floor windows. Try as she might, she couldn't see inside. Couldn't see any movement. Disappointing. "Why didn't you just shimmer us inside the house?"

Even in the dark, Xander's scowl packed serious wallop.

"Haven't been inside."

She recalled Niklas telling her a demon could only shimmer to where they'd already been. That must have been really irritating, having such an annoying restriction placed on someone who otherwise would have nearly unlimited power.

She leaned forward, pushing the door open a little farther. "How are we going to hear anything out here?"

"Shhh!" Xander took her by the shoulders and shoved her deeper into the shed.

He turned back to the door and scanned the yard. Gideon shot her a warning look and joined him.

Undeterred, Carly slipped around Gideon, excitement flowing through her veins. "Are we going to sneak into the house?" She reached past Xander, pushing the door open just a tad farther. "I bet the back door's not locked," she whispered. "Why would it be? After all, all the bad guys are already inside." She surveyed the house, scanned the trees. A small well house stood halfway between the shed and the house, slightly to the right of their line of sight. On the far left, a huge machinery shed loomed at the bottom of the hill. The large, sliding doors were open. Inky darkness filled the interior.

She pointed at the well house. "We could shimmer over to the—"

Two rough hands clamped just above her elbows and lifted her clear off the ground. Xander deposited her on her feet, hard, at the back of the shed. He bent close, until his nose all but brushed hers.

"Shut. Up." Each syllable was a slow, furious hiss. "You will not speak another word, not even to tell us the shed is on fire. You will stay *inside* this shed. You will not follow us into the house, or I will tie you up and gag you right now. Do. You. Understand?"

Carly blinked at him, wide-eyed, lips compressed. She nodded, unwilling to push her luck. She'd never heard Xander talk so much all at once. Judging by the way Gideon was staring at him, Xander's abrupt loquaciousness was a new development for him as well. She wondered if he spoke to his wife this way.

He released her and moved back to the door. Gideon stepped closer, reached out as if to touch her, as if to offer comfort, but then dropped his hand to his side with a sympathetic smile. Shrugging, he turned to follow Xander from the shed. Carly crept to the door and peered through the slim opening. She watched as the two of them crouched behind the well house. They seemed to be arguing about something, and then they darted for the back door. With the stealth of the world's best cat burglars, they slipped inside the house undetected.

Carly waited impatiently for their return. Minutes passed. And more minutes still. She toyed with the idea of slipping over near a window and peeking inside. It just wasn't fair that she'd gotten this close to an actual demon nest and couldn't get a peek inside. After her experience with the Master—Ronové, she corrected—and his minions, you'd think she would have had enough excitement of the demon variety. Apparently not. Her curiosity was killing her.

Xander's warning gave her pause, though. Much as she trusted him not to hurt her, thanks to Niklas's protection, he still scared her...a lot. But when another ten minutes passed, and she'd not seen a hint of them, her curiosity began to grow again. She edged toward the door, ready to push it a little wider, when voices broke the stillness.

Carly peered through the gap in the doorway. Her jaw dropped. They were hideous.

"Gusion said she's not to be killed. He *didn't* say we couldn't have a little fun with her before we turn her over though, now did he?" A squat demon with green scales and black horns chortled.

"I heard she's easy on the eyes. Wonder what else she's easy on?"

"Aw, now, why would you worry about something like that?" The first demon swung an elbow at the second. "You prefer 'em screamin' and fightin'."

Their companion, a tall human-looking guy with black hair, chuckled darkly. He turned his head. His eyes flashed in the dark, red as Hell's flames. Carly drew back into the shadows of the shed. A chill ran through her. They were talking about her.

The repulsive trio crossed the yard, their lewd remarks cut off as they entered the house.

Carly was reaching for the door again when a sudden explosion shattered the silence. Wide-eyed, she scrambled to peer out the crack in the doorway. A second explosion followed close on the heels of the first. Light flashed, and soon she heard the hiss and crackle she had come to associate with those wicked plasma balls. Xander and Gideon were in trouble.

She had to help them. But how? She frantically searched for a weapon of some kind. If she could only get her hands on something—

A particularly loud explosion rent the night. She craned her neck to see the house better. The back door of the house burst open and Xander rushed out, dragging Gideon's limp body behind him, blasting plasma balls over his shoulder. Xander was still in human form, but Gideon...Gideon was not. At least, she assumed that was Gideon. She couldn't imagine Xander taking such care with one of the demons from the nest. And the sight terrified her. Creatures poured out after them were anything but. Gideon's shirt was charred and smoking. And beneath, his flesh sported gruesome claw marks and livid burns. He was gushing blood, and his head sagged at an odd angle. She couldn't tell if he was conscious or not. But he wasn't making any move to help Xander, so she assumed not.

She grabbed the iron handle, but Xander glanced her way and jerked his head sharply. She drew her hand back, the warning look on Xander's face imprinted on her mind. One more crackle and hiss, then silence filled the air as Xander and Gideon vanished. Shaking, Carly tiptoed to the back corner of the shed, slowly sank to the ground, and wrapped her arms around her drawn-up knees.

They would come back for her, she told herself. They hadn't abandoned her. They just hadn't dared lead the other demons to her hiding place. Gideon had been injured. Xander had to see him to safety first. Then he'd come back.

It didn't matter that he didn't like her. He'd still come back for her.

He will.

Oh, Gideon! Please, let him be all right.

He'd become such a dear friend, going out of his way to keep her entertained, to be a shoulder when she needed one. She thought of his endearing grin, and the way he called her "darlin'" in that wonderfully Southern drawl of his. His penchant for sitcoms. And the raw, fragile hope he placed in an ancient amulet and the possibility of *someday*. A tear escaped her. Dashing it away, she dropped her forehead to her knees.

Please, let Gideon be okay. Tears clogged her throat. Death was no friend of hers, and yet it had visited her all too often.

Please, don't take Gideon. Don't punish him for being my friend.

No, she couldn't think like that. Couldn't give in to the terror.

She also couldn't cower in the corner like some frightened child, even if that was what she felt like. Xander and Gideon had been convinced that they might be able to learn something important by coming here. Obviously, something big was happening tonight. They'd been forced to leave. But she was still here. Maybe, if she was really careful, she could figure out a way to help.

She crawled to the door and peered out into the night. Biting down on a knuckle to keep herself from crying out in fright, she watched through a gap in the planks near the door as a cluster of demons crossed the yard and entered the house. Nine. All in hideous demonic forms. Petrifying.

Two left. Three more arrived. Five left. Six arrived. The farmhouse began to look like it had a revolving door. But she diligently wiped her eyes and kept tally. Until Xander came back for her, she'd just sit right there and count and listen. Just in case.

And she would *not* fall apart.

Niklas. Oh God, Niklas, I need you!

****

"Carly!" Her name left his lips as soon as he materialized in the kitchen at the farm. Panic balled in his chest like a block of ice. He didn't know why. "Carly!"

Even as he raced into the living room, he knew she wasn't there. He'd shimmered there out of habit. After all, this was where she was *supposed* to be.

But she wasn't.

He should have just used the bond and shimmered directly to her side.

Stupid. Stupid.

But the pull of the guard stones he'd given her confused him. They were there, somewhere. And yet *she* wasn't.

Just as he prepared to shimmer to her, the air near the fireplace distorted. Xander shimmered into the room, his arm wrapped around Gideon's waist. Gideon hung at his side, limp and unresponsive, his arm thrown over Xander's shoulders. Gideon looked as if he'd gone up against a legion of Lucifer's best and lost.

"Where the hell did you take her?" He flew across the room and grabbed Xander by the front of his shirt. "Goddamn it, what did you do with her?"

"At the nest, in the shed." Xander grimaced, shaking him off before lowering Gideon to the floor.

The air distorted again, and Sebastian appeared in the room.

"What the hell, Seer?" He threw a bag on the floor at his feet. "You think Asher is gonna keep feeding us information like this—good, solid leads, I might add—if you keep flaking out like that?" He broke off as soon as he got a good look at the scenario unfolding before him. "What's going on?"

"You took her to a nest? Son of a—"

"She's hidden," Xander said. "We got intel—"

"I don't give a good goddamn about your intel. You had no business—"

"She wanted to go. Knew we wouldn't leave her here unprotected."

"You should have told her no. You would never have taken Kyanna someplace like that."

Xander shot him a guilty look as that accusation hit its mark. "The nest has close to thirty with more arriving. They're going to perform a summoning. Tonight. Whatever this is, it's a hell of a lot bigger than we thought. Ashïek was there. He shimmered before I could take him out."

At the mention of Ashïek's name, Sebastian's eyes turned black. He clenched his hands at his sides as his nostrils flared.

Ashïek, a powerful general in Lucifer's army, was a slippery bastard. He'd gone head to head with Sebastian on more than one occasion. Only Lucifer's interference had prevented a battle to the death between two of his most powerful generals.

"I don't give a flyin' rat's ass," Niklas bellowed.

Xander heaved an aggravated sigh. "I'll take you, just—"

Niklas went still. His focus turned inward. A fresh wave of fear congealed in the pit of his stomach.

"Take care of Gideon. I don't need you."

"You've never been to the nest."

"I don't need you to find my woman," he exploded, ignoring the bemused glance Sebastian and Xander shared. "We're bound in blood. *Redimio Cruor Ritus*."

Niklas scowled at Xander, ignoring the dawning look of alarm now passing between Xander and Sebastian, and Gideon's pained moan. "You've done enough damage. Stay here and take care of Gideon."

"I got your back, Seer," Sebastian told him, his eyes still black. "I'll follow you."

Niklas skewered Xander with one last seething look, and then he turned his focus inward.

Using the connection he'd forged between them with dark magic, Niklas shimmered directly to Carly. He found her, there in the shadow-filled shed, crouching by the door. Tears rolling down her face as her lips silently moved.

He dropped to his knees beside her and pulled her into his arms. With a muffled cry, she buried her face against the side of his neck. Murmuring soothing sounds, he smoothed his hand over her hair. "Shhh, it's okay. I'm here. You're safe."

Relief—so overwhelming at finding her there, unharmed—flooded him, temporarily blocking the urge to light into her for pulling such a ridiculous, dangerous stunt. Cupping her face, he wiped her tears away with his thumbs. His lips found hers, and she stretched up, locking around his neck in a death grip.

His arms slipped around her as he changed the angle of the kiss. Emotion surged and buffeted him. How could she have put herself at risk like this? Never mind that Gideon and Xander had allowed it. Thank God she was safe. If she'd been discovered, the things that could have happened to her—

Behind him, Sebastian cleared his throat. Brimming with fury, Niklas released her. He rose and turned to face Sebastian, letting Carly scramble to her feet on her own. He didn't trust himself to touch her again, not right now. He'd probably strangle her.

"They've begun the ritual," Sebastian said. "Feel the power in the air surge?"

Damn it. They had a narrow window of time there to halt the ritual. And if it was Stolas this nest thought to call forth, then stopping the summoning was crucial. Much as he hated to think about leaving Carly there in this shed, he didn't see any alternative. It was impossible to tell how far into the ritual they'd already gotten. Seconds mattered now.

"Stay here," he barked at Carly.

"Wait." She grabbed his arm. "They've been going in and out of the house right and left since Xander and Gideon left. I don't know how many were in there to start with, but so far close to thirty have come, and only a few have left. And I heard a couple of them talking about summoning some prince."

Niklas swore again. Upwards of forty demons were still in that house. He wanted so badly to shimmer Carly away from this place. As far away as he could. But if the nest succeeded in bringing Stolas to Earth, there would be no safe place left. The Earth, all of it, would burn.

Xander shimmered inside the shed, right beside Sebastian. Niklas's fury boiled anew.

"Where's Gideon?" Sebastian demanded.

"Woke up and took off. Human form couldn't heal fast enough. And you know he's not safe around anybody in demon form."

Niklas opened his mouth. He didn't exactly know what he'd been about to tell Xander to go do with himself, but voices just outside the shed drew his attention. He signaled for silence with a raised fist and leaned closer, peering out the doorway.

"What's this about?" A deep, layered voice snarled in the ancient demon tongue. Not far away—five feet, maybe. Then they came into view. "I just razed a village near San Juan when Gusion summoned me. I'm missing the best part right now." The demon ground his fist into his palm. "This better be worth it."

"It's a summoning," replied another in the same language. "Glasya summoned me from Minneapolis. Wouldn't tell me who though. Hey, you think it's the prince?"

His companion shrugged.

Damn it!

Carly pressed against his back. She was shaking like a leaf. He closed his eyes and groaned inwardly, torn between the urge to wrap himself around his woman and shimmer her to safety and his righteous duty.

Chapter Seventeen

Carly peered around Niklas, feeling safer than she had any right to. All because he was there now. Carly couldn't understand a word that was being said by the demons passing by, but it wasn't hard to tell that whatever they said, it wasn't good. Niklas and the others bristled with aggression. She'd assumed they'd return to the farm as soon as Niklas came for her. It hurt her to think of Gideon. He must be in terrible pain. She wanted to be there for him, her friend, help him in any way she could. She'd heard Xander tell Niklas that Gideon had gone demonic and left—Niklas had explained they heal faster in demonic than in human form—but still, she thought he'd surely come back soon, and he'd feel better if only he weren't suffering alone.

Niklas glanced first to Sebastian, then to Xander. "We have to go in now."

"Stolas?" Xander rasped.

Niklas nodded confirmation. Seconds ticked by. Seconds they didn't have.

He pressed his lips near her ear. "Stay inside the shed. And, for the love of God, do not follow us inside the house." Despite the pressing urgency, he dropped a swift kiss to her lips.

At Xander's angry hiss, Niklas broke the kiss and rejoined Sebastian and Xander near the door.

Right before her stunned eyes, the three of them *morphed* into their demonic forms. Despite herself, Carly pressed herself against the wall, her hand lifted to cover her gaping mouth. She'd seen Niklas in this state once before, but it was still a shock.

Beside Niklas, Xander transformed into a nightmare. Red-skinned, black horns and claws, much like Ronové, except Xander's tattoos—Cryptoglyphs, she corrected—were much more extensive, calling to mind Niklas's explanation about a demon's legend, their glory being displayed this way. *Holy cow!* His Cryptoglyphs were…mind-boggling. And everything about Xander was *sharper*. Pointed horns. Sharper, longer claws. Jagged teeth. Pointed chin and ears. Piercing red eyes.

And Sebastian—

My God!

Sebastian shifted into, perhaps, the most fearsome of all. He grew nearly a head taller than the others, his muscles—everything about him—bulging to twice its normal size. His skin turned dark gray. Thick horns grew from the sides of his head, spiraling up and back. His eyes were black as coal. Monstrous fangs sprouted in his open mouth.

With chilling purpose, the three of them stepped out into the night. Unable to stop herself, Carly rushed forward and, clutching the doorframe for support, watched them cross the yard. Sebastian flexed his shoulders and shuddered. Massive, black wings unfurled behind him. They glinted in the glow cast by the yard light like some kind of metallic, feather-shaped plates.

Wings. The wings of Vengeance.

The three of them crossed the yard, Xander on the right, Niklas in the middle, Sebastian on the left. Unlike earlier when it had been just Xander and Gideon, there was no rushing now, no furtive dash. No, they crossed the yard like generals going off to war. Regal. Determined.

Deadly.

A set of demons stepped from the doorway, glancing up in the middle of their conversation. They froze for half a second, their mouths hanging open. Before they could turn and run, before they could raise an alarm, before they could defend themselves, Niklas and Xander let loose a plasma ball each, incinerating the unlucky duo where they stood.

A plasma ball flew from one of the second story windows, aimed directly at Sebastian. His wings curled around him like armor. Carly tensed to scream, fearing she was about to witness the first of them fall, but the plasma ball melted into a puff of harmless embers, fluttering to the ground. Sebastian shook the ash from his wings. Then, with a loud whoosh, those black wings stretched wide. He soared into the night sky. Carly lost track of him for a moment. And in the next instant, the demon sniper in the window screamed as Sebastian plucked him from his perch.

In midair, his great wings making deep, surprisingly slow *thwap-thwap* sounds, Sebastian ripped the sniper's head from his body with his huge, bare hands and claws. Sebastian dropped the sniper to the ground like a broken toddler's toy, already forgotten. Tucking his wings around him, Sebastian slipped inside the house. Though Carly could have sworn a lifetime passed during that heart-stopping sequence of events, in reality, the whole attack had lasted little more than a handful of seconds.

First Niklas, then Xander stepped over the glowing piles of ash still smoking on the doorstep. They disappeared inside the house. Explosions rent the air. Fire and smoke began billowing from the windows. The house shook, and the foundation cracked. Too afraid to close her eyes, Carly clutched the doorframe until her fingers went numb.

Please, please, please let them be okay.

A demon staggered from the house, screeching, his body engulfed in flames. Two steps across the yard, he burst into a puff of ash. Another leaped from the same second story window Sebastian had entered only moments before. He, too, was lit up like a marshmallow held too close to a campfire.

Demon after demon began pouring from the house now. Like rats fleeing a fire. Xander stood in a broken-out first floor window and began hurling plasma balls at his fleeing prey. Every plasma ball that left his hand unerringly found its mark. But demons streamed from the front and sides of the house as well. In the distance, they dropped beneath a firestorm in the front yard.

A dark, sinister sound cascaded through the night, and she glanced up. Sebastian stood on the tallest peak of the roof, flinging plasma balls down on the demons on either side of the house, laughing diabolically as his victims fell, bursting into smoking embers. The sight of him up there, fire-filled palms lifted to the night sky, wings spread, smiling maniacally, almost sent her to her knees.

Oh my God. Oh my God!

How could that be Sebastian? The rakishly

handsome man who'd sat on the kitchen counter and called Niklas 'dude'?

When the last demon had fled the house, and the yard was covered in smoking piles of ash, Xander and Niklas exited the house from the rear. Sebastian dropped from the roof. Before they reached the well house, the three of them turned in unison and paused. Holding their arms out to their sides, they conjured plasma balls in their palms. Slowly, they lifted their arms skyward. The plasma balls grew, built, burned white-hot. A dark chant rose on the night wind. Demonic voices. Demonic language. And then they let loose the plasma balls. The house exploded. The ground beneath her feet lurched and shuddered.

Satisfied, the three of them turned as one, morphing back into human form. As they strode across the yard toward her, backlit by the blazing ruins of the farmhouse, Carly was struck speechless with awe. The three of them. Formidable. Dangerous.

And God help her, sexy as hell.

Dashing from the building, she raced toward Niklas, preparing to throw herself into his arms. Fury rolled from him in waves. He caught her by the wrists, stopping in his tracks. Glaring down at her, he shimmered them back to the farmhouse without giving her any warning.

He released her as soon as they materialized, like one would after picking up a hot frying pan. Niklas stormed to the far side of the kitchen, putting the length of the room between them. She clutched one of the straight-backed chairs at the table for support, gasping for air. The room continued to spin, and so she dropped weakly to the chair and squeezed her eyes closed tight.

Blinked. Drew long, deep, steadying breaths.

A moment later, Sebastian and Xander shimmered into the kitchen. Sebastian glanced from Niklas to Carly. "You okay?" He dropped to one knee beside her, laid his hand on hers as he frowned at her in concern. Niklas growled warning, but Sebastian ignored him. "You're white as a sheet." He conjured a glass of water near her elbow on the table. "Drink, Carly," he urged. "Slowly."

She tried to comply, but her hands were shaking so badly she set the glass aside for fear she'd dump it all over herself. Sebastian patiently, insistently lifted the glass to her lips himself while he smoothed his free hand up and down her arm. Gentle and soothing.

She couldn't wrap her head around the fact that this gentle man, one who looked so like a Viking god, was one and the same as the dark, winged terror up on that roof.

"Good. Good." He set the glass aside and took her hand as he said, "Now breathe. Just breathe."

"Get your hands off her, Vengeance," Niklas snarled, whipping around and stalking toward them. He sounded like a wounded animal. A rabid, wounded, feral animal.

"Cool off," Xander barked, stepping between Niklas and the bristling Sebastian.

Just like that, Niklas transformed once again into the huge, fearsome monster that had stormed into the park that first night, ready to battle to the death. Xander braced himself, but he did not transform. Sebastian shot to his feet and hurried to stand, shoulder to shoulder with Xander, forming a protective wall between her and Niklas.

Fear filled her. Not fear of Niklas, but fear *for* him. If he hurt one of his friends, he would never forgive himself.

He lifted his hands, palms blazing with plasma balls. Galvanized, she leaped from her chair and darted around Xander and Sebastian. She rushed forward, eluding their startled lunges for her, and raced to head Niklas off. Without giving it a second thought, she launched herself at him. Wrapping her arms around his neck, her legs around his waist, she clung to him for all she was worth.

Pressing her cheek to his, she whispered into his ear, over and over, "I'm sorry, Niklas. I'm so sorry. It was all my fault. Please, come back, Niklas. For me. I need you. Please, come back. I'm sorry."

At first, he stiffened. His hands found her waist in a punishing grip. But still she clung, resisting his effort to pry her off him with all her might. She could hear Xander and Sebastian behind her, frantically urging her to release him and to back away slowly. She heard them trying to calm Niklas, reminding him that he didn't want to hurt her.

Xander even taunted him. "It's me you want, Seer. Put the female aside."

"Please," she whispered, ignoring them. "Please, Niklas. Remember the meadow. Remember how you held me." His grip lightened, and he stopped pushing at her. "That's it, Niklas. Remember how you kissed me." She pressed gentle kisses to his cheek and the side of his neck. "Remember how you made love with me? Come back to me."

His hands slid around, cupping her bottom. A deep purring rumbled up from his chest.

Xander and Sebastian went abruptly silent. Then, cautiously, Sebastian advised, "Ah, Carly." He cleared his throat. "You, ah, you don't want to be doing that."

Ignoring Sebastian, she arched her back, rubbing her breasts against Niklas's chest. He growled, low and deep. But *this* wasn't a growl of challenge or threat. Leaning back, she cupped his cheek in one hand, balancing herself by keeping one arm wrapped around his neck. He supported all of her weight in the palms of his hands. Effortlessly. His enormous erection pressed demandingly against her.

Staring deep into glacier eyes, she sternly demanded, "Niklas, you must change back now. Do you hear me? I can't be with you like this. You would hurt me. You must change back."

He blinked at her, confused at first. Denial. Resistance. He shook his head. But then his attention drifted to her mouth, to where her body pressed against his.

"Now, Niklas. Change back, now."

Reluctant understanding.

He transformed back, right there in her arms. Behind her, she heard Sebastian's surprised exclamation. Heard Xander's snort of disgust. She didn't care. She pressed her lips to his and kissed Niklas with everything she had in her.

Chest heaving, he eventually set her on the ground.

"I'm fine," he told her. Turning his burning gaze to Xander, he warned, "Don't *ever* put her at risk again. For *any* reason."

Xander appraised him for a long moment. At length, he conceded with a curt nod.

Niklas captured her left wrist, lifted it for his

inspection. His eyes slowly lifted to hers, and she cringed. To say he was upset was an understatement. For a moment, she feared he might go demonic again. Holding his hand out, palm up, he conjured her jewelry. Without a word, he fastened the necklace around her neck, the bracelet on her wrist. But as he took her hand in his and positioned the ring at the tip of her ring finger, his eyes met hers.

"Never take this off again," he demanded.

"Never again," she dutifully repeated. He pushed the ring into place, gently. Firmly. Niklas captured her chin in his hand, lifted her face and planted a possessive kiss on her lips.

Releasing her, Niklas faced the others. Stiffening once more, he spoke quietly to Carly. "Go upstairs."

Glancing over her shoulder at Xander and Sebastian, Carly shook her head. Xander was angry. Very, very angry. Sebastian looked as if he didn't know whether to laugh or swear.

"I'll stay," she insisted, turning to stand at his side. If his friends were going to catch hell for what had happened, so would she. It was just as much her fault as theirs.

"Damn it, Carly. Go upstairs."

Now she glowered at him. "I'm not going upstairs. I said I was sorry that I took the guard stones off. We will deal with this together."

"Oh, we *will* discuss that later. Now, go upstairs. Xander, Sebastian and I have much to discuss."

Planting fists on hips, she squared off against the three of them. "I'm not some child to be sent to her room as a punishment. I'll stay. I'll stand besi—"

"Damn it, woman," Niklas exclaimed a moment

before he snagged her wrist.

Without warning, the room swam before her eyes. She got that horrible falling sensation as he shimmered them to the bedroom upstairs. She was still fighting to regain her equilibrium when he growled, "You will remain here while I deal with Sebastian and Xander."

"Niklas, wait," she pleaded. "Sebastian wasn't even hear earlier. It was my fault. Don't—"

"Xander knew perfectly well the consequences of taking you to a nest. He would never have taken his own mate to one, he should not have taken mine."

Her mouth fell open. She didn't know how to respond.

And the next thing she knew, she was staring at the closed door. Alone. Her mouth snapped closed. She sucked in an outraged breath through flared nostrils. Marching to the door, she jerked on the handle. And jerked. The door wouldn't budge.

"Niklas!" Carly bellowed, slapping the flat of her hand on the door. "You let me out of here right now, do you hear me? Niklas! Sebastian!" She pounded until her palm stung. Desperate, she even tried calling, "Xander!" Nothing. She should have known better. Carly kicked the door until her toe throbbed, railing, shouting, "Damn you! Just you wait, Niklas!"

Chapter Eighteen

Niklas could hear her shouting, and cursing him, as could everyone else in the room. The sound of her small fists banging on the door echoed all the way downstairs. For such a little thing, she had one hell of a temper. She was going to hurt herself. Frustrated, he strode toward the table, intending to light into Xander for his dangerous stunt. Halfway there, he heard a loud crash and flinched.

What in the name of Mother Mary was she *doing* up there?

Grimacing, he pulled out a chair and took a seat, waiting for the others to do the same.

"Never again, Slayer."

Xander gave him a gimlet stare.

"You treat her with the same kid gloves you'd treat Kyanna with from now on, you got me?"

That managed to get a reaction out of the fearsome warrior. Both dark eyebrows arched. Eventually, when Niklas refused to back down, Xander nodded. Beside him, Sebastian let out a muffled curse.

"Where'd Gideon go?" Sebastian asked. Every demon in the room was an alpha, but Sebastian was the only one with any kind of diplomatic skills. Changing the subject before Niklas could take Xander to task any further was probably a good idea. The last thing they needed right now was to be at odds with each other.

Xander shrugged, not as in he didn't care about Gideon, but as in he had no idea where the Demon of Temptation had gone. And Mikhail was still MIA. Just freakin' brilliant.

"*Redimio Cruor Ritus?* A binding ritual?" Sebastian pulled the chair from the table, spun it around and straddled it. "Seriously, dude?"

In for a penny, in for a pound. These two had had his back more times than he could count. As he'd had theirs. He owed them the truth. But he wouldn't regret his decision, no matter how difficult it might make his life now.

"It's done."

"I get that, but *why*?" This from Sebastian. Xander, who had a mate of his own, apparently didn't need to ask.

"Because I had to." Raking a hand through his hair, he fought to find the right words. "I don't expect you to understand. Hell, I don't understand. Or I didn't at the time. It was just something that I—I needed do. I had to know she would be safe. No matter what happened. I couldn't trust stones and crystals to do the job." He glared pointedly at Xander but didn't push the issue. "Keeping her safe has become more important to me than anything else."

"Anything?" Leave it to Xander to cut straight to the heart of the situation.

"Anything," Niklas repeated, not batting an eye. The look he sent across the table challenged Xander to pursue that particular point. He'd made his choice. Nothing Sebastian said, or anyone else, for that matter, was going to change how he felt.

"She's human." Conjuring a soda, Xander

succinctly summed up his argument on the subject in those two fatalistic words.

"Do you think I don't know that?" Angry now, Niklas slammed the table.

Xander lifted a brow and took another long, serene sip of his soda. Heaving a sigh, Niklas leashed his temper. Point taken. In a calmer tone, he tried his best to explain his guilty conscience, and these jumbling, volatile emotions, to comrades who wouldn't judge him. He knew any objections they presented would be voiced purely for the sake of trying to help him. Because that was what they did for him. And that was what he did for them.

Brothers-in-arms.

Friends, whether they cared to admit it or not.

"Sorry," Niklas muttered. "I know she's human. I know she'll die. But there's a connection. One I couldn't shake even before I performed *Redimio Cruor Ritus.*"

"She's grown attached to you too, dude. A blind Garnoch could see that." Sebastian flexed his hands and tapped the tabletop. "Don't get me wrong, I like her. I do. She's feisty. But she's human. Not a demon, or a Halfling, even one however-many-times-removed, like Kyanna. Our world isn't safe for her, Seer," he added gently.

Niklas was silent for a moment. It didn't sit well, knowing that she could be in danger just by association. "I know that. Lucifer's balls, don't you think I already know that?"

"You lost your way," Xander rasped.

Niklas leaned back. Hadn't he been wondering that, deep down, since the moment he'd scooped her up in that park and carried her back to his apartment? Was he just using her as an excuse? Had she just been the catalyst for a choice that had been a long time coming? "I don't know," he answered truthfully.

"You lost your way," Xander repeated. Then he floored Niklas by announcing, "Just as I did. She will be your way back."

"How can you make this decision?" Leave it to Sebastian to be reasonable. And to not understand. He didn't have a mate.

Too bad his body and emotions where Carly were concerned were anything but reasonable.

And that was before he'd factored in his beliefs, his faith. Once he added in all he'd done over the course of the last two hundred years to redeem himself, once he'd taken into consideration the sacrifices he'd offered, sacrifices he'd given in vain, or so it would seem more and more of late, his faith had begun to falter. He could admit that, at least to himself.

But he still couldn't bring himself to view keeping Carly as turning his back on God. It wasn't the same. He could still have both.

Licking his lips, he bit the proverbial bullet. "You might as well know the rest. The bond is permanent."

"Holy hell, are you sure?" Sebastian conjured a stress ball. Rolling the squishy bit of rubber in his hands, he peered at Niklas. "I thought, given time, the *Redimio Cruor Ritus* wears off." He glanced to Xander. "Right?"

"Usually," Xander confirmed, eyeing Niklas curiously.

"I altered some of the elements of the rite. Actually, I altered most of them." Seeing he was going to have to take them through this one step at a time, he heaved a sigh and went over every step of the process, noting every crystal and every stone he'd used. He held his hands up, displaying the scars across both his palms, and told them he'd used a Bloodrite Athamé, one of thirteen sacred daggers designated specifically for blood-bound or sacrificial rituals, one he'd stolen directly from Lucifer's personal stash. Rituals that could never be undone.

And he told them of the scrolls he'd stolen from Lucifer's grimoire.

That last brought a stunned, speechless stare from Sebastian. You could have knocked Xander from his chair with a feather.

"Dude," Sebastian said once he found his voice.

"There's more."

Xander rolled his eyes and shook his head, and Niklas vehemently craved a beer. Something crashed again overhead, telling him before the night was through, he was going to be wishing for a case of something a whole lot stronger, but he resisted that particular temptation. He never went past his self-imposed limit of one can. *Never.* A demon with lowered inhibitions was a menace to himself and everyone around him.

"Something happened during the rite. I don't know exactly how it happened. But I can't see her aura anymore."

Sebastian went absolutely still. His mouth hung open, his eyes wide. Xander's response was much more predictable. He frowned.

"I can still see other humans' auras. Just not hers."

Sebastian stood up and began prowling the

confines of the kitchen. "There has to be a way to reverse this. A way to—"

"No." Niklas cut him off. "There is no way. I don't want to reverse anything."

"Are you saying you want to stay bonded to this mortal woman? To always have her there in the back of your mind? To always be drawn to her?"

"Giving up," Xander said quietly, appraising him with shrewd eyes over the rim of his soda can.

Sebastian skidded to a halt, whipped around to stare at Niklas in obvious shock.

"I'm not giving up," he denied. "Do I still want absolution? Yes. Do I still hope to find my way back to God's grace? Definitely! But Carly has come to mean something very special to me." He paused, licking his lips. No, those words weren't adequate for the emotions she stirred in him. "Something I can't explain. You should understand this, Xander. It's important to me that you understand, both of you. All of you. She's not a consolation prize because I've given up on redemption.

"And I'm not settling. I know she'll—" Sweet Mary, it was hard just speaking the words aloud. "I know someday she'll die. I know that I'll have to stand by and let it happen, there's nothing I can do to stop it. But being with her is something I have to do."

"Are you stepping away from the legion?" Sebastian braced his hands on the back of the chair, leaned forward. "Is that what you're trying to tell us? That you want out?"

"No." Swearing, Niklas pushed back from the table and crossed to the counter. He settled back and crossed his arms and his ankles. "I don't want out. Xander didn't leave, and neither will I. I intend to stay. I intend to continue on the path that I've—that we've all—chosen. But I'm going to do it with her by my side. I need you to accept that. Accept her."

"And if we don't?" Xander tilted his head, staring Niklas down. Waiting.

Niklas restrained himself—barely—from leaping across the table and shoving his commitment to Carly down Xander's ravaged throat. Niklas had accepted Kyanna. All the others had too. Why couldn't Xander accept Carly? But forcing the issue with violence wouldn't help. He didn't want to have to choose between his comrades-in-arms and the woman he'd claimed for his own.

The woman he'd fallen in love with.

Dear Lord! That admission sent a jolt of adrenaline coursing through his system. His eyes widened, and he went deathly still.

He loved her.

"I won't give her up," he stated. It would be one of the most difficult things he'd ever do, but if his hand were forced, he'd choose her.

"I hate to sound like a broken record, Seer," Sebastian spoke up, "but again, our world isn't safe for her. Even Kyanna has some defense against our kind. Carly has nothing."

"She has me," he barked. "Besides, our world *is* her world. The battles we fight are for people just like *her*. The innocents we save are *her* kind. I can protect her better if she is with me, with us."

Xander was silent for quite some time. Niklas was patient, though, knowing how Xander liked to brood. Eventually a nefarious grin curled the edges of

Xander's lips.

Sebastian took the bait first. "What?"

"Mikhail."

Niklas didn't know whether to grin or groan. On one hand, Xander had just given his stamp of approval, Xander-style. On the other, he'd reminded Niklas that, while Carly had met and accepted Gideon, Xander and Sebastian, she had yet to meet the most fearsome, the most antisocial, of them all.

Great. Just frickin' great.

"Tick tock," Xander said, vanishing his empty can. Meaning they had too much on their plate to sit around chatting like old women for much longer.

"Yeah, yeah, slave driver," Sebastian complained, softening his accusation with a half grin. "I'm headed to Michigan. After you took off, Asher gave me the location of a descendant of the Guardian of the Sword of Kathnesh. Asher claims the descendant should be able to sense the sword, should be able to track it. The descendant is *like us, but just doesn't know it,* according to Asher, whatever the hell *that* means. So, the sword might not be off the table after all."

"A puzzle?" Xander glanced between them. "Or a clue?"

"I guess we'll find out, huh?" Turning to Niklas, Sebastian grinned. "Well, lovebirds. Do you need me to beat you on the backs and congratulate you?"

Carly chose that moment to resume her pounding and cursing, stomping on the floor for good measure. Something else crashed. Sweet Lord, she was demolishing his room. "I think"—Niklas glanced at the ceiling, wincing—"wishing me luck might be more appropriate."

Laughing, Sebastian shimmered from the room.

As soon as he was gone, Xander pushed his chair back from the table, but he didn't rise. Tilting his head to the side, he pressed, "When she dies?"

Xander saw far too much.

Lifting his chin, Niklas drew a deep breath. "What would you do if something happened to Kyanna?"

Xander's lips compressed. "I'd follow her."

They were of a like mind. When their mates died, they would leave this world behind. The only difference was Xander, having committed the ultimate sacrifice and been given the forgiveness he'd sought for so long, now had a soul. Or rather part of a soul...the soul he shared with Kyanna. Two halves of one whole. When he died, he would follow his love into Heaven's waiting arms.

When Niklas died? There would be no Heavenly hereafter, no following his love.

He would find Oblivion and nothing more.

"Are you going after Gideon?" he asked, pained by the thought of eventually being separated from Carly and having no way to fight it.

Xander gave a terse shake of his head.

"Do *I* need to go after Gideon?"

Brooding, Xander finally shook his head.

"You think he'll come back on his own," Niklas surmised.

Xander nodded.

"Then I guess I'll hang here, try to smoke Ronové out." He pushed his hands deep in his pockets. "With any luck, Glasya or Gusion will tip their hand."

Xander glanced to the ceiling. He offered a slight nod, and a groove formed in his cheek. As close to a congratulations and a smile as Xander would get. And then he, too, shimmered away.

Squaring his shoulders, Niklas decided to take his time and walk up the stairs rather than shimmer into the room. He'd never dealt with a furious woman. Incoherent, occasionally. Terrified, usually.

Fury would be a new experience for him.

****

Her fist hurt. Her toe throbbed. Her palm stung. And her throat was raw from screaming. Damn him. How could he do this to her? She wasn't some naughty child to be put in a time out. She was an adult woman, capable of contributing to their missions. Hadn't she been the one to keep track of the comings and goings at the nest after Xander and Gideon had left her there? She hadn't cowered in the corner and blubbered. She might have felt like it, but she hadn't. She was responsible for her own actions and her own choices. If she wanted to take afternoon tea in the middle of a freakin' nest with Lucifer and all his cronies, then she damned well could.

A creak on the stairs warned her of his imminent arrival. Seething, she reflexively scanned the room. He wanted to treat her like a child? Then, by God, she'd damned well give him what he wanted. She launched the brush the moment the door opened. The bristles bounced off his shoulder, denying her the satisfaction of having drawn first blood.

But the act of throwing the missile, in and of itself, had been fiercely liberating. She'd never, *never* been one to throw things when she got angry. She'd never been one to lose her temper. Not until she'd met this infuriating, bullheaded, autocratic—

Aim better, Carly told herself, picking up a bottle

of lotion. She hurled the bottle and smiled maliciously as it slapped against his hip. The cap came off and white, creamy lotion splattered up his chest and across his neck. Lock her up, would he? A few inches to the left, and he would have been singing another tune...in a whole new octave.

"Get out, you rotten, tyrannical jerk."

Rather than retreating as any wise man would, he entered the room and slammed the door behind him. "Damn it, Carly," he snapped, ducking as a glass shattered against the wood at his back.

"How *dare* you"—she flung a vase, filled with water and wildflowers, at his head—"lock me in my room! Of all the—"

He'd ducked again, but water showered over him. More shards of glass tinkled onto the floor.

"You deliberately put yourself in harm's way—"

A hefty collection of works by Sir Arthur Conan Doyle met the center of his chest with a gratifying thud. Niklas sucked in a sharp breath, instinctively catching the book.

"I was trying to help." She scoured the room for anything else light enough to throw but heavy enough to bruise. She grabbed a tennis shoe off the floor, wound up like a major league pitcher and let 'er rip. "I'm not a child, damn you!" Carly shouted as the shoe clipped his ear. "I will not be treated like one."

Snagging the shoe's mate, she stood, chest heaving, her face pulsing with heat. He was gone.

That sneaky, despotic, arrogant, son of a—

Tempered steel wrapped around her from behind, pinning her arms to her chest, caging her. Struggling, she cursed him, calling him every dirty name she could think of. Niklas tucked his chin into the curve of her shoulder, pressed his cheek to the side of her neck and held on for the ride.

At last, when she was exhausted from trying to throw him off, when she'd depleted the anemic parameters of her cache of vulgar vocabulary, she stilled. Just to be defiant, though, she held herself stiffly, refusing to melt into him the way her body begged.

"You scared me half to death, *tá'hiri*," he whispered against the side of her neck, pushing the side of his forehead to the edge of her jaw. "I was so afraid I'd be too late. I couldn't lose you like that. I just couldn't."

His quiet, agonized words accomplished what no amount of brute force could. It defused her anger. Slowly, muscle by muscle, she relaxed into him. She turned in his arms and slid her palms up his chest to frame his face between her hands.

Staring deep into his ice-blue eyes, she tried to explain. "They needed to go. There was something very important happening at the nest, and they didn't want to leave me here alone and break their word to you. I didn't mean to scare you. I—" She broke off, eyes widening when she realized how close she'd come to telling him her feelings.

But she wouldn't lay that kind of burden on his shoulders. He was meant for greater things.

"You what?" He searched her face, frowning.

"I-I overheard two of the demons talking. They said I'm supposed to be taken alive." She swallowed, adding, "They said that just because I wasn't supposed to be killed, that it didn't mean they couldn't have a little fun with me before they turned me over."

"I won't let them get to you again, *tá'hiri*." He brushed the hair from her brow, tracing the lines of her face with his steady gaze. "Swear to me you will never, *never* take these guard stones off again."

"I won't take them off again. I promise," she vowed, smoothing her fingertips along his cheek. How it was going to kill her to let him go. "Niklas—"

His lips sealed over hers. The kiss was filled with desperate need. A need so jagged, so deep and consuming, she couldn't defend against it. Her fingers tugged at the waist of his T-shirt, eager to feel his velvet skin once more. Lifting his arms, he let her draw his shirt up and over his head. His lips only left hers for the barest of moments before returning to ravish her senseless. And, although he could have vanished her clothing in a heartbeat, he took his time physically stripping each article away. Slowly. Methodically. Fingers stroking, lips and tongue sampling every inch he unveiled. Seducing her with every touch.

Her nimble fingers coasted over his ridged stomach, skimmed over his hips, glided down the outside of his thighs. His jeans pooled around his ankles, and she couldn't resist taking him in hand. Every steely inch of his length was rock hard and velvety smooth. With a stifled groan, he kicked off his pants, swept her up in his arms and turned to the bed, impatient now. But when he laid her down and bent over her, she planted her heels and pushed against his shoulder, toppling him onto his back. Tongue tangling with his, she straddled his waist, rolling with him.

The engorged length of his erection throbbed, pulsing against her, fueling the fire in her blood. He arched his hips, rotated them, transparently doing his damnedest to slip inside her. But she moved with him, tantalizingly out of reach, prolonging his torture as she denied him entrance. His fingers dug into her hips as he battled to guide her. She gripped his shoulders, savoring the raw strength of him.

She tore her lips from his, only to skate kisses along his jaw, nibble at his earlobe, nip at his neck. She pushed against his shoulders and leaned back to stare at him from beneath lowered lashes. His chest rose and fell on deep gasps for air. His pulse hammered at the base of his throat. Sliding her hands across his chest, she slipped her wet cleft along his manhood, smiling sensuously at the agonized groan she forced from him. And she savored the power of his desire.

Now *this* was exhilarating.

His eyes were dilated with passion. Hungry. Fixed on her. Burning her. Following her every move. The muscle running along his jaw leaped and bunched. His grip tightened, and his muscles quivered beneath her touch.

Her gaze slid to his chest. Her hands followed. Skimming. Savoring. Mouthwatering muscles wrapped around his shoulders and ran over his arms. They flexed, bunched, and her breathing grew that much faster. That much more labored. Beads of moisture prickled along his forehead. She knew he was battling for control. She'd never witnessed this level of desperation from him before.

And he was losing the fight.

Intoxicating.

How close was he to losing it completely? How little effort would it take to push him over the edge?

Between her thighs, his rigid staff pulsed and throbbed. Ground against her, slipping along the drenching wet heat of her body. How long could she prolong this? His hands flexed on her hips, slid up and around, down, converging on the sensitive nub at the apex of her thighs. His thumbs found her, stroking and slicking over her, and she lost the thread of her thoughts altogether.

Sucking in a sharp breath, she reached behind her, arching her back as she braced her hands on his thighs. One of his thumbs continued to work over her as his hot, slightly-abrasive palm pushed, none-too-gently, up over her stomach and covered her breast. He tweaked her nipple, and her head fell back. Her eyes drifted closed. Her hips began to undulate of their own accord. Her quivering core slid over him, ground against him. Throbbing for relief. Aching. Hollow.

Niklas shifted beneath her, sitting up. His lips found her nipple as the tip of his erection came close, oh, so close, to entering her. But not quite. He pulled his hips back, wrapping his arms around her waist as he drove her insane with his mouth. And suddenly he was the one tormenting her.

Sinking her fingers into his hair, she moaned. She didn't care about power anymore, or about who wielded it. She only wanted him. Inside her. Now.

The thick head of his erection pressed to her core at last, slipped just inside her slick entrance. "I need you, *ma'ilc cho'ckta*."

She didn't know what those words meant, but the fervor with which he whispered them against her skin set her blood on fire. He feathered burning kisses up her neck. He anchored one arm around her waist and cupped the back of her head, dragging her mouth down to his. "Please, Carly," he whispered feverishly between soul-deep kisses, "let me in. Let me love you."

Why did those words feel so portentous, as if he were talking about far more than this moment in time?

In reply, she tilted her hips and took him inside her in one long, mind-blowing thrust.

His mouth fell open, his eyes rolled back in his head. A guttural sound escaped him as his arms clutched her so tightly she could barely breathe. She watched him, savoring his reaction. He filled her, stretched her, sent her head reeling and her body spiraling into ecstasy.

This was what she'd been born to do, she realized dimly. She'd been born to love him, love Niklas and no other. Wrapping her arms around his neck, she poured her heart into her kiss, stunning him immobile.

He pulled back, breaking the kiss to look up at her. Wonder shone in his eyes. And still she kept moving, kept the pressure building. She couldn't stop now, couldn't calm the emotion boiling through her any more than she could stop breathing. She rode him breathless.

His hands trailed down her back and over her thighs, pulling her legs around him, guiding her until she locked her ankles behind him. This new position left her vulnerable, completely at his mercy. Niklas cupped her bottom, rocking her up and down his shaft on a slower, steadier rhythm. She could still feel the power pulsing inside him, the hungry greed. But somehow, after that initial thrust, he'd managed to harness it, focus it. He suckled at the side of her throat, murmuring words in a deep, dark, layered voice, words in the ancient demonic language she'd come to recognize.

Moving so quickly she wasn't sure if he'd flipped them over or simply shimmered them, Niklas pressed her back into the pillows. His muscular back flexed beneath her fingers. His hips rolled. Deep, powerful. Sublime. Fiercely controlled.

Lines of strain etched his face as he peered down at her. His teeth were clenched. He held his body in strict check. His gaze was so serious, peering straight through to her soul. Oh, he was a sight to behold.

And then he began to move with determined purpose. She was lost. The words slipped out despite her resolve. Words she knew better than to say. Carly was helpless, boneless. Mindless with need. The first crest of her orgasm peaked, shattering her. Sealing his mouth over hers, he swallowed her screams and followed her over the edge.

Chapter Nineteen

Once his heart was no longer in danger of exploding, he lifted his head from her shoulder. "What did you say?"

She sprawled beneath him, unmoving, eyes closed. Only the rapid rise and fall of her chest indicated she was still in the land of the living.

"Carly," he demanded, pushing up on his elbows. He held her head between his hands, willing her to meet his gaze. He wouldn't let the fact that he was still buried inside her, and still hard enough to take advantage of the situation, distract him. Hope, golden and warm, flooded his chest, making it difficult to draw sufficient breath. Had he heard her correctly?

Had it only been wishful thinking on his part? He had to know.

"What did you just say?"

"Wh-what?" She pried her eyes open and peered up woozily at him. And then, it was as if understanding dawned. Her eyes slowly widened as her mouth fell open. She blinked, quickly trying to turn her head, trying to squirm away. "I didn't...I don't know what you're—"

"Oh, no you don't," he growled, capturing her chin, forcing her to look at him. "You said you love me."

She looked panicked, and vaguely ill.

"*Tá'hiri*, say it again. Please." Why he needed to hear it so badly he didn't know. He knew she had feelings for him. He'd already made up his mind that he was going to keep her. But to know that she loved him as he loved her?

His heart did wild cartwheels.

She stared up at him, lips adamantly pressed closed, her expression filled with consternation, for so long that he nearly gave up hope.

"All right, damn it," she snapped ungraciously. "I fell in love with you, okay? I love you." She pushed futilely at his shoulders, but he wasn't about to budge. "I slipped, all right? Now just forget it."

"Slipped?" Baffled, he stared at the bewitching, bewildering minx. He'd never forget the sound of those three words coming from her precious lips, not if he lived a thousand years more.

"Yes," she hissed. "But it doesn't matter anyway."

"Doesn't matter?" Shaking his head, he frowned at her now, pinning her hands to the mattress when she tried to shove him off and shamelessly using his body to hold her in place. "How can you say it doesn't matter? It makes all the difference in the world."

"Well, it shouldn't." She closed her eyes, but a tear slipped out.

"*Tá'hiri*—"

"No." She scowled up at him. "I know there's no future between us. But I won't regret being with you, Niklas. Do you hear me? The one thing I learned in this life is to never live with regrets. To tell the ones you love that you love them. Oh, I tried not to love you. Lord help me, did I try." And oh, was she mad about that. It was written all over her precious face. "But it was just no damned use. You wormed your way into my heart, and I haven't been able to pull you back out. So okay. I love you. There, I said it. Now don't go complicating things."

He could feel his expression melting. *"Ma'ilc cho'ckta.* I love you too. I want—"

Eyes wide, she jerked her hand free and clamped her hand over his lips. "Don't say that!"

"Why not?" Niklas mumbled against her palm.

"Because you can't."

"I can, and I do," he argued, shaking her hand off when she tried to muffle his declaration again.

"No. You. Can't," she insisted frantically. "You've worked too long and too hard to give up now."

Give up? Not her too. "I haven't given up anything."

"I refuse to stand between you and Heaven. Between you and God." Shoving angrily at his shoulder, she finally succeeded in making him move.

He rolled from her, dropped back against the pillows and pressed his thumb and forefinger to the bridge of his nose. Carly scrambled from the bed and darted for the dresser.

"This is ridiculous," he muttered, pushing up to a sitting position. He leaned back against the headboard and watched as she pawed through the drawer that he'd previously conjured full of lingerie.

Maybe someday, a long time off from now, of course, maybe he'd find the humor in the situation. Wasn't it the man's role to panic at the first mention of that dreaded four-letter word? Just now, however, confusion and hurt had too tight a grip on him, leaving no room for amusement.

He groaned aloud as her luscious bottom jiggled while she hopped and wiggled her way into a tiny bit of lace that passed, just barely, for panties. He should have kept her in bed and loved her into submission. He should have kept himself buried deep inside her and—

Turning, she scowled at him. "You just wipe that lecherous smile off your face and get those ideas out of your head." She wrestled a lacy scrap of cotton over her breasts, making them bounce and look especially plump, which in turn made his heart beat just a little harder. "I knew this was a bad idea. I should never have given in—" Her words trailed off, muffled beneath the folds of the T-shirt she got tangled up in.

"Come back to bed, *tá'hiri*. We'll talk about this in the morning." After he'd spent the night convincing her that loving him, and being loved by him, was something she couldn't live without.

Cursing, she tugged the shirt down and turned to search for a pair of shorts. The soft globes of her bottom distracted him again.

She mumbled something beneath her breath. He caught the words *forgiveness* and *sin* and *mistake*.

"Carly, damn it." He sat up. "Talk to me."

She kept right on searching, pointedly ignoring him.

He vanished the shorts in her hand, and the shirt off her back. There, that was better. If she wouldn't argue with him naked in bed, then across the room clad in mouthwatering lingerie would do in a pinch. Smug, he crossed his arms behind his head, reclining once more, and let his gaze wander.

Gasping, she stared down at herself. Scowling, she whirled around and snatched up another shirt.

He vanished it before she could pull it over her head.

"Knock it off," she snapped, grabbing another shirt with one hand as she leveled a finger at his chest. "Damn it, stop it. Just stop."

Seeing that she wasn't about to fall back in bed, he conjured clothing for them both.

Satisfied, she leaned back against the dresser. "I won't stand between you and redemption, Niklas. Don't use me as an excuse to quit trying."

"I'm not using you as an excuse," he snapped. Sweet Lord, he was tired of that allegation.

"Then how could you forgo redemption, how could you set yourself up for that kind of pain?"

"Pain? What are you talking about?"

"I'm going to die, Niklas. Someday I'm going to die. How could you give up on redemption, give up on forever in Heaven for something...temporary?"

Temporary? There was nothing temporary about the way he felt about her. This, what was between them, was forever. If anyone would know, he should. How dare she try to make this less than it was?

"I didn't tell you I love you to trap you, or to make you feel guilty."

"No, you weren't going to tell me at all, were you?" He climbed from the bed, his own temper surfacing.

She bit her lip. "No, I wasn't," she admitted, her soft voice cutting him like a poisoned sword.

He swore. Long and creatively. She turned back to him, her brows lifted.

"Don't do this, Niklas," she pleaded. "Don't, please."

"Don't what? Don't hope? Don't want a future with you? Don't love you? Too late." He paced the room. He wanted to go to her, wanted to shake some sense into her. But he didn't trust himself to lay hands on her, not just yet, anyway. "This can work, Carly. We can—"

"No, we can't, Niklas." She raked a shaking hand through her hair. Then she stormed to the window and threw it open. She filled her lungs before turning to confront him. "Will you age?"

"I can make myself look older. I could—"

"But it wouldn't be natural for you," she interrupted. "You could go back to looking like you do now at any time. But I can't. I have a shelf life. An expiration date. Sooner or later, my body is going to age. I'm going to die. I can't live like that, waiting, knowing the pain I'm going to eventually cause you. And I won't let you throw away all you've worked so hard for. I won't make you start all over—"

"Enough!" He slammed his hand against the wall. Every word out of her mouth drove barbed spears through his heart. "I won't let you slip away. Not now. Not later. I will find a way. Do you hear me? I'm keeping you."

Shaking her head, eyes huge and filled with tears, she wrapped her arms around herself and turned away. "You can't keep me, Niklas. You are meant for better things."

He could see her drawing away from him. He could see it in her eyes, in the rigid set of her shoulders. And it terrified him, because without her there was no future. No hope.

No point.

He'd had no experience with these emotions—the love between a male and his mate, the irrational fear, the unwarranted jealousy, the desperate need to possess—not before her. He'd never even been tempted to let a human mean anything to him. She held his future, his very heart in the palm of her hand. And she was throwing it all away because of some misguided notion that his salvation meant more than she did.

And he didn't know how to stop her. God, what he wouldn't give to be able to read her aura right now, to have *some* advantage. Some way to sway her.

Going with gut instinct, he accused, "You know what I think? I think this isn't about me, and it's not about forgiveness. At least, not about mine."

Her head snapped up and she whirled around, glaring at him. "I don't know what you're talking about."

"The hell you don't. This is about you being too afraid to love someone else. Being too afraid to let someone else love you." Clenching his fists at his sides, he refused to yield to the expression of shock and devastation twisting her features. He was fighting for them, for their future. He'd fight dirty if he had to. "You've lost loved ones. I understand that. I realize you're afraid to lose anyone else. But you're the one who said you don't want to live with regrets. Won't you regret not giving this a chance? Not giving *us* a chance? We—"

"Stop!" she shouted, pressing the heels of her hands to her eyes. Slicing her hand through the air in front of her, she glowered at him. "I couldn't live with myself knowing I'm the reason you can't return to Heaven."

"So what? You think once I'm gone *you* can just go on as *you* did before? Will you go back to living with your memories? Will you go back to burying yourself in work? Don't you want more for yourself?" Tears sprang to her eyes, but he couldn't stop now. He couldn't let her deny her feelings and her fears any longer. Panic drove him. "What will it take, Carly? Will you ever stop being afraid to let someone love you? Trust me, Carly. Trust *in* me. Give me the chance to show you that we can overcome—"

"Death? You think there's some way to stop it? I'm supposed to ignore reality? Ignore the way my body will change, ignore the pain, the regret, the anger and resentment I will someday see in your eyes every time you look at me? I'm just supposed to trust you on this?" she demanded. She paced across the room, jerking at the door handle. When it continued to stick, she pointed angrily at it. "You can't even trust me enough to unlock the door."

To prove a point, he flipped the lock with a mental flick, and waited for her to bolt. Instead of fleeing, she clutched the door handle like a lifeline and dropped her forehead to the wood panel, her shoulders slumping. But she remained in the room, and his hope surged once more.

"I didn't mean to make you feel like a prisoner. Look, I had to talk to the others, needed to make them understand that I've decided to—"

"No, you shut me up in this room rather than let me stand at your side," she cut in. "It just proves my point. You want to make these decisions on your own. But you aren't prepared to make *this* decision. And I won't live my life pretending the impossible could someday happen. You're old as time, and you've probably seen every corner of Earth in your pursuit of evil. But when have you ever actually watched someone you truly love die? That's what you would end up doing with me. Watching me die."

"Why can't you get past that—"

"Because I have seen it, Niklas. I watched him die, knowing there was nothing I could do. The helplessness. The fear. The raw grief. And knowing I was going to be all alone...the anger, the resentment. I won't put someone else through that," she snapped. "I won't put you through that. I won't let you put yourself through it. Not when you have more important things to worry about."

How had this spun out of control so damned quickly?

"That's just"—Lord in Heaven, she had him so frustrated, he was all but stuttering—"just stupid. People grow old and die together all the time."

"That's just it though. You won't grow old, will you? Not naturally. So, you know what? It's just too bad. Because that's the way it is. I'm making *my* decision. I won't let you give up Heaven just to watch me age and die. I won't do it."

"Carly—"

She glared up at him, her jaw set stubbornly, and repeated, "No."

He seethed. How could she just arbitrarily make this decision for the both of them?

Plopping on the edge of the now made-up bed, she scowled at him. "You'll get over this, get over me...and I'll get over you too. It's just the stress of the situation, the heat of the moment drawing us together."

"Is that what you honestly think? That what's between us isn't real? That I don't know my own feelings?" Niklas snarled, clenching his fists again and shoving them deep in his pockets. How could she discount what he felt for her?

"I'm not saying that. What I'm saying is that this, what's between us, is a bad idea. What I'm saying is that you've worked too hard and too long to redeem yourself to throw it all away for something that won't last. When you fell, by your own admission, you looked at the world, not as a wonder, but as a treasure trove waiting to be plundered. Now? Now you look at it as a responsibility, a weight hanging around your neck. Eventually that's exactly what I would become. And that would destroy me."

Clawing, suffocating pain sizzled through his veins. She was slipping right through his fingers. Raking his hands through his hair, he stomped across the room, stomped back. Her words hung heavy between them.

"You can't return to Heaven if you stay with me. You will earn your forgiveness, Niklas. You can't set it all aside, not for me." She pinned him to the spot with a look that was much too knowing. "You've never forgiven yourself for turning your back on God. Never forgiven yourself for all the things you did when you fell, have you?"

Her arrow struck far closer to the target than he felt comfortable admitting, even to himself. "You don't know the things I did—"

"And whose fault is that? You know everything about me. Everything. Because I trusted you with all of it. And you listened. But you offered damned little about yourself."

"Because my life has been all about death. For the last two hundred years, I've existed for the sole purpose of saving the world I ruined," he said, exploding.

"Saving the world *you* ruined? All by yourself? Really? You're a demon, Niklas. Not omnipotent. Not God." Carly threw words he'd once used on her back at him. "That's why you're so defensive. You can't forgive yourself."

"I'm defensive because you made this about me, about my absolution," he growled. "And you're trying to change the subject. We were talking about you and this ridiculous fear of yours."

"Is it really a ridiculous fear? You don't exactly have the safest of professions. You slay demons, Niklas. Literally. You could die just as easily, leaving me behind just like my..." Her voice trailed away, and she shook her head, her eyes suddenly haunted. "Either way, we're bad for each other."

Out of control. This whole conversation had spun completely out of control. He had to get them back on the right track. Somehow. He had to get her to admit to this fear she had. Only then could he get her to move beyond it and accept him and their future together.

"No, this is about you being afraid to love me. Afraid I'll leave—"

"No," she retorted, pushing to her feet. "This is about me letting you go."

"You've been doing that right from the beginning," he said, the realization knocking him back on his heels. "I fell in love with you, and all this time, you've been deciding it was over."

Her face went pale. "I didn't ask you to—"

He snatched up a book, hurled it across the room where it crashed against the wall and exploded in a shower of loose pages. "You love me. Damn you." He pointed a trembling finger at her. "You love me. But you can't wait to get rid of me. You understand me so well, but you don't know a damned thing about me."

He grabbed the end of the dresser and upended it, tossing it across the room as easily as he'd tossed the book. Gasping, she leaped back, staring at him as if she'd never seen him before while the dresser crashed into the wall, splintered and broke apart. And that, too, made him mad.

Damn her. Damn her for doing this. Damn her for making him care and then pushing him away. The fear in her eyes drove him crazy because, for once, that fear was *his* fault. "You're wrong, *tá'hiri*. I do know death. Intimately. For so long I've *become* death. I've become its greatest weapon. And it's become a black void inside me, consuming me little by little until I fear there will be nothing left of me. But when I touch you, when I hold you, when I make love to you…there's so much life, so much hope. The light swallows up the darkness. There is no death. There's no fear, no pain. There is only you."

"Niklas, don't—"

"Don't what? Don't be angry? Don't be hurt?" He faced her, throwing his arms out. "Don't take it to heart? Again, too damn late. *I love you!*" He slapped the flat of his hand against his chest. "I want something for me! *I want you.* I want to spend the rest of your life loving you. But that's *my* damn problem, isn't it?"

"Niklas—"

Unable to listen to another word, he shimmered

from the room. She'd ripped his heart from his chest and left it in bloody shreds at his feet. What more was there to say?

Chapter Twenty

Niklas paced the kitchen, clenching and unclenching his fists. The demonic urges inside him pulsed and shook with rage, darker and more violent than normal. How could she say such things? How dare she give him her love, and then brutally rip it away? Damn it, he'd devoted the better part of a century to snatching innocent victims from demon rituals and sacrifices. He'd saved souls. And forgiveness? How dare she lecture him on forgiveness?

How could she deny him? How could she deny what they could have together?

Judas Priest's "Painkiller" exploded in the room.

"Where have you been?" Niklas barked into the phone.

"Busy," Mikhail snarled back. "What crawled up your ass and died?"

"You talked to any of the others yet?"

"Yeah, Sebastian brought me up to speed. Hope everybody saved up their frequent flyer miles. No telling where the Chosen One's gonna pop up."

"Great," he muttered, suddenly feeling drained, and more than a little dismayed at the fact the relics no longer held such urgent priority for him. Not since Carly had tossed his feelings back in his face. Not since she'd made it clear she didn't want what he had to offer.

Defeated, Niklas pulled a chair from the table and dropped onto it. He propped both elbows on the table and dropped his forehead to the palm of his hand.

"Gideon called. Said he'd be back to the farm." Mikhail paused, shifted the phone. "Pretty damn quick would be my guess."

Niklas drew a deep breath and willed some of the tension to drain away. A part of him was still furious with Xander, and Gideon as well. They'd had no business putting Carly in jeopardy as they had. But hearing that Gideon would be back with them soon—particularly since he'd been walking such a razor's edge between salvation and self-destruction lately—well, Niklas hadn't realized he'd been so worried until the weight lifted from his chest.

He dragged a hand over his face. "When are you headed in?"

"Probably about the same time as Gideon. I got one stop to make, and then I'll be there."

"Fine." Niklas eased back in the chair and conjured a beer. After the day he'd had, screw his one beer limit. Right now, he'd be willing to tap a keg. "I'll see you when you get here."

He disconnected the call and immediately thumbed in Asher's number.

Three rings, and then a flat, "Yeah?"

"I need a favor."

"Favors don't come cheap."

"I'm aware of that."

"What's the job?"

"Ronové."

"You want Ronové's head, you're gonna pay—"

"I want him alive," Niklas interrupted.

Asher's bark of laughter was mirthless. And short. "Are you kidding me? Do you know what that demon is capable of?"

"Right now, I'm capable of a whole lot worse."

A heavy moment of silence passed. Finally, Asher sighed. "Where? When?"

"There's an old warehouse on the outskirts of Ridgefield. 1226 West Clayton. The sooner the better." Niklas tipped the beer to his lips, guzzled. "How much is this gonna cost me? You want it wired to the same place as last time?"

Another long silence.

"Not this time. I don't want money." Apprehension balled in Niklas's gut. Asher's only god was cold, hard currency. But he didn't want gold for this? Hell and damnation. Niklas chewed the inside of his lower lip when Asher continued. "Someday, I'm gonna ask a favor from you. It's gonna be big. And you're gonna give me exactly what I want, no qualifications. No questions asked."

Dangerous as hell.

Asher was one ruthless SOB with no loyalties to anyone save himself. A cutthroat mercenary who sold his vast array of services to the highest bidder, regardless of which side of Hell they resided on. Kidnappings, coups, theft—though never of the petty variety as only those that could pay exorbitant prices could afford him—extortion, assassinations and flat-out murder. Those morally questionable activities and more factored among Asher's specialized talents.

What's more, Asher could go where Niklas and his legion could not. He could pass through nests without anyone giving it a second thought. While a return trip to

Hell meant a certain, immediate, and extremely painful death to Niklas and his companions, Asher could swagger straight into Lucifer's hall on pretenses of "business" and no one would bat an eye.

And, depending on how you chose to view it, Asher had one more point in his favor. He wasn't squeamish. He did whatever it took—*whatever it took*—to get the job done.

Asher *never* failed.

Rumor had it he'd even stolen an angel right out of Heaven, wrapped her up in a bow and hand delivered her to Lucifer himself.

Niklas had considered using Asher's services to capture Ronové right after he'd initially saved Carly, but then discarded the idea as unnecessary. Niklas had thought he'd have plenty of time to capture Ronové himself. Now, casting a glance at the ceiling, he weighed his options as despair ate a hole in his heart. Now he just wanted it finished. It didn't matter what marker Asher called in. If Niklas had lost Carly…well, then, he'd already lost everything. What else was there to lose?

"Deal."

"Blood oath?" A white scroll appeared before him.

"Blood oath," Niklas vowed. He spread the scroll open and scanned the contents. Clear-cut. Precise. No loopholes. That was Asher for you. Satisfied, he pierced his thumb with his switchblade and pressed his bloodied thumbprint at the bottom of the parchment. The scroll immediately disappeared.

"He'll be there," Asher said. And then the phone went dead.

Shoving the device into his back pocket, Niklas

paced the kitchen. Every now and then, sounds of movement came from overhead. Absently, Niklas rubbed at the ache in his chest.

Memories assailed him. The time they'd shared in the meadow. The intimacy. Her expression when she'd spoken of her family. The pain and fear in her eyes when she'd talked about losing them. The same fear that had glimmered in her eyes when she'd told Niklas that they could have no future together.

She loved him, damn it. She did.

I know she does, damn it.

She was just afraid of losing him. Afraid he'd leave her as her family had done. And she'd somehow managed to convince herself that if he stayed with her, he'd never be accepted back into God's grace. Niklas slammed his fist into his palm, ground flesh against flesh. Gnashing his teeth, he stormed from one end of the room to the other.

Then more memories filled his head. Her voice, crying his name in the throes of her surrender. The expression on her face in those heady moments while their bodies were joined. The soft lines of her face as she slept, head resting on his chest, sated with their lovemaking.

No, he wouldn't give up so easily.

He wouldn't let her drive him away. Much as it abraded his sense of self-awareness, she'd been right. About some things, at least. She'd been right when she'd said he hadn't forgiven himself for the things he'd done after his fall. He wasn't sure if he ever would, for he'd done truly atrocious things.

But that didn't mean he couldn't change. That didn't mean he couldn't be what she needed. He wouldn't let it end like this. He was keeping her, damn it. No more second-guessing for either of them. No more excuses. No more denial.

He wasn't going to let her get away. Not like this. One way or another, he would make her see she belonged to him. That they were going to be together.

With renewed determination, he shimmered into the bedroom. Carly had drawn the drapes. She lay on her side on the bed, curled into a tiny ball. Her slight shoulders shook.

"*Tá'hiri*," he called softly, lowering himself to the bed beside her. He settled his hand on her hip.

She rolled away, scooting back against the headboard, refusing to meet his gaze. "I think"—she hiccupped, shoving a palm across her cheek—"we've said all that needs to be said."

"Not even close." He slid closer, then stopped, frustrated when she slid farther away. At this rate, she was going to end up on the floor. Holding his palms up, he motioned his acquiescence. "Okay, I won't come any closer. Just listen, all right?"

"Please, please don't do this, Niklas. Don't make this any more difficult than it already is."

He conjured a box of Kleenex and offered it to her. She snatched one out and pressed it to her nose as she accepted the box with her free hand.

"I won't let you go like this, *tá'hiri*." He clenched his hands into fists on his lap to keep from reaching for her. And he deliberately kept his voice calm and gentle, but oh so determined. "I refuse to believe that God would be so cruel as to give you to me, only to yank you away like this."

"God? God didn't—" She sputtered, gaping at him

through wide, red-rimmed, swollen eyes.

"Yes, He did," he argued. "He works in mysterious ways, remember? I believe He gave you to me. I'm meant to protect you. To keep you safe. You are my mate. But more than that, I'm meant to cherish you. And to love you."

"Oh, don't twist this around." She sobbed, burying her face in her hands.

"What if *you* are my second chance, *tá'hiri*? What if you're His reward for all I've done, all the lives I've saved and all the good I've done since becoming Earthbound? Would you deny me that?"

That gave her pause. Hope soared, only to smash against the hard wall of her stubborn denial. Shaking her head, she mumbled against her palms, "You're only seeing what you want to see. You're not being fair. How can you—"

He snatched her hands from her face and held her wrists. "Would you stop being so damn hardheaded?"

How he wanted to shake her.

"I won't give you up." He glared into her eyes, fierce. Unbending. "You are mine, and I *won't* lose you—" Niklas felt a familiar chill skate up the back of his neck. Carly's eyes went wide, and she let out a bloodcurdling scream.

Heaving a frustrated sigh, Niklas barked over his shoulder, "Couldn't you wait for me in the kitchen?"

Mikhail's response wasn't exactly fit for polite company.

Thankfully, Carly had ceased screaming. But her mouth continued to hang open. And she hadn't blinked.

"Breathe," he reminded her, clamping down on the urge to roll his eyes.

He lifted her chin with the back of his knuckle to close her mouth before twisting around to glare at Mikhail. "As you can see, I'm a little busy—sweet Christ, couldn't you have at least stopped by your own room long enough to take a shower and clean up?"

Mikhail appeared to glower at him. Forbidding. Deadly. Then again, that was Mikhail's normal expression. Easily closing in on seven feet tall, Mikhail's frame was packed with lean muscle. Bald. Tattooed. Heavily scarred from a battle with a nest of Ralsha Demons, acid-spitting, bat-like creatures covered with pus pockets filled with poison. His clothing was charred...and still smoking in places. Blood splattered his face, neck and chest. His right hand was liberally coated with viscous fluid that slowly dripped onto the floor. He looked as if he were fresh from the battle.

Niklas sighed. At least he'd come in human form.

Mikhail opened his mouth to reply, no doubt with another offensive, provoking comment, when Niklas's phone began to ring. Mercenary's "Endless Fall."

"Damn, that was fast." At Mikhail's lifted eyebrow, Niklas absently remarked, "I contracted Asher to bring Ronové in. If I'd known he'd work so quickly, I'd have contracted him way before now."

Carly slid off the bed and eased closer to the door. Cursing, Niklas shimmered to her side and latched on to her wrist as he flipped the phone to his ear. "Yeah?"

"The package has been delivered. Sorry, I'm fresh out of bows."

"We'll be right there."

Turning his focus to Mikhail, he shoved the phone into his pocket. "Asher has Ronové at the old warehouse on the outskirts of Ridgefield. Call the others and have them meet us there."

Mikhail's frosty gaze swept to Carly, then fell to where Niklas held her wrist firmly manacled in his hand. One eyebrow slowly arched. He let out a long, slow breath. And then he disappeared.

"Wh-who was that?"

"Mikhail."

"War, right?" Her voice shook, and Niklas could have kicked Mikhail for his tactless entrance.

"War," he confirmed.

Drawing an unsteady breath, she tugged at her wrist. He refused to relinquish it. Pulling her around to face him, he anchored a hand on her waist. She opened her mouth to protest, but he quickly sealed his lips over hers.

But she was ready for this tactic and jerked her head back before he could sweep her away on a rising tide of passion.

"Niklas, that's not going to change my mind," she warned, shoving at his chest. But he was undaunted. He released her wrist, sank his fingers into her hair, and cupped the back of her head, holding her still for his ruthless invasion.

Her mouth clamped tight. He nibbled. He teased. He feathered kisses across her lips, coaxing them to soften, tempting them to open. The moment she acquiesced, he swept his tongue inside her mouth and poured every ounce of emotion boiling inside him into his kiss.

Before long, she clung to him, kissing him back with equal fervor. Soon, they were both breathless and needy. One heartbeat away from falling back into bed.

Reluctant, Niklas drew back. Cupping her cheeks, he stared deep into her beguiling eyes, pleased to see his kiss had left her bemused. "This isn't over, Carly. *We* aren't over." He couldn't resist one last, intense brush of his lips against hers. "I. Will. Not. Lose. You."

****

Carly rubbed trembling hands up and down her arms. That had gone wrong. All wrong. And now, somehow, he'd managed to shake her resolve. And who could blame her? She couldn't think straight when he kissed her like that.

What if you are my second chance, tá'hiri? *What if you're His reward for all I've done, all the lives I've saved and all the good I've done since becoming Earthbound? Would you deny me that?*

She tried to tell herself that he'd only said those things to get his way. But it was difficult to ignore his arguments, especially when they gave her exactly what *she* wanted as well.

Damn it. He didn't fight fair.

And now here she was, more confused than ever. What if he was right?

She wrenched the door open, tromped down the stairs and made a beeline for the kitchen. Tea. She needed a nice, strong cup of tea and a good book. That always settled her. She'd read for a while, let her brain clear out and her blood cool and then she'd be better able to consider the situation.

In short order, she curled up on the sofa with a suspense novel and a cup of herbal tea. It didn't take long to realize her usual escape just wasn't going to cut it. Already on chapter three, she couldn't remember anything she'd read. She closed the book with a huff and picked up her tea.

Ugh, too sweet.

She must not have been paying attention to how much sugar she'd dumped in.

Dissatisfied, restless, she set the cup aside as well and pushed to her feet. Prowling around the living room, she debated whether it would be a good idea to go for a walk. She ought to be safe enough. After all, there were numerous ward stones scattered throughout the grounds. And they'd already captured Ronové.

Surely, it must be safe. Niklas hadn't left a babysitter with her this time. Did she dare risk it?

Making up her mind, she strode toward the kitchen, her goal the back door. She made it halfway across the room when the air in the corner distorted. She paused, thinking perhaps Niklas had changed his mind about having someone stay with her. Hopefully, he'd sent Sebastian. She wasn't in the mood to put up with Xander and his sullen stares and uncomfortable silences. And Mikhail was just too damn scary.

Maybe Gideon had come back—

The tall, blond rock star from the woods solidified.

Gusion!

His expression was distinctly pained, and he looked a bit green around the gills. But he was there, inside the farmhouse. Fierce. Determined.

Carly's eyes went wide as he smiled grimly and took a step toward her. She raced across the living room, anxious to put as much space between them as she could, as she scanned the room for something to defend herself with. Her eyes lit on the teacup. She hurled the still steaming cup at his head. Hot liquid splashed over him, and he howled. The lamp soon followed the cup, as did the book and the end table. She didn't waste her breath screaming. Instead, she pivoted to run.

But he was already there. A brutal hand clamped onto her shoulder and spun her around, right into a huge fist. Searing pain exploded along her jaw. And then her world went dark.

Chapter Twenty-One

Niklas shimmered inside the warehouse. Mikhail materialized at his side a spare moment later. Dust motes floated in the air around them. Anemic shafts of light filtered down from broken, dingy windows some twenty feet up along the west wall. Spotlighted in one of those beams of light, bound to an old, metal chair bolted to the floor, was a beaten and battered Ronové.

Once again, Niklas marveled at how quickly Asher had accomplished a task that would have put most other demons on the wrong side of Oblivion.

Asher lounged against a wall a short distance away, muscular tattooed arms and chunky biker boots crossed, a distinctly bored expression on his strong face. A face, Niklas was sure, that many a female had fallen victim to, tossing her virtue carelessly at his feet for nothing more than a smoldering glance or one of Asher's infamous, irreverent grins. He'd cut his hair since the last time Niklas has seen him. Of course, that had been some thirty years ago. His customary ponytail had been replaced by a close-cropped military cut. He sported a trimmed goatee now as well. His mocha-colored skin glistened with a fine sheen of sweat. His dark brown eyes were remote. Chilly. A long gash on his forearm looked new, but was healing rapidly, as was a charred burn on his thigh.

Though he'd assumed an air of lazy indolence,

everything about him from his broad shoulders to his narrow hips, from his toned physique to his military-grade, black fatigues screamed predatory mercenary ready to spring into action at the drop of a hat.

Niklas glanced at Ronové again. Something suddenly struck him as odd. Ronové seemed to have been captured and frozen in the middle of transforming, trapped somewhere between human and demon form. Overall, he'd retained the shape of a man, and yet his horns, fangs, and claws were visible. Niklas hadn't realized that was even possible.

"How are you containing him?" Niklas asked as he and Mikhail approached Asher. "And how are you keeping him in human form? Or rather, semi-human?"

Asher pushed away from the wall and tossed a small glint of silver across the distance. Instinctively, Niklas caught the projectile. He turned his hand over and examined the small skeleton key.

"Don't take the cuffs off unless you're planning on letting him loose." Asher fingered the long pink strip of scar tissue—a freshly healed cut—over his right eyebrow. He shot a narrow-eyed glare in Ronové's direction. "I'd just kill the SOB and have it over with if I were you though."

"Binding cuffs?" He'd heard rumors of such things, but he'd assumed they were nothing more than myth. He, of all people, should have known better than to assume myth did not equal reality. Niklas dropped the key into his pocket.

Asher gave a brief nod. "They're unbreakable and restrict his abilities. While he has them on, he won't be able to shimmer, create plasma balls or transform."

"How'd you capture him mid transformation?" His

puzzled gaze flicked to the still unconscious Ronové.

Asher just smiled. Wholly evil. Wholly unrepentant.

"Uh-huh," Niklas murmured. "What's he dosed with?"

The sooner they brought him back to consciousness, the sooner he'd get his answers. Certain venoms affected a demon's system like poison, while others worked as a sedative. With a guy like Asher, you never knew what to expect.

"Nothing," Asher gloated. Holding his hands up, he flexed his fists, and examined his scraped and swollen knuckles. "If I wasn't such a greedy demon, I might have said this job was on the house. I rather enjoyed myself."

"Still could," Niklas remarked absently, his attention already on the demon cuffed to the chair. By the time Niklas was through with him, Ronové would be spilling every secret and tidbit of info rattling around in that primitive, useless brain.

"I didn't enjoy myself *that* much."

Though he was anxious to begin questioning Ronové, Niklas couldn't help but admire Asher's efficiency, not to mention his work ethic. "I know Xander mentioned this to you before, but I'm suddenly feeling the need to extend another invitation. Anytime you want to join our ranks—"

Asher held a hand up. "Appreciate the offer, but I work better alone."

"All the same, consider it a standing offer."

Asher dipped his chin once. "Don't forget our agreement."

"I won't," Niklas assured him, ignoring the

speculative glance Mikhail sent his way.

Asher's head tilted. His focus seemed to turn inward. And yet, he appeared hyperaware of his surroundings. "And that's my cue," he murmured a split second before he vanished.

Across the room, the air distorted. Xander, Sebastian and Gideon suddenly appeared. *Ah, yes.* Another of the mercenary's little quirks, Niklas recalled. Crowds made Asher twitchy.

Gideon scanned the area before returning to Niklas. "Carly?"

"She's at the farm. Now that we have Ronové, she'll be safe. I didn't want her near this."

Sebastian let out a loud, impressed whistle as soon as he noticed Ronové. "Sweet!" Chuckling, he rubbed his hands together in anticipation as the five of them converged on Ronové.

Niklas conjured a bucket of ice-cold water and took great pleasure in tossing it, bucket and all, in Ronové's face. Ronové came instantly awake, spitting and swearing.

"Arghh," he bellowed and wrenched on the cuffs, but, true to Asher's word, they didn't budge. "I'm gonna cut off your balls and shove them down your throat. I'm gonna—" He jerked violently, doing his damnedest to rip the chair from the floor. It didn't budge either.

Niklas snapped Ronové's head back and to the side with the back of his hand. Blood sprayed across Sebastian's white T-shirt. Sebastian didn't seem to mind. "What you're gonna do is answer my questions, you skeezy SOB."

"Fuck off." Ronové spit a fang and a mouthful of

blood at Niklas, who agilely dodged to the side at the last moment.

Mikhail smiled, evil incarnate, as he popped his knuckles. "I was hoping you'd say that."

Mikhail set to work on Ronové, not the brutal beating one might expect, but a subtle application of pain in all the right places, slowly straining tendons until they tore, leisurely exerting pressure until bones snapped. Ronové snarled and screamed, his chest heaving, sweat dripping down his grimacing face. Gideon and Sebastian stood on the sidelines, making helpful suggestions. Niklas had just decided to step in before Ronové was rendered completely unable to speak, when he realized he felt...*wrong*. His connection to Carly made him uneasy all of a sudden. He couldn't pin down exactly what it was, but something seemed *off*.

The back of his neck prickled, but he was torn. Mikhail had finally begun to wring answers from Ronové. Still, he had the strangest urge to go to Carly. To verify with his own eyes that she was all right. He'd almost decided to shimmer back to the farm, just for a moment, when her name tripped from Ronové's lips.

Niklas seized Ronové by the throat. "What about Carly?"

"She's a pretty little thing, isn't she?"

Squeezing, Niklas restricted Ronové's airflow until the demon began to turn a mottled shade of purple. Only Sebastian's restraining hand prevented him from snapping the demon's head off his shoulders.

"Her skin was so soft. I bet she's soft as silk between her—"

Niklas shattered Ronové's nose. Once again, blood

sprayed, this time catching Gideon. The Demon of Temptation arched an eyebrow at Niklas. "Thanks," he drawled.

"You had that coming," Niklas growled, fisting Ronové's hair and jerking his head back.

"You all in on the action? The five of you pass her around like a piece of—"

This time, when Niklas's fist connected, it knocked Ronové unconscious.

Backhanding Ronové awake, Niklas demanded, "Why are you after Carly?"

"Woman saw too much," Ronové hissed. "I didn't have a choice. I had to take her out."

"Well, you failed, didn't you?" Niklas got right up in his face. "You'll never get to her now."

Ronové sneered, making the fine hairs on the back of Niklas's neck stand straight up. "You think I'm the only one gunning for her?"

Niklas's blood ran cold.

"Who else?" He had his switchblade in his hand and was pressing it to Ronové's throat before he realized what he was doing. "Who else?"

Grinning, his teeth bloody, Ronové pushed his throat against the blade until blood began to run in a steady rivulet. This time it was Xander who pulled Niklas back.

"The nest in South America?" Xander grated, applying steady pressure as he twisted one of Ronové's horns.

"I don't have anything to do with that nest," Ronové howled. "I don't know why they're gathering. Glasya…that's Glasya's nest."

"And the one near Ridgefield?"

Ronové pressed his lips together. Gideon grasped Ronové's other horn and twisted hard, cranking until it snapped clean off. A crimson arc shot across the room for a moment like an arterial spray. Ronové screamed.

"Gusion," Ronové panted. "Gusion's nest. Don't know anything else about that one."

Niklas glanced at Xander for confirmation. He gave a subtle nod. Ronové was telling the truth.

Sebastian stepped up to the plate. "What about the Sword of Kathnesh? Where is it?"

Ronové looked him dead in the eye and hissed through the pain, "I don't know what you're talking about."

"Lie," Xander stated flatly.

Sebastian snapped Ronové's remaining horn off at the base. Blood sprayed and Ronové screamed again.

"Let's try this again, shall we?" Sebastian rolled the amputated horn between his thumb and his first two fingers right in front of Ronové's glassy, agonized eyes. "Now, tell us about the sword."

Chest heaving, he spat out, "Screw you, Vengeance."

"The hell with this," Niklas muttered, snatching the horn from Sebastian. He drove the poisonous point through Ronové's thigh, lodging the tip in the metal seat below him. "Tell us about the damned sword!"

Ronové's eyes rolled back as he gasped for air. "Okay, okay," he sobbed. Blood dribbled from the corner of his mouth, soaking the front of his shirt. "He has it. Stolas has the sword. He has to have the other relics to wrest control from Lucifer. All of them. Must follow the Prophesy."

The Prophesy? So Stolas *did* believe the old

prophecy was true. Not only did that make Stolas crazy, it made him fanatical.

But they already knew this.

"*Where* is it?" demanded Xander.

Ronové shook his head. One last stab at resistance.

"Where is the sword?" Xander shouted as he pressed his thumb into Ronové's shattered collarbone.

"It's in Hell. Hidden in the borderlands of M—" A blur of gray fur launched itself between Gideon and Sebastian. A flash of silver. And Ronové's head rolled to the floor.

Niklas caught a fleeting glimpse of Dimiezlo as the creature landed on his hooves some twenty feet away. His beady, black eyes scanned them as they gaped, too shocked to move, and then he shimmered away.

What the hell!

The five of them stood in a circle around the headless body, staring at the spot where Dimiezlo had disappeared. Since the beginning, Dimiezlo had been Ronové's faithful servant. Only a handful of demons could exert that kind of control over an Animagi Demon, motivating him to this level of betrayal.

Stolas.

A chill ran down Niklas's spine as Ronové's words came back to haunt him. *You think I'm the only one gunning for her?*

"Carly," Niklas whispered. Centering his focus on the farm, he shimmered into the living room. The others appeared in the room less than a moment later.

Niklas's stomach dropped as he surveyed the room, the scattered objects. The overturned table. The shattered cup. "Carly!" he bellowed.

Blood. Carly's blood, splattered across the wall.

Oh God!

Where was she? He couldn't detect her essence there in the house. But her guard stones were there, somewhere.

Just as that thought formed, Gideon called his name in a strangled tone. Niklas whirled around, his eyes going wide as Gideon held up Carly's broken necklace and bracelet in one hand. Her ring in the other.

He flew to Gideon's side and snatched the jewelry from him. The clasp on the necklace had been shattered. The bracelet had snapped between two links, as if torn from her wrist. He scanned the room, lingering on the blood on the wall. Bending, he scooped up the ring she'd sworn never to take off again.

Why had he ignored those uneasy sensations?

He looked around the room again for some clue. The splintered coffee table, the broken lamp. She'd resisted. Even as terror gripped his insides, twisting mercilessly, pride blossomed in his chest. His girl was a fighter. More importantly, she was a survivor.

But he'd ignored the tug. He hadn't kept the promise he'd made her.

He'd failed her.

Closing his eyes, he strained to find her. Why was it so difficult? Opening himself up, absorbing the lingering essence in the room, he gasped aloud.

He was struggling to find her because she was no longer on this plane.

Icy fear swamped him as he cast his senses farther.

He staggered back a step and clutched the back of the sofa for support as he turned incredulous, horrified eyes to his companions.

"Where is she?" Gideon demanded, grim, ready to

do battle.

"Hell," Niklas whispered. "She's literally *in Hell*."

Closing his eyes, he centered on her essence. But a hand on his shoulder popped his eyes open. Damn it, he had to get to her. Had to save her.

"It's a trap," Xander warned.

"I don't care!" Niklas exploded. "She's my woman!"

"Then we all go," Sebastian barked.

He shook his head. He couldn't put the others at risk. "If something goes wrong—"

"Then we'll be there to back you up," Mikhail interrupted.

"Damn it, don't you understand?" Niklas glared at each of them in turn. "It *could* be a trap, and I can't guarantee I'll be able to bring you back this time. You could be stuck there. *In Hell!*"

Gideon laid a hand on his shoulder. "I'm going."

"She is your woman. She is one of us," Xander rasped. "We will not leave her to Gusion."

If anyone would understand Niklas's desperate need to save Carly, it would be Xander. He had a mate of his own.

Seeing the cold determination glinting in their collective eyes—determination and loyalty—Niklas was humbled by their support. Humbled by this united display of friendship.

Nodding, he held his arm out. Mikhail clasped his elbow. Sebastian and Xander grabbed hold of his forearms. Gideon touched his shoulder.

Closing his eyes, he struggled with all his might to lock on to Carly. Shimmering with one, even two others was difficult enough. Taking all of them with him was pushing him to his limits. But they could not sense her as he could, so they had no idea where to go. There was no other way.

Sulfur burned his nostrils. No matter how long he'd been gone, that smell was never forgotten.

Sweet Christ, how I hate that smell.

The minute his feet touched solid ground, the others released him and all five went into a defensive stance. The hall was dim, lit only by the ambient glow of torches. He'd been here once before. Millennia ago. But he knew this place.

Gusion.

The demon would die.

A huge, rough, black slab of granite rested in the middle of the room. Carly lay upon it like a virginal offering sprawled on the altar of a monster. He'd dressed her in a thin covering of white lace and nothing more. So help him, if the demon had touched her—

What they'd done to Ronové would look like child's play.

Her eyes were closed, and she was deathly white. Smears of crimson trailed over her forehead and down her right temple. Her left wrist lay at an odd angle. Beneath the sheer white material, horrendous bruises had already begun to form across the side of her rib cage. Matching color marred her thigh and the side of her face. Her eye had begun to swell. Oh God, she had so many bruises. Her knee was scuffed and bleeding.

He rushed forward, prepared to snatch her up and shimmer her away, when Gusion appeared on the opposite side of the altar, a long, thin sword poised inches above her vulnerable neck. His grin was depraved, malevolent. Niklas skidded to a halt.

"At last, the great Seer has returned." Gusion glanced behind Niklas. "And look. He brought along his little friends to play."

"I'll kill you, you son of a bitch," Niklas snarled.

"Maybe," Gusion softly allowed. "But not before I kill her."

A roar of rage bellowed up from the depths of Niklas's soul. Every step he took was an inch closer that the blade came to her delicate skin. Carly slowly roused. Blinking, she frowned and made to rise, until the sharp edge of the blade nicked her skin. She gave a tiny whimper and flattened herself back against the granite.

"Let her go," Niklas demanded.

"Niklas?" Carly called groggily, slowly tilting her head just the tiniest bit so that she could search for him.

"I don't think so, Seer. It's been a while since I've had a taste of anything this delectable."

Niklas advanced, filled with fury.

"Back off," Gusion snarled. His blade dipped closer, drawing another fine bead of crimson.

Niklas froze, taking in her face, her wide, glassy eyes. A mistake. The sheer terror in her eyes was nearly his undoing. The urge to change came upon him in such a sudden surge it was almost impossible to deny.

But...

If, God forbid, but *if* something went wrong, he didn't want the last thing she saw to be the monster within him. And so, for her, he battled the change and faced off against Gusion not as a beast, but as a man.

"Okay. Okay." He lifted his hands in supplication. "Tell me what you want. Just let her go."

"Hmm." Gusion's black eyes gleamed. "What I

want..."

Behind him, he could hear the others shifting restlessly. *Please don't let one of them do anything rash.* He looked at the blade. It was still much too close to her neck.

"You, Seer," Gusion finally drawled. "Or, rather, your head, to be exact. You will offer yourself in her place. Willingly. No resistance."

"No," Carly gasped, whipping her head around, cutting herself further.

The sight of crimson trickling along her pale throat ripped through him. His claws shot out. His fangs began to lengthen. His eyes began to burn, foretelling the imminent change in him. "Lift the damn blade," he roared.

Gusion arched a brow in warning, but he complied, sparing Carly precious inches of breathing room.

"If I agree, you'll let her go? And the others? You'll let them all go?"

Grumbling erupted behind him, but he ignored it. Carly protested. But he ignored her too, intent only on Gusion.

"I will," Gusion vowed. "I'll let her go as soon as the others shimmer from here."

"They all go together. With Carly."

"No, Niklas. Don't do this. Don't!"

Gusion considered Niklas's demands, ignoring Carly as well. A slow, gruesome smile curved his lips. "They can't all shimmer between realms, can they? Only you, Temptation, and the Slayer can. I'd almost forgotten that little fact." His sly gaze tracked to Xander. Calculating. "Hmm."

Niklas's eyes narrowed and he tensed. "If you even

think about double-crossing me—"

"I was just making an interesting observation."

Niklas didn't believe him for a minute.

Gusion smiled. Cold. Satisfied. "I'll let them go."

"Xander?" Niklas called over his shoulder.

A long pause. A grudging reply. "Truth."

"And you'll just accept my word that I'll stay?" Niklas pressed.

"Oh, yes. After all, honor is what you're all about now, isn't it?"

Niklas didn't believe that for a minute either. There was more to it than that. Gusion had to have something up his sleeve. But what? The bastard smiled, tracing a finger over the curve of Carly's bruised, bloodied shoulder. Everything inside Niklas went taut with the need to maim and kill.

"After all, I got to her once," Gusion gloated. "I can get to her again. And the next time, she won't be in quite such pristine shape when I'm done with her."

"Get your hands off her," Niklas snarled.

Gusion tsked in dramatic disapproval. "Do we have a deal?"

"Deal," Niklas spat.

"No!" Carly sobbed, struggling to sit up again. Gasping, she clutched her ribs and fell back against the granite. "Please, Niklas," she wheezed. "Please, no—"

"The others will agree to the deal as well. Once I let her up, you will bow before me, willingly place your neck beneath my blade. And the others will leave."

When silence fell in the room, Niklas glared over his shoulder. "Agree, damn it," he ordered, desperate. She was in such pain. Couldn't they see how badly she was hurt? Why did they hesitate? If only he could hold her one last time. If only he could tell her what was in his heart.

Could Gusion see the way his hands shook?

Mikhail, cold and stoic, snapped, "Agreed."

"Dude, there has to be another way."

"Don't do it, Sebastian," Carly begged. "Don't let Niklas do this—"

"There isn't any other way," Niklas argued, talking over her. When no reply was immediately forthcoming, he spared a glare over his shoulder. "Damn it, Sebastian."

"I don't like this, Seer." Fury boiled in Sebastian's black eyes. "Son of a—"

"Vengeance!"

"Agreed," Sebastian snarled.

"Gideon?"

Silence.

Frustrated, he glowered. "Gideon!"

But Gideon wasn't looking at him. He was staring at Carly. His expression torn. It was then that Niklas realized how close they had become. Not intimately, as lovers were. But they shared a depth of feeling, true friendship.

On the slab, Carly shook her head despite the proximity of the blade, silently pleading with soulful, tear-filled eyes. "No, Gideon. Please, no," she whispered.

"Gideon," Niklas snapped, finally gaining his attention. "I've never asked anything of you before, never anything personal. But I'm asking you this now. I'm begging. Please, Gideon. Take her from here and keep her safe. Watch over her. For me."

"Gideon, you can't agree to this." Carly's voice

broke on a sob. "Niklas is your friend. You can't turn your back on him."

The muscle running along Gideon's jaw jumped. Niklas had put him in a truly difficult position, and he regretted that. The weight of this decision had fallen on Gideon's shoulders. Not only was he going to have to choose between one life and the other, but he was also going to have to choose which heart to shatter, in essence destroying them both.

"Touching, touching," Gusion drawled. "I'd clap, but, as you can see, my hands are a little busy. Now, let's get on with the show. This blade grows heavy and I'd hate to *slip*."

Gideon's attention drifted back to Carly. His eyes were sad. So, so sad. And Niklas wondered if this would be the tipping point, the final straw that pushed the Demon of Temptation over the edge.

"I'm sorry, darlin'." Gideon turned to Gusion and his expression hardened. "Agreed."

"No!" Carly screamed, struggling in earnest now. Tears streamed down her face. Gusion merely slammed her back against the granite hard enough to make her head bounce. She fell silent for a moment, unmoving, and Niklas tensed, fearing Gusion had knocked her unconscious. Or worse. But then she gasped and dragged in a shuddering breath.

"And now the great Slayer," Gusion smiled. The bastard knew he'd already won. He was just rubbing salt in the wound.

Xander was silent for a long moment. Though he didn't take his eyes from Gusion, he addressed Niklas. "You really want it to go down like this?"

"You'd do it for Kyanna. It's like that for me." He

paused, searching for the right words to make them all understand. To make *Xander* understand. *God, please let him understand.* "I want her safe, whatever the cost. Just like when you protected Gideon at the nest. I want you to leave me behind."

Tilting his head, Xander gave a tiny shiver, and then finally—grudgingly—replied, "Agreed."

Gusion took hold of her upper arm and dragged her off the slab, unmindful of her injuries. She paled further as she wrapped one arm around her ribs. The other arm hung uselessly in Gusion's grip, her wrist bruised and swollen grotesquely. Niklas had no idea how she was still conscious.

She tried to stumble to him, but Gusion denied him that final contact as he jerked her back. "I don't think so," he murmured. "No sense testing honor."

"Niklas," she pleaded, her voice hoarse with pain. Tears poured down her cheeks unchecked. "Please don't give up. Fight. Fight for us. We do belong together. We do," she cried as Gusion shoved her into Xander's arms. "I love you, Niklas. Don't leave me like this."

His head came up like a shot. *Now* the woman was going to admit that she loved him? *Now* she was going to admit that they belonged together?

Now?

They were seriously going to have to work on her timing.

"Mikhail," Niklas barked. "You have to heal her as soon as you get her back to the farm."

Mikhail nodded once.

"Xander." Niklas turned to the grim-faced demon. "You know what you have to do. Get her out of here."

"No!" She fought against Xander, and Niklas could see she was only hurting herself further.

"Carly," he snapped, his focus finally landing on her. If this didn't work, he needed her to know what she meant to him. "*Tá'hiri*, I'm sorry, but it has to be this way. Forgive Gideon, this isn't his fault. It isn't any of their faults." She stubbornly shook her head and continued to fight Xander's hold. "Carly," Niklas growled, "Listen to me, damn it." She stilled, finally, and faced him. But she couldn't contain the sobs. "I told you before that I existed to right the wrongs I've done. And that may have been true. Before. But then I met you. Now, I know the truth." He dropped to his knees in front of Gusion. His steady gaze held hers. "I exist only for you."

A fresh wave of tears poured down her face.

Niklas met Xander's hard stare and nodded. Sebastian and Mikhail reached out and laid their hands on Xander's shoulders as he wrapped his arms more firmly around a struggling, screaming Carly. Drawing a deep breath, Niklas clasped his hands behind his back and lowered his head.

Chapter Twenty-Two

"No!" Carly screamed.

And then Niklas was gone. Or rather, she was. Xander shimmered them back to the farm. He released her the moment they solidified. Mikhail moved forward, catching her in surprisingly gentle arms.

"No, take me back. We have to go back. You can't just leave him there!" She flailed, fighting Mikhail until the pain became too much for her, and she collapsed in his arms, sobbing. "Please, please, go back. Take me back. Please!" Her pleading gaze met Gideon's tortured stare. He reached for her, only to let his hands drop uselessly to his sides.

"They're already gone, Carly." Mikhail smoothed his hand along her shoulder. Comforting. Gentle. "This is the way Niklas wanted it. He wanted you safe. Away from the fight. Protected. Xander and Sebastian have already gone back."

Carly glanced around. Xander and Sebastian *were* gone.

Oh God, please don't let them be too late.

Her vision swam, and she swayed on her feet. Gideon moved closer, his expression concerned, as Mikhail scooped her up and laid her carefully on the sofa.

"Niklas wouldn't fight with you there. He wouldn't risk getting you hurt, not even by accident." Mikhail eased her hair off her brow. His cool-eyed, methodical stare searched her features, probing for injuries. The earlier, momentary lapse in his tough-guy persona was gone as if it had never happened.

"You have to go back." She grasped Mikhail's arm, desperate. She looked between Mikhail and Gideon. "You have to help them."

"We can't," Gideon said. The lines around his mouth were grim, his eyes bright with worry.

"I-I don't understand." She hiccuped, blinking up at Gideon in confusion as he dropped to his knees beside her. Once more, he reached for her. The cold pass of his hand through hers brought a tormented expression to his face, and he drew back again.

"You don't realize where you were, do you?" Gideon asked. He glanced to Mikhail, watched him carefully smooth his hands along her scalp, down her neck and over her shoulders, healing her from the inside out. Her flesh warmed, tingled. Mended. "You were in Hell, Carly. Gusion took you *into Hell*."

And Mikhail couldn't shimmer between planes like Xander and Niklas could. But why hadn't Gideon gone?

"Why didn't they take you with them?" she asked, frantic. "Why didn't they take you to fight?"

"This is the way Niklas wanted it," Gideon reminded her. "Mikhail had to stay here to heal you. And Niklas wanted me to stay here, for you. To protect you."

He didn't say it out loud, but she could see it in his eyes. They were there for another reason. If Sebastian and Xander failed and Gusion killed Niklas, if Gusion double-crossed them, then Mikhail and Gideon would be there to guard her. A last line of defense.

"But they went back for him? They'll get there in time? They'll save him?"

"We would never abandon one of our own." Mikhail scowled at her as if she'd offended him on some sacred level. But his hands were cautious as he lifted the wrist Gusion had taken such glee in breaking.

"But—"

"Shhh," Mikhail hissed. He closed his eyes and held his palm over her injured arm. A deep furrow formed between his brows. His lips compressed and bleached of color, as did the rest of his face. Warmth surged. Building to heat. Nearly unbearable. And then the pain in her arm was no more. But she didn't care. The only thing that mattered was Niklas. That he was safe. That he was alive. That he *stay* that way. Mikhail moved on to her ribs. Perspiration had broken out across his forehead. She struggled to sit up. She had to *do* something. She just couldn't lie there, waiting.

"Lie back," Mikhail ordered, his voice a harsh rasp now. His breath was labored. He eased her shoulders to the cushions and replaced his hands on her ribs. Once more heat built, but she was numb to it, too filled with dread. To busy struggling with her fear for Niklas to notice the miracle Mikhail was accomplishing with his bare hands.

At last, Mikhail sat back on his heels. His expression was strained, stoic. She pushed up to a sitting position, nearly out of her mind with helpless fear. Niklas wasn't there. He wasn't safe yet.

The air in the corner of the room distorted. Mikhail and Gideon both tensed and shot to their feet, ready for battle. A moment later, Xander and Sebastian staggered into solidity, supporting Niklas between them. All three were bloodied and singed. Wounded. Their clothing blackened in places. But Niklas was in far worse shape.

Carefully, they lowered him to the ground. Carly flew off the sofa and scrambled to his side. Mikhail and Gideon followed. Sebastian and Xander dropped to the floor. Panting. Wincing.

"Oh God, Niklas," she cried, desperate to hold him but afraid to touch him. He was bleeding everywhere. Gashes. Burns. Blisters and blackened flesh. His chest was barely moving. "Open your eyes. Open your eyes for me. Please!"

He moaned. His head lolled to the side. Cupping his cheek, she pressed a soft kiss to his brow. "Please, Niklas. Please!"

She pleaded with Mikhail, "Do something. Fix him. Fix him like you fixed me."

"I cannot," he said quietly, never looking away from Niklas's face. "I cannot heal others of my kind."

"He needs a soul then, right? He needs to feed on a soul?" Desperate, clutching Niklas's hand in hers, she glanced from Xander to Sebastian. Mikhail. Gideon. "A soul would heal him. You have to get him a soul." In that dark moment, she didn't care where they got that soul—just that they saved him.

"No time," Xander rasped.

"Something's wrong with him," Sebastian quietly warned her. "He should have already begun healing. If nothing else, the more minor of his injuries should have already begun to mend, but they haven't. He's not healing."

Sobbing, she bent over him and pressed a trembling kiss to his lips. Her tears fell upon his cheeks as she pressed the flat of his palm over her own heart and pleaded with him. "Niklas, you have to feed. Now. Do you hear me? I won't let you die like this, Niklas. Take whatever you need. Please."

His fingers twitched. He turned his head. "*Tá'hiri*," he whispered.

"I'm here." She sniffled, quickly dragging the back of her forearm across her face, blinking away the sheen of tears. "I'm right here, Niklas. You have to feed now. Do you understand? You have to feed."

He twitched again. But she didn't feel him drawing her essence. Instead, he slid his shaking hand up the side of her neck, cupped her cheek. But he was too weak, and his arm fell back. Snatching his hand up, she pressed his palm to her chest once more.

"Please," Carly begged, sobbing. Her lips continued to move, silently willing him to take what he needed, take all she had so that he would live. But tears and terror clogged her throat, preventing all but helpless sobs from escaping.

His lips moved. She leaned closer, until a faint wisp of breath slipped along her ear.

"I love you," he whispered.

"Niklas? Niklas!" She leaned back, scanning his face. He wasn't breathing.

He's not breathing.

Shaking him, she screamed his name over and over. She wouldn't let him go. Not like this. She beat on his chest. Swore. And then she dragged in a breath, struggling to calm herself.

Terrified, she glanced to Gideon, Xander. Then to Mikhail and Sebastian. Each, in turn, looked thunderstruck.

He's not dying like this.

She wouldn't allow it.

Carly started CPR. Over and over she followed the steps she'd learned in a class a long time ago. A-B-C. Airway. Breathing. Circulation. Check for pulse, check breath. Chest compressions. Two breaths. Compressions. No. That was wrong. Just compressions now, she remembered. Lots of compressions. Fast compressions. Frantic, she wouldn't stop. Not until he came back.

Tears streamed down her face. Sobs erupted from deep in her chest, torn from the back of her throat. But still she pressed on. Until the motions were mechanical. Her mind locked on the process, refusing to recognize and accept reality. One, two, three, four…fifteen, sixteen, seventeen…twenty-eight, twenty-nine, thirty. At length, strong arms wrapped around her, dragging her off Niklas's unresponsive body. Fighting like a she-wolf protecting her pups, she screamed, swore, scratched, struggling madly to get back. She had to keep his blood circulating. Had to keep oxygen pumping to his brain.

"Shhh, Carly." Steely arms caged her, rocked her, as a rough voice rasped against her ear. "Shhh. He's gone. Let him go."

"He can't be gone. He told me the only way for you guys to die was to lose your head. He's still got his." She sobbed hysterically. "He's still got his! I don't understand. He's not gone. He's not. He can't be gone! I need him."

"Darlin', I'm not sure we understand either," Gideon offered from nearby. Then his voice softened, as though he were speaking to someone else, someone closer to him. "Shouldn't his body have ashed by now?"

Ashed? As in turned to ashes? The very idea struck terror into the very heart of her, and she fought with renewed strength.

But he hadn't yet. Did that mean they still had time? Still had a chance to change this?

Oh please, God! Please! Anything you ask, I'll do it. Just please, please...

She glanced around the room, at Gideon and Sebastian, at Mikhail. Twisting in his arms, clutching the front of Xander's shirt in her white-knuckled fists, she pleaded, "Can't you do something? Bring him back somehow? He had scrolls, Lucifer's scrolls. Dark magic. Something in there has to bring him back!"

They stared at Niklas. As if they'd never seen him before. As if they couldn't figure out what to do next. Grief, she realized, slowly going numb. They stared at Niklas as she'd stared at the caskets of her mother and father. Her uncle's. They were trying to process his death. Through their grief, her own finally engaged. Sobbing, she collapsed against Xander. Strong arms banded around her as Xander's chin dropped onto the top of her head.

****

A warm, gentle light bathed Niklas. The soothing sense of peace washing through him was so pure, so true he could little fathom it. And he knew he was not alone.

Oh, I know this place.

Tears of joy pricked his eyes, even as fear and longing tightened his chest.

"Father?"

I am here. And I am pleased.

A sob caught in his throat. Though he knew he would see nothing beyond the light, he continued to search the warm glow. A hundred questions darted through his mind, too swiftly for him to pin one down. A hundred things he wanted to confess. A hundred things he needed to give thanks for. He opened his mouth but, overwhelmed, he could only make inarticulate sounds.

Be at peace, Niklas. I know all that is in your heart.

He calmed without conscious effort.

And the *knowing* filled him. That certainty that only He was capable of giving. He had, at last, achieved forgiveness.

You have earned the choice I give few others.

The answer filled his heart before it could form upon his lips. "Carly! I choose Carly. I ask only to be bound to her, my life force be linked to hers. I would age as she does. I would die with—"

Soothing calm swept through him once more. Though He didn't speak, Niklas could feel He was pleased.

You shall be as Xander is. You are my own warrior once more.

Another wave of peace washed over him, love in its truest form, and then the light receded.

His battered body jolted, surging and shaking as if struck by lightning. Touched by the very hand of God Himself. Niklas convulsed and then gasped, dragging in a huge rasping breath.

He opened his eyes. And he wondered if he hadn't gotten sent to some wrong dimension by accident. There sat Xander of all people, holding Carly, rocking her, gently patting her back...*comforting* her...while she sobbed as though her very heart had been torn from her body. The sight of her grief, raw and unfiltered, robbed him of speech for a moment. The others stared at him in a slack-jawed daze.

"Carly?" he managed to croak.

A wave of murmurs, both shocked and relieved, swept the room, but her reaction was the only thing he truly registered. Her head whipped around, and she gasped. Her shoulders shook and jerked in time with the great sobbing breaths that heaved through her. Her eyes were puffy, nearly swollen shut. Her face was soaked from the tears that continued to roll down her cheeks. Her nose was red, and her face was splotchy.

She looked like the sun and the moon and the stars all rolled into one. She looked like Heaven.

"Niklas?" she whispered, as if afraid she was hallucinating. Then louder, "Niklas!"

Before he could speak, before he could even sit up, Carly wrenched free of Xander's arms and threw herself on top of Niklas. Her body heaved as she sobbed his name and peppered his face with wet, salty kisses. Her hands frantically patted at him, all over, as if to make sure he was real.

"I love you! I love you! So much. I do! I'll tell you every day. So often you'll get sick of hearing it, I swear!" she gushed between kisses. "I'll tell you whatever you want to hear, just please, please don't leave me again. I love you a thousand times."

He smiled beneath the onslaught, and even tried to capture her lips with his, but she was just too fast, too overcome with relief and happiness, and her haphazard kisses connected with eyelid and nose and chin.

Distantly, Niklas felt the press of stronger hands on his shoulder, his wrist, his ankle and heard words of thanks and reassurance murmured and he was doubly grateful for his blessings. His family. His band of brothers.

Carly squeezed him tight and, at last, held still long enough to press her cheek to his. Though his arms felt like wet noodles, he managed to get them around her.

This…this right here…the woman in his arms was what he'd come back for.

His mate.

The love of all his lives.

Chapter Twenty-Three

Carly leaned her elbows on the wrought iron railing. The sultry Mediterranean breeze wafted over her skin. In the distance, sailboats and yachts skimmed through the crystal waters. Birds screeched, wheeling looping circles in the clear, azure skies. Closing her eyes and lifting her head, she drew in the crisp scents, savored the warm sunshine on her skin.

Twenty-four hours had passed since Niklas's brush with death. She shuddered, still feeling a little sick to her stomach at the mere thought of how close she'd come to losing him. Close enough to know she didn't want to spend another second without him in her life, no matter the risk, no matter the consequences. Her love, *their* love and the connection the two of them shared, was stronger than death.

He'd survived the battle, but he was still recovering from the worst of his injuries. Slower than was normal, or so Mikhail and the others had stated. Several times and with a great deal of concern. She didn't care. He was alive, and she intended to spend the rest of her life showing him exactly how much she loved him.

The rustle of movement behind her caught her attention, and she turned. Niklas stood in the open French doors, smiling, his eyes devouring her.

"You should be resting," she scolded.

He held his arms open, waiting. "I missed you,

ma'ilc cho'ckta."

"I haven't been away from your side for more than ten minutes." Laughing, she moved into his embrace and carefully wrapped her arms around his waist.

He smoothed the backs of his fingers over her cheek and dropped a soft kiss to her lips. "A lifetime, surely. One minute without you is a minute too long."

Carly laced her fingers through the hair curling over his collar. "I'm glad you feel that way. Because you're never getting rid of me again. I intend to be a thorn in your side for the rest of my days."

"The rest of *our* days," he corrected. Laughing, he swept her up in his arms, smothering her face with kisses. "And I have every intention of holding you to that promise, sweetheart."

Carrying her back inside, Niklas set her on her feet near the bed and drew her in for another long, soul-branding kiss. Concern for him overrode her passion for the moment, however. She'd come too close to losing him. So she pushed carefully at his chest until he let her ease her lips from beneath his.

"Niklas, you can't carry me around like that. You'll reopen your wounds. Let me see...are you okay?"

"I'm fine, *tá'hiri*, completely healed."

She tsked, convinced he'd reinjured himself despite his assurances otherwise. She pushed the hem of his shirt up. The golden skin on his abdomen still showed the bright red, nearly ten-inch-long slash where a poisonous Animagi horn had cleaved his flesh, but the wound hadn't reopened. Powerful muscles rippled and flexed as he readjusted his hold on her. And then he vanished his shirt, baring the rest of his magnificent physique to her hungry eyes.

Unable to resist, she drew her hands over his chest, lightly fingering the dozen or so other wounds he'd sustained, which were also in various states of healing. Satisfied he'd not harmed himself further, she couldn't resist brushing down the rigid muscles of his stomach. With a knowing smile, Niklas drew her down beside him on the edge of the bed. But when he tried to urge her to lie back, she resisted.

"If you're healthy enough for *that*, then you're healthy enough for explanations." She'd agreed to wait until he was out of danger to demand answers for what had transpired after Xander and the others had whisked her to safety. And answers as to what had happened in those life-altering moments between his last breath as a demon and his first breath as...well, as an *other*. Not quite angel. Not quite human. That same strange category, she'd since learned, that Xander had fallen into when he'd absorbed half his wife's soul and tied his life force to hers.

Warriors of God.

Niklas tucked a lock of hair behind her ear, and then slipped his hand into hers. "Fair enough. Let me start at the beginning. Gusion did have a trap set. But you weren't the only bait. He knew the others would come back for me. So he had backup. Lots of it and...well, it was a hell of a battle. But I don't want you to worry. Gusion is dead. The last thing I did before that Animagi gored me was to send Gusion to Oblivion. And Ronové...well, he lost his head too. They will never come after you again.

"I won't lie to you and tell you this is all over. We still need to stop Stolas and his uprising. And we have to find the rest of the relics. But I want you with me, by my side for whatever comes next."

"But how—"

"Be patient." He lay a finger against her lips. "*Try* to be patient. I'll answer all your questions, at least as best as I can. But while I do, I just"—he slid across the bed, pulling her with him, and lay back, tucking her into his arms—"I just need to hold you."

Curling into him, she absorbed his warmth, the feel of his hard muscles wrapped gently around her, the scent of him, spicy masculine musk. She'd thought she'd never feel this again. Tears welled once more. Sniffling, she swiped at her eyes with the back of her hand and tipped her head to peer at him through damp lashes.

"Okay, where was I?" He pressed a kiss to her forehead and smiled at her. "I didn't die. But I—my consciousness, I guess—returned to Heaven…at least for a few moments." Her eyes widened. She sucked in a sharp breath and opened her mouth, but he silenced her with a swift kiss. "Please, *tá'hiri*. Patience."

She drew in a deep breath and nodded. But then a thought occurred to her, and she blurted, "What about the bond? The one you forged in your little black magic circle. It is—"

"The bond is not gone." His hand slid along her back in a long, consoling stroke. "Not completely. But it has changed. I promise, I will get to it all."

Frustrated, she pressed her lips together.

"I returned to Heaven, in a way, because of you. Because I finally carry true love in my heart." He squeezed her. "And, because of that love, and because I would continue to do His will here on Earth, I was given a choice."

"To stay or to come back," she guessed.

"To stay, or to come back. As a Warrior of God once more," he clarified. "A Warrior of God, and your mate."

Twisting around, she wiggled up until she could lean over him. She couldn't resist asking, "You had what you wanted, Niklas. You returned to Heaven. How could you give all that up? Why would you come back?"

"Because the only thing I truly wanted—my only reason for existing—was still here. You're still here. You, Carly. You are the only thing I want. The only choice I could make was to come back and be with you. I want to spend the rest of *my* life with you, loving you, making a family with you, if you'll have me. Heaven can wait a little while longer," he reassured her with the smile of a confident believer.

"You really gave up your immortality for me?" Her voice was little more than a whisper of indignation. Of disbelief and awe.

"If I had come back a demon, or an angel, it would have made no difference. When you died—whenever that might be, I wouldn't have been far behind. I refuse to exist in a world without you. Oblivion would be better than that. Be with me, Carly. Share your life with me. Be mine, now and always."

She stared at him, silent. Speechless.

A Warrior of God? She could scarcely wrap her brain around it.

"But—"

"No buts, sweetheart. I want you with me always. No more fears of dying. No more of these crazy ideas about standing in the way of my redemption. You saved me, Carly. You're the reason I'm still here."

She nodded.

He went on to explain that he no longer needed to siphon souls to stay alive, stay strong, and he had retained some pretty wicked abilities. Just as Xander had. However, he could now be wounded, or killed. Just like Xander.

He'd come back. From Heaven. For her. He was here now, in her arms, and she was too grateful to split hairs. Tears of joy pricked her eyes.

"Say something, Carly." A slight crease formed between his brows.

"On one condition," she stipulated, sniffling, impatiently swiping the tears away with the back of her hand. "I'll be yours on one condition."

Niklas tilted his head and regarded her with narrowed eyes. "Condition?"

Pushing herself higher up, she narrowed her eyes and scowled threateningly. "Absolutely no more bordellos for you, mister."

"Love, the only woman I want for the rest of my life, is you." He pulled her down and sealed his lips over hers in a kiss clearly meant to demonstrate his claim.

He succeeded.

"Say yes, my love," he urged. "I want the words."

"Yes, Niklas. I will spend the rest of my life loving you." Before he could sweep her away on another kiss, she smiled and traced the curve of his lower lip with the tip of her finger. "So tell me the rest."

"I made only one request before I was returned." He searched her face, and he grinned, as though vastly pleased with the bargain he'd struck, whatever it might have been. "I asked that my life force be tied to yours, as Xander's is to Kyanna's. I will grow old with you. And when you die, I will follow."

A frown creased her forehead as the ramifications sank in. "Niklas, no. You shouldn't have—"

"Too late, the deal is struck." He nuzzled the side of her throat. "There's more."

She shivered in response. Seeming to take that as encouragement, he let his hands begin to roam. Her breath caught.

"And as far as our bond goes..." Grinning wickedly, Niklas rolled and pinned her beneath him. "I could tell you." He used his splayed fingers to fan her hair on the pillow. "But I think *showing* you would be far more effective."

He took his time removing her clothes, lavishing each inch of bared skin with sensual attention. Niklas worshiped her with such devotion that her head was soon spinning, and she was poised on the brink of orgasm by the time they were both naked.

He positioned himself between her thighs and braced his elbows on either side of her head. His fingers slid through her hair, cupping her head as he waited for her to open her eyes and look up at him.

And when she did, she caught her breath. *His eyes!*

They flickered a startling, brilliant, sapphire blue.

So serious. So *intense.*

"I love you, *tá'hiri.*" Slowly, deliberately, he eased inside her in one long, seamless thrust. "For the rest of my life"—he rotated his hips—"in this life and every moment beyond." Gliding in, gliding out, he added, "I will love you, and honor you, and cherish you. And you *will* be marrying me, by the way. In a church."

"*In a church*," she echoed, smiling dreamily.

"In a church," he repeated, as if the mere words were too unbelievable to credit. "You are my heart, my soul. My reason for existing."

His lips sealed over hers, capturing her sob. His thumbs tracked the trails of tears slipping down her temples as he kissed her with such tender passion that her heart flip-flopped. By infinitesimal degrees, Niklas deepened the kiss, turning it into a glorious blaze of soul-fusing fervor. Breaking the kiss abruptly, he held her head between his hands and peered into her eyes, unwavering. Compelling.

Tiny sparks, like little shockwaves of static electricity, erupted all over her body. Her nerve endings sizzled with awareness. And deep inside, molten heat soared, erupted, drenching her body in bliss as she'd never experienced. She clung to him and screamed his name.

Niklas gave a hoarse shout near her ear as his body went rigid and his shaft spasmed deep inside her.

Carly lay beneath him, panting, limp. Dazed. At length, when she finally recovered her senses and located her voice, she pressed a gentle kiss to his jaw and queried, "Was *that* the change you were hinting about?"

"One of them," he murmured, smiling against her temple.

"*One* of them?" Good God, if he had any more surprises like that in store for her, their life together was destined to be woefully short. She was likely to expire from sheer pleasure. She could already see her gravestone. *Here lies Carly*—she didn't exactly know what her last name would be as he had none; that was another of many things they needed to discuss— *Beloved wife of Niklas, loved well and gone too soon.*

"Mmhmm," he mumbled, nibbling at her earlobe.

"At the risk of looking a gift horse in the mouth and asking too many questions..." His snort of laughter earned him a stiff-fingered poke in the ribs. Still buried deep inside her, his erection pulsed, making her catch her breath before she could go on. "What other changes are there?"

He rotated his hips and began anew the rhythm that was as old as time. Her eyes went wide, and she gasped softly. Moaned low as he set that stunning shower of sensual sparks cascading throughout her system once more. Only magnified.

"Oh, I think I'll just keep surprising you," he promised, his eyes smoldering, his grin wicked.

Epilogue

Gideon let the door slam behind him. He dragged his gaze around the smoke-filled barroom. The place was called Purgatory. Some twisted part of him found humor in the name. It was, after all, what his life had become. Not exactly Hell, but Hell was certainly within spitting distance. Only a smattering of demons loitered around the half-empty bar tonight. Just as well. He wasn't in the mood for company. His great loophole had been a bust; any scraps of hope he'd managed to hold on to this long had evaporated.

No. *Evaporated* wasn't the right word. *Evaporated* was benign. *Evaporated* implied there was nothing left. That he was empty. And he was anything but empty. Quite the contrary, in fact. He was so very full. Full of despair. Full of hate. Full of fury.

Full of the need to destroy.

He seethed with it.

Never had he felt this all-consuming rage, not even after his fall. Not the whole time he'd followed Lucifer. And not since he'd thrown off Lucifer's despotism.

After all these centuries of not being able to touch or be touched—after all these years of trying to convince himself it didn't matter, that this was the price he had to pay to redeem himself—he'd really thought he'd found a way around his curse. And having failed, he couldn't find it in himself to care anymore. About himself. About the imminent threat to humankind. About his brothers-in-arms. About redemption.

He was done trying.

Bellying up, he slapped a pouch of gold down, pointed at a bottle of the most potent demon brew ever created, and snapped his order to the horned Animagi behind the bar, following it up with a snarl. "Keep 'em coming."

At the first glance Gideon's way, the barkeep's eyes widened, and stayed that way. Working his way over to Gideon, he cautiously set a full bottle of demon brew and a shiny shot glass in front of him. And then he slowly backed away, like one would a motion sensitive bomb.

Shooting him a disgusted look, Gideon snatched up the bottle, foregoing the glass altogether. He skulked across the room to settle in at a table in the corner. After shoving one of the chairs back with the toe of his boot, he dropped onto it, kicked his feet up on the seat of another and twisted the cap off the bottle, breaking the seal.

Several long swigs later, he grimaced and lowered the bottle to the table with a loud thump, turning his attention to the room at large. The place looked like it had two-stepped through the 1950s, crashed into the 1960s, tripped and fell face-first through the 1970s, and landed on its rear end in the 1980s, keeping a bit of each time period as a memento. Purgatory was the kind of place that most sane demons gave wide berth to. Tossing a mental shrug, he chugged another quarter of the bottle down, hissing as it stripped away yet another layer of his empathy. What the hell, he wasn't there for the ambiance. He was there for the brew and some peace and quiet. It wasn't as if he was ever going to have a family to worry about. While he and the other fallen demons had formed a loose brotherhood of sorts, they were a far cry from a tight-knit family unit. Xander's Kyanna had begun to grow on him, and Niklas's little human had wormed her way under his skin. But it was getting damned hard to paste a smile on his face and pretend to be happy as he watched the cozy couples make googly eyes and fawn all over each other.

Damned hard to watch them *touch* each other when he'd never again know the touch of a woman. Never again feel a woman's warmth. Never experience anything more than pitying looks and sympathetic smiles.

His loophole was closed. Permanently.

God, he was pathetic.

Tossing back another mouthful, he savored the sting. Brew was the only thing that could warm him now, and he intended to swim in it, swim until he burned. He glanced over to the pool table. A couple demons stood there, cues in hand, staring at him. His gaze traveled to the chrome and vinyl booths on the far wall. The three occupants there were staring at him too. Even the barkeep continued to keep a wary eye glued to him.

What the hell was their problem? Hadn't they ever seen a demon drink brew before?

He reached for the bottle again, and that was when he finally looked at his own hand. It was caked with drying demon blood. Frowning, he glanced down at himself. His jeans had a big rip in one knee and a slash across the thigh. The other pant leg was singed along the seam and splattered with more blood. His shirt looked as if he'd used it to mop up after a *gar'umprtach'ta* orgy. Unmoved, he flicked a chunk of demon skin from the waist of his T-shirt. The cuts on his knuckles were beginning to heal. As were the slash across his bicep and the gash in his thigh.

He could have cleaned up a bit before coming there after the last battle, he supposed. Still could. But why bother? The blood just saved him the hassle of having to blow off the next female that came sashaying in his direction. He could look all he wanted. She could look all she wanted. But in the end, lookin' was all that was gonna get done. And that just bit the big one. He drained the bottle, slammed it on the table and motioned for the barkeep to bring another. What the hell was wrong with all of them? So he was a little bloody. So what? Were they demons or were they human?

He took a certain amount of satisfaction from his bruised and split knuckles, remembering the way that demon had begged for mercy and wet himself. The darkness churning inside his soul wasn't buried so deep just now. In fact, it simmered just below the surface, eager to be set free once more this night. Had been for a while now.

His eyes narrowed at the duo by the pool table. The cues dropped to the floor and bounced before rolling under the table when the two demons vanished. Next, he glowered at the demons in the booths. Only one had the good sense to leave. The other two looked as if they were eager for a fight. Well, he'd be happy to oblige them, whether they deserved to die or not.

He was sick and tired of hunting for relics. Disgusted and resentful over having to watch his buddies get paired up with the girls of their dreams. He wouldn't even be pitiful enough to ask when it would be his turn. 'Cuz the answer was goddamned never. Not with his curse. Gideon laced his fingers together and stretched his arms out in front of him, cracking his knuckles. If Dumb and Dumber over there wanted a fight, well bring it the hell on.

In a matter of minutes, Purgatory lay in ruins. Tables were shattered, chairs were smashed, smoking holes dotted the walls and demon blood was splattered everywhere. Tiny fires speckled the floor and walls. The ceiling tiles sagged in the corner and above the broken pool table. Gideon stalked back to his table, the last man—well, *demon*—standing, and plopped back down, barely winded and more than a little disappointed. They hadn't put up near enough of a fight to suit him.

He turned to glare at the wide-eyed barkeep. "I thought I told you to bring me another damned bottle."

Don't Miss the other titles in Brenda Huber's Chronicles of the Fallen Series!

THE SLAYER
Chronicles of the Fallen, Book 1
The darker side of his nature just can't let her go.

Born of heaven, forged in hellfire and damnation, Xander roams the earth as an unlikely protector of the innocent. Grudgingly embroiled in a demon uprising, Xander must help his brothers-in-arms recover four Sacred Relics rumored to be Lucifer's downfall.

The stakes are simple. If he fails, a new regime will assume control of the underworld and the boundaries between hell and earth will crumble. If he succeeds, long-awaited salvation could be his. But when a beautiful innocent is caught in the crossfire, the price of redemption could be too steep.

Kyanna Hughes is a hereditary Guardian, sworn to protect a sacred Relic at all costs. From the cradle, she was taught to hate all things demon, but her unwanted attraction to Xander turns everything she's been taught upside down.

The danger she faces involves more than her heart. For Kyanna is not only a Guardian, but a keeper of secrets so dangerous, that to keep them out of demon hands even the angels in heaven would see her dead...

A word about the author...

Brenda Huber lives in Iowa with her husband, her two children, and her very spoiled dog, Sam. You can learn more by visiting her on her website (www.brendahuber.webs.com), or by following her on Facebook (http://on.fb.me/1F4VsNc).

~*~

Look for these titles by Brenda Huber

Now Available:
Mine
Cravings
Shadows
Queen's Chess

~

Texas Series
Texas Bride
Texas Blaze

~

Chronicles of the Fallen
The Slayer
The Seer

~

Coming Soon:
Temptation

CPSIA information can be obtained
at www.ICGtesting.com
Printed in the USA
BVHW080328130819
555664BV00023BA/2260/P